Brea

Breaking Boundaries
By
Jason Hanson

Breaking boundaries

Breaking boundaries

1

Toby stood paralysed, gripped by fear and consumed by panic. Rational thinking eluded him, yet there was a high-pitched scream echoing deep in his subconscious, urging him to regain control and take action. It was instinctive, yet transient as the conflict between subconscious and conscious raged on. His panic was for the present, his fear for the future and the inevitable consequences he would face. He had worked with many clients experiencing anxiety, who would exhibit symptoms such as palpitations, racing thoughts, shaking, and as more than one client had described, being crushed by the weight of the air. He wondered if this was what it felt like for them before an overwhelming feeling of disbelief displaced this thought. This was much easier to deal with when it was somebody else's experience he thought. He wondered if this was some sort of twisted karmic humour for listening to, and hearing patients without truly being able to understand their experience, their emotions. As this thought began to grow, an attack of guilt grew with it. He had experienced anxious thoughts before; exams, his wedding day, his first client; even the best man's speech he had been pressured into giving, much to the chagrin of his wife. As Toby recalled the angst he had felt that day, he was suddenly struck by a moment of clarity. Nothing in his past came remotely close to inducing the feelings he was experiencing now. This

Breaking boundaries

magnitude of anxiety, which now seemed to replace the very cells of his being, trivialised all before it. Why would this be karma? He was a good person, a loving husband and a dedicated professional. In his teenage years, he had made a decision that he wanted to help people and had spent several years working towards this. Of course, he wanted to have a comfortable lifestyle and afford the finer things, but who didn't? Why would this be karma? Regathering his thoughts, he became conscious of the moment again. The room had ceased spinning and was back to its normal size, not that it had actually shrunk in the first place, he thought, before chastising himself for allowing his mind to venture in an irrelevant direction, given the scene that lay before him. He took a deep breath, shook his head and surveyed the room to see what he could use to stem the bleeding. The body appeared lifeless, but maybe, just maybe, there was still hope. Do people continue to bleed after death? he wondered. Refusing to get into that internal debate, Toby reached for a towel he had spotted folded neatly on a shelf in the corner. It occurred to him how out of place a neatly folded towel looked in a scene enveloped in chaos and disarray. As he did this, another intrusive thought entered his head. Why was he going to such lengths to save a rapist, an abuser, somebody who had inflicted suffering and misery on his family? He wanted to believe it was solely down to saving a human life, just like any Good Samaritan would do but was conflicted by a

Breaking boundaries

strong sense of self-serving, selfish, self-preservation. After all, he was present in a room with blood smeared on his hands, which he had instinctively wiped on his shirt, standing over a person who had been stabbed more than once. The last hour had been a blur for him, but despite the mental tangents and the out-of-place orderliness of the towel amongst the disorder of the room, he had crystal clear clarity on one important point; his fingerprints would be all over the knife.

Whatever the outcome, whether they lived or died, this would be a life-changing moment, and one which Toby knew would remain with him. He briefly saw the irony in a therapist needing therapy to explore a traumatic event and found once again he was putting himself in the position of his clients. How did they deal with trauma, with adversity? It always felt so much easier when he wasn't emotionally invested in a situation and could detach. But this was very real, and at this moment, there was no detaching for Toby. This wasn't a therapeutic setting, and it wasn't a safe place. This was real life and in fact, as far removed from a safe place as you could get. How he yearned to be back where he was comfortable, exploring other people's trauma rather than living his own. He wanted to scream, but nothing came out; needed to move, but was frozen to the spot. It felt like time was standing still, or was it moving quickly? As the sweat poured down his face, panic consumed him, and he could

Breaking boundaries

feel his grasp on reality slipping further. He felt a loss of control and realised whatever *this* was, it was genuine and all-encompassing, like nothing he had experienced before. Toby knew he had to try and gain some perspective and quickly. He thought about how he would work with clients around removing the emotion from the situation and willed himself to do the same. Still nothing. Toby, alone with his thoughts was startled by a noise and a scream behind him. 'We have to leave here Toby… NOW'. The voice was that of Olivia Stanton, a thirty-three-year-old woman. The individual lying face down in a pool of blood on the floor beneath them was Olivia's forty-two-year-old husband, Eric, the father of their six-year-old son Tyler. What added more complexity to an already desperate situation, was the fact Olivia was one of Toby's clients. He already knew he had contravened so many ethical boundaries and couldn't even begin to think about how he would ever be able to explain or justify this. He could just imagine the conversation with his clinical supervisor, Richard. *'So I ended up at the home of one of my clients standing over a limp, blood-soaked body, but other than that things have been good and not much has happened since we last spoke, how are you?'* Toby let out a nervous laugh. He felt sure there was little chance his career would survive this. It was over. He forced himself out of the dark humour to turn to Olivia. She was almost unrecognisable from the soft-spoken individual he had first met, who had always taken a

Breaking boundaries

great deal of pride in her appearance. Instead, he was now looking at somebody dishevelled, saturated in what must have been a concoction of blood and sweat. Toby thought to himself that she just needed the tears now to complete the cliché. *Dark humour again.* Wasn't this how the emergency services coped with traumatic experiences... by making light of them? He wondered how many times he had discussed the importance of clients finding their own coping strategies. He wondered how many times they had asked him what he would do in their position, and he had told them what may work for him may not work for them, that part of the therapeutic process was about them finding their own answers. Besides, he couldn't imagine any amount of mindfulness would serve any purpose in the scenario he now found himself in. Yet right now all he wanted was somebody else to give him the answer, tell him what he should do, and get him out of this situation. Toby, as a professional had vanished, instead this was Toby, whose bravery and strength of mind it seemed, had almost regressed into that of a child. The child who needed somebody to make this right, to remove him from the nightmare he was facing. There was an irony that he spent a good deal of his time explaining that his job was not to fix situations for people, yet here he was wanting nothing more than somebody to come and fix this for him; to take it away, make it better. He desperately wanted to go back just a couple of hours so he could make a very different decision.

Breaking boundaries

He knew however, this wasn't about one bad decision. There had been a series of events leading up to this moment and several points where Toby felt he could have, or indeed should have, made very different choices. But he hadn't, and here he was now having to live with those choices and their consequences. He had managed to get himself into this situation and he knew realistically that he couldn't enlist the help of anyone else to get him out of it. As he looked at Olivia, he was overcome with a pang of sadness at what she had experienced. Accompanying this though was a feeling of guilt around whether he had in some way either consciously or unconsciously brought them both to this point and put them in this situation. As he questioned his professional integrity, the guilt turned to anger, anger at Olivia for involving him in this. It was no longer simply about his profession, but also about the impact, this would have on his personal life, on his marriage, on Beth. His thoughts turned to his wife, the beautiful, kind and loyal Beth. How would she feel once she found out about what he was involved in? They had been together for fifteen years and had always enjoyed a close and happy marriage. This would inevitably feel like a betrayal, and whilst it was one thing considering the impact this would have on him, the thought of how this would affect Beth was heart-breaking and not something he could even bear to consider. Then, he was present again and knew that whilst any actions from now would have consequences, inaction was

Breaking boundaries

simply not an option. He turned towards Olivia and for the first time in what seemed like an eternity, was able to hear the words come out of his mouth.

'How do we just leave him? Look at him, look around you, you can't just walk away from him.'

Toby wasn't hiding his anger.

'This was an accident. We can clean up any traces of us being here and leave. We have the perfect alibi, I was in a therapy session with you. We both corroborate each other's story.'

'You're asking me to commit perjury for you?'

'I'm asking you to do what you know is right.'

'Take a look at the body just inches away from your feet. What about any of this is right?' Toby snapped back. His anger was raw, almost certainly coming from fear he thought, and he wasn't done.

'This is your husband, the father of your child, how can you live without conscience at what's happened, what you've done? How will you be able to look your son in the eye knowing you just walked away and left his father to die?'

'We don't have a choice. This looks bad, really bad, and if we call the police now and are here when they arrive, this won't end well for us.'

'Look at the scene Olivia. There's no hiding what's happened. Whatever we do next will have consequences of some sort. There are several possibilities, all of them bleak.'

He felt his voice raising, his tone was changing. Toby had always prided himself on being self-aware. He now recognised there was a deeper

Breaking boundaries

sense of anger replacing the panic. He was struggling to even look at Olivia. He knew her background, he'd been seeing her as a client for several months now. He knew the marriage wasn't a happy one and she had disclosed being subjected to abuse throughout. So why couldn't he sympathise? Why was he struggling to grasp her apparent lack of emotion? His thoughts again turned to Beth. Would she be so cold towards him in the same situation? Would she be happy to walk away from his limp body, in the process hiding the truth, living a lie? But this wasn't about Beth, it was about him and Olivia and of course, Eric and Tyler. He was reminded that however grave the situation was, it was vital he try and find some rationality. This proved difficult and the fact he was standing at a crime scene with all the evidence pointing directly at him, seemed surreal. He turned to Olivia, his voice now more controlled.

'What do you suggest we do?'

'This was an accident, Toby. It wasn't anybody's fault, I had to defend myself. You know what I've been subjected to over the years, the emotional abuse, the physical violence, the infidelity. Don't feel sorry for the son of a bitch.'

Olivia's voice felt cold and without remorse.

'You think he deserved this?' Toby said in a quiet, disbelieving voice as his head turned from the body on the floor to Olivia.

'You think I deserved what he did to me for all those years?' she retorted sharply. Olivia was

11

Breaking boundaries

deflecting and Toby knew it. It was a technique he used often in therapy when he felt clients were seeking answers from him and he wanted to empower them, to find them for themselves. Suddenly *he* felt like a client, a vulnerable one, and he didn't like it.

'We're wasting time. We need to make a decision... and quickly,' she added.

Toby turned as if to move toward the door. He was stopped in his tracks by Olivia grabbing his arm, tightly. This wasn't the first time she had done this.

'Toby before we leave here, we have to make sure we are straight with our stor...'

Toby cut her off abruptly, shocking her in the process.

'Your husband is lying in a pool of blood in front of you, in your marital home, and your main concern is getting our fucking stories straight? What the hell is wrong with you?'

He had never spoken to her like this before, why would he? Their relationship had been a professional one, although there had been moments when he had questioned whether Olivia was close to overstepping the boundaries. He didn't ordinarily swear, but the situation was grave, and pleasantries were the last thing on his mind. Even if by some miracle, he was able to practice again, his relationship with Olivia was over. He no longer cared about causing offence and had felt up to this point he had been incredibly restrained, considering

Breaking boundaries

the desperate situation they found themselves in. Olivia placed her hand on his shoulder and rubbed it gently for a moment, appearing to change tact, perhaps to placate him. She needed him on side.

'Toby, I know you didn't want any of this, and I feel bad that I got you involved, but this isn't your fault. We cannot control what has happened, but we can control what happens from now, *we* control the narrative.

The police will be suspicious, I need to make this look more believable.'

Toby stared at her for a moment with a look of disbelief.

'You're talking about tampering with a crime scene, fabricating evidence. If you're honest, I can help you. You have access to your case notes. They reflect your disclosure about the abuse you have been subjected to and the impact this has had on you. *They* will corroborate your story. Think about this.' He had hoped to change her mind, to persuade her to do the right thing, but her mind was made up.

'I can't risk it. If they don't believe me, I lose everything. No, there's only one way out of this, and it's not by calling the police, well not right now anyway,' she replied softly.

'Olivia, I....'

The soft tone quickly disappeared as she cut Toby off with an assertiveness he had not witnessed in her previously.

Breaking boundaries

'Tyler is visiting his grandparents for the holidays, which buys me some time. This is how it has to be.'

'Just like that huh?'

'We have no choice. Think of Beth.'

'Don't bring my wife into this,' he snapped angrily.

'I'm sorry, I'm trying to help you here Toby.'

'Help me?'

'I don't want either of us to suffer. You have been a great therapist and have really helped me, showing me kindness and affection. I've grown quite fond of you, but you already know this.'

Toby thought about all the boundaries Olivia had overstepped in that one sentence, then smiled inwardly. He wondered why Olivia showing affection towards him seemed to be the first thing that came to mind considering the severity of the situation they were both facing.

'Toby?' Her voice was soft and gentle again and for a moment he caught a glimpse of the Olivia he had got to know in the therapeutic setting.

He had put his head in his hands, something he often did when he felt he needed perspective. But this wasn't about perspective, not in this moment. He had regressed. As a child, he used to do this to try and disappear, to pretend a situation wasn't really happening. He knew the psyche was powerful as a kid, but as an adult, he was acutely aware this was very real and wasn't disappearing. Again, that thought *action has consequences, but so does inaction.* Toby knew he had to quickly assess the lesser of two evils and make a decision. Finally,

Breaking boundaries

after a few moments of silence between the two, he turned to Olivia.

'I need to use the bathroom.'

He didn't. He just needed to be somewhere else right now, anywhere but here. More importantly, he wanted to be away from Olivia. He was struggling to even look her in the eye such was his disdain for her right now. He wondered if he had sounded convincing.

'Really?' Olivia said in a tone which Toby struggled to place. Panic? Confusion? Perhaps suspicion? Maybe it was a combination of all three, but one thing Toby was sure about was that this Olivia was very different to the vulnerable, abuse victim he had worked with over the last few months. She was much more confident and assured, but at this stage, he felt that the vulnerability was masked by panic, and this was her way of dealing with an unimaginably frantic and desperate situation. He didn't reply.

'Okay, do what you have to do. There's a toilet on the ground floor, through the hallway over there, second door on your right,' Olivia said gesticulating as she directed him. As Toby turned to walk away, she shouted after him.

'Toby!'

He turned to look at her but didn't answer.

'Don't be long.'

He moved through the hallway, his eyes noticing every last detail on the walls. He thought about the years of practice, all the clients he had worked with,

Breaking boundaries

all the disclosure which had taken place in his safe and comfortable setting. He found himself longing for that environment right now. It was more than just a safe place for his clients. It was *his* sanctuary, *his* safe place as well. Then he was struck by a thought. He had worked with difficult clients but never had he regretted meeting any of them, regardless of their levels of engagement, their occasional projection or even the nature of their disclosure. He had worked with perpetrators as well as victims and had embraced the challenge of having clients who perhaps contravened his own value system. But right now, right at this moment, as he surveyed the hallway, he regretted ever meeting Olivia Stanton. Now out of view, he paused for a moment. He removed his phone from his pocket and stared at it intently whilst trying in vain to gather his thoughts.

Minutes later Toby walked back down the hallway and into the living room, the scene of the crime. For a moment they simply stood and stared at each other with no words exchanged. Those few seconds felt like hours to Toby. If he didn't like silences in therapy, he certainly didn't like them here. He was out of his comfort zone but needed to hold things together. Thoughts of Beth again entered his head as he wondered what would happen next. The ever-devoted, sweet and innocent Beth who showed nothing but kindness and compassion to others. The woman who had loved him unconditionally for years and had always stood by him. He wondered how

Breaking boundaries

she could ever stand by him through this and thought about how in an instant so much could change. The ripple effect. He couldn't even imagine how many lives would be affected by his actions. Toby knew this thought process would be his downfall. Now was no time for sentiment or emotion. He had to be lucid and remove any feeling from the situation. He had to find a mental toughness he had never had to display before; one he was not sure he even had. He had to take control, for Beth, for his family, and for himself. He wondered why he hadn't put Olivia into that equation. Wasn't she a victim here? The outcome didn't change the events leading up to it. Still, for some reason, Toby found himself unable to sympathise. He looked down and realised his fists were clenched so hard, his hands were bleeding from where his nails had dug in. He was angry, perhaps hadn't realised until now just how much so. How could he have been so naive as to allow himself to be placed in this situation where he had had to take such drastic action, almost certainly ending his career, possibly even his marriage in the process? Olivia had been waiting, well not simply waiting; he could see that things had been moved but showed no surprise. She had already told him her story had to be believable. This had meant her trying to make the scene look even more like a struggle, like a brutal and prolonged attack she had been forced to defend herself from. Olivia came and stood next to Toby. When she

Breaking boundaries

opened her mouth to speak it was direct with no trace of emotion.

'Ready?'

'I think I'm going to be sick,' Toby mumbled, before making a hasty retreat back to the bathroom.

Minutes later, he reappeared.

Olivia looked at him and smiled.

'Are you ok?'

Toby took a deep breath.

'It's time to leave' he replied in a more controlled tone. Olivia left the house first, through the back door, the same door through which Toby had entered a while earlier. The property was detached and on its own grounds, which meant being seen was less of a problem. Toby reached for the door handle before turning to survey the kitchen. He was fearful of what he was leaving behind but more fearful of what awaited him outside. He now had to live with what he had done and even if he escaped punishment, there was no escaping his conscience. Naturally, his eyes were drawn to the clock on the oven, still illuminating the kitchen. Olivia was now waiting outside. He tentatively reached for the door handle, turned it slowly and exited the house.

Breaking boundaries

2

Toby was woken by the sound of his alarm. Reaching across his bedside table he hit the snooze button, groaned, and closed his eyes in a vain attempt to squeeze out an extra ten minutes. As a student, he didn't particularly like going to bed, but equally, once he was there he didn't like getting out of it either. It wasn't that he specifically disliked mornings, simply that he enjoyed student life and wanted to maximise his time at university with little regard for responsibility. This was his final year and he was entering the final term. Toby knew the time was fast approaching when he, as his parents kept reminding him, would have to exit education and make his way. He was fortunate that he came from an affluent background where he had been given an allowance through university and (much to the jealousy of his friends) had also had the luxury of owning a new car, a present for his eighteenth birthday. Whilst Toby did not feel uncomfortable with the lifestyle he had been afforded, he was acutely aware that some of his friends at university hadn't had the same opportunities he had, and occasionally felt embarrassed by this. He only had to look down the hallway at Mac, an insular individual who had struggled financially throughout university to the extent that Toby had been convinced he was more likely to see a minimum-wage job than graduation. Mac came from a single-parent family and Toby always felt bad for him. His

Breaking boundaries

clothes were old, well-worn, almost diametrically opposed to the designer labels Toby wore. Toby had an allowance, Mac a night job; Toby had a car, Mac used public transport when he could afford it and walked when he couldn't; Toby had two loving parents who provided emotional support, Mac had lived with his father who did not want him to go to university and placed no value on education. In his mind, it took three years away from earning. Mac had once confided in Toby that his father had threatened to cut him off if he decided to go to university and break the family tradition of entering employment straight from school. As far as Toby knew, Mac's father had made good on that promise. Seeing Mac made Toby feel grateful, a sense of humbleness and appreciation for what he had, and how it could be so intrinsically different from what other people had. Though he enjoyed a good relationship with his parents, on the occasions when they would argue, Toby used the thought of Mac's position as an incentive to not allow things to escalate. The thought of not having their support made him anxious and induced a feeling of sadness. Whilst he welcomed the financial contribution, he was more appreciative of being able to pick up the phone and call his mum if he was having a bad day. He enjoyed their conversations, and she had a very natural ability to help him identify the positive aspects of almost any situation. Toby would speak with his mother several times over the course of a week and she was his go-to if

Breaking boundaries

anything was on his mind. He felt no shame in having such a close bond with her, and even the label of *'mummy's boy'* did nothing to deter this. She appreciated how hard his father worked, but wasn't materialistic and would sacrifice a nice car for more family time in an instant. Her family was her only focus and whilst it was never said in front of him, he could tell his father sometimes felt she mollycoddled Toby. There had been occasions he had noticed an exchange of looks between them when she had been comforting him, something which made him feel uncomfortable. He hated the thought of his parents arguing and often wondered what this might look like as he had never witnessed it first-hand. He wasn't sure whether they did argue, but if they did, Toby felt they did a good job of keeping it private, not allowing any ill feelings to overspill into the time they spent together as a family. He was proud of the person his mother was and the relationship they enjoyed. She was, in his eyes, the kindest person he had ever met and he knew without a doubt she held the family together, well respected on both sides. Toby's relationship with his father was a little different. Rather than be his natural self, occasionally around his father, he would catch himself seeking approval and validation. He was close to his mother, but his father had been a role model for him growing up and he was desperate to make him proud, even if he didn't want to be like him in some areas. His father was an accountant and had worked his way up through the firm which

Breaking boundaries

he had been at for twenty-five years. Whilst he loved his family, Toby knew he was extremely career-focused and there was never a plan for more than one child. Toby sometimes questioned whether there had actually been a plan for him, but his mother had assured him that from the early days of her and his father dating, he had always been part of their future. Sometimes Toby felt grateful he hadn't had to share the love of his parents or even his toys with others, whilst on other occasions, he felt lonely and wondered what it would have been like to have a sibling. Somebody to play games with, rather than either playing on his own or against a computer; somebody to build dens with; somebody to go out exploring with. He was very conflicted when it came to this subject, and though he didn't resent his parents for their decision, or his father for being career focused when he entered adolescence, he had determined that his career would be secondary to his own family. Toby envisaged having a large family but knew a stable career was essential in being able to provide for them. This was where he saw his father as a role model. He worked hard, displayed great dedication, and always found a way through adversity. He had once explained to Toby that he was effectively a hermit whilst at university himself and very much lived by the mantra that it was a place to study and that it was about enhancing your knowledge, not your social life. This was perhaps another area where Toby and he differed. Toby took his

Breaking boundaries

education seriously, but right now he was still unsure what he wanted to do. He had never spoken openly to his father about his career aspirations because in truth he wasn't sure what they were. There had been vague ideas he had considered in passing, but nothing definitive. He also quite enjoyed the social aspect of university. There had been nights where he had woken up in strange places, nights where he had got into a little mischief, and nights he couldn't remember at all. He felt this was part of university, part of growing up, and that enhancing one's social life was just as important as enhancing one's knowledge. Whilst he wasn't sure exactly what his chosen career would be, one thing he did know was that he didn't want to follow his father into accounting. He hated maths and found it a struggle at school. His father had tried to encourage him to study it at college, but in a battle of wills, on this occasion, it was Toby who was the victor. He ultimately chose to study English, Psychology and History, subjects which piqued his interest.

Although he had not excelled at college, Toby had done enough to receive firm offers of acceptance from four out of his five university choices. Ultimately, he chose a university far enough away from home that his parents wouldn't be in a position to just drop by unannounced, but still close enough that it wouldn't be too much of a problem for him to get home, or his parents to get to

Breaking boundaries

him, should he need them. In his later years, Toby would single out his college experience as being one of the most influential factors in his choice of university course, and subsequently his career. He had enjoyed all of his subjects at college, but when it came down to discovering what prompted him to opt for Psychology, it wasn't a case of what, it was a case of who...Georgina Sampson. He remembered the day he had first laid eyes on her. She had stood out to him as a fresh-faced sixteen-year-old girl with a captivating smile and optimism that you couldn't help but admire. They had both had the same idea of going to such lengths to avoid being late, that they had arrived early, long before others. Toby was a little shy, but he felt an immediate connection to Georgina, mesmerised by her. That first meeting had been etched in his memory.

'Hi, I'm Georgina,' she had said holding out her hand.

'Toby,' he replied feeling a little unsure but shaking her hand, nonetheless.

'I'm feeling a little anxious about this, I sometimes struggle with meeting new people.'

'You can't tell,' Toby said in a way that made Georgina let out a nervous giggle.

'My mum says I need to push myself when it comes to social situations and meeting new people. She says it will help me.'

'Push yourself?'

Toby sounded confused.

Breaking boundaries

'Yeah, I struggle with social interaction sometimes, it doesn't come naturally to me.'

Toby pondered for a moment. In front of him was this energetic young girl who had gone out of her way to introduce herself to him, a stranger. She struck him as confident, not socially awkward. This didn't make sense to him. Georgina noted the look on his face and broke the momentary silence.

'It seems crazy right?'

He was glad of Georgina's interjection but still felt bad and a little embarrassed with the way he had responded. Toby wasn't sure what to say next and was relieved that Georgina had appeared to grab the initiative and further the conversation.

'Do you live locally?'

'Relatively. I am about twenty-five minutes away by bus. How about you?'

'I live a little further out. My mum drives me here. It was part of the deal with her allowing me to come to college.'

'Deal?'

'She's very protective. She didn't think I was ready for college but said I could come here as long as she was able to drive me. She was worried I might fall in with the wrong crowd. She thinks I am impressionable and easily led.'

'Are you?' he said with a grin.

Georgina smiled and paused for a moment.

'I guess it depends on what mood you catch me in.'

'Does your mum not trust you?'

Breaking boundaries

'You could say that, but it's also other people she doesn't trust. You see my mum is a very suspicious person and trusting people doesn't come naturally to her. She sees the bad in society, in people in general, and believes that often even when people are nice, there's a hidden agenda, a darker motive.'

'She sounds paranoid' Toby said flippantly. He soon wished he hadn't when he saw the look on Georgina's face change.

'I'm sorry, I didn't mean anything by it,' he said nervously.

'It's ok, you weren't to know, but my mum is borderline for having a paranoid personality disorder.'

'What does borderline mean?'

'It basically means not all professionals agree. Some have diagnosed her with a PPD, whilst others feel she simply has unresolved trust issues.'

'What do you think?'

'I think we need to get inside the classroom before all the seats are taken…and call me George.'

Toby hadn't noticed the other students arriving whilst they had been deep in conversation, neither of them had. He paused and wondered how long they would have been oblivious to their surroundings had the conversation not become awkward. There was something about her which was strangely alluring, but he also got a sense there was much more beneath the surface. It wasn't necessarily anything she had said, more perhaps her body language and the things she hadn't said.

Breaking boundaries

There was something about her mother that she didn't feel comfortable discussing. Toby wondered if George's smile and friendly nature were masking something, but before he could give this any further thought, she grabbed his arm, handed him his bag, and walked him into the classroom, still smiling. The rest of the day went quickly for Toby, and whilst he had enjoyed all of his classes, the English lesson was the one he had enjoyed the most. The bus journey home had given him time for some quiet reflection on his first full day at college. He quickly realised it wasn't the lessons he had enjoyed; it was meeting and spending time with Georgina Sampson. He'd had a girlfriend in school and remembered how upset he had been when she had ended their six-month relationship. Unable to face her, he had skipped the classes they shared for a week, which hadn't gone unnoticed, and had ultimately drawn the wrath of his father. He smiled as he thought back to the contrasting reactions from his parents. His father had been furious, reminding him of the importance of his education. He had highlighted how Toby's future began with his GCSE results which would ultimately shape his college and university ambitions. His mother was more understanding and placed an arm around him. He loved both of his parents and looked up to his father, but at that moment, he had just needed somebody to talk to, and his mother had provided this. Toby had always felt he got the best of both worlds when it came to his parents. His father was

27

Breaking boundaries

motivated, well connected and very focused on his career. He might not be the type of dad who would sit down and put an arm around you when you were sad, but he also wasn't the type to miss your school plays or football matches. Toby was drawn back to George. This felt very different to the feelings he had had for his girlfriend. These emotions were different to anything he had experienced with any girl previously, but he didn't know why, and it frustrated him. He hated not having the answers and felt confused. George was pretty, he knew this, but that wasn't it. There was something else he couldn't put his finger on. Was it the smile, which had a way of drawing you in, a smile that could make you believe in the darkest times that everything really would be okay? Was it perhaps that innocence, a social clumsiness almost that made her alluring? Toby changed direction. Maybe it wasn't anything physical, but more about her personality. She seemed genuine and sincere, kind, and open. Suddenly he was struck by a thought he felt uncomfortable with. In the little time they had spent together that day, he had learned she had difficulty in social situations, and her mother had a mental illness. He wondered if what he was feeling was pity. Toby didn't like the idea of being a saviour rather than a friend. He suddenly felt consumed with a sense of guilt as he began questioning his feelings. If what he felt was pity, was he looking down on her, judging her situation? But how could he hold these thoughts when he knew so little about

Breaking boundaries

her? He was brought back into the moment by the jolting of the bus and the realisation this was his stop. As he headed for the bus doors, he zipped up his coat in anticipation of the harsh wind which had begun to pick up. The weather always felt cooler out in the countryside, and today had been particularly cold. He exited the bus and began the ten-minute walk along the country lane which would take him to his front door. He enjoyed the fact he lived in the countryside, although by his own admittance, it could get lonely sometimes. The walk could be very cold in the winter and though he had desperately tried to cling to the summertime, autumn had now arrived, and with it, the inevitable cold snap. Snow in these parts wasn't uncommon and when it did fall, it made the journey increasingly more difficult as the buses would not venture this far out. This would mean Toby having to walk to the main road to catch the bus, adding a further fifteen minutes to his journey time. In plummeting temperatures and adverse conditions, this thought had little appeal to him. As he entered the house he was greeted by his mother who asked him about his day. He wondered whether this was out of courtesy or intrigue and considered whether or not to mention his new friend. Ultimately, he decided not to, instead simply telling her it had been okay before retiring to his room. The next few weeks saw Toby and George grow closer. He was very fond of her and had now dismissed any previous thoughts that this was fuelled by pity. The truth was he liked George, he

Breaking boundaries

liked spending time with her, he enjoyed their conversations, having fun and not taking things too seriously. Whilst they were only friends, Toby was harbouring hopes that they may become more. There was an attraction for him, and he looked forward to spending time with her in the classes they shared. Even on the days when they didn't have any classes together, they would frequently meet for lunch and just hang out. Just before Christmas however, something changed, and Toby's perception of George being infallible and unwavering in the face of adversity was shattered. Whilst most people hated Monday mornings, Toby looked forward to them. He had English up first which meant time with George. He couldn't think of a better start to the day, the week, and approached the corridor with his usual vigour. As always, he was there early. Ordinarily, he and George would arrive twenty minutes or so before class started to allow themselves the time to catch up, whilst consuming the obligatory energy drink. Usually, George would be there to greet him. Her mother would have to drop her off at an earlier time so she could get to work afterwards. Today however was different. As Toby approached the classroom there was no sign of George. He thought she may just be running late, but as the beginning of the lesson drew nearer, there was still no sign of her. Toby felt subdued and distracted during the lesson. He had sent her a message, but there had been no response. He was despondent and felt sure he hadn't taken anything

Breaking boundaries

in from the lesson. It was at this moment Toby realised his feelings for George were stronger than he had previously acknowledged. Though only one lesson, he had missed her presence. He thought of George when they were not together and spent much of the weekend exchanging messages with her. Suddenly spending time in his room on his own didn't feel so isolating. In fact, he had withdrawn from family time in the evening in favour of talking to George. Toby exited the classroom caught in the usual melee of people scrambling for the door to grab a snack before the next class. He stood in the corridor for a moment, staring at his phone. Why hadn't she responded? Toby found a quiet spot and decided to call George...voicemail. He deliberated for a moment and then hung up without speaking. He sent her another message asking if she was okay but now wondered if this was in hope rather than expectation. The college day ended without any response from George, leaving Toby filled with a variety of emotions. Actually, he didn't know what he was feeling but knew there was something in the pit of his stomach which was causing him distress. That evening Toby couldn't focus and tried on several occasions to call her none of which yielded any success. He now just wanted the day to end and hoped when he awoke, he would have something from her, anything. He didn't know what love felt like but wondered if it was something like this. It wasn't simply physical attraction, it was how she made him feel when they were together, it was

Breaking boundaries

her smile, her calming nature, and her warm generosity. It was all of these things and Toby knew with a large degree of certainty, he was going to tell George how he felt, hoping she felt the same way. That night Toby was restless. He didn't sleep particularly well, his thoughts dominated by the girl who was his motivation for getting out of bed on the bitter winter mornings and braving the cold to get to college. Throughout the night he had continuously reached for his phone, but any expectations were quickly disappearing.

The clock displayed just after seven in the morning as Toby was abruptly awoken by his alarm. It didn't feel like he had been asleep for long and he knew the day ahead would be a challenge for this very reason. He reached over in vain to hit the snooze button, but instead knocked it to the floor and had to get out of bed to retrieve it. Eyes still bleary, he picked up his phone, waiting for a few seconds for them to focus accordingly. Still nothing. Tuesday was one of the days he and George didn't have classes together, but would still meet up for lunch. He showered, pulled on his clothes and left for the bus stop, with only a cursory glance towards his parents on his way out. Whilst his father was oblivious, Toby's mother was astute, she knew him well. He knew there would be questions later and wondered how much he was comfortable telling her. Perhaps she could offer some insight, or perhaps this was one thing he wasn't ready to talk to

Breaking boundaries

anybody about. He reached college and headed for the main doors. Deep in thought, he was startled by somebody jumping onto his back, covering his eyes in the process.

'Guess who?' said the voice with giddiness and excitement which felt out of place for this time in the morning.

'George!'

Toby spun around and hugged her, after a few seconds realising it was tighter and with more feeling than it ever had been previously. He worried she may have picked up on this and let go promptly. This wasn't the right time to have *that* conversation with her. He had missed her, worried about her, but that feeling in the pit of his stomach was a very different one now. He paused for a moment.

'Where have you been, I tried to call you, sent you messages. Are you okay?'

'Aww Toby, you're so sweet, were you worried about me?'

Toby knew she was teasing him but felt a little awkward. He also felt angry at her for putting him through this and now seemingly trivialising his emotional struggle over the last twenty-four hours.

'George I'm serious, what happened yesterday?'

'I wasn't feeling well and switched off my phone so I could sleep. No big deal.'

'No big deal?' Toby thought. Throughout the entire day and night, he had been overcome with concern and worry. He had lost sleep and disengaged from his parents. He was more worried

Breaking boundaries

about the latter and didn't relish the awkward conversation which would undoubtedly come later. It may not be a big deal to her, but it was to him. Toby wondered if he should verbalise this, but simply smiled back at her and kept those thoughts to himself, agreeing to meet for lunch later. Lunch had been nice, but George had not wanted to talk about her absence. Toby respected this and hadn't pushed. They had instead talked about the looming deadline of an assignment and argued in jest about which of them was least prepared. Throughout the day Toby was again distracted in his classes, but this time for a different reason. Something didn't feel right to him. He and George were close and opened up to each other about the most personal of things, things which neither had disclosed to anybody else. Why was she suddenly so dismissive, completely shutting down on him?

'Come and sit with your mum'.

Toby had been deep in thought and oblivious to his mother asking him how his day had gone. She was perched on a chair at the breakfast bar, having momentarily ceased what she was doing in the kitchen. Toby got up from the sofa and went and sat next to her, bracing himself for what was about to come.

'Tell me about it,' she said warmly, with a sympathetic tone.

'About what?'

Breaking boundaries

'Toby I'm your mother and I know when my boy isn't feeling himself. Now is one of those times.'

'Am I that obvious?'

'Not to your father, he's oblivious', she said with a smile.

They both broke into laughter and that eased a little of the anxiety Toby had been feeling.

'There's this girl.'

'George?'

'How did you know?'

'Are you kidding? it's the only person we ever hear about. I was starting to think there were only two of you at that college.'

His Mother smiled. A smile which grew wider when she saw her son blushing.

'We get on really well, but yesterday she didn't come to college. She didn't answer my calls or respond to my messages. Today she just dismissed it like nothing happened, and it feels a little strange.'

'Strange how?'

'Well, we talk all the time and then she ignores me and completely shuts me down when I ask her why. I don't understand.'

'Maybe she had a bad day, honey. We all have them. If you have a close relationship, don't push her. You may well be worrying over nothing and don't want to upset this girl if you like her.'

'Who said I like her?' Toby asked coyly.

Toby's mum reached out and put her hand on his shoulder with a smile.

Breaking boundaries

'You did Toby, with all the things you just said and the things you didn't. Give her time, respect her boundaries and I'm sure it will be fine sweetie.'

Toby simply smiled without replying. That evening he was much more conversive with his parents and family time involved playing a board game. Whilst he had won, he had felt like this was a little contrived, a hollow victory. It seemed a deliberate attempt to cheer him up, orchestrated by his mother no doubt. But he didn't mind, after all, it had taken his mind off George for a while. He retired to his room at around ten and set his alarm for the following morning. He considered the conversations he had had with both George and his mum. Something still didn't feel quite right, but he wasn't sure what this was. He glanced at his phone, switched off his light and entered a much-needed sleep.

Several weeks passed, which saw the two grow closer still. They never spoke about George's absence, and with things seemingly back to normal, Toby hadn't thought about it in a while. If it had entered his mind, he thought back to his mother telling him that sometimes people just have a bad day, and this was enough to satisfy his curiosity. He felt his mother was very wise, so when she spoke, he listened. She was usually right, and Toby had no reason to believe this time would be any different. Much to Toby's annoyance, his mother was able to read him, and therefore all attempts he had made to

Breaking boundaries

deny he had a crush on George, were in vain. But was it a crush or was it love? Whilst his mother may recognise he had feelings for George, did she know the depth of these? Did he?

He wasn't sure why he had omitted to tell his mum about his true feelings for George. She was always understanding and never teased him about these things. Still, something had made Toby close up, and if he was uncertain what this was, he felt sure he would struggle to get anybody else to understand. His confusion came from the fact that quite simply, he wasn't able to define what he and George were. On the one hand, it felt like they were more than friends, but on the other, there had been little to suggest they were a couple. George had cuddled up to him at the cinema and there were those moments when they had hugged before parting, where he felt they had held on a little longer than friends ordinarily would do. Then there were those lingering looks which told a very different story to the narrative they were simply friends. Still, they had never had this discussion. Toby often wondered if George was waiting for him to make the first move. He felt confused, but one thing he was clear on was there was a connection between them, and this connection was like nothing he had felt before. Christmas was approaching, the weather had turned, and Toby had spent the last couple of days trudging his way through the snow to get to the bus stop. He could try and convince himself that his attendance was due to a pride in his work and a

Breaking boundaries

commitment to his education, but he knew the real reason he had such endeavour when it came to college, was George. This was the final week before they broke up for the Christmas holidays and Toby and George had made plans to skip class to see a movie. A new release they had both been eager to see was the choice, but Toby was more excited about the company than the movie. He liked the cinema, but more so now because he knew that George would usually cuddle up to him and this closeness, the feel of her face pressed against the side of his, the warmth of her hands holding his, this...this was what he looked forward to more than anything. That morning Toby raced to the bus stop, barely even acknowledging his mother on the way out. She smiled as he hurtled past her, knowing by now that Monday mornings meant Toby's attention was on only one thing, well one person to be precise. He arrived at college and headed through the main doors, along the corridor and toward the common room. Knowing the risk associated with being anywhere in the vicinity of their classroom when they had no plans on entering it, Toby walked cautiously and with his head down. George had needed to see her tutor first thing, however, so it made sense to meet inside, but at the opposite end of the college where it would be unlikely, they would run into their teacher. With the icy cold weather and treacherous conditions Toby had experienced on his journey, he was now feeling even more grateful for this decision. He approached the meeting point and

Breaking boundaries

removed his bag from his shoulder. No George. She was usually the first one there, but he wondered if perhaps she had already gone to see her tutor. He took his phone from his pocket to see if she had messaged him. She hadn't. Toby felt a sudden wave of panic, a sinking feeling in the pit of his stomach. He tried to call her, but it went straight to voice mail. Her phone was either switched off or she was somewhere where there was no reception, he thought. He looked to see if she had been online recently, but she hadn't. He was now feeling incredibly anxious and that feeling he had become acquainted with several weeks back, emerged once again. He tried to calm and rationalise the situation. It was only ten past nine in the morning, perhaps she was running late and her phone had drained its battery, this wasn't unheard of. Nine-thirty approached and passed. The corridor had become busier, but Toby felt completely alone, now consumed with a feeling of dread. He was in no frame of mind to endure a class, so reached for his rucksack, placed his phone back into his pocket, and headed for the exit. Once outside, he began to feel sick. He felt sad. He still wasn't sure what love was. His mother had once told him the best way to find out if you love somebody is to think about how you feel when you're not with them. At the time this had felt like a curious concept to Toby. Surely, he thought, the feeling when you are with somebody is more of an indication of how you feel about them than time spent away from them? Now here in this

Breaking boundaries

moment, in the arctic conditions, feeling isolated, Toby realised what his mother had meant. He loved spending time with George, but perhaps it was the time away from her that gave away the depth of the feelings he carried for her. He realised there had been only two occasions in his life where he felt lost, and not in control of his emotions. Both of those were recent, and both involved George. Perhaps he did love her. But how could that be? They hadn't even officially begun dating yet, although Toby knew there was more to their relationship than just friendship. He headed away from the college campus, found a bench and contemplated what to do next. Even if he had wanted to go to class, he would have been so preoccupied, there would be little chance of him taking anything in. He couldn't go back home as his father had opted not to go into the office today and this would raise too many questions. He often felt his father was more committed to his education than he was, though he would never say this to him. The movie wouldn't be the same without George and there weren't many shops in the centre, certainly not enough to kill several hours. His options were limited. Then a thought entered his head. He knew where George lived. He could go and see her, just to make sure everything was okay. But what if she wasn't? What if she wasn't there or didn't want to see him? Toby was plagued by this inner conflict as he sat weighing up both sides of the argument. The desire to go and see her, just to see her, to see her smile,

Breaking boundaries

to touch her hand, to make sure she was well. Then there was the fear of her telling him something he didn't want to hear, or him seeing something he wouldn't wish to see. Toby had no idea what this could be, he just knew he was keen to avoid it. He was still deliberating as he got onto the bus and asked for a return ticket to George's village. If nothing more, the journey would kill some of the time required to then allow him to return home, his parents being none the wiser. The journey seemed to last forever and for Toby, alone with his thoughts, anything that gave him this much thinking time wasn't good. He had no idea what he would say and was still considering what to do as he approached George's front door. He knocked and stood back. No answer. He knocked again, this time a little louder. Still nothing. He was shaking and now felt nauseous. Unsure what to do, he found himself heading around the back. George had told him previously her bedroom faced out onto the garden, and she would frequently stare out at the picturesque countryside, which she felt was cathartic. Toby smiled as he recalled pretending to know what that meant, but having to ask his mother later. He tried knocking on the door next to the conservatory. Still no reply. He knocked louder again but felt uncomfortable in doing so. He turned despondently and began walking back to the front of the house. He had no idea what he would do now and felt worse than he had earlier in the morning. Then as he glanced up, something caught his eye,

Breaking boundaries

something in George's window. The curtain had moved, or were his eyes simply showing him what he wanted to see rather than what he was actually seeing? Suddenly without consciously thinking about it, he yelled her name, then a second time louder, and with more desperation. His heart appeared to skip a beat as he saw a figure appear in the window. George opened it a little and popped her head out.

'George!'

'Toby, what are you doing here?'

'You didn't show up, I couldn't reach you, I was worried.'

George raised a smile, but Toby could see that it took effort and it faded quickly.

'Toby, it's really sweet that you care, but you should go.'

'Go? Why?' Toby said both with confusion and sadness. He felt vulnerable and was unsure how else to respond.

'Toby there are things you don't understand about me.'

'How can I understand them if you don't tell me?'

'It's complicated.'

'I thought we were friends, maybe...' Toby caught himself, but George had picked up on that last word...*maybe*.

'Maybe what Toby?'

'Nothing, it doesn't matter?'

'You raised it, it matters.'

Breaking boundaries

He was now feeling extremely nervous. He had dreaded having this conversation but worried he had been backed into a corner.

'I'm not sure what to say,' he replied hesitantly.

'Wait there and give me a minute,' she shouted.

Toby was certain that minute was the longest of his life and there was no indication of what was about to happen next. Should he be honest with George about how he felt and risk rejection? Or should he make something up, but always wonder what could have been? This didn't feel like a particularly easy choice. He felt if making decisions like this was part of being an adult, he wanted no part of it. George appeared, disrupting his thoughts. She was still in her night-time attire with no makeup, and hair which she had just tied up quickly. Toby had never seen her like this before, but his pulse was racing, and as he stared at her he realised just how much she meant to him. He had only known her for around three months, but it felt like a lifetime. He gazed at her in silence as she motioned him to come inside. Still unsure what he was going to say, Toby smiled, took her hand, and stepped inside, closing the door behind him.

'That's Dylan, my older brother,' she said noticing Toby staring at a photograph on the mantelpiece.

'I didn't know you had a brother, you've never mentioned him,' Toby replied in a slightly confused, yet inquisitive manner.

Breaking boundaries

'He doesn't live with us, he left for the army three years ago and it really affected my parents. They were very much against the idea, but he was determined to go.'

'Do you miss him?'

'We used to be close, he always looked out for me, but I could tell he began to change and as much as I didn't want him to leave, I knew he needed to, for his own good. So yeah, I do kind of miss him, but more the person he used to be when we were growing up if that makes sense?'

'I guess so,' Toby said, not fully understanding.

This wasn't something he had ever experienced, but he could see that it affected George just by the way her tone and facial expression had changed when she had begun talking about her brother. Toby felt a sudden feeling of angst as there was an awkward silence between the two. He didn't know what to say now and was hoping George would break the silence.

'Toby there are things about me you don't know, well one thing in particular.'

The overwhelming feeling of panic took hold of Toby once again. At this moment in time, he was unsure whether he wanted to hear whatever it was George was about to tell him. He did a good job of disguising how he was feeling, and what he was thinking, managing to reply calmly.

'Okay.'

'I have bipolar disorder.'

Breaking boundaries

'Bipolar disorder?' Toby had heard the term mentioned previously but had no real insight into what it meant. He knew it wasn't a physical illness, but any knowledge beyond that was lacking. George could see Toby looking perplexed and smiled at his innocence.

'It means my moods are not always stable. Sometimes I feel great, on top of the world and energetic, but occasionally I feel really low like I can't get out of bed and see little point to anything. On those days I struggle to see or even speak to anyone. I don't have any control over which George is going to wake up in the morning.'

Toby felt a sudden relief. It hadn't been about him, she hadn't been ignoring him, and it didn't mean she didn't like him. No, this was about her and what she was going through. Then the relief turned to guilt. He felt selfish. He was more concerned with what he was feeling than what she was experiencing. He couldn't imagine how it must feel to not be in control of your moods. Sure he had on occasions felt down, but he had always had an explanation behind them, which removed any uncertainty. George on the other hand had no idea from one day to the next how she was going to be feeling when she woke up. Unaware of whether his face had given away his thoughts, Toby spoke up, his voice cracking.

'George that must be awful, I had no idea.'

'Of course you didn't Toby, I decided against announcing it in the college bulletin.'

Breaking boundaries

Toby laughed, but when he looked at her, barely able to raise a smile, he got a feeling he didn't like. He could see George's struggle and all he wanted to do was hold her, tell her he loved her and make things better. Only one of those things was a real option for him so without saying a word he put his arms out and pulled her in for a hug, which seemed to last forever in his mind. He felt a sense of anger; anger that George was having to experience this through no fault of her own; anger at the fact he had no control over her condition and could not make it better; anger over the fact she had not told him, instead suffering in silence. They sat huddled together on the sofa for a while with no words spoken. At one point Toby had heard the faint sound of sobbing and pulled her closer towards him, resting his face on the top of her head so tightly he could smell her hair. That conflict again. He was desperate to take George's pain away, swap her tears for that smile he had been so captivated by since the very first time he saw it. However, he also didn't want this moment to end and had never felt as close to somebody as he did right now to George.

'Are you okay?'

'I guess,' George replied rather sullenly.

'Your mum being protective, the deal she made with you, not feeling you were ready for college. It's because of this isn't it?'

'Ah Toby you do listen to me,' she said teasing him with a friendly tickle.

Breaking boundaries

'Always'. Toby smiled, jumping back, before realising he probably looked like a kid with a crush.

'Mum is always afraid that I may have a sudden episode whilst at college, although on most occasions I know when I wake up what sort of day I'm going to have. She can tell too; she knows me well. She just feels more reassured taking me to college herself rather than me using public transport. I guess the journey helps her to gauge how I'm feeling,'

'Can your mood change at any time, and does it change frequently?'

'That's a bit of a myth. Some people believe that with Bipolar your moods will change many times during the day. It doesn't happen like that. I can go a few weeks or even months where I feel okay, but then without any reason or explanation I can have a few days where I can't get out of bed and struggle to function.'

'So you have no control over how you feel?'

'That's the hardest part. For most people, there is an explanation for their moods. For me, there is just a label.'

'What causes it?'

Toby was mindful that while he didn't want her to feel like this was an inquisition, he was curious and had a genuine interest. He desperately wanted to understand.

'Some people believe it's psychological, others don't believe in it at all. The Doctors tell me it is to do with the chemicals in my brain. There's an

Breaking boundaries

imbalance and it impacts my mood. I take medication which helps, but it doesn't cure it.'

Toby reached out and grabbed her hand. He didn't know what to say but was glad he now knew. At least he had an explanation and his mind no longer needed to take him in countless directions.

George went into more detail about her condition and whilst Toby asked occasional questions, he mostly stayed quiet and just listened. Although they were talking and they had been physically close, George was far removed from her usual effervescent self, but Toby didn't mind. Now he knew why and that was okay with him. The trepidation had now transformed into sorrow, yet also determination. Sorrow at what George was going through and determination because he was committed to helping her through this, doing everything he could to be a supportive friend. That Christmas had seen them finally disclose their feelings to one another. George had bought Toby a photo frame, which would later be occupied with a photograph they had both loved, taken on a day out at a theme park. He had bought her a necklace with two hearts intertwined showing each of their names. She had been overcome with emotion and had vowed never to take it off. Their relationship blossomed and the two had become inseparable throughout college. Whilst George knew on occasions her condition would be a struggle, she felt happier knowing Toby was there to support her, and Toby in turn felt better now he understood what

Breaking boundaries

George was experiencing. They had rarely argued, and Toby had firmly believed they would be together forever, but university would prove to be a difficult hurdle to get over, and ultimately, the distance between them had taken its toll on their relationship.

Toby stared at the picture of himself and George, which rested at the side of his bed. His life at university was very different to the one he had back home and he would sometimes catch himself craving for his college days. He remembered that feeling he would experience at the beginning of every day, knowing he was going to see her. It had always been about George, from the first time he had laid eyes on her. Things felt so much simpler back then for him and he longed for a return to those days. That sixteen-year-old boy was now a twenty-one-year-old man and things had changed. George had opted to stay at home and seek employment whilst Toby had enrolled in a university some seventy-five miles away. As George didn't drive, this in itself had presented as a barrier and Toby's willingness to make the journey each weekend had waned over time. Every weekend became every other weekend and soon this became monthly as the two had begun to drift apart. At the end of Toby's first year, he had been offered a summer job on campus which he had seen as a great opportunity to earn money and gain work experience. George hadn't seen it the same way,

Breaking boundaries

instead feeling that Toby was abandoning her. It wasn't a heated argument. He and George didn't work like that, but it was enough for them to agree that the relationship had run its course and they were perhaps moving in different directions. There had been tears and regret, but no cross words. They had remained in touch but spoke less these days. Toby had not dated anybody since, and to his knowledge neither had George. He remembered his college days with fondness and the fact he still had the picture of him and George by his bed reminded him just how much he had loved her, and still did. Toby was brought out of his nostalgia by the sound of his phone ringing. He looked at his clock, which with tiring eyes, he could just about make out displayed one-thirty in the morning. Who would be calling him at this time? As he reached for it, he glanced down and saw it was his father's number. A sudden dread filled him. His father wouldn't call at this hour unless something was wrong. After pausing briefly, he got out of bed and pressed to answer.

'Dad?'

For a moment there was silence. Then the sound of sobbing on the other end of the line, but no words. Panic set in, his dad never cried.

'Dad, what's happened?' his voice now much less controlled. It was breaking. After a moment his father finally spoke.

'Toby, it's your mum.'

Breaking boundaries

Toby's heart sank. He didn't want to hear anymore.

'Toby I am so sorry, but your mum has passed away.'

Toby dropped to his knees with his head in his hands. Not his mum. The person he had been so close to throughout his life, the one constant; the one person he could always turn to; the one who would never judge and was happy with Toby just being Toby.

'Dad, what happened, was she ill? Why didn't you tell me?' he managed, fighting back the tears.

'She wasn't ill, well not in the physical sense anyway.'

Toby was confused. What did his dad mean by this?

'I was working late this evening and then went to an office party afterwards. I wasn't drinking but the party ran on late into the night. I got home and I found her. She had...' His voice broke and any concerted attempt he may have been making to try and stay composed for his son gave way. He began sobbing hysterically, they both did. Words were exchanged but nothing coherent through the grief. Eventually, his father was able to regain his composure and answer Toby's question although Toby wished he hadn't.

'How did she die?'

'Toby, that's not important.'

'How did she die?' Toby repeated, now raising his voice in a manner in which he had never done so

Breaking boundaries

previously to his father. After taking a deep breath, his father responded, quietly.

'She took her own life.'

Toby listened in disbelief. He couldn't accept what he was hearing. His mother had always been so happy. It was inconceivable she would do something like this. Suicide was for people who felt depressed, people who had nothing, people who felt like there was no way out. His mum wasn't depressed, and she had everything. It didn't make sense.

'How? She was always so happy. Mum would never do this. It must have been an accident. She would never leave us.'

'I don't have the answers right now, I'm sorry.'

'I'm coming home,' Toby said assertively.

'Toby it's late and you're in no fit state to drive. Come home tomorrow morning.'

'I can't sleep now.'

His father, realising there was little point in arguing, didn't offer any resistance.

'Please be safe, I'll wait up for you,' he replied calmly.

Toby quickly grabbed a bag, threw some clothes in it, and looked intently at the picture of him and George.

'I need you, George,' he said aloud before closing his door and heading out of the building to his car. They hadn't spoken in a while though, and Toby wasn't sure whether this was the right time to be changing that.

Breaking boundaries

The weather was bad, but Toby paid little attention to it as he made the drive back home. His mind was consumed by a mixture of sadness, hopelessness and confusion. He would later recognise that he had also felt angry at his mother for leaving him, more so for not being open with how she was feeling when she had spent years encouraging Toby to do just that. The journey seemed to take forever yet Toby had no recollection of it as he pulled up outside his house. He could see a light on in his father's study so knew he had kept his word and waited up for him. He didn't head there immediately though, having entered the house quietly. Instead, he went and sat at the breakfast bar for a moment, in the same seat he had sat so many times before, having a conversation with his mother whilst she prepared a meal. He couldn't stay there long, it was too much for him, so physically and emotionally drained, he headed down the hallway to his father's study. His father was sitting, a tumbler of whisky in one hand, and a photograph of himself and Toby's mother in the other. Toby had never seen his dad emotional, but by the redness of his eyes and the marks on his cheeks, believed he had likely not stopped crying since their conversation on the phone a short while back. His father stood and offered Toby a sympathetic and despairing look. The two stared at each other for a moment before embracing in a heartfelt hug, something Toby had experienced a hundred times

Breaking boundaries

with his mother, but never with his father. It felt strange yet comforting. He knew at this time, and perhaps for a while after, he would need his father, and his father would need him. There was nobody else, it was now just the two of them and whilst he felt guilty for thinking it, his father was the main link to his mother, and right now he needed that link, something to hold on to.

Neither Toby nor his father felt in a position to sleep and so the next few hours were spent with Toby desperately trying to piece together what had happened. It was emotional, but this was raw for them both. The situation didn't make sense to Toby, and his father opening up about his mother and some of her difficulties in the past left him feeling confused and wondering whether he really knew her. His father disclosed he had always hoped Toby would never become aware of his mother's hidden battle, something he had grown more optimistic of the longer time went on. He explained to Toby how his mother had suffered from depression for years but had kept it well contained, only allowing it to surface in private. Throughout the early hours of the morning, Toby was suddenly introduced to somebody who didn't even resemble his mother. He felt disillusioned but was more overcome with overwhelming sadness and a sense of guilt that whilst his mother had always been there for him, he never had the opportunity to be there for her. He questioned whether his decision to go to university

Breaking boundaries

and leave the family home had created a void for his mother, a void she was unable to fill and whether this had ultimately become unbearable for her.

'This was happening long before you decided to go to university Toby,' his father said pouring them both another drink.

'How could I not know? How did she hide this so well from me?'

'She hid it from everybody, even me most of the time. I had no idea this had resurfaced. The last time I saw her really struggling was over a year ago. We talked it out and she seemed okay after that.'

'It went away?'

'I'm not sure it ever really went away. I see that now, but I didn't at the time. Perhaps I was just convincing myself everything was okay.'

'If I hadn't gone...'

Toby's father interrupted him, placing a hand on his knee.

'Listen, this isn't your fault. Nobody could see this coming, not even the professionals.'

'Professionals?'

'Your mum had been seeing a therapist on and off for years.'

'How could I not know?'

'She didn't want you to know. She didn't want anybody to know. To my knowledge, I was the only person she had ever opened up to. Your mum was a very private person, but you know she put her energy into others. She was such a good friend to those around her, always more concerned with

Breaking boundaries

other people than herself. That was the wonderful thing about her Toby. But I often wondered whether she neglected herself.'

The realisation that he was talking about his beloved wife in the past tense suddenly overwhelmed Toby's father. He bowed his head and began to cry. Toby moved over to him putting his head against his father's. He didn't know what to say and knew no words could describe how they were both feeling, the enormity of this loss. They stood for a moment in silence, then with a sudden outpour of emotion they gripped each other tightly as if the reality of the situation, had suddenly hit them at the same time. They remained like this for several minutes and by the time tiredness had set in, it was just after six.

Toby had never been to a funeral before and had never imagined his first would be that of his mother. The service was emotional but uneventful. People Toby had either never met before or hadn't seen in a long time had all come together to mourn the loss. He had looked around the crematorium and been amazed by just how many people had been touched by her. Neither he nor his father had been religious, but there was something quite spiritual about the gathering. This left him with contrasting emotions. He was happy his mother had been so loved by so many but felt sad beyond words that she was no longer here. He had smiled to himself as he thought the one person he would want to support him

Breaking boundaries

through a funeral, the one person to tell him everything would be okay, was the one person who couldn't. He had hugged many people but had spoken to barely anybody. He had sat with his father at the front and they had been the last to leave. He and his father hadn't spoken much on the way home and a week later Toby was on his way back to university. Although he had valued the time with his father, he had struggled to be in a house where he had so many memories of his mother. Neither of them had coped well. He didn't want to leave him but felt he had to. He had tried to encourage his father to take some time out and go away for a while, but whilst Toby struggled to be close to the reminders of his mother, for his father, this was all he had. On the drive back to university, Toby thought about his mother and her illness. He wondered how many more people suffered in silence, believing they had nowhere or nobody to turn to. He considered how bad things must get for people to feel like the only option is to end their own life. He paused for a moment and wondered whether he could have done something, anything. Tears flowed down his cheeks as he imagined her final moments, alone and feeling there was nobody to turn to. He wiped his face and thought about his future. As he recalled how George had once told him that people always make life-changing decisions in the wake of a traumatic event, he smiled. He made a promise to himself at that moment that he would dedicate his life to helping

Breaking boundaries

others. He would do all that he could to prevent suffering and be that person who was there to listen. He hated the thought of other people suffering as his mother had. He hated the thought of the resulting grief suffered by loved ones. He needed to make a difference, to do everything he could to prevent others from feeling the way his mother had, the way he and his father were feeling right now. It was at that moment that Toby decided where his future lay, and two years later he began his career as a Psychotherapist.

Breaking boundaries

3

Toby rose from his seat and walked over towards the door. The knock had been a tentative one, but still enough to startle him as he had sat immersed in his book. He liked to read in between clients. It was his downtime, a method he had used for several years now to allow himself to detach from the previous session, before readying himself for the next. He mostly read fiction, light-hearted and easy reading which would hold little resemblance to real life. His profession, by its very nature, would usually contain sensitive subjects raised by vulnerable individuals. After all, people didn't come to therapy to talk about how wonderful their lives were, they came in most instances because they'd reached a point where they had exhausted all other avenues. Toby had worked with some difficult cases and was always grateful for his supervision with Richard. Somebody had once asked him how he managed to do the job he did, and he had explained to them it was only possible because of his clinical supervisor. It was Richard who had recommended Toby find something in between sessions to allow a moment to be himself and switch off from being a therapist. This single piece of advice had been instrumental in his self-care. It was late Monday afternoon and the individual who was entering his practice was thirty-three-year-old Olivia Stanton. This was her first session and whilst he was well practised, he had awaited her anxiously, yet also with intrigue. This

Breaking boundaries

seemed to be his default reaction to all new clients ahead of their initial session.

'Hi Olivia, I'm Toby, please take a seat.'

Olivia sat down anxiously, and Toby noticed her looking around the room. This was a natural reaction to a first session, particularly if it was also the client's first experience of therapy. Toby was well-trained and prided himself on his comforting nature. The first thing he did with any new client was to introduce himself and try and make them feel as comfortable as possible. He was aware for somebody new to therapy that this was an unfamiliar and sometimes daunting environment. He had put a great deal of thought into the layout and décor of his practice in an attempt to make it as relaxing and welcoming as possible. Therapy was a big step and Toby had nothing but admiration for anybody who took the decision to enter into it. Placing your trust in a stranger and showing vulnerability in the process wasn't an easy thing to do. He noticed her looking at his attire, more specifically his ripped jeans. He smiled.

'These are ok to wear in the summer, but it's a little cold on the knees come winter,' he said still maintaining that smile. Olivia let out a nervous giggle. The therapeutic relationship was one of if not the, most important factors in any therapy.

'You don't look like I imagined,' Olivia said with an anxious smile.

'How did you imagine I would look?'

'I'm not sure. Don't therapists wear suits?'

Breaking boundaries

It was Toby's turn to laugh, but he was mindful not to do this mockingly as the last thing he wanted was for Olivia to feel silly.

'The concept of therapy involving a client lying on a couch with a man in a tweed suit standing over them with a clipboard is a little archaic now.'

Olivia laughed, this time, less nervously, Toby observed. He liked to spend the first ten or fifteen minutes with a new client just getting to know them and breaking the ice. The superficial things.

'I always thought therapy rooms would be more formal, more clinical.'

Toby offered her a glass of water.

'My job is to break down barriers, not create them,' he replied.

'I like that.' Olivia said now appearing to relax back into her chair. Toby spent the next few minutes introducing both himself and his practice. He talked her through the confidentiality agreement and explained how her data would always be kept private. Whilst he felt it was important to humanise himself, he was mindful of oversharing, and was particular about what he did and didn't disclose to his clients. He was happy to tell them how long he had been a therapist and the fact he had moved here from further afield, but his personal life he kept just that. Though it had never happened to him, Toby had known instances where boundaries had been blurred due to therapists oversharing. In training he recalled his lecturer recounting a story where a therapist had overshared to such an extent

Breaking boundaries

with one particular client, that questions had been raised about whether they had effectively become the client themselves. No, this was something Toby was very firm on. He enjoyed working with all of his clients, but the relationship was strictly a professional one. The emotional investment was for those fifty minutes, and it was about them, not him. His job was to provide a safe environment where he would ultimately learn as much about his client as they were prepared to allow. However, this was not a two-way process and Toby had always been very cautious in this area. Talking about his practice, setting expectations, and boundaries, and even discussing payment methods made Toby feel uncomfortable. The latter he hated, and regardless of his years in practice, he felt as awkward discussing it now as he had with his very first client. He didn't believe in putting a price on mental health and was keen to avoid therapy feeling like a transaction. He had chosen to go private because it allowed him to have more control over his client work. He felt some therapists overcharged, and for Toby, it was about enhancing people's emotional well-being, not his bank balance. Besides he was able to vary his rates to allow more people access to private therapy and had worked with some clients in precarious financial positions for free in the past. He was proud of what he did and enjoyed making a difference. After losing his mother and his experience with George, he had wanted to dedicate

Breaking boundaries

his life to helping others, and his life as a Psychotherapist allowed him to do just that.

'Would you like to tell me a little about yourself, Olivia?'

'What would you like to know?'

'What would you like to share?'

Olivia looked at Toby for a moment, seemingly unsure what to say next. There was a momentary silence and Toby sensed Olivia having shown glimpses of relaxing, was now feeling out of her comfort zone. He smiled.

'Why don't you start by telling me about Olivia?'

She looked at Toby, pushed her hair from over her eyes and sat back in her chair.

'Well, I'm thirty-three years old, have been married for seven years and have a six-year-old son. What else would you like to know?'

Toby smiled once more. In his mind, a reassuring smile at the right time could help to relax his clients. This was something he tended to use more with new clients when he was building that relationship. He had been through therapy himself and whilst he could never determine how somebody else was feeling, he knew how it had felt for him.

'I know what you're thinking,' Olivia said breaking the silence.

Toby looked at her curiously.

'And what's that?'

'That I married because I was pregnant.'

'Did you?'

Breaking boundaries

'I don't know,' Olivia replied shrugging her shoulders.

A pause. An uncomfortable one at that. Toby knew when clients looked down or away in silence, it often meant they were thinking, exploring. When they look directly at you, they are expecting you to speak and this early into the first session, Toby felt he should be doing very little speaking. Olivia again flicked back her hair and then began to plait it. Toby's first impression was that this was a nervous reaction. He had seen similar reactions many times over, almost always in that initial session when clients are unsure of what to expect and how to interact with him. He thought about how in a different environment this could be seen as quite a seductive act but quickly displaced this thought. He sat upright, uncrossed his legs, and paused for a moment wondering whether Olivia was going to speak. Realising this wasn't forthcoming, he broke the silence. A recurring thing for Toby throughout his years of practice had been his discomfort with long silences.

'Olivia, why don't you tell me what brought you here today?'

'Where do I start?'

Rhetorical, but still necessitated a reply in Toby's mind.

'Where would you like to start? This is your time; you can spend it however you like.'

'My marriage isn't a happy one. Eric, my husband, isn't a particularly understanding man. He

Breaking boundaries

struggles to control his drinking, and in those instances, most often his temper too. I am usually left with the options of either appeasing him, staying completely out of his way or…'

Her voice trailed off. Toby noticed her body language become more rigid. He knew what she was alluding to, but he wasn't about to make assumptions. No, the work had to be done by her, but ultimately this was their first meeting, and he wouldn't push.

'I can't imagine how that must feel for you.'

'Pretty awful, I mean it doesn't happen all the time, but it's enough to have taken its toll over the years.'

'Years?'

'It began when Tyler, that's the name of my little boy, was two. He was kind enough not to lay a finger on me whilst I was pregnant.'

She laughed. Her humour was camouflaging a deeper trauma, he thought. He had worked with clients who had displayed humour when exploring their trauma. It was their way of coping and as Toby had always maintained, people finding their own way in their own time is what's important. Right here in this moment, his client was nervous, quite possibly traumatised. She was confident but also vulnerable.

'How long have you been together?'

'We met when I was twenty-five. He was thirty-four and he seemed like a nice guy. I had just come out of a relationship of five years and wasn't in a

65

Breaking boundaries

rush to enter another. I worked as a dental nurse at the time and he'd come into the practice one day to repair the printer. He's an engineer but has his own business. He's successful by all accounts. We got talking and suddenly we were out on our first date. As I say, he seemed a genuinely nice guy and it felt like he was really interested in me.'

'I see.'

'We had been together about a year and I fell pregnant. At the time I was questioning the relationship and in all honesty, looking for a way to end it. But instead, I married him. How about that for a U-turn!'

That laugh again. Toby could see the angst on Olivia's face. He couldn't imagine feeling trapped like that. Going from planned separation to marriage and parenthood in the blink of an eye.

'I love Tyler with everything I have, but him coming along certainly complicated things. Christ, what sort of a mother am I putting this on my son?' Olivia said exasperated.

'Do you feel like you're blaming your son?'

'You ask a lot of questions. When are you going to give me some answers?' Olivia said with a smile.

'Is that what you think therapy is about?'

Another question.

'I'm not so sure what it's about, or even why I'm here, to be honest.'

'Why *did* you come here today?'

Toby realised the inflexion on the word *did,* changed the meaning of what he was trying to

Breaking boundaries

convey and became momentarily concerned he may have unintentionally antagonised or offended his client. Whatever the intention, it seemed Olivia had not taken offence, or at least she didn't show it. She looked at Toby tentatively, drew breath and spoke in a composed manner, almost a whisper to begin with.

'I came here because I am struggling to accept my situation. I came here to try and gain some perspective and maybe find some strength to remove myself from a situation where I don't feel like I am in control; remove myself from an environment where I am being physically assaulted; remove myself from a cheating, manipulative and overbearing bastard, to get my life back and rediscover *me*. I want to be *me* again.'

Toby could see Olivia's body language change. Her tone of voice had transitioned, and the volume had increased significantly almost to the point of shouting. She was angry. This would be coming from a place of pain, fear, or frustration, or perhaps a combination of the three. He sat back and listened intently. He knew Olivia had much more to say and had no intention of interrupting her when she had gained the confidence to open up. This was her time, not his. She continued.

'I have endured this for four years. I have had to, for the sake of my son. I don't want him to be from a broken family. My parents separated when I was nine and I know how it affected me. I don't want this

Breaking boundaries

for Tyler. You have no idea what I have had to put up with. The humiliation, the pain, the fear.'

'I'm sorry.'

'Why are you sorry? You don't control me, beat me, monitor my every move.'

Toby was taken aback by her sharp retort. He had experienced this type of response before, but for some reason, this felt different. He paused for a moment. It didn't feel like a long time, but it was long enough for Olivia to notice. She inhaled slowly and then responded, now in a calmer and more measured tone.

'I'm sorry. I didn't mean to make you feel uncomfortable or take my situation out on you. This isn't your fault and I know you're here to help. It's just I have never spoken about any of this to anybody. I'm not sure what I am supposed to feel or how I am supposed to act.'

'This is a safe space, Olivia. Whatever you feel, whatever you disclose, whatever emotions you're combatting, it's okay.'

'I feel vulnerable.'

'It's okay to feel vulnerable.'

'Thank you, it's not a position I ever thought I would be in... being vulnerable that is. I always thought at some point I would need therapy!'

She smiled as she said this, and Toby wondered what deep trauma her humour was masking. Clients who tended to use the most humour were usually those with more deep-seated troubles.

Breaking boundaries

He glanced at the clock. The session was only twenty minutes in, not even halfway through, yet it felt like he had been in the room with Olivia for hours. He would have time to reflect on this later and considered whether this was something he would speak to Richard about, but right now he was client-facing, and he needed to be present.

'It sounds like you've experienced a great deal of trauma. I can't imagine how that must feel for you,' he said with a sympathetic smile.

'I feel completely trapped.'

'Trapped?'

'When we met, as I said, I was a dental nurse. I had my own home, a good job and was financially secure, and independent. Once I fell pregnant, Eric suggested I move in with him to his three-bedroomed house. This seemed a practical option as my flat was hardly conducive to family life, even though I was still unsure about the relationship. I guess I hoped that having a child may change the way I felt about him.'

'Did it?'

'No, and talking about it now, I'm realising that the control started before Tyler was even born. How could I have not seen this at the time?'

'Hindsight is much more accurate than foresight. When we are emotionally invested in a situation or person, we don't always see certain things. Or we do, but we don't recognise them in the way we perhaps do when we are reflecting on something after the event.'

Breaking boundaries

Olivia looked at Toby with a slight look of puzzlement on her face.

'I'm not sure I understand what you mean,' she said.

Toby sat up and leaned forward in his chair. This was something he occasionally did if he was clarifying a point. He wasn't sure why, but it felt comfortable and didn't appear imposing.

'Sometimes things are done subtly. If my wife tells me I look good in something, should I take that as a compliment?'

'I guess so.'

'What happens if she is vociferous about what I am wearing whenever I leave the house?'

'She has insecurities about you being out?'

'Perhaps. And what if that opinion escalates into a display of anger should I disagree with her?'

'She is trying to control what you wear?'

'Okay, so we have just moved from complimentary to controlling in two sentences.'

Toby noticed Olivia staring at him like she was deep in thought and processing what he had said. He felt like this had resonated with her. He enjoyed offering up thought-provoking questions to encourage his clients to look beneath the surface. He wondered if she realised at that moment just how much therapy was going to bring up for her. Toby had now resumed his position sitting back in his chair. It was Olivia who broke the silence.

'How are people so convincing?'

'Convincing in what way?'

Breaking boundaries

'Like they show one persona for a while, draw you in and then it's like…' She paused.

'Like what?' Toby asked.

'Like they flick a switch and just become somebody totally different.'

'I wonder if they do change, or simply change back?'

Olivia looked at Toby in a manner which suggested his words had struck a chord with her. Toby recognised this but said nothing. He didn't need to elaborate further. He was sure if this had resonated with Olivia like he thought it had, she would pick this up and run with it. He wasn't wrong.

'So you're suggesting he has always been abusive, he just hid it from me?'

Toby looked at Olivia carefully. He didn't make suggestions, he asked questions. This was something he was always very clear on with his clients. He didn't provide answers, he provided a safe environment where clients could find their own. He didn't fix people, he facilitated them fixing themselves if indeed they felt like they needed to be fixed in the first place.

'It was a question, not a suggestion,' he said gently.

'But I think it may be true.'

'Then you're finding your own answers.'

Olivia smiled. Now a much more relaxed smile. She seemed to be displaying less anxiety and more confidence. It could take clients several sessions to feel comfortable and some clients Toby had worked

Breaking boundaries

with felt that wave of anxiety before every session right up until the point they were discharged. Olivia was thirty minutes into her session and considering what she had disclosed and how she had presented at the beginning, Toby was amazed she had relaxed so quickly. *Like a switch being flicked*, he thought.

'I'm not sure what's harder to accept, the violence, the control, or the fact I didn't see the pattern at the time, the warning signals. I just let this happen, didn't I?'

'Do you feel you let it happen?'

'Well I didn't do anything about it did I?'

'Is that the same as allowing it to happen I wonder?' he asked.

'Surely when people are in a relationship and they realise it's abusive, they should just walk away?'

'Many don't.'

Olivia began looking around the room once more, before settling her eyes back on Toby.

'I don't understand. Why would you willingly keep yourself in that situation?'

'I wonder if it always is willingly,' Toby replied.

'So people are forced to stay in their situation?'

'There are many reasons people remain in abusive relationships, none of them a reflection on the victim.'

'Don't you think that's weak?'

Olivia spoke the words rather coldly. Toby noticed but didn't acknowledge it. He saw his job as more than simply listening to what was being said. Toby was astute and observant when it came to things

Breaking boundaries

such as body language and tone of voice, especially when these seemed inconsistent with a client's general demeanour. If he were to answer this question, he needed to be careful. He was consciously aware that he had to avoid disagreeing with his client, whilst also not appearing to trivialise or make judgments on abuse victims.

'I have worked with abuse victims who have sometimes taken that label on themselves, but I wonder whether we are oversimplifying an often complex situation?'

'Do you ever work with abusers?'

'I have done.'

'I don't know how you can.'

Toby paused for a moment and considered his response. He wanted to say that in his experience, behind all abusers, somewhere lies a victim. An explanation, not a justification. However, he knew there was a chance this could be misinterpreted, a risk he was simply not prepared to take. The benefit of him addressing this question was significantly outweighed by the potential of harming the therapeutic relationship. This was about his client, not his practice. It was about somebody presenting as an abuse victim. She was not an abuser. It would be wholly inappropriate for him at this moment to present abusers as victims. He took a breath and sidestepped the question.

'Olivia, do you feel weak?'

'I don't know, I guess so. I wonder why I've stayed for the amount of time that I have, why I

Breaking boundaries

didn't leave when this all began. I have always been independent and assertive. If you talk to my friends, they would tell you I would be the last person to endure this. I feel too embarrassed, too ashamed to even talk to them about it. Maybe that's why I am here, somebody who doesn't know me, who won't judge me.'

'Do you feel like people would judge you?'

'I guess so. I've just made those same judgments, haven't I? People wonder I wonder, why not just leave? Or once you have left, why go back? But it's not that easy, is it? I feel so conflicted. Determined yet resigned in the same breath. How do people end up in this situation?'

'What do you think?'

'I honestly don't know.'

Toby noticed her voice begin to crack, her body language visibly changing in an instant. She was displaying that resignation she had just spoken about. It felt like she was accepting this as not only her present but her future too. Toby knew in any situation there were only ever three options, which were to accept it, to change it or to leave it. As he looked across the room at Olivia Stanton, he wondered how many of these options she felt were available to her. He glanced at the clock, noting only fifteen minutes were left of the session. When clients were engaging, he felt like sessions passed him by in no time, but when they were more reserved and reluctant to communicate, the hands on the clock appeared to move backwards. Olivia

74

Breaking boundaries

had been engaging, and very open for the first session, but he couldn't determine whether the time had passed him by or not. First sessions didn't usually work like this. After the initial introduction and discussion of confidentiality, Toby liked to keep the first meeting on a less profound and more superficial level. This was primarily because clients wouldn't have a great deal of time to explore any significant disclosure. He didn't like the idea of them opening up wounds and then being left to effectively deal with them on their own in between sessions. Then a thought passed through his mind. Why hadn't this first session progressed in the same way as others? What was it about Olivia Stanton that had allowed him to become so immersed in her narrative so quickly? The session had begun intensely and there was no indication this was about to change. Toby, for a moment, felt overwhelmed. He had worked with a lot of clients over the years but couldn't recall feeling like this only thirty-five minutes into a therapy session with a new client. Before he could allow himself to explore this thought any further, Olivia spoke. Toby felt relieved, almost grateful. He had plenty of time away from his clients to reflect on his own practice. He had Richard. He felt angry at himself for becoming entangled in his thoughts and wondered whether this had impacted her therapeutic experience. He recognised the magnitude of anybody reaching out for help and felt inspired by those who did. There were many therapists within the area, but she had taken the

Breaking boundaries

time to actively choose him. There was a reason for this.

Distracted again. He looked at Olivia as she began to speak.

'It's a mess, right? I bet you haven't worked with many people like me before?'

Toby smiled, but behind the smile was a curiosity, a slight nervousness. He had worked with many people like her, yet nobody like her. This didn't make sense and for the first time since he began his career, he felt uncomfortable. He didn't let it show.

'I've worked with a lot of people, and while a lot may share similar symptoms and afflictions, all are unique in their own way. We all have different ways of coping.

'So you've worked with others who have been in my position before? How did they cope? How did they get through it?' Olivia asked.

'All situations are different and what may work for one individual may not work for another. A strategy may provide a safe resolution for one person, but that same strategy may put another in grave danger.'

'That's why you don't give answers right?'

'There are many reasons why therapists don't provide answers, the main one being we don't necessarily have them. Remember you are the expert on your relationship and no therapist can know you better than you know yourself. What we aim to do, is to work with you to find your own answers. Does that make sense?'

Breaking boundaries

Olivia nodded but looked disappointed. Her body language had changed again. She slumped back in her chair and let out a sigh. Toby was finding it difficult to read her. She had originally presented as vulnerable but had quickly relaxed into the session and portrayed a confidence, manifesting through a display of anger towards her husband as well as herself. She appeared to fluctuate between confident and downtrodden. This was quite common, but ordinarily, that oscillation would be seen at varying stages of the client's journey, however, in this instance, this palpable change was taking place during a single session. Toby broke the silence.

'If I could wave a magic wand for you right now and make everything better, what would have changed? What would or would not be happening and how would things feel for you?'

'Why do you ask me that if you don't fix things?'

'Because I am wondering whether your answer will provide you with a starting point of what you would like to get out of therapy.'

'You're good,' Olivia said breaking into a smile.

Toby smiled back, but it was a tentative smile. Compliments made him feel uncomfortable in any circumstances, but more so in practice. He was acutely aware of professional boundaries and how easily they could be contravened, even without intention. He said nothing.

'I guess I really need to talk to somebody about my situation. As I've said, I've never disclosed any

Breaking boundaries

of this to anybody, and I am thinking it has built up to a point where I no longer feel I can cope.'

Toby looked at Olivia, now displaying that same shyness and vulnerability she had when she first walked into his practice less than an hour ago. He remained silent. He sensed she had more to say and didn't want to disrupt her flow. She continued.

'I want to leave him, need to leave him. It's just...'

Her voice broke off and Toby sensitively gestured towards the box of tissues located on the small table at the side of her chair. She took one out, wiped her eyes and then blew her nose, apologising in the process.

'I'm just not sure what I can do. I don't know how to escape. When I talk about it, it makes it real, and it sounds so much more frightening when I hear the words out loud. His temper frightens me, but I'm more concerned for Tyler.'

'Has he ever hurt your son?'

'No, I don't think he would do that, but Tyler has seen him angry with me and I can see how it upsets him. I had to go through that as a child and I don't want him to go through the same. As his mum, surely my job is to protect him?'

'You were raised in an abusive household?'

'My father was very handy with his fists. I witnessed that for a while, powerless to do anything. Eventually, he left.'

'Is that how you feel now, powerless?'

Olivia clasped her hands together, put them under her chin and leaned forward. She looked at

Breaking boundaries

Toby, but only for a brief moment before lowering her head into her hands. She looked exhausted and said nothing. Toby again glanced at the clock, which was behind Olivia. There were only five minutes left in the session. Usually, at this time, he would wait for the client to pause and then highlight the session was drawing to a close. For Toby, those last few minutes were extremely important in trying to help the client transition from the therapeutic setting back into their everyday life. He didn't like simply ending a session abruptly, without having a few minutes to see how the client was and giving them that opportunity to breathe and gather their thoughts before leaving his practice. He had once likened this to blood donation, whereby afterwards you have that time when you can have a drink, a quick snack and relax before driving home. Olivia had opted against answering his question, instead remaining silent. Toby saw this as his opportunity to begin the process of ending the session.

'Olivia, we just have a few minutes left, I'm wondering how you're feeling?'

'Beat up. Sorry perhaps not appropriate, but you get what I mean don't you?'

'I can only imagine how difficult it must have been for you. Therapy can be incredibly draining, emotionally and physically.'

'I feel like I have made a start. Does it get better from here?'

'I wish I could tell you the therapeutic journey was a linear one, but unfortunately, it can be quite

Breaking boundaries

tumultuous. It's different for everybody though,' he said trying to set her expectations without dampening any optimism she may have.

Olivia smiled at him, and Toby realised she had said this in hope rather than expectation. She had experienced a lot of trauma, and if she had been in an abusive household for a prolonged period, would sadly be all too familiar with turbulence. She would likely only be a casual and infrequent acquaintance of consistency or serenity. Olivia made another appointment before thanking him for his time, reaching for her coat and exiting his practice. Toby sat for a moment and reflected. He removed his glasses and stared at the wall. He had occasionally experienced first sessions like this in the past, but something about that one, about Olivia Stanton, had left him feeling emotionally fatigued. The first appointment usually involved getting to know clients, learning a little about their background and understanding on a very broad level what had brought them to therapy and what they wanted to achieve from it. This had taken a very different path and he was confused as to why. He remained deep in thought until his phone sounded, making him jump in the process. It was Beth letting him know she was in the midst of preparing tea. Toby rose from his seat and walked towards the door of his practice. He paused and stared intently at the vacant client chair where Olivia Stanton had been sat just moments earlier. His eyes remained focused on that spot for a few minutes until he was

Breaking boundaries

finally able to shake himself out of the daze. He locked the practice and headed towards his car, still thinking of his last session, still thinking of Olivia Stanton.

Breaking boundaries

4

Toby opened the door and entered the house before removing his jacket. As he was doing so he was met with a warm greeting from Beth. This was *his* therapy he thought. Every evening without fail Beth would greet him at the door with a smile and a hug. It was five-thirty in the evening and Toby, having endured a treacherous car journey home, was extremely happy to see that smile. Although he always looked forward to returning home to Beth, today he felt like he needed that smile more than ever. Whilst he had tried to convince himself it was due to the ten-minute homeward journey spanning over half an hour, he knew this wasn't the case. The real reason of course was Olivia Stanton. Something had happened in that session which had left Toby feeling uncomfortable, but the reflection on the journey home had provided no answers.

'You look exhausted, are you ok?' Beth asked with a slight look of concern. On a professional level, Toby was very limited in what he could disclose. On a personal level, he kept as much away from her as possible. He'd always endeavoured to keep his profession and anything accompanying it, in his practice. It wasn't that he thought Beth couldn't handle the impact his work may have on him, more that he didn't feel she should need to. Besides, he had Richard, somebody who knew the world of psychotherapy in depth. Richard could understand what it was like to be

Breaking boundaries

faced with the things which may impact Toby, as he was exposed to that very same environment himself. He had once thought how well Richard knew him as a psychotherapist and yet Beth, the person closest to him than anybody else, knew very little about him as a professional.

'I'm ok. The journey home was a little gruelling and after a long day in practice, that was the last thing I needed,' Toby replied with a smile he knew she would see straight through.

'Did you come via Charring Bypass? Maggie was saying earlier there are temporary traffic lights there and it was causing quite a disruption.'

'Well, it would have been lovely if Maggie could have told me this about forty-five minutes ago.' Toby said grinning. He was fond of Maggie. She had been a very close friend of Beth's for ten years since they had moved here and was a frequent visitor to the Reynolds household. Beth shot him a sympathetic look, rubbed his shoulder affectionately and turned to retrieve the tea from the oven. Though she was always modest, Beth was a fantastic cook. Toby had once teased that the main reason he had married her was for her culinary expertise and that if she ever left him, he would starve. As they sat opposite each other enjoying the extravagant chicken dish Beth had prepared, Toby felt distracted. Whilst he was empathic, he knew the importance of leaving client work in the practice. He was a psychotherapist, not a saviour. He devoted fifty minutes to each of his clients. This did not

Breaking boundaries

extend to his home life, and he had always been good at maintaining those boundaries, creating that distinction. But he *was* distracted, and Beth noticed.

'You seem preoccupied.'

'Why do you say that?' he replied, wondering how much his face had given away.

'Because you still haven't figured out that you're nibbling on a chicken bone honey. The meat is long gone.'

Toby looked down and laughed. He smiled at her, but the smile was a front for uncertainty and confusion. Although he had always thought Beth shouldn't have to deal with the effects of his work, Toby felt sad that he didn't open up to her more. He had never lied to her, but when it came to his profession, he worried that he was effectively keeping things from her, hiding how he was really feeling and masking some of the darker thoughts which had occasionally passed through his mind. Mostly, he was able to pull himself through difficult sessions and he was hopeful this too would pass as the evening progressed. He looked at Beth and reached for her hand across the table.

'I'm sorry, it was a tough day today. I was just sitting reflecting on one of my sessions.'

'You know you can talk to me Toby, right? I know you are bound by confidentiality and can't talk about your clients, but talking about how you're feeling doesn't betray their confidence. Remember that.'

Toby squeezed her hand and tried to give her a reassuring smile, although he was certain she didn't

Breaking boundaries

believe it to be genuine. Beth could read his body language and his general demeanour incredibly well. He had always maintained she would make an excellent therapist and had once raised this with her. She had baulked at the idea, joking that two therapists in a household would make it an unbearable environment. She squeezed his hand back and offered a comforting smile. Hers was genuine.

'Mr Reynolds you are one stubborn individual. You expect others to unburden themselves, and yet you do not afford yourself that same courtesy.'

'I have Richard.'

'You also have a wife,' she responded quickly.

Beth never really raised her voice yet had a way of being assertive in a controlled manner. This was one of those occasions. It was one of the many reasons Toby had fallen in love with her. She had a presence but in a very relaxed way. She didn't get angry; she didn't get frustrated, and she didn't judge. She was his constant, the calming voice at the end of a difficult day. She was the voice of reason in his sometimes-confusing world. She reminded him a lot of his mother. Whilst he loved everything about her personality and character, he was also extremely wary of it. What he loved the most, he also feared the most. That which brought so much joy within also induced a deep anxiety. The happy moments provided a constant reminder of much darker ones.

Breaking boundaries

After the meal, they had sat with a movie before retiring for an early night. Toby had fallen asleep relatively quickly but had woken up with his mind active. He looked over at the clock. It was just after two. Outside, the streets were silent, the solid darkness interrupted only by sporadic lighting. He loved the tranquillity. It was one of the things which had attracted him and Beth to the house originally. Whilst it wasn't geographical isolation, there were only a handful of houses on the street, and being overlooked in any capacity was never an issue. Toby looked over at Beth, sleeping peacefully, seemingly without a care. He wondered what she was dreaming of. As he lay there and watched her breathe, he smiled to himself and considered how lucky he was to have somebody as wonderful as her to share his life with. It wasn't her physical appearance, although Beth was naturally beautiful. No, it was who she was as a person. She had always offered unconditional love and unwavering support. Toby would tell his friends it wasn't love at first sight but rather love at first sound. Of course, there had been that initial attraction, but once he had spent an evening talking to her, he knew she was the girl he wanted to spend the rest of his life with. He had quickly fallen in love with her sincerity, her intelligence, her humour and of course, that smile. Toby tilted his head as he smiled. He wondered what she would think if she woke up now and saw him looking at her in this way. She had lovingly labelled him as goofy, and Toby wondered

Breaking boundaries

whether this is what she meant. He felt awake and knew he wouldn't be getting back to sleep any time soon so quietly pulled back the covers and climbed out of bed, being careful to avoid the one creaky floorboard in the bedroom. As reserved and thoughtful as Beth was, Toby knew better than to disrupt her from her slumber. The only times he recalled Beth being remotely cranky were the occasions when for various reasons, she had had a disturbed night's sleep. He reached for his dressing gown, put on his slippers, and silently made his way out of the bedroom and down the stairway. He poured himself a glass of milk and walked quietly into the conservatory. He took a seat, not just any seat, but his favourite seat, a beautifully crafted papasan chair, positioned right in the corner under the window. He sat thoughtfully and gazed outside. It was a clear night, the moon was prominent, and the stars were spectacular. Whilst Toby had never studied astronomy, he couldn't help but admire the constellations and had spent many hours staring up at the sky on those clear nights. He found it cathartic, and finding ways to relax was extremely important in his profession. As he sat there, he reflected on his day. This wasn't uncommon, though Toby liked to limit the amount of personal time he dedicated to anything related to his practice. He had seen five clients that day beginning with bereavement, and ultimately ending with domestic abuse. Several hours had passed since Olivia Stanton's appointment and Toby felt he was now

Breaking boundaries

more able to remove the emotion and look at things objectively. He wondered whether during the session he had been picking up on Olivia's emotions. Had he been feeling her anger? her despair? her frustration? It was natural for him to feel empathy for his clients, sometimes sympathy. He had always maintained it was difficult to be desensitised to certain topics in therapy. More importantly for him, he thought any desensitisation could lead to a lack of empathy, something which would almost certainly impact the relationship with his clients. Toby was happy he was still impacted by some sessions. He felt it humanised him and meant he cared, and ultimately, that's why he did what he did. His thoughts quickly turned to Beth. Ordinarily, regardless of the day he had had, her comforting nature, just her presence, was enough to elevate his mood. Yesterday was the first time they weren't enough, and Toby was struggling to find an explanation for this. He had always been efficient at separating himself as a therapist from himself as a husband and felt upset he had not been able to do so in this instance. On occasions, if he needed to reflect, he would remain in his office at the end of the day to prevent the need to do this at home. Beth had been with him through his journey into Psychotherapy. They had met in Toby's final year of his post-graduate degree, but the relationship remained platonic; one of close friendship, and didn't develop into a romantic one until a year later. As Toby had become smitten with Beth very quickly,

Breaking boundaries

he had found it particularly difficult to spend so much time with her. The way he felt about Beth, he had only ever felt about one other person, George. It was because of the experience with George that Toby had held back from Beth. In the first few months, he wasn't entirely sure how she felt about him. Some days he believed she wanted the friendship to blossom into something more, whilst others, he felt like she had little interest in him romantically. Regardless, Toby had kept his feelings guarded. Whilst he and George had separated amicably, it had impacted him, perhaps more so than he had originally realised. As a result, Toby had been reluctant to enter into another relationship and hadn't dated anybody since George. That wasn't to say there hadn't been occasional mornings when he had woken in the company of another, however, Toby had been very careful to avoid anything which could lead to him being hurt. This had been a conscious and concerted effort and something he had managed to stay on course with. That was until he met Beth. There had been several occasions when Toby had wondered if he should open up to her about how he felt, but ultimately he had remained tight-lipped. In the end, it had been Beth who had made the first move, declaring her love for Toby over a meal after a visit to the cinema. He had known at the time Beth was his soul mate. It wasn't something he could put into words. They simply went together. They didn't argue and shared many of the same values and beliefs. However,

Breaking boundaries

whilst their outlook on life was very similar, their upbringings had been quite different, and Beth's past had been one of tragedy and trauma.

At fourteen, on a humid August evening, Beth had attended a family gathering with her parents and younger sister. As a family, they had been close, and Beth had revelled in her role as an older sister. Lara at the time was only five, but rather than Beth feeling worried about no longer being the centre of her parent's world, she had taken on a very protective role as a sibling. In later life, Beth would question whether Lara was planned due to the age gap, but growing up she was just pleased to have somebody else in the household. The gathering had been for the engagement party of her older cousin, who in Beth's mind had chosen well. Her partner was both charming and handsome, but also had a lot of money, Beth thought, considering the car he drove. The party had begun at six, however, the decision had been made beforehand to stay only for a couple of hours due to Lara. Whilst she was a placid child, she of course did have her moments and one of the contributing factors to these moments was a lack of sleep. The following day would see an early start as they were making the long drive north of the border to see Beth's grandparents. Whilst some of her friends at school used to complain about having to visit grandparents, it was something she had always looked forward to. They had played a prominent role in her life and as

Breaking boundaries

a young child, she had spent many weekends staying over at their house. The lure wasn't just her Grandmother's cooking or her grandfather's sense of adventure, it was the fact they were always there and always treated her with such importance. Even when Lara came along, her grandfather would still take Beth out exploring in the woods, whether it was seeking out the wildlife, or searching for hidden treasures. She had never forgotten the way she felt and the wave of emotion which had overcome her the day they had moved away. Her grandfather's site had closed and when faced with the options of relocating or unemployment, he had felt there was little choice but to move. From that moment, the ten-minute walk to their house suddenly became a four-hour drive. She had gone from seeing them most evenings to only a handful of times per year, and it had affected her badly. They would of course still speak over the phone, but it hadn't been the same and Beth aged just ten at the time, had felt like part of her world had been taken away from her.

The party had been nice, yet uneventful, however, Beth had spent the night catching up with her other cousin who was only a year older. She didn't get to see her much and Beth had pleaded with her parents to stay a while longer. Reluctantly they had agreed, but by ten, her father had determined their night was coming to an end. Lara was asleep and they would have to navigate getting her in and out of the car without her waking. They

Breaking boundaries

would be rising shortly after six the following morning and her father had said the last thing he needed on a four-hour journey was a crabby Lara. The drive home was only around twenty minutes and as her father had consumed several alcoholic beverages, her mother was the designated driver. This wasn't something that happened often, but Beth always liked it when her mother drove. She thought her father was far too cautious and enjoyed the sometimes-erratic nature of her mother behind the wheel. The journey had been peaceful until Lara had suddenly awoken agitated. Beth had tried to console her from the back seat, but Lara had become frantic and there was simply no reasoning with her. Her father had also tried and failed to placate her, Lara repeatedly screaming for her mother. Beth's mother had turned around momentarily to try to calm Lara and reassure her soon they would be home. Whilst her eyes were only off the road for a matter of seconds, it was enough for the car to drift onto the opposite carriageway. Suddenly noticing the flashing lights and repetitive sound of a horn from an oncoming vehicle, Beth's mother had jerked the car back to the left in an attempt to avoid a collision. In her panic, she had overcompensated and lost control. The car careering down a ditch at an alarming speed was one of the last things Beth remembered. It had eventually come to rest in a secluded field. She had remained conscious for just a few moments, but in those moments she realised two

Breaking boundaries

things in the eerie silence: It was ten-fifteen in the evening and the front windscreen had a large hole in it. The next time Beth was conscious, she found herself in a hospital bed with her grandparents sat either side of her. It had taken her a while to open her eyes and become fully aware of her surroundings. She had little recollection of the accident or even the evening as a whole. It had been her grandparents who had broken the news to her that both her mother and father had tragically died in the accident. They didn't go into detail at the time. Beth was fourteen and having to face up to growing up without her parents. The small ray of light in a now very darkened world for Beth was seeing Lara, accompanied by a nurse, walk into her hospital room. She had survived the accident. Beth made a promise she would always be there for Lara, and they would never be separated. This was a promise Beth had always kept and even after both were married in later years, they would remain inseparable, bound together by tragedy. Whilst Beth didn't like to talk about that night, she had told Toby that several days after she and Lara had gone to live with their grandparents, she had overheard them talking about the accident one night. In between the sobs, she had been able to make out that her father after taking off his belt when turning to attend to Lara, had been thrown from the vehicle and killed instantly. Her mother had been taken from the scene alive but had passed away in hospital in the early hours of the following morning from her

Breaking boundaries

injuries. Beth never told Lara what she had heard. Toby had initially questioned whether Beth suffered from survivor's guilt, but he had learned the guilt she was carrying wasn't from surviving. She had pieced the night together, and, in her mind, the car had crashed because of her mother being distracted due to Lara screaming. She reasoned that Lara was screaming due to being over-tired, something which would have been avoided had they left the party at the originally planned time. Her parents had been reluctant to extend their stay at the gathering but had relented due to Beth's persistence. For her it was simple... her actions had caused the death of her parents. Beth had carried this with her since the night of the fatal accident which had left her orphaned at fourteen.

Toby was powerless as a professional. He couldn't be her therapist, though he had encouraged her to see somebody. His pain, however, came from the fact he felt powerless as her husband to take away her pain and suffering. Beth was conflicted. Part of her was trying to suppress her recollection of that night, but her guilt was opposing this, ensuring she remembered. The sporadic reminders along with the feelings they induced would serve as a punishment, and Beth felt she deserved to be punished. It was difficult to believe somebody with such exuberance could mask such anguish. As far as Toby knew, Beth had never disclosed the events of that night to anybody, not even her closest

Breaking boundaries

friends. She didn't like to talk about it, but Toby would occasionally catch her looking withdrawn and vacant, and knew that in these moments, she was again that fourteen-year-old girl on that fateful night. He looked at the clock and realised that he had been so immersed in Beth's past, he had lost track of time. He wondered whether he had had the same vacant look she did when she would drift away into her past. Thinking about Beth's childhood and the impact this had had on her had taken his mind off the previous day and Toby felt a small sense of relief for this. He smiled as he thought of Beth teasing that he wouldn't be able to handle a client like her, but wondered if there was some truth to it. He hadn't handled Olivia Stanton particularly well but had no idea why he felt this way. She had left saying she felt lighter and had made another appointment. Surely, he thought, that would constitute a good session? But it wasn't about the session for Toby, it was about his reaction to it. Being awake at three in the morning still reflecting, in his mind, made him question that reaction further. Whilst he had been thinking about Beth and her tragic past, Toby suddenly realised he had woken up thinking about Olivia Stanton and would be going back to bed thinking of her too. Now consumed by conflict and guilt, he picked up his glass and finished the remainder of his milk, making his way into the kitchen in the process. He placed his glass next to the sink, turned off the already dimmed light and made his way up the stairs. As he got back into

Breaking boundaries

bed, making sure to carefully pull the covers over him so as not to wake Beth, he glanced over at his beloved wife. The peaceful smile had now left her face and her body was beginning to shake. Her lips were quivering with the occasional murmur passing through them. He placed his hand gently on her forehead and stroked her in a soothing motion. He wondered what must have happened to turn that peaceful smile into an expression of anguish. This wasn't about her dreams, of course, he had no control over them. It was about the trauma he knew Beth was living with. He felt sure that at this moment Beth was that fourteen-year-old girl once again, reliving the night of the accident. Though she had been able to exercise a degree of control over the guilt in her conscious day, she was much more vulnerable in her sleep. She had told Toby that she would sometimes return to the scene of the accident in her dreams, usually when she had woken up in a cold sweat, screaming. Toby had actively encouraged her to make an appointment with a therapist, however, Beth had always played down the impact it had on her. She didn't believe she was unique; that everybody had nightmares about their past occasionally. Toby knew that therapy would be difficult for Beth because she would be faced with reliving the trauma. The things which had either been unconsciously repressed or consciously suppressed would be brought to the surface and Beth would have to deal with them. He knew Beth better than anyone and was consciously aware this

Breaking boundaries

process wouldn't fit with who she was. She wasn't the kind of person who dedicated her time to worrying about a situation. She was practical, logical, and would instead focus on finding a solution rather than exploring the cause. Her philosophy had always been that you can't change what has already occurred, but you can find a way to move through it. It was something else Toby loved about her. He couldn't help but admire her resilience and outlook on life even if he did feel it didn't always work in her favour. Beth had now stopped shaking and the peaceful look had returned to her face. He wondered where she was now and thought wherever it was, it was more peaceful and less traumatic than where she had been just moments ago. He leaned over and kissed her, before turning onto his side, briefly thinking about his appointments for later that day. With a final glance over his shoulder at his wife, Toby closed his eyes and entered a much-needed sleep.

Breaking boundaries

5

It had been a month since Toby had begun seeing Olivia Stanton. The concerns he had felt after the initial meeting had dissipated somewhat, largely in part due to some wise words of encouragement and reassurance from Richard. Olivia appeared less anxious in her sessions, and Toby, under Richard's tutelage, had explored the concept of whether much of what he had been feeling, had in fact come from picking up on her display of emotions. This wasn't uncommon in his line of work and whilst it was something he had encountered previously, he hadn't felt it to that level before. Still, he had been satisfied after exploration that it wasn't anything he should be unduly concerned by. It was Saturday morning, and as much as he loved what he did, Toby very much looked forward to the weekend, feeling it was his time to recharge and ready himself for the week ahead. He knew much of his attention during the week was dedicated to his clients, and had promised Beth she was his only focus at the weekends. Saturday morning meant Toby could lay in until seven, although this wasn't much of a victory considering he was up only an hour earlier during the week. He chuckled as he thought of this and was reminded of his student days when there was only one seven o'clock in his waking day, and it wasn't in the morning. After eventually pulling himself out of bed, and dressing in his casual attire,

Breaking boundaries

Toby headed downstairs for his morning coffee. Beth was already up and was presently sitting at the breakfast bar staring out of the window into the garden. Toby approached her quietly not wishing to disturb her, deep in thought, but as he got close she extended her right hand to hold out a cup of coffee.

'How did you know I was here?' Toby asked her quizzically with a smile.

'Woman's intuition' Beth replied giggling.

'Really?'

'No, I heard you get out of bed fifteen minutes ago.'

'Why the travel mug?'

'The travel mug is because I knew you'd be scrambling for the door to get to your gym session.'

'Shit, I'd forgotten about that.' Toby said exiting the kitchen, but not before kissing her forehead and reminding her how wonderful she was.

'Have fun and don't forget you're collecting the birthday cake for Sasha's party tomorrow, from the bakery.'

'Ah, the spawn of Satan.' Toby said with a wide grin.

'She's four Toby and just has some emotional needs, that's all.' Beth replied in a manner which left Toby wondering whether he had genuinely offended her. He moved back into the kitchen and wrapped his arms around her, kissing her neck in the process. He then turned, picked up his bag and left the house. Whilst he teased Beth about her niece and personally felt she had quite complex

Breaking boundaries

behavioural issues, Toby was sensitive around the subject and kept much of what he thought to himself. Sasha was his niece, but more importantly, she was Lara's daughter. When it came to anything involving Lara, Toby didn't push. It wasn't that he thought Beth would take Lara's side in the event of any animosity, he just didn't want to put her in that position, particularly after what she and Lara had been through as children. He knew the strength of their bond and had no inclination to put that to the test. Toby didn't dislike Sasha, but she reminded him of why he had actively decided parenthood wasn't for him soon after meeting Beth. He wasn't sure why this was but wondered whether it was perhaps the fact he didn't want to share her with children. He smiled at the irony that she now shared him with his clients.

Toby closed the front door and opened the boot of his car, placing his gym bag carefully in the small space in and amongst other things, which had no place really being in his boot. Saturday morning was *his* downtime away from all things related to work. He wondered what his personal trainer had in store for him today. Last week he had left feeling exhausted but knew this meant it had been a good session. He wasn't overweight, in fact, he was in good shape, considering his penchant for all things sweet. For Toby it wasn't about his physique, it was about getting interaction with somebody who wasn't a client and wasn't a family member. After a week of

Breaking boundaries

being sat in the therapist's chair, he quite liked being a client himself, an irony not lost on him. He had realised some time ago he didn't need a personal trainer, he just enjoyed having somebody who didn't know him and who would keep the conversation light. And after a week of often highly emotive disclosure, what Toby yearned for, was something light, superficial and without agenda. He pulled into the car park of the gym, managing to grab one of the last available parking spaces. One of the things he had come to realise was that everybody seemed to want to be at the gym early on a Saturday morning. He wondered whether people still went out on a Friday night, and then realised he could add himself to that category. As he entered the gym, his personal trainer, Dan, who had been waiting for him, rose to his feet with a smile and greeted him.

'Sorry I'm a few minutes late,' Toby said apologetically.

'These things happen don't worry. Besides, it gave me chance to have a breather from my last client. It was only her first session and I think she worked me harder than I worked her. She headed straight for the pool once we'd finished. You can't help but admire that enthusiasm.'

Toby laughed and settled into his warmup with Dan. This was the type of conversation he enjoyed. Listening to somebody else talk about their clients made him momentarily forget about his own. He only saw Dan for an hour per week but cherished

Breaking boundaries

that time and knew he benefitted more emotionally than he did physically. His training session seemed to pass quickly and both he and Dan were happy with the progress he had made. Toby had managed to obtain a personal best on the rowing machine whilst also adding an extra ten kilograms to his previous best on the bench. He now felt refreshed and focused, regardless of the day having started in a disorganised manner. Whilst it was less than twenty-four hours since he was in his practice, any thoughts of client work were in the distance. Once Toby left the practice on a Friday afternoon, he would begin the transformation from therapist to individual and had perfected using the journey home for this very purpose. This had been one of the things which had hit him so hard just over a month ago when he had been unable to shake that session with Olivia Stanton. It wasn't solely surprise and confusion which had enveloped him that evening, but also disappointment. Showered and refreshed, Toby reached for his gym bag and headed out of the changing room door. He turned to his left and walked towards the café for his obligatory coffee. Whilst he would never pass himself off as a coffee connoisseur, this was Toby's drink of choice, almost a vice he had thought on occasions. He had heard people say they couldn't function before a morning coffee, but Toby had never felt like this was the case for him. He enjoyed the taste and liked to sample different blends. The percolator he had received for his birthday from Beth two years ago,

Breaking boundaries

had become a prized possession. Finding a vacant table, Toby took a seat and ordered his drink. He sat peacefully taking in the surroundings, waiting with an almost childlike excitement for his drink to be served. Suddenly his tranquillity was disrupted. A shiver ran through his body.

'Toby?'

He turned sharply to see Olivia standing behind him smiling, her wet hair tied up in a bun, looking slightly lighter than he remembered. In her left hand was a light blue holdall, which didn't look long removed from its packaging. In her other hand was a handbag, not so new, but elegant all the same. It wasn't the first time Toby had encountered one of his clients away from his practice, but it was a rare occurrence, and each of those occasions, like this one, had elicited the same response; trepidation and discomfort. He was always clear with clients in their first session about chance meetings outside of therapy. Privacy and confidentiality extended outside of the practice, which meant Toby would not acknowledge a client unless they first acknowledged him. There were two key reasons behind this. Firstly, he needed to protect the privacy of his client and by engaging with them away from the safe and confidential setting of his practice, he was potentially putting their privacy at risk. This risk was heightened if they were in the company of others. Toby hated the thought of a client being forced to explain who he was due to something he had said or done. Secondly, from his perspective, his clients

Breaking boundaries

were just that, clients. For Toby, it was important they see him only as a therapist, not as a friend. He was very particular about maintaining the boundaries between his professional and personal life. This was also one of the reasons he was so guarded at home and disclosed little about his profession to his wife, much to Beth's annoyance. Regardless of seeing numerous clients who lived or worked within close proximity, Toby had not seen a client away from his practice for quite some time. Previously in these situations, he had remained polite but had avoided being drawn into engaging in any detailed conversations. This was a technique he had often used in therapy, but still, it felt strange in this situation. He smiled politely and spoke, hoping the awkwardness he was feeling would not show.

'Olivia, how are you?'

An open question, yet just a pleasantry. He didn't want to engage with his client but realised this wasn't a passing hello. They stood facing each other and some form of exchange appeared inevitable.

'I know I'm probably not supposed to speak with you outside of our sessions, and I must admit this feels a little awkward, but I didn't want to ignore you,' she replied, not answering his question.

Toby felt better knowing that Olivia had also recognised the boundaries and was relieved he wasn't the only one feeling awkward right now. Just as he was about to respond, his coffee arrived,

Breaking boundaries

which for Toby was a welcome distraction, and the opportunity he needed to excuse himself.

'Latte? Nice choice, but I prefer Jamaican Blue Mountain or a nice Nicaraguan coffee.'

Toby looked at Olivia with surprise but wasn't sure why. Was it so inconceivable that a client could have knowledge and enjoyment of coffee?

'You know your coffee.'

'I know what gets me up in the morning, and what keeps me awake in the evening,' she said with a smile.

'My percolator is my best friend in the morning,' Toby replied, seeming to now relax into the conversation. But he didn't want to relax into the conversation. It was nice not to feel anxious, but the longer he remained talking to her, the more likely it was the anxiety would return. Client time, he reminded himself, was during the week. This was his time and he valued it as it allowed him to be himself, not a therapist.

'I once visited Brazil. The most memorable part of the trip was the coffee. Not sure what that says about the rest of the trip.'

'Perhaps it's more of a reflection on your love of coffee,' Toby said politely.

Taking a sip from his cup whilst having an internal monologue about how to remove himself from this conversation, Toby looked at the clock over Olivia's left shoulder. He wasn't sure whether this had been an involuntary cursory glance, or whether he had intended Olivia to notice him doing this, which would

Breaking boundaries

provide him with an opportunity to leave; leave without being unwittingly rude and without damaging the therapeutic relationship with his client. She noticed.

'I'm sorry, I'm disturbing you in your own time.'

'You're not disturbing me,' Toby replied. But he knew this was a lie. She was disturbing him. She had also given him a way out of the conversation, an opportunity for some reason he had declined. Was it really a way out? What were his options? He either risks offending her or remains in an uncomfortable situation he had been trained to avoid. He thought of the different ways he could have responded to politely excuse himself and wondered why they hadn't entered his mind a few moments ago. He willed his coffee to cool so he could drink it quickly and make a hasty, yet polite retreat. The coffee did not comply. For a moment there was an awkward silence. Toby hated these in therapy but hated them even more when he was out of his comfort zone. Olivia broke the silence and as much as Toby felt relieved, he had hoped the silence would lead to her leaving the conversation. It didn't.

'Toby, I wanted to say thank you for what you have done for me in therapy. I feel so much better about things and it's because of you.'

Toby blushed.

'I simply provide a safe environment,' he replied.

'I think you're doing yourself a disservice, Toby. The questions you ask, the observations you make,

Breaking boundaries

they have helped me to look at things from a different perspective and I'm feeling stronger for it.'

Toby smiled tentatively at a compliment which made him feel more awkward because of the environment he was in. Clients would sometimes make comments during the session if Toby had asked them a particularly thought-provoking question which had struck a chord positively. Occasionally they would voice their gratitude at the end if they thought it had been especially positive for them. Toby wasn't overly comfortable with this, mainly because he wanted to empower his clients to make any necessary changes themselves, explore their own difficulties and find their own answers. He knew the dangers of them becoming overly reliant on him and would remind them, when necessary, not to overstate his role in their journey, and understate their own. He believed quite simply, the client needed to end their therapeutic journey knowing it was they who had made the changes, and they who had developed the strategies to allow them to continue their progress. This wasn't his practice though; this wasn't during or after a session. This was a weekend, his time, and not a place where he felt at all comfortable conversing with a client on any level, more importantly, not one who had raised the topic of their therapy. Professionally and ethically, he didn't believe he had contravened any boundaries, yet this feeling of discomfort grew. At that moment and with that thought, Toby decided he needed to end the

Breaking boundaries

conversation and excuse himself. He took a few sips of his coffee, burning his mouth in the process and turned back to Olivia. But something caught his eye, a burn on her arm. She had worn short sleeve tops before and it occurred to him that he hadn't noticed this before. He was perceptive, he was trained to be. He had spent years studying his clients' body language, their appearance, the words they spoke, and the things they omitted. He would have surely noticed had this been there previously. It looked red and hadn't begun to scab over. This was fresh and had been done recently.

'I burnt the tea.'

'I'm sorry?' Toby replied confused.

Olivia had noticed him looking. He hadn't been diplomatic enough and felt angry with himself.

'I burnt the tea, he burnt me. He thought that was a fair exchange.' Olivia smiled, but Toby could only imagine the emotional anguish, as well as the physical pain that such an experience must have inflicted upon her.

'I'm sorry. Have you had that checked out? it looks painful.'

'I'll be fine, it's not the worst thing he has done.'

Toby realised he had now been drawn into a conversation with Olivia. He hadn't been careful, had broken all of his own rules, and as a result, now felt like he was in a moral dilemma. It would be awkward and potentially damaging for Toby to cut the conversation suddenly at this point. Whilst it had certainly not been his intention, Toby had indirectly

Breaking boundaries

played his part in what was happening now. Through intrigue or concern, Toby's actions had put Olivia into a situation which had effectively forced her to explain. In practice, Toby would see the fact Olivia felt comfortable enough to disclose this so readily as a good thing. It would signify she trusted her therapist enough to be open, to show her vulnerability. This was something which could take a significant period of time with some clients, whilst others would never reach this stage. But this wasn't his practice, it was a public place; He wasn't her therapist right now, he was somebody she had bumped into. This was a place where he was the client, and that's why he enjoyed it so much. He didn't want to be a professional here, he didn't need to be. He could simply be himself and rely on others to be the professionals. He felt a dull ache in the pit of his stomach and wondered whether it was trepidation around the situation he found himself in, or simply the abdominal workout he had completed less than an hour ago with Dan. Deep in thought, he was interrupted by Olivia.

'He was once kind enough to give me a helping hand down the stairs you know. Dislocated my left shoulder in the process.'

She gave a wry smile, which wasn't uncommon for abuse victims. Using humour when talking about traumatic events was sometimes an attempt to minimise the severity of the situation, allowing them to be able to live with the effects more readily. Toby knew this could sometimes leave the trauma

Breaking boundaries

unprocessed, which may be more damaging, but it wasn't his role to provide his clients with coping strategies. He simply provided the environment which would allow them the opportunity to find their own way through.

'Olivia, I don't know what to say.'

He wasn't lying. Toby had been completely caught out by the situation and for a brief moment felt out of his depth.

'You don't have to say anything. This isn't your problem and I shouldn't be talking to you about this, certainly not here. I only wanted to say hello and thank you for all the support you have given me.'

Olivia suddenly looked frightened and vulnerable and at that moment Toby felt an overwhelming sense of guilt. Had his carelessness forced Olivia into a discussion she hadn't wanted to have? He had now backed himself into a corner and felt angry about the dilemma he was now facing. He felt responsible for stirring up the emotions Olivia was now displaying, and if he removed himself from the conversation now, he was effectively leaving her to deal with that on her own. He reminded himself again this was not a professional environment and certainly not the place for a conversation of this nature. He thought for a moment and then smiled sympathetically.

'You're right, this isn't the right place for a conversation of this nature. Perhaps it's something you wish to explore further in your next session. It sounds like you have been through a lot.'

Breaking boundaries

'Everybody has a story to tell Toby. Many people have had traumatic experiences in their lives. The stories are often the same, it's just a different narrator.'

'I'm not sure what you mean.'

'I'm not unique. You've probably heard many stories like mine in your line of work.

Toby thought for a moment.

'Even though experiences may be similar, the impact on an individual can vary dramatically. We all handle things differently and that's why not everybody who has experienced adversity ends up in therapy. Does that make sense?'

'So, I'm one of the ones who couldn't handle it and needed therapy huh?'

Although she laughed as she said this, Toby still felt the need to elaborate.

'Therapy may form part of a coping strategy for one person, but not for another. We don't all cope in the same way.'

'I feel like I should be paying you here.'

'For what?'

'Your words of wisdom.'

'That statement is only fifty per cent accurate,' Toby said with a smile. He felt less anxious now but wondered whether he was picking up on Olivia's demeanour which was now much more relaxed. He reached around, picked up his cup and finished the last few sips of his coffee, grimacing as he realised it was now tepid at best. Olivia noticing this, drew in

Breaking boundaries

a deep breath through her teeth as if sympathising with his experience.

'Cold?'

'Well its time in the coffee machine is now a distant memory, we'll put it that way,' Toby responded.

Olivia let out a laugh as she bent forwards to pick up her gym bag, which she had placed on the chair at the table Toby had been seated at.

'I'd better head off now, Eric will be wondering where I am.'

'Are you sure you're going to be okay? It looks sore,' Toby said looking directly at the burn on her arm.

'I'll be fine, she replied pausing for a moment and offering a grateful smile to him.'

'Thank you, Toby.'

'For what? I haven't done anything.'

'More than you think.'

At that, Olivia turned and walked through the sliding doors and out into the car park. Toby reflected for a moment as he watched her walk off into the distance. He felt sorry for her and had a genuine concern about her well-being, physical and emotional, but he couldn't allow himself to get pulled into wanting to save her. As he left the gym and approached his car, he suddenly felt uneasy and conflicted. She was his client, but this was not a scheduled appointment. Had he seen this during one of her sessions, he would have explored this further with her no doubt. Although he felt like he

Breaking boundaries

hadn't probed and had avoided an in-depth discussion, he still questioned whether he engaged more than he should have, and made a conscious decision to speak with Richard to seek reassurance. Richard was good at this and very rarely, not that Toby gave him reason to, had he shown any frustration or disapproval towards Toby's practice. He was kind, knowledgeable and extremely laid back. He had been in the profession himself for thirty years and Toby felt lucky he had come across him when he had been starting as a trainee.

Taking out his keys and placing his bag into the boot, Toby climbed into his car and pressed the ignition. How he loved the sound of the engine. Beth would tease him about what his clients would think of his enthusiasm for fitness and fast cars. He would say in defence, always good-natured, that he was good at keeping personal and professional separate, that the two would remain strangers to one another. Then he had a thought. Had the two just had their first meeting? Had he inadvertently muddied the waters between a professional and personal encounter? He had tried to remain professional, courteous, and formal with Olivia, but she was his client, and this was a gym, not a professional setting. Brief small talk about a workout would have been one thing, but in a public place, this escalated into a conversation about domestic abuse. How could he have allowed himself to be put into this position? Toby now felt angry, not towards

Breaking boundaries

Olivia, but towards himself. He couldn't control what she said but had control over how, or indeed if, he responded. He had made a conscious decision to engage, and whilst he knew this was for the right reasons, he believed it was the wrong decision. Toby pulled out of the car park and accelerated. Just as he was gathering speed and relaxing into his journey home, he noticed the lights turning red in the distance. As he slowed to a halt, he looked down to change the radio station. Upon looking back up he noticed Olivia, in and amongst a group of other pedestrians, crossing the road in front of him. She recognised him and smiled, giving a cursory wave in the process. He paused for a moment but didn't respond with anything other than a polite smile. He watched Olivia walk off into the distance and wondered what she was walking into. That uncomfortable feeling had now returned.

Breaking boundaries

6

'I'm not sure how to answer that. How *am* I doing? Okay, I suppose.'

'Suppose?' Toby asked.

Her response had been vague, almost cryptic. He was experienced and knew when to remain silent and when to probe. Usually, when a client used the word 'suppose', in his experience, it meant there was something there to be explored, something they wanted to discuss, but were trying to find a way in. Sometimes, he thought they just wanted to know he was listening, that he cared. Other times, he felt they may be pondering how far they wanted to go with something which may be especially sensitive. As he sat back in his chair, hands clasped together and placed under his chin, he was pretty sure he knew his client well enough to know she wanted to explore this. She was seeking reassurance it was okay to do so, he thought. Whatever the reasoning, Toby didn't believe anything said in a therapy session was done so by mistake or coincidence. He had learned that sometimes clients are in essence, seeking permission to feel vulnerable. He found this particularly true among those who had been in controlling relationships and hadn't been used to making their own decisions; those who had had to actively seek out permission in most aspects of their daily lives; those who had seen their self-confidence and self-esteem eroded over a period of time to such an extent, they believed they were not worthy

Breaking boundaries

of any self-care, or even any love. For those people, simply getting to therapy was a monumental step forward and just making that decision in itself had therapeutic benefits. Olivia Stanton had made progress Toby thought. She had ostensibly relaxed into her therapy, feeling comfortable enough as the weeks progressed to display a range of emotions and feelings. From anger to sorrow; fear to assertion; laughter to tears. This was quite natural, and Toby had reiterated how the therapeutic journey was not necessarily a linear one. She had accepted this, but her disappointment had not gone unnoticed by him. Olivia sat across from Toby, arms now folded, and rested her eyes on him after spending a while looking down at the floor. She opened her mouth to speak, but nothing more than a sigh came out. He could tell she wanted to say something but was trying to figure out how best to do this. Toby relaxed back into his chair and crossed his legs. He didn't interject. If she was deep in thought, the last thing he wanted to do was interrupt that thought process. Instead, he remained quiet and offered her an encouraging smile. A moment later Olivia finally spoke.

'Eric was working away this last week. He only came back at the weekend. Things had been calm, until Sunday night.'

Toby sat silently; eyes focused on Olivia. His face was expressionless. Whilst he knew reactions could be quite natural and sometimes unconscious, Toby made a concerted effort not to show a tangible

Breaking boundaries

reaction regardless of the severity of what he might be hearing. The therapy was about them and their feelings, it wasn't about him. Olivia continued.

'We were invited to a family barbecue during the day and of course, Eric saw this as a valid excuse to drink…excessively.'

'I see.'

'The afternoon was quite pleasant. *Eric* was actually quite pleasant, but then he always is when he is getting what he wants.'

Toby nodded.

'Good food, nice weather, alcohol, the centre of attention. Isn't that what all men want?' Olivia looked at Toby. He couldn't determine whether she was waiting for him to speak, or just gauging his reaction. He said nothing.

'The day started fine, but then it always does until Eric and alcohol become more than just casual acquaintances. I wouldn't say every time he drinks he gets abusive, but on most occasions when he gets abusive, he's been drinking. I have often thought if I was somehow able to control the drinking, I would have a very different husband. But then I am reminded of the occasions when alcohol hasn't been involved and I have still ended up in the firing line.'

At this, Olivia paused and bowed her head. She had placed her hands on her knees and was pulling at the thread of the ripped jeans she was wearing. Toby had now come to recognise she did this when she was feeling anxious. This was her way of

Breaking boundaries

distracting herself, momentarily focusing on something else other than her situation. By the time she raised her head, her eyes were red. She was visibly upset, and he could only imagine how difficult things must be for her. 'If you would like a tissue, please help yourself,' he said gesturing towards the box positioned neatly on the table next to her. She took one, dabbed each of her eyes and then blew her nose before carefully folding the tissue and placing it in her pocket.

'Thank you, sorry.'

'What are you sorry for?'

'For wasting your time. You must wonder why I come here and talk about the same things every session without doing a damn thing to change my situation. It must be so frustrating for you.'

'Why would I be frustrated?'

'Because you must look at me and wonder why when you're trying to help me, am I not helping myself.'

'I'm here to provide a safe and confidential place for you. That time is about you, and only you. My feelings, thoughts and any hypotheses don't factor into that equation. Therapy is never about the therapist.'

'How do you manage it?' she asked.

'Manage what?'

'Not having an opinion.'

'I didn't say I don't have opinions, but my job is to neither express them directly or indirectly in a way that could influence my client.'

Breaking boundaries

Toby realised Olivia was in the process of deflecting. She had started to recount a difficult experience and it had become too painful for her. He didn't control what his clients spoke about, but he wouldn't be acting ethically if he allowed the sessions to become a reciprocal conversation. This wasn't a balanced engagement between two friends; it was therapy. She had sat back in her chair, considering his response to her. For a moment she said nothing, but her eyes had a curiosity in them. She took a deep breath, as if to ready herself, and leaned forward.

'I thought I could get through this. I thought I had the strength to leave him, but he will always be part of my life, won't he? Sometimes I worry I may resent Tyler because he is that link between Eric and me that can never be broken. How awful must I be to even think that? But it's true, isn't it? If I didn't have Tyler, I could walk away and never look back.'

Toby didn't reply. He could see Olivia was deep in thought and had an inkling she had just opened the tap and was ready to flow. With little pause, Olivia continued.

'Tyler wasn't planned you know.'

'I see.'

'I was never certain I wanted children. We hadn't discussed it and always practised safe sex. For various reasons, I didn't use contraception, but Eric did. That's perhaps one thing I will credit him with. He was always careful.'

'You changed your mind?'

Breaking boundaries

'I had it changed for me.'

Toby noted the change in Olivia's body language. Her face looked pained, almost ashen. She began pulling at the threads on her jeans again, a little more frantically this time.

'Are you ok?' he asked.

'I'm sorry, this bit is painful for me to talk about. I always knew at some point I would need to talk about this, but I also knew no amount of preparation would make it any less uncomfortable.'

'Olivia, there are no expectations in therapy. You don't have to discuss anything you don't wish to. This is your time.'

He tried to give her a reassuring smile but wasn't sure how successful he was.

'We had been at a festival and had a good time by all accounts. The relationship was still in its infancy really and at this point, I didn't have any undue concerns. It's perhaps one of those where you look back and see certain things, which retrospectively look different to how they did at the time. We had both consumed quite a lot of alcohol throughout the day and had gone out for food later that evening. We returned home around midnight and I was feeling exhausted. I went to the fridge to grab a drink to take up to bed. Eric walked up behind me and ran his hands up my skirt. We had always had a healthy sex life, so this was nothing unusual, however, I was tired and sex was the last thing on my mind. Do you know what I mean?'

Rhetorical, but still Toby nodded politely.

Breaking boundaries

'I told him I was tired and in no physical state to have sex, but he persisted. His hands were now placed around a very intimate area, and I was feeling a little uncomfortable. I moved his hand and wriggled away. This seemed to anger him, and he began shouting hurtful comments at me, telling me I had dressed provocatively and had led him on. I was stunned. This wasn't the person I knew and I didn't know how to respond. I was fearful of antagonising him further so I decided I would try and calm the situation by removing myself from it. I tried to step around him and head off to bed, but he grabbed me and threw me down onto the sofa.'

Toby braced himself. He knew what was coming next. It didn't matter how many times he had heard disclosure of this nature, it never became any easier.

'Before I knew it, he was inside me. I asked him to stop, but it was like he didn't hear me. He didn't wear protection and it didn't last long. Perhaps that's the one thing I should be grateful for.'

'I'm so sorry.'

'So there you have it. Tyler was the product of rape.'

Rape. This was one topic Toby had continually struggled with. When he had made his career choice, he had known it was inevitable he would encounter victims of rape, and he knew this would be emotionally challenging for him. Regardless of his experience, this was still a subject that Toby struggled to process, though his clients would never

Breaking boundaries

be aware of this. Over the years he had focused heavily on his own body language and liked to think he had become adept at responding with empathy but without opinion. It was vital for Toby that his clients did not feel judged in any way. Their time with him was just that, their time, not his. Therapy wasn't about him and how he was feeling, he had Richard for that. Therapy was only ever about his clients, and they needed a space to feel vulnerable without the added worry of how their therapist was feeling. Olivia leaned forward and put her head in her hands, scrunching her hair. After a few moments, she looked up at Toby, eyes red and mascara smudged. She again reached for a tissue. For a moment there was silence, aside from occasional sniffling from Olivia. Then taking a deep breath, she continued.

'He never mentioned it. It was like it never happened. To this day we have never spoken about it.'

Her speech slowed. She had just relived a terrifying ordeal and was in shock. Then the disbelief turned to anger.

'The son of a bitch carried on without a care in the world, completely unaffected. Didn't even break stride the whole day, or any time after for that matter. I mean who can do that? How can somebody be so callous?'

He wasn't expected to answer this. Nothing he could say or do in this situation would make it better for her. She was reliving the trauma, and this was

Breaking boundaries

going to hurt like hell for her. Besides, he could see she had a lot more to say and the last thing he wanted to do at this point was to stem the flow. The fact she felt comfortable enough to open up about something so incredibly traumatic was a good sign.

'Do you know what I remember more than anything about that night? It wasn't the smell of his inebriated breath; it wasn't the fact I had no control over what was happening; it wasn't the physical pain as he thrust with what can only be described as anger. No, it was the look on his face as he took what he wanted. He seemed to get off on my submissive state. Not submissive through choice, but through a resignation that there was no point in fighting it. He even whispered in my ear that he knew I liked role-playing. It was like he was justifying it. Was that his way of being able to live with what he did, to convince himself that this was a sex act I was complicit in?'

'You didn't consent Olivia, and even if you did, the moment you asked him to stop and he didn't...' Olivia didn't allow Toby to finish.

'I should have done more to stop it.'

'You feel you could have done more?'

'Yes. I could have scratched, kicked, screamed at him. Something, anything. I just froze and allowed him to do what he wanted.'

'Why do you think you froze?'

'I guess through shock and disbelief initially, but there was a fear there. I looked into his eyes and saw something I'd never seen before, and it

Breaking boundaries

frightened me. I was petrified of what he may do if I antagonised him.'

'Olivia, if you were frozen through fear, did you have any conscious control over your actions I wonder?'

'What do you mean?'

She looked up at him confused.

'Allowing something to happen would ordinarily involve a conscious decision. If you were paralysed by fear, do you believe you were in a position to make such a conscious decision?'

'No. Maybe. I don't know.'

Olivia lowered her head into her hands and began to sob uncontrollably. Digging up an old trauma was never an easy thing to do. This had been without a doubt the most emotion she had shown in her therapy, and Toby wondered whether this was the moment she had been building up to since she first walked into his practice just over two months ago. She slowly lifted her head to look at Toby, the smudged mascara now smeared down her cheeks. She opened her mouth to speak, but there was nothing coherent amongst the sobbing. Her breathing slowed; she was beginning to calm down. Still, no words were spoken, with the silence broken only by the now more sporadic sobs. Whilst this was something Toby had become accustomed to, it was still never easy for him to see. As she gathered her thoughts and reached for the tissue box once more, Toby found himself imagining what it must be like for her right now. She felt trapped in an abusive

Breaking boundaries

relationship and had carried a secret for nearly seven years, that her son had been the result of a vicious rape. He thought about the choice Olivia would inevitably be faced with as Tyler grew of age. Does she open up to him about his father, or keep her secret to prevent his illusions from being shattered? It wasn't out of the question that a bad husband could be a good father, but if this was the case, would Olivia allow herself to acknowledge this? If Tyler had a close bond with his father and Olivia threatened this in any way, he may vilify her and sympathise with his father. Toby wondered if this was something she had consciously thought of and whether it would be something she would be prepared to risk. Olivia composed herself and spoke.

'I know you must be sitting there wondering why I married him after this and why I have stayed with him?'

'Not really. I'm sure you had your reasons.'

'It sounds kind of surreal when I say this out loud, but he was so convincing at pretending it hadn't even happened, I began to question it myself. I'd also had a few drinks. Maybe it didn't happen the way I thought if you get what I mean.'

'What made you change your mind?

'About two months ago Eric was invited to a leaving party for a colleague. Naturally, I was expected to go. On the way there he turned to me and said with a look I will never forget, that he hoped I would let my hair down because when we

Breaking boundaries

had been drinking, he enjoyed the sex games we played. And in that instant, I knew. That look on his face. I knew the son of a bitch remembered every single detail of that night seven years ago.'

Toby, for a moment, didn't reply. In his mind, he had already done the maths. The correlation between Olivia's realisation, and her reaching out to him for therapy couldn't be a coincidence. If this was the case though, why had it taken her two months to open up about it? Toby looked at the clock and noticed the session was coming to an end, alerting Olivia to this.

She looked at Toby, still bleary-eyed and tried in vain to raise a smile. He could see this in itself took a lot of effort. It had been an incredibly emotional session for her.

'How are you feeling?' he asked sensitively.

'I don't know. Numb, I think. I'm not sure what I expected to feel after talking about…you know.'

Toby gave her a sympathetic look. He felt sad for her. Olivia continued.

'I could lie and say I have never really thought about this, but the truth is, and this is the hardest part, that every time I look at Tyler, I'm taken back to that night. The sight of my own son reminds me of rape. How do you think that feels for me, Toby?'

'I can't even begin to imagine,' he replied. He wasn't lying.

'I just don't know where to go from here. Talking about this is too painful, but what's more painful is having the light of my life, the very reason for my

126

Breaking boundaries

existence, and the motivation to get out of bed each day, also be the constant reminder of a brutal ordeal I was subjected to. How is that fair on him? Why should he suffer because of his father's actions?'

'Do you think he suffers?'

'I hope not, but then sometimes I question myself.'

Toby looked up at the clock again. Time was now up, but how could he simply cut her off here? He needed to draw the session to a close, but he needed to do this sensitively. He was in a difficult position now and he knew it. His natural response ordinarily would be to probe around the type of questions Olivia was asking herself, but this was the end of the session and asking an open-ended question now would extend it. Alternatively, he was mindful of simply disregarding her response and didn't wish to come across as insensitive and unfeeling, which could have an adverse effect on her willingness to open up about things in the future. Olivia decided for him.

'Recently Tyler and I were having breakfast and I was watching him eat. He was eating with his mouth open and I snapped at him for doing this, explaining the importance of etiquette to him in the process. I saw the look on his face change in an instant. He had been smiling and enjoying his food, but suddenly he looked subdued. I felt guilty and later wondered why I had reacted in the manner I did. I mean sure, it was annoying, but he is just a child and it felt like such an overreaction on my part. And

Breaking boundaries

then it hit me. It wasn't about what he was doing. It wasn't even about him. It was whom he reminded me of...his father. At that moment Toby, he reminded me of his father, and I didn't like it. Of course, then I started to wonder how many other times I had scolded him for something which wasn't really about him.'

Toby didn't get a chance to respond. Olivia tapped her hands on her knees, stood up slowly and thanked him with a warm smile.

'I've taken up enough of your time Toby, thank you for listening.'

The session had only run over by five minutes, but this wasn't his concern as Olivia left the practice. Toby relaxed back into his chair for a moment, deep in thought, but his reflection on the session with Olivia was about to take a concerning turn for him. He thought about her situation, about Eric, about the rape. He knew it was Eric who had the upper hand. He had been in control that night, and he was still in control now. But that was what this was all about, he thought, control. The verbal abuse, the physical violence, the rape, the words whispered. This was all about him exercising control over her. The son of a bitch was calculated, and Toby felt consumed by a wave of sudden anger, perhaps on Olivia's part, perhaps due to his own values. His mother had taught him as a child that the two most important things in life were to be kind and respectful. She had reaffirmed more than once, that people have different experiences and opportunities in life, but

Breaking boundaries

those experiences don't automatically make people any better or worse than others. He had no idea about Eric's background. He could be a victim himself for all he knew, so how could he explain the depth of these feelings? Without warning he was reliving Olivia's ordeal with her, trying to piece together how it must have been for her to feel so helpless. In his mind, he saw the pain in her face, the tears, the paralysis, the fear. But it didn't stop there. He had no idea what Eric looked like but had formed an image of him, grinning, no, laughing, with a crazed look in his eye. The enjoyment and satisfaction clear, but whether that was due to sexual gratification or the very thought of being in control, perhaps not so clear. Then suddenly the scenario took an unexpected, dark turn, something which frightened Toby and would lead to him questioning his ability to continue in the profession. Up until this moment, this was like a movie scene playing in his mind, but this was about to change. He was there. He was no longer seeing this through a camera lens but through his own eyes. He was there. Bursting through the door having heard Eric's raised voice, he had headed straight for him. The sight of Toby had been enough to deter Eric who had then backed away from Olivia. He hadn't been confrontational; it didn't fit his profile. He had prevented the rape, prevented Olivia's ordeal from becoming any more terrifying.

Breaking boundaries

Toby snapped himself back to reality unaware of where his thoughts would have gone had this continued. That thought, that intrusive thought, he had been her rescuer, and this worried him. Aside from wondering if he saw Olivia as somebody who needed saving, the more pressing concern was the fact he was a therapist, he was *her* therapist, not her protector. Yet at that moment, in his mind, he had suddenly been present in a very different form for her. Toby had never encountered anything like this before and was hoping Richard would be able to provide him with an explanation, and reassurance. He sat in silence for a moment, wondering what this meant, questioning his own practice. He wasn't any closer to finding an answer when he was disrupted by his phone, a welcome disruption in the form of a message from Beth. Feeling confused and anxious, Toby rose to his feet, turned off the lights and walked out of his practice. As he strolled to his car, he didn't notice the overcast skies which had now replaced a warm summer's day. He considered how he would approach supervision at the weekend. Then a strange paradox hit Toby. Never had he looked forward quite so much to supervision, but also never had he feared it so much either. Still, deep in thought, Toby opened the car door and placed his bag on the passenger seat. Starting the engine, and looking up to the skies, he suddenly became aware of the incoming weather, and he didn't relish the journey home.

Breaking boundaries

7

Richard gestured towards a chair and Toby sat down. In the years he had been seeing him, he was still yet to determine how he actually felt about sitting in the client's chair. On the one hand, it felt strange, but on the other hand, it felt nice to have the time dedicated solely to him. Richard sat opposite him with his wavy black hair and freshly trimmed beard, wearing a grey suit and open white shirt. He dressed well Toby thought and looked younger than his years. But fashion sense aside, Richard had a reputation for being an excellent therapist himself and Toby valued him as a supervisor. He was in awe of his knowledge, not specifically about his profession, but just in general. He was well-read, continually looking to add to his already impressive credentials.

'How are you, Toby?'

'I'm doing ok…I think.'

'You think?'

'I have an interesting case at the moment and it's causing me some concern. The fact I haven't spoken about her before is perhaps also a little worrying. I need to process what's happening and haven't been able to do this on my own.'

'Okay.'

'She's thirty-three and I've been seeing her for around eight weeks. She elicits feelings within me that I don't fully understand, yet know they are causing me concern. The feelings aren't romantic,

131

Breaking boundaries

but there is something, and I felt this in the first session. I spent a lot of time reflecting on why that particular session had had such an impact on me.'

Toby paused for a moment and looked up at Richard, who was sitting forward in his chair resting his hand on his chin. Richard was listening attentively and Toby wondered what he would think of him by the end of the session. Richard's opinion, more than most, meant a lot to Toby and he considered very carefully how he would convey his dilemma to him. Toby continued.

'In her last session, she disclosed to me that she had been raped by her husband. She has previously told of being subjected to physical and emotional abuse and feels her husband exercises control over her. What adds further complexity is that her son Tyler who is six, was the product of the vicious rape she described.'

Again, he paused, looking up momentarily. Richard had not moved, nor had his expression. Toby knew he was focused on what he was saying, and wondered what his first thoughts on the situation would be. He felt like he was looking for approval to continue.

'After the session, that's where it starts to get complicated.'

'I see.'

'I sat for a moment reflecting on the session and suddenly had this conscious thought of preventing her ordeal…of saving her.'

'Saving her?'

Breaking boundaries

'I had seen her pain and upset, and in the moment, I just wanted to take that away from her. In those short minutes, it was like I had gone from watching the movie to being in it. I save her, I prevent the rape from happening. I'm worried about what this could mean.'

Richard nodded, making a brief verbal acknowledgement in the process. He cleared his throat and spoke.

'You've named her son, yet not her. Why is that?'

Toby was shocked. Why hadn't he disclosed her name? Why was he so secretive?

'Her name is Olivia,' he said hesitantly.

Richard smiled at him, but Toby knew there were already seeds of doubt.

'You've ruled out erotic transference, so it's not an erotic feeling coming from her, but is it transference? Is this something she is putting onto you do you think?'

'I did question whether I was picking up on what she was feeling.'

'Does she want you to rescue her Toby?'

This question took Toby by surprise, and Richard noticed his retreat into the back of his chair. Did she want Toby to rescue her? This had not been reflected in the things she had said, but what about what she hadn't said? Toby paused and made a considered response, which he wasn't sure actually answered Richard's question.

'I usually get a good read of my clients and build on this understanding as the therapy progresses,

Breaking boundaries

but with her, I'm all over the place. Maybe that's part of the issue here. Maybe I'm frustrated because I can't read her, or I have read her wrong. She oscillates between somebody who is incredibly vulnerable and somebody who exudes confidence. Of course, this isn't uncommon over a period of time, but never before have I seen this fluctuation during a single session.'

He paused, expecting Richard to speak, but he remained silent and Toby knew he was waiting for him to answer his original question. In therapy, Toby would avoid answering questions directly, as that wasn't his role. However, therapy was about his clients, and supervision was about him, about his practice, and to process this he needed to be honest with Richard, with himself.

'In some moments, when I see this vulnerability, this helplessness, it does feel like she is wanting to be saved. Then there are other times when she is displaying that tenacity and confidence where it feels like she is saying *'I'm ok, I'm in control, fuck Eric'*. The difficulty is the speed at which she can move about between these two personas.'

'What was her presenting issue?'

'She originally came wishing to process the prolonged abusive relationship she was in, stating she wanted to find the strength to remove herself from that environment.'

Richard now sat back in his chair and looked at Toby rather quizzically. Toby knew this look. He

Breaking boundaries

knew Richard was about to throw a curve ball at him, and he needed to be prepared.

'With that confidence, you are describing she has displayed, what is she wanting to achieve from therapy? What goals do you think she has?'

'She has spoken about the build-up over years with a reticence to open up to anybody about her situation, her ordeal. Holding onto this had become overwhelming for her and she had felt to stop it from eating away at her, she had to tell somebody. But it's more than this. She said she needed therapy to give her the confidence to leave her relationship, to be free of her situation.'

Richard, waiting for Toby to finish speaking, leaned forward and poured them both a glass of water. It was a warm day and Toby joked he would prefer a cocktail with plenty of ice. Richard had responded by telling him the bar was a work in progress. Having relaxed back in his chair now, Richard took a sip of his water and then offered his insight.

'It sounds like the goal of her therapy for her is to build her own self-confidence to leave her marriage, however, does she have a safety plan in place? If she were to leave now, where would she go, what provisions has she made? I'm wondering whether she is at the end stage and therapy is the final piece of the jigsaw for her, or whether she is just in the planning stages and therapy allows her to explore her options.'

Breaking boundaries

Toby uncrossed his legs and let out a deep breath. He was an experienced therapist, how had he not considered this himself? Why had he not recognised the fact there had been no mention of forward planning by Olivia? He felt frustrated but hid this from Richard.

'Thinking about it now, her disclosure has been centred around the present and the past. There has been no mention of future planning.'

'The rape was six years ago, right?'

'Yes'

'Has there been any escalation or de-escalation in controlling behaviours since then?'

'She has spoken about him being controlling in some areas, but her main concern has been the occasions when alcohol is involved. These are the occasions when his anger has manifested itself in the form of physical violence. I am quite interested to understand why she disclosed the rape when she did. At the beginning of the session, she pre-empted the tone, by telling me that she knew what she was about to say needed to be said at some point, but she still didn't feel comfortable with it. I wondered whether she had been building up to this, or even, whether actually, this was her main goal of therapy…to externalise her rape ordeal and its impact.'

Richard cleared his throat and took a sip of water, before focusing back on Toby.

'So from what you're saying it sounds like there is no suggestion his behaviour has escalated, with the

Breaking boundaries

worst event taking place some six years ago. Is she in fear for her life do you think?'

'She says not and I did ask her this at the beginning. I also asked her about any fears she had for Tyler. Interestingly, she acknowledged that Eric was a good father to him. One of her concerns is Tyler picking up certain mannerisms and behaviours from his father. She said these aren't necessarily bad, but it's more her reaction to them.'

'Tyler reminds her of his father?'

'Yes. She provided an example where she believed she overreacted based on the fact that at that moment, she didn't see Tyler, she saw Eric. It wasn't about the action; it was about whom the action reminded her of.'

He stopped for a moment and took several sips of water. It was a warm day and any liquids were most welcome. Richard looked at him intently, but more out of intrigue. Toby took a deep breath as if to order his thoughts, and continued.

'When she was disclosing this, my only reaction was one of concern. What if this escalates and Tyler is in danger, not from his father, but from his mother?'

'Ok, so Olivia doesn't feel like she is in any imminent danger, there's been no escalation in the violence or other abusive behaviour. Why do you think she chose that moment two months ago to come to therapy?

Toby leaned forward, chin resting on his hands and sat deep in thought, considering a measured

Breaking boundaries

response. The truth was, he didn't know the answer to Richard's question. Well, he had an idea, his hypothesis, but when he had asked his client the same question Richard was now asking him, she had given a very vague response. He sat up and produced an answer that he felt must have sounded as vague as the one Olivia had given him.

'I think she was feeling overwhelmed.'

'You think? Did you ask her?'

'I did. She just said that it was the right time. I saw the look on her face, her body language. I heard the hesitancy in her voice. At that point, I knew there was much more under the surface, but didn't want to probe.'

'What are your thoughts about Olivia, what do you really think about her?'

One thing Toby had learned during his time with Richard was his ability to occasionally throw up a question that he wasn't expecting. This was one of those occasions, and it made Toby uneasy. He smiled at the irony of his unease amplifying upon the very realisation he was feeling uneasy in the first place. Richard knew him and knew him well. Toby couldn't lie. Why would he? He needed perspective, and open dialogue with Richard was essential in helping him to understand why he was feeling this way.

'She's a very interesting person. I have no romantic feelings, but if I were to describe her, I would do so as a well-dressed, attractive young woman.'

Breaking boundaries

'When you say romantic, are you using romantic in a sexual sense?'

Toby looked up, stunned. An overwhelming sense of guilt enveloped him. Was there a sexual attraction to Olivia? He exhaled slowly.

'I'd like to think not.'

'You can say there are no romantic feelings, but this doesn't mean there isn't a sexual feeling. If this is erotic transference, remember we have no control over it, until we become conscious of it. This can happen to any therapist at any time, regardless of gender or sexual orientation. Toby, if you are getting erotic transference, that doesn't make you a bad person or a bad therapist. It happens, and it's important to remember this is not your stuff, it's your client's.'

'Do you think I have a sexual attraction to Olivia?'

'I don't know, but there's a difference between sexual attraction and erotic transference. Attraction is your stuff; erotic transference is Olivia's. Do you find her sexually attractive?'

With every question Richard asked, Toby's discomfort increased further. This right here was one of the most difficult questions he had been asked. He did find Olivia attractive, but admitting sexual attraction to himself, never mind anybody else, left him with a moral dilemma. He had always been faithful to Beth. How could he begin to process having a sexual attraction to somebody else? Whilst Toby braced himself, he was diplomatic in his

Breaking boundaries

answer. This was to protect himself more than anything else.

'I acknowledge she is an attractive young woman.'

'Ok, think about it this way. What is one question you would like to ask her, or one thing you would like to say to her, that you could never say to a client?' Richard asked.

Another one of those questions which caught him out. He could see by the look on Richard's face, that he had picked up on it too. Eyes glazed wide, looking around the room, searching for an answer, he responded, without even looking up. He had been honest, but it left him feeling despondent.

'How can I take this pain away from you?'

Richard gave a mutter. He was waiting for Toby to expand.

'I'm struggling to understand my feelings. I've worked with several hundred clients, and I don't know what it is about Olivia Stanton that is making me feel like this. Why do I feel the need to fix her or, perhaps her situation because that's not my role as a therapist?'

'So here's the thing Toby. Does she want you to take her pain away? Is this ultimately what she really wants from therapy?'

'I think she needs to find a way out of her situation.'

Richard looked at Toby, with a hint of a smile.

'Needs? Is that your opinion or hers?'

Breaking boundaries

'I don't know. Maybe she just wants me to validate what she is feeling?'

Toby was squirming and suddenly didn't want to be in supervision anymore. He was feeling emotionally fatigued and regretted his decision to push himself into confronting this. Richard was good, in fact, he was brilliant. That was the problem. If you simply wanted somebody who was agreeable, then he wasn't for you. He challenged sensitively, but it was more about his ability to read body language and hone in on specific words which stood him out from others. If Toby was holding anything back, Richard would notice. He drew a deep breath, expelling slowly.

'There's something else.'

'Something else?'

'Yes.'

There was a brief pause as Toby readied himself.

'A few weeks ago, I bumped into her when I was leaving the gym. I had just finished with my personal trainer, waiting for my coffee, and there was a tap on my shoulder.'

Richard was focused but had a look on his face which made Toby feel slightly uncomfortable. It wasn't one of judgment, more of intrigue where this was going. Since that day, Toby had not even wanted to acknowledge it had happened, yet here he was about to revisit it in its entirety.

'She acknowledged the boundaries which was reassuring and even gave me a way out of the conversation. Then I saw something.'

Breaking boundaries

Richard's intrigue now looked palpable.

'And what was that?'

'I saw a burn, fresh. My eyes naturally gravitated towards it.'

'She saw you looking, didn't she?'

Toby nodded slowly.

'I then felt compelled to comment on it. Suddenly we were engaging in a conversation, almost like we would in the therapeutic setting, but in a different environment.'

'BPD?'

Toby knew what Richard was alluding to here. People with borderline personality disorder could have unstable and intense relationships with others, which sometimes create issues with boundaries.

'I did consider it.'

'If it's BPD she will have boundary issues within all of her relationships. If that's not the case, what is it about her therapeutic relationship with you, which may create boundary problems?'

Toby sloped back into his chair. This felt almost as uncomfortable as the situation he was describing. He looked at the clock. Only twenty minutes left of his supervision. A scant consolation he thought. Richard remained quiet waiting for Toby to answer. Whilst he didn't feel comfortable with long silences in the therapy room, Richard was quite happy with them, so holding out for Richard to speak wasn't an option.

'I was very clear in the first session with her regarding boundaries, as I am with all clients, and I

Breaking boundaries

felt reassured she acknowledged this in our chance meeting.'

'You mentioned she gave you a way out. Was she testing you do you think?'

'Do you have any suspicions about this client?' Toby asked quite curtly. He had no idea why he had asked this question and was wary of what Richard may reply with. Did he have suspicions and need them validated, or was he looking for Richard to reassure him?

'Most of what you have said causes me concern, Toby. You have, on occasion, seen clients before, at petrol stations and supermarkets and haven't engaged on this level with them. Ordinarily, noticing something such as a burn would have presented to you as a red flag, a reason to shut the conversation down. Instead, here, you dropped your physical and emotional boundaries and I'm curious as to why.'

Toby was hoping this was rhetorical as he didn't have an answer. Before he could think of an answer Richard followed up with another question.

'Does she remind you of anybody?'

Toby hadn't expected this and wondered what the purpose of the question was. Who could Olivia remind him of?

'She has a warm smile and is somebody whom I could imagine people would gravitate towards. However, I know there is a deep sorrow that lies behind that smile.'

Breaking boundaries

Then it hit him, not an epiphany as such, but certainly a sudden realisation strong enough to shock him.

'Holy shit, my mother.'

Richard didn't break stride.

'When you think of her, where do you get those feelings?'

'Physically?'

'Yes, where do you experience those sensations?'

'I guess in the pit of my stomach.'

'Where have you experienced that before?'

Toby slowly looked up at Richard, as though he had just unearthed something which had been buried for quite some time.

'Only twice in my life...George and my mum. I couldn't help George, and I couldn't save my mum.'

'We can't save everybody Toby, and some people don't want to be saved.'

The anxiety had now subsided, replaced by a sense of sadness at the thought of his late mother, and also of George who had been his first love. They hadn't spoken in years and he wondered what had become of her, how her life had turned out.

Richard sat upright and shuffled in his chair.

'Toby, this therapy seems to have no direction. You're eight sessions in and in most cases at this stage, would be looking at closing out the therapy. There seems to be no evidence of this with Olivia.'

He knew Richard was right, he usually always was. His supervision was drawing to a close and he

Breaking boundaries

felt like he perhaps had more questions than answers. He finished his water and wondered what Beth's day had been like. Thinking of Beth always made him smile, and right now, in one of the most emotionally draining supervision sessions he had ever experienced, he needed something to make him smile. He drew his attention back to Richard, who was still speaking and wondered how much he had missed. Richard continued.

'If you were to say to Olivia that you were looking at discharging her within the next six sessions, and asked her what she felt she needed to explore and achieve within that time, how do you think this would be received?'

Toby found himself once again taken by surprise. He hadn't even considered discharging Olivia, and now found himself consciously wondering why this was the case. Richard sensed his hesitation and offered a follow-up question before Toby could produce anything coherent in response.

'Ok, let's go back a step. How do *you* feel right now thinking about closing Olivia's case in six sessions?'

Toby looked intently at him and wondered why he had asked this specific question. What had Richard picked up on?

'I have become quite fond of her as a client, but that's not unusual when I have built up a good therapeutic relationship with somebody.' He paused and suddenly felt like he was having to defend himself by qualifying his initial response. Why did he

Breaking boundaries

feel he was on the back foot here? There was no judgment coming from Richard, so he thought this must be about his own guilt. But why would he feel guilty? He hadn't acted inappropriately at any stage and whilst boundaries perhaps needed realigning, he had maintained his professional ethics throughout. So why was there something niggling at him when it came to this client? Richard knew him well and could tell he was holding back. Toby had no choice now, but to be honest with him, but more importantly with himself.

'I think there would be a sadness, but perhaps not in a conventional way.'

'In what way then?'

'I think I fear her and the impact she has had on me.'

There it was, a sudden release. He felt like this is what he had been building up to for several weeks now, his crescendo. He had perhaps known subconsciously that there was something different about Olivia Stanton, something he had never experienced in any other client previously, but he had been afraid to admit it to himself. He threw his arms up in the air as he openly stated that he would have no idea how Olivia would react, but sensed it may not be wholly positive.

'You've worked short-term therapy with many clients Toby, in which time you have set therapeutic goals, and worked to an ending. You have also worked with clients for over a year and felt elated when you were finally able to discharge them.'

146

Breaking boundaries

Richard stopped. He didn't need to say anything further. Toby knew exactly where he was going with this but again found himself with no answer. He had come to supervision to try and understand why he was faced with this situation but was feeling more and more confused, lacking in answers and insight. Now Richard leaned forward, looking more serious than Toby recalled ever having seen him.

'Toby, where do you hold your code of ethics here? Does she need therapy, or do you need her to be in therapy?'

Toby was unexpectedly overcome with an uncomfortable feeling in the pit of his stomach like he had been struck with force by a powerful instrument. The mention of the word *ethics* hit him hard. He couldn't begin to imagine that he had overstepped the boundaries of therapy to this degree. His shoulders were now sloped, and his posture gave the impression of somebody who was defeated and had little left to give.

'What do I do?'

'She is your client Toby, but if it were me, I would be looking at closing out the case sooner rather than later. I'm not altogether sure where this is leading, but I sense if you thought it was anywhere positive, we wouldn't be having this conversation.'

'I guess.'

'I'd be interested to know what made her choose you as a therapist. Also, if she has had any previous experience with therapy, what happened within those sessions and with those other therapists?'

Breaking boundaries

'You think she sought me out?'

'I couldn't say for sure, but it's not unheard of. If she has the ability to elicit feelings in you that you have previously attached to George and your mother, then that's not healthy for you. And if she has the ability to grey the boundaries, that's not healthy for her.'

Toby looked up at the clock. Time was up. He had never felt so relieved to end supervision. He found himself wondering whether this was what his clients felt during therapy. As he rose to his feet and reached for his coat, Richard put his hand on his shoulder.

'Toby, tread carefully. It's not ethical to simply end the therapy abruptly with her. But also keep in mind, it isn't ethical to continue working with her indefinitely with no objective. You're a good therapist, I know you've got this.'

Toby smiled momentarily but didn't respond. He shook Richard's hand and exited the building. The trees in the car park were now swaying vigorously and the dark clouds had made it feel much later than it was. He paused for a moment and wondered whether a brisk walk around the block may help him to clear his head, and then decided against it. As he strolled across the car park, he felt the first drops of rain and realised he had made the correct decision. He reflected on the last hour and a half with Richard and pondered on the decision he had to make. It was easy for Richard to urge him to look at ending the therapy with Olivia, he wasn't emotionally

148

Breaking boundaries

invested, Toby thought. And there it was, those two words... *emotionally invested*. They cut through Toby like a surgeon's scalpel. Suddenly in this moment, Toby was realising his fear. He *was* emotionally invested in this client. She was George, she was his mum, and she was even Beth in some respects. All the people he loved, he saw in Olivia. As he sat in his car, he shivered, not at the cooling temperature, but at the realisation, he was uncovering complexities within his relationship with her. He was learning things about himself that he didn't like. He had no idea what he was going to do moving forward, but he knew he had a battle on his hands, and considered whether he now regretted meeting Olivia Stanton. With that thought fresh in his mind, Toby started the engine, took a deep breath and sped out of the car park, windscreen wipers swaying frantically from side to side in a vain attempt to counteract the tropical shower, which had just begun.

Breaking boundaries

8

'Jack, it's Beth. I'm trying to reach Toby; his number isn't connecting. Could you grab him for me please?'

'I would if he was here Beth'.

'He's left already? You must have gone easy on him!'

'Not exactly. He never arrived. He called me earlier this morning to say he was running a little late, but I haven't heard from him since then.'

'That's not like him.'

'Maybe he's broken down? The signal out here isn't great, if he's out in the countryside, he'll struggle with any reception,'

'How long ago did he call?'

'About four hours.'

'And you're not worried?'

'I've never worried about Toby. He's incredibly smart… and streetwise. You know that right?'

'Maybe, but…' she said hesitantly.

'What is it?'

'Have you noticed anything different about him recently?'

'Different how?' Jack asked with genuine curiosity.

'He seems preoccupied. I know his job is emotionally fatiguing, but he's always been good at keeping his work in his practice.'

'You see him more than me.'

Breaking boundaries

'I know he talks to you. I don't want to pry; I just want to know if there is anything I should know about,' Beth said with a calmness perhaps not befitting of the situation.

'Like what?'

'I don't know. Just anything which has made you think he may be in some sort of trouble.'

'Trouble? Beth this is Toby we're talking about. I can't think of anybody I know, who is more risk averse.'

'Jack, knowing your circle of friends, that doesn't say a great deal! You may be right; I just have a bad feeling something is happening he isn't telling me about.'

'Beth...' Jack paused. 'I don't know if this is relevant, but a few weeks ago, he mentioned he was working with a client like no other he had worked with. That was the first time he had ever spoken about a case with me on any level.'

'I know he wouldn't have given you any more than that, but I don't suppose he mentioned how long he had been working with them?'

'Sorry. He just said she was a particularly interesting case.'

'She?' Beth said sharply.

'Why do you say it like that?'

'Because if it's the case I am thinking of, then the timeline would make sense.'

'I'm not sure I follow.'

'The point, on reflection, where Toby started to appear distracted, not his normal self. He would

151

Breaking boundaries

never talk about the specifics of a case, but occasionally, he will tell me if he is working with a particularly challenging client.'

'Did he mention this specific case?'

'Not really, but I distinctly remember the evening a few months back when I first noticed he looked troubled. I don't know, maybe not troubled, but certainly deep in thought, like he was there physically, but emotionally he was vacant.'

'And you think it's this client?'

'I can't be sure, and at the time, I wasn't unduly concerned, but when I piece other small things together, I'm left wondering how much this is affecting him.'

'I'm not sure what to say. Toby and I are close, but he doesn't talk to me about that sort of stuff,' Jack replied almost apologetically.

'And even if he did, I wouldn't expect you to betray his confidence. I guess I just want to know what's going on in his world. He dedicates so much time to his clients, I worry he neglects himself.'

'He knows what he's doing. Could you be worrying over nothing?'

'Maybe, I don't know,' Beth said with uncertainty.

'If I hear from him, I'll let you know.'

'Likewise.'

'Take care, Beth.'

'Bye Jack.'

Breaking boundaries

9

Toby removed his phone from his pocket. It was Jack calling. Jack was an old friend of his, a farmer who had taken over the day-to-day running of the place just a year earlier when his father had first become ill. When Jack's father passed away shortly after his diagnosis, Toby had taken it quite hard. They had maintained a good relationship and he had always been fond of him. Jack's dad would tease Toby, frequently telling him he sat in a chair all day to avoid manual labour. Toby got his humour and knew whilst they didn't have much in common, there was a deep, mutual respect. He also knew Jack's father always appreciated the friendship he had with his son. They had known each other as children, attending the same school, but whereas Toby had gone off to college and university, Jack had stayed local and begun helping his father out more frequently on the farm. Regardless of the different paths their lives had taken, they had always maintained contact, and he listed Jack as one of his closest friends. Though Jack had always had a passion for the family business, Toby got the impression that his dedication was now more to do with his father's memory and preserving his legacy, than his love of farming. That was one of the problems with Toby's profession, he could pick up on things without a word being spoken. Professionally, this was an asset, but on a personal level, he found it to be a burden. There were times

Breaking boundaries

when he wished he was just oblivious, times when he realised things, he wished he hadn't. With Jack, he sometimes heard the despair in his voice, a resignation at what his life had become. On the outside Jack exuded positivity, a warm smile endearing to all who came into contact with him. On the inside, Toby feared there was a dark sadness consuming him. Jack had been close to his father and hadn't taken his death well. Toby had been there for him, and had talked him through the grieving process, reassuring him that he would find his own way through, in his own time. He had remembered thinking at the time that it was so much easier working with a grieving client than a grieving friend, something made more difficult due to him being in mourning himself. Jack wasn't a talker, and would frequently tease Toby about his profession, but Toby knew he was still hurting. It wasn't what he said, it was what he didn't say. He had only spoken to Toby once about it, on the day of the funeral. Jack was divorced and lived alone, having little time for anything else in his life beyond the farm. Like Toby, he had no children. His mother was relatively local, but they were scarcely more than cordial after she had walked out on him and his father when Jack was just seven. She had attended the funeral of his father, but the exchanges were uncomfortable and felt more like pleasantries between two old acquaintances, than heartfelt dialogue between a mother and her son. Toby felt he was lonely, not

Breaking boundaries

that Jack would be receptive to this theory, and always tried to find time for him where he could.

'Tobes, fancy doing some real work?', Jack said laughing.

'*Tobes*' was Jack's nickname for Toby in school. It had stuck, and Toby didn't mind, though Beth hated it, and Jack knew better than to use it in her presence.

'I do real work every day Jack, with people who can hold a conversation.'

'I'm offended.'

'You're never offended,' Toby quipped.

'You're right, I'm only offended by people I actually like.'

'Ah touché,' Toby said with a smile. It was clear to see where Jack got his humour and relaxed demeanour from. It was the same banter Toby used to enjoy with Jack's father. Having not spoken to Jack in a while, he had missed their light-hearted exchanges.

'What do you need buddy?'

'The heavy winds last week have left one of my fences damaged. I tried to do a temporary fix, but it now needs replacing and I could do with a bit of muscle.'

'So, you phoned me?' Toby said bursting into laughter.'

'No, I couldn't locate the muscle, so I called you instead. I thought you could give me some moral support, you know do your head thing to give me a

Breaking boundaries

positive mindset, some motivation,' Jack replied mockingly.

'So many things wrong with that sentence, I wouldn't even know where to begin,' Toby replied.

'So, you'll come?'

'I promised Beth I would go shopping with her today.'

'So....'

'So, I'll be there in half an hour and owe you one for getting me out of it,' Toby said still grinning.

He knew Beth would understand, and she was more than happy tackling the shops on her own. Besides, it meant she could utilise the credit card without him questioning her purchases. Toby felt he was just financially cautious, whereas Beth felt he worried too much about money. Just as he hung up, Beth entered the room, hands cupped around her ears as she put in her earrings. She was dressed casually in just a pair of jeans and a jumper, but Toby thought she looked radiant.

'You look beautiful.'

'Why Mr Reynolds, what are you after?'

Toby breathed in through his teeth, partly in jest, and partly because he didn't like breaking plans with her.

'Jack called. He needs some help on the farm. There's a fence that needs replacing. He needs some muscle.'

Toby said the last part with a grin.

Breaking boundaries

'I'm assuming he couldn't find it, so he called you instead?', she said smiling. Toby tried to maintain a straight face to feign hurt, but couldn't manage it.

'Jack said the same thing, you'll give me a complex.'

'It's absolutely fine darling. Go help Jack. I will be just fine on my own. I'll take my best friend instead.'

'Lara?'

'Your credit card.'

At this, she grabbed him and gave him a long kiss on the lips, with exaggerated, accompanying sound effects, before briskly heading out of the room. Toby stared at the door for a moment and considered just how much he loved her, how fortunate he was to have her in his life. She was funny, non-judgmental, and extremely caring. She had a beauty that went way beyond her physical appearance. Beth was a beautiful person, with a kind spirit.

Toby looked down at the speedometer and hit the brakes. It was easy to speed in this car, and whilst he enjoyed the power it had to offer, he was also mindful he was in a very rural area, which inevitably meant narrow roads with sharp corners. Just as he slowed down, he was alerted to the low fuel level, via a loud tone and accompanying message on his console asking him if he would like to be directed to the nearest fuel station. He was confident he had enough fuel for the journey but didn't like running on empty. He looked at the options with a slight frustration at the inevitability of having to take a

Breaking boundaries

significant detour. Naturally, he selected the closest, which happened to be a supermarket some ten miles in the opposite direction to where he was heading. He reasoned with himself that he could take a little time and grab a bite to eat at the café. He had rushed out without breakfast, and his stomach was now reminding him of this very fact. He called Jack, who had teased that it would be Toby who would need refuelling by the end of the day. He would be a little later than anticipated, but the days were longer and he didn't need to rush home. Pulling into the car park, Toby sighed at the volume of cars already taking up spaces. Opting to park out of the way, for a quicker and easier retreat, he switched off the engine and headed for the entrance, but not before double-clicking the lock button on the key fob to activate the alarm. As he took a seat in the less busy café, he was faced with an important decision. Did he opt for a lighter breakfast involving a Danish and a coffee, or knowing he was going to be expending energy for the next few hours, did he fuel up on a cooked breakfast? Toby didn't really do hot breakfasts, and when abroad usually elected to go for a more continental start to the day. But he was mindful it was going to be a long day and wasn't sure when he would get the opportunity to eat again. In the end, he reached a compromise with himself, after much debating, and ordered scrambled eggs on wholemeal bread. High protein, high fibre and more filling than a Danish he thought. He took his seat at

Breaking boundaries

a table near the window and gazed at passers-by. He enjoyed people watching, and though he knew he shouldn't, also profiling. Perhaps it was to do with his profession, perhaps it was just simply his character, but Toby would occasionally find himself making assumptions about the lives of strangers, their character, likes and dislikes, relationship status. Beth found it intriguing and sometimes they would have fun with it. A somewhat dull Christmas party they had attended the previous year, had been injected with much-needed laughter by profiling some of the guests on the dancefloor. It wasn't judgment for Toby, it was about keeping his mind sharp and studying behaviour. His practice was as much about deciphering non-verbal cues and omissions, as it was about listening to what was being verbalised. His concentration was suddenly broken by a young boy screaming for his mother. He had entered the café area extremely distressed and in a panic.

There was only a very slight coherence between the sobs. Toby immediately recognised the child was having a panic attack and could only imagine what it must feel like to be alone at this age, unable to find a parent in a place filled with strangers. The young boy was frantic, now screaming. A small crowd had gathered, which Toby knew would only amplify the panic of the child. He knelt to the child's level and gently placed his hands on his shoulders, so he was looking him directly in the eyes.

Breaking boundaries

'Hi, my name is Toby, can you tell me your name?'

'My mummy,' he cried, still inconsolable.

'Have you lost your mummy? It's ok, we will find her together, I promise.'

Usually, he avoided making promises, simply because he knew that in life there were no guarantees. Bad things happened, and sometimes even with the best endeavour, there was little you could do to control them. This was different though. Right now, he was faced with a young child overcome with panic and his only priority was to reassure him to help that panic subside. If that meant making a promise, then so be it. Besides, it would be relatively straightforward to reunite a child with their mother in a supermarket, he thought. He would simply look for the frantic mother. He offered a comforting smile to the boy, staying at his level in the process.

'Where did you last see your mummy?'

'She was getting milk and fell'

'She fell?'

'She yelled loudly and fell over. Then she was quiet, and then I ran because I was frightened.'

Toby realised the boy was not lost. He hadn't strayed from his mother's side or even run off in a tantrum. He was afraid. He had seen his mother collapse and was scared, and confused. Toby got back to his feet and began peering around to see whether there was a crowd gathered anywhere. The café had music playing, so it wasn't out of the

Breaking boundaries

question that he wouldn't hear any commotion. He needed to tread carefully here, the situation wasn't as clear as it may seem. If he took the boy to find his mother, he risked creating trauma for him, and that was something which could follow him into adulthood. He imagined the irony of him working with this child in twenty years because of how this situation had affected him. However, he needed to reassure him and ultimately locate his mother. After deliberating for a few moments, Toby decided he would take the boy to one of the staff in the kiosk, whilst he located his mum. There didn't appear to be any panic within the store, so he didn't believe it was serious, but still, he wanted to be sure for the sake of… Toby stopped and realised he still didn't know the boy's name. Toby bent down and smiled at him.

'I'm going to take you to wait with that lady over there in the shop, whilst I go and find your mummy. Is that ok?'

There wasn't a verbal response, just a hesitant nod. This was understandable given the situation, as well as the child's age.

'Are you able to tell me your name?'

'Tyler!'

Toby spun around quickly. The response hadn't come from the boy, but from a woman who had just hurtled past him, almost knocking him over in the process. She looked unsteady on her feet. They ran towards each other and embraced.

Breaking boundaries

'Where have you been? I've been so worried about you. You know never to wander off.'

The boy didn't have time to answer, as his mother pulled him in for another hug. Then she got to her feet and turned towards Toby. Suddenly her face dropped, perhaps in shock, perhaps in relief. Toby couldn't' place the expression, but he could certainly place the face.

'Olivia.'

'Toby, what are you doing here?'

'You know Psychotherapists also eat breakfast and occasionally shop right?'

Toby wondered whether this was the right moment for humour, but he knew this was often his default response when he felt uncomfortable.

'Of all the people he could have run into Toby, I am really glad it was you.'

'He said you'd fallen,' Toby said as more of a question than a statement.

'I felt a little faint and fell over whilst picking up some milk. I believe for a few minutes I was a little confused. It's no big deal, I think I just stood up too quickly.'

'That's a nasty cut on your face.'

'Please Toby, you sound like the manager I have just spent several minutes being lectured by. He wanted to call an ambulance.'

'Would it be a good idea to get yourself checked out?'

'Now you sound like my therapist.'

Breaking boundaries

Toby couldn't help but smile. Whilst he wouldn't describe himself as comfortable, he felt less awkward than he had when he had seen her at the gym previously. He wondered whether this was due to the fact she was injured, as well as it not just being the two of them.

'I'm fine honestly, don't worry.'

Just as she said this, Olivia staggered forward, only remaining on her feet thanks to the counter she had been standing next to.

'You really should get checked out; I'll call you a taxi.'

Olivia looked at Toby like she was about to argue with him, but a sudden tug on her arm from Tyler deterred her.

'I don't want to take a taxi Toby, I'll drive myself.'

'That's not a good idea.'

'It's the only way I'm going to the hospital as I'm not getting in a taxi. A friend of mine was once driven to a secluded spot by a taxi driver and narrowly escaped an attack. I've never taken a cab since, and I don't intend to change that now.'

He understood her trepidation and didn't want to force the issue.

'I'll drive you.'

'I couldn't ask you to do that.'

'You didn't ask, I offered.'

'Are you allowed?'

There was a sweet naivety about Olivia that Toby couldn't help but warm to. It was a valid question, but Toby's oath was always to take evasive action if

Breaking boundaries

a client was at risk. Getting into a car in her current state would put both her and her son at risk. Toby couldn't, without conscience, allow this to happen. And if he didn't see her as a client at this moment, he was taking the same action he would with anybody else. Either way, he reasoned with himself, he was doing the right thing.

The nearest hospital was about twenty minutes away. Toby reached into his pocket and retrieved his phone. He needed to call Jack. He felt bad for letting him down but was sure he would understand under the circumstances. No reception. Frustrated, yet unsurprised, Toby slipped the phone back into his pocket. He would call later, once he had dropped Olivia and Tyler at the hospital. The day was still young, and although he was already late, he thought he might still be able to get to Jack's by lunchtime. Toby hated hospitals. He associated them with death, and he didn't do death particularly well. The rare occasions where he had had to visit a hospital, served as a reminder that his professional traits, did not necessarily transfer into his personal life. He also hated the waiting around, and the bureaucracy. The wait to see the doctor, the wait for a second opinion, the wait for a scan or treatment. Waiting. As he took his seat he looked around. It wasn't busy, but Toby still knew Olivia would be looking at hours rather than minutes. He looked over at Tyler, who was happily busying himself in the small children's area over in the corner. He was

Breaking boundaries

close enough to be monitored, but at a distance whereby he could play independently. Toby watched him for a moment, playing innocently with little regard for his surroundings. He wondered how much of his mother's sadness and despair he picked up on. How much of the dysfunctional home life that Olivia described, was he exposed to? He felt a sudden overwhelming sadness for him. Here was this six-year-old boy who adored his mother, completely oblivious to so much. Would he ever know how unhappy his mother had been in his younger years? Would he ever know the toxicity of the relationship between his parents, the two people he likely adored more than anyone else? Would he ever know some of the pain, emotional and physical, his mother had been subjected to, and his father had propagated? Would he ever know his father was a rapist and that he was the product of a brutal attack? The choice Olivia faced was very simple, yet also enveloped with complexities. Either Tyler lives a lie and maintains that relationship with both of his parents, or he learns the truth, which would almost certainly have a profoundly negative impact on his relationship with his father. Toby couldn't imagine what it must be like to be in that position, and he suddenly felt sympathy for Olivia's dilemma.

'He's my world.'

Olivia had noticed Toby staring at Tyler.

'I can't imagine how frightened he must have been today.'

Breaking boundaries

'It broke my heart to see him like that. Not something you ever want to see as a parent.'

'I can only imagine.'

'Did you ever want children? I'm sorry that's a rather intrusive question,' she said, quickly backtracking.

Toby smiled, knowing that answering the question would inevitably take him down the route of having a personal conversation, something he was keen to avoid. He had brought Olivia to the hospital as someone who dedicated his life to helping others. He could never sit idly by and watch anybody struggle. He had done this as much for Tyler as he had for her, but his deed was now done and he knew he must leave.

'I must go now. Will you be ok?'

'I'll be fine. Thank you, Toby, I really appreciate your kindness.'

Olivia stood up to call Tyler over. Suddenly she stumbled and fell back into her chair. Instinctively, Toby reached out to grab her to soften the fall but only managed to grab a handful of her sleeve, which slipped through his fingers. By this point, Tyler had returned from the play area and was now beginning to panic at the sight of his mother slumped back in her chair with the colour having drained from her face.

'Olivia!'

Toby was worried she may be about to have some sort of seizure and ran towards the reception desk shouting for help. The receptionist ran from

Breaking boundaries

behind the desk and disappeared through a door. Moments later she reappeared with a man in a white coat walking with pace towards the chair Olivia had collapsed in. Toby was amazed at just how composed he looked. He appeared to take it all in his stride and didn't seem at all phased by what was happening in front of him. Toby thought he would probably see significantly worse than this every day, but still, he couldn't help but admire his calmness. Toby reached for Tyler to remove him from the situation. Hell, hadn't he seen enough? Maybe not just today either.

'She'll be okay Tyler, the doctor is going to make her better, don't worry.'

'She's going to die isn't she?'

A concept of death at six years old? Toby felt his heart skip a beat. He was just a child. He shouldn't have any understanding of panic, of trepidation and certainly not of death. He was far too young for any of this.

'She isn't going to die. She is just feeling a little poorly, and that man in the white coat is going to make her better.'

'Promise?'

Toby looked down at Tyler. He was just a kid. A kid who was genuinely frightened of his mother leaving him. As much as Toby fought against making promises he had no control over, Tyler needed reassurance right now. Nothing could make Toby want to compound his panic.

'I promise.'

Breaking boundaries

Tyler smiled. Toby was sure Olivia would be fine, but still, he felt uncomfortable he had been forced into making a promise he had no control over being able to keep. He knew he couldn't leave now. This was beyond professional ethics. These were exceptional circumstances, and for the first time, he didn't feel uncomfortable being in Olivia's presence away from the therapy room. He knew if Beth was here right now, she would be much more likely to commend his kindness than question his boundaries. At this, he suddenly realised he had not spoken to Beth since he had left earlier that morning. He would usually let her know once he had arrived somewhere and wondered whether she would worry he had not done so in this instance. Whilst he and Beth didn't live inside each other's pockets, they had decided at an early stage in their relationship, no matter where they were, they would make every attempt to speak every day, something they had rarely broken. He would call her later to explain. Right now he could make a good case for his priorities lying elsewhere.

'I think your mummy could probably do with a nice drink. How about you and I go and get her something nice for when she wakes up?'

He didn't know what else to do, what else to say. The doctor didn't look unduly concerned, but still, Tyler didn't need to see this, whatever *this* was. As he made his way to the vending machines in the hallway, Toby felt a tap on his shoulder.

'Are you the husband?'

Breaking boundaries

He felt embarrassed but wasn't sure whether this was for himself or Tyler.

'No, I'm...'

He hesitated and then the reality of the situation hit him. What was he? How did he introduce himself? He couldn't say he was her therapist as not only would it breach confidentiality, but it would also quite likely raise questions about what a therapist was doing at the hospital with a client and her son. But he wasn't a relative, and he wasn't a friend, so what was he? Toby paused for a moment, a brief moment in actuality, but it felt like a long time to him.

'She collapsed in the supermarket. I was there, I guess.'

'You guess you were there?'

'Yeah, I mean I was there. Sorry, just a little shaken by all this,' Toby replied, feeling like he was being interrogated.

'Do you happen to know who her next of kin is?'

'I'm afraid I don't, but I am happy to stay with her and her son until she is stable.'

'We really should let her next of kin know she's in hospital. I'm sure somebody somewhere is worried about her.'

'Is it serious?'

'I am not qualified to answer that, I just sit behind a desk.'

Toby detected a hint of sarcasm or even resentment in her voice, but this wasn't the time to address it with her.

Breaking boundaries

'She is going to be transferred into a side room now, where the doctor will be able to give her a more thorough examination. Once she is settled, I will let you know.'

Toby wasn't sure how to respond. He wasn't a spouse, a relative of any sort, or a friend. He wanted Beth, needed her. She was his calming influence, his reassurance, and he needed this right now, but he knew it wasn't viable to call her at this time. He would have to wait. He looked up at the clock. It was just before one. He had been due at Jack's first thing, and now it was highly unlikely he would make it at all. They had been here for a couple of hours now, though it hadn't seemed like it. *The waiting.* Toby was again reminded why he hated hospitals so much.

He purchased himself a coffee and Tyler a soft drink. They had decided against buying a coffee for Olivia, Tyler instead convincing Toby she would prefer a bar of chocolate. Whilst Toby had relented, he had a strong inkling this was more for Tyler than his mother.

Toby and Tyler were escorted through the double doors and guided through a corridor. They were then shown into a room, and greeted by a smiling Olivia who was now sitting up in her bed. Toby noticed she had regained the colour in her cheeks and was now looking significantly better than she had a short while ago.

'How are you feeling?'

Breaking boundaries

'Been better, been worse.'

Toby smiled but didn't maintain eye contact with Olivia. Instead, he found himself nervously looking around the room. This didn't feel right to him. He knew he had been okay up until being mistaken for her husband. Now, everything was telling him he shouldn't be here, but whilst nothing about the situation felt comfortable, something was compelling him to stay, at least for a while, to make sure both Olivia and Tyler were ok. He had convinced himself this was solely about an innocent child caught up in a world of complex family dynamics that no child should ever be subjected to. He worried however, it wasn't just about Tyler, and whether empathy had now become sympathy. Though he knew he couldn't control his feelings, how he responded to such feelings, however, was something he did have control over. Olivia, noticing his awkwardness, spoke softly.

'Thank you for all your kindness, I'll be fine now... we'll be fine.'

She looked over at Tyler, who had curled up on the reclining chair in the corner and fallen asleep. He looked so peaceful, now oblivious to the drama which had surrounded him today. Toby reflected on losing his own mother and recalled how it had felt for him. He had been an adult though, emotionally more mature to handle it. Tyler hadn't lost his mum, but Toby had remembered his words as the doctor approached and knew his fear of being without her had been very real.

Breaking boundaries

'Not a care in the world,' Toby said now focusing back on Olivia, who had just taken a sip of water.

'He is such a sweet little boy. I know all mothers will say this about their child, but he is amazing, my rock. I try my best to protect him you know. I don't want him exposed to some of the things I've had to endure.'

'It must be incredibly difficult.'

'More so than you may think. He picks up on things, I know he does.'

Toby looked at her but was careful not to come across as though he was pitying her.

'I can't imagine how difficult it must be for you.'

'He doesn't know I come to therapy you know.'

Toby looked at her inquisitively.

'Eric. He doesn't know. I'm not sure how he would take it.'

Toby said nothing. Olivia continued, but he wasn't sure he wanted to hear more. He looked over at the clock on the wall. Every moment he was here with Olivia he felt more guilty about Beth not knowing his whereabouts. Least harm, most good, he thought. Olivia and Tyler had needed him more than Jack today. He was being overly self-critical and he knew it, but this was what made Toby the person he was. He cared, sometimes too much, which meant when the inevitable happened, and he couldn't help somebody, he took it personally. Beth had often said Toby's altruism was a gift, yet a curse of equal measure. His thoughts were interrupted by Olivia.

'I lied to you, Toby.'

Breaking boundaries

'I'm sorry?'

'I told you a lie when we first met.'

Toby turned to look at her. Internally, he was screaming at himself, to acknowledge, but not engage, to close the conversation down and leave. He could no longer justify being in this room. Olivia was fine and recovering; Tyler was safe, comfortable and sleeping. He had done his good deed for the day. If he engaged her now, he felt certain she would likely disclose something which he should only hear in a professional setting, or perhaps as a friend. This wasn't a professional setting, and he wasn't a friend.

'It's not unusual for clients to keep things hidden from their therapists. I should be going now,' he said politely.

Olivia looked up at him, but this time there was no smile. She looked deeply troubled. For the moment, she didn't respond. Toby smiled as he turned his head towards the corner of the room, where Tyler was sleeping quite contently.

'He looks incredibly comfortable. It must have been a really difficult day for him. Take care of yourself, Olivia. I'll wait to hear from you once you're feeling better.'

Toby headed towards the door and reached for the handle. As he did so, Olivia shouted after him.

'When we first met, you asked me if I feared Eric, and I told you he would never hurt Tyler. I lied.'

He halted, before slowly loosening his grip on the door handle and turning back to face her. He wasn't

Breaking boundaries

sure how to respond, or whether in fact, he should. He hadn't contravened any professional boundaries, but he was struggling to justify still being in this hospital room. He sympathised with Olivia's situation, but no more or less than he did with any client he worked with who had encountered such challenges in their life. As he stood deliberating what to do next, Olivia continued, but in a quieter and more controlled tone now. She had his attention.

'Last year on Christmas Eve, we hosted a family gathering. Naturally, Tyler was excited, not just because it was Christmas time, but because he loves spending time with family. As always with these types of events, Eric saw this as an excuse to have a few drinks.'

Toby was quiet, focused, and comforted by the fact there were no expectations on his shoulders. He would simply do Olivia the courtesy of listening, before finding a reason to excuse himself. Olivia continued.

'By the time everybody had left, Eric was drunk. Tyler was still excitable, running around with one of his cars. I guess he wasn't looking where he was going as the next thing I knew, Eric's freshly opened can was all over the floor. He completely lost it, and as much as I tried to calm the situation, there was no reasoning with him. He lurched for Tyler and hit him with force around his head. Tyler was inconsolable, I felt powerless. When he fell asleep, I called the police, but when they asked me for my

Breaking boundaries

address, I panicked and put the phone down. I was worried about what may happen to us if we angered Eric any further. I should have reported it. I should have let them come and take the bastard away. I didn't protect my son.'

'It must have been an incredibly difficult decision to have to make,' Toby responded.

'Maybe part of it was self-preservation. Maybe I didn't want him to turn his attention to me. Maybe I convinced myself he would feel so guilty about what he did to Tyler, that he would never do it to me.'

Toby remained quiet. He knew that when it came to abusers, guilt was a complex subject. Abuse was often about power and control, but also about justification. To protect themselves from shame, abusers would commonly justify their actions, which would ordinarily place the blame on others. He had told Richard that there didn't appear to be any escalation in Eric's behaviour but now felt reasonably sure this was not the case. At that moment, Toby wondered how much more there was, how much she had either suppressed or chosen not to actively speak about. He could see she genuinely believed, hoped, that the abuse would simply just stop, and though he knew this was unlikely, he had no interest in shattering that hope. She looked up at him and smiled.

'Naïve right?'

'Whatever decision you made, I'm sure you did it for the right reasons. It's not about judging the outcome.'

Breaking boundaries

'What do you mean by that?'

'We don't have the foresight to determine an outcome, we simply base our decisions around what we know, what we think, or what we feel at the time.'

'But I made the wrong decision.'

'You're judging yourself on the outcome. Think about what was happening at the time, the reasoning behind your decision.'

'I hoped it would keep Tyler safe.'

'So you decided not to involve the police due to a concern about the impact it may have on the welfare of your son?'

'I guess so.'

'So it's the intention you need to focus on, not the outcome.'

Olivia raised a faint smile at Toby, before moving her eyes over to Tyler, still peacefully asleep in the corner.

'You're very wise.'

'I learned things the same way as everybody else.'

'Ah so you're human after all', Olivia teased.

'I have to go now, but I am glad you're feeling a little better than when you first arrived. Do you have somebody to help with Tyler?'

'I have a friend who will come and collect him if they keep me in. Hopefully, that won't be the case and I'll be able to get home later today.'

Toby wondered what Olivia would go home to. If Eric's behaviour had indeed escalated, he would

Breaking boundaries

likely display little sympathy for her traumatic experience or her health. He couldn't help but wonder what the future would hold for her and Tyler, and felt a degree of sadness as he looked at the young boy asleep in the chair, safe and comfortable...for now.

As he headed out of the hospital doors and towards his car, Toby thought about his time as a therapist. In all his years of practising, he had rarely encountered a client outside of his practice, and on the sporadic occasions this had happened, it was a courteous acknowledgement. Here he was now, having seen Olivia twice in a few months, beginning with a chance encounter at the gym, and culminating in him driving her to the hospital. He paused for a moment and took in the surroundings. There was a slight breeze, which blew the tree branches rhythmically. It was the tranquillity Toby noticed most. It felt so peaceful, so calm. He thought about how that contrasted with Olivia's life for a moment. As much as he told himself he was a professional, and wasn't there to fix people, he was also human and displayed a great deal of empathy. He took one final look around, drew a deep breath and then slowly got into his car. He plugged his phone in to charge and sat there wide-eyed as the notifications began to filter through. He had several missed calls from Beth, and Jack, too. He felt somehow that this part of the day had been relatively straightforward when compared with how

Breaking boundaries

he was going to explain its events. As he drove out of the car park, he looked up at the window of Olivia's room and wondered how bad things really were for her. Yet he also questioned why she was so disjointed in her disclosure. Then suddenly, he braked and ground to a halt as a thought struck him. Each of the times he had encountered her away from the practice, there had been a common occurrence. Whenever he had made a move to leave or end the conversation, she had done or said something to stop him in his tracks and keep him engaged. Why was this? Had she formed an unhealthy attachment to him? Was she simply lonely, and he was the one person who listened to her? Did she see him as her rescuer? After a brief pause, he shifted the car into gear and drove off slowly, still deep in thought. That thought hadn't disappeared minutes later when he was finally able to call Beth.

Breaking boundaries

10

'What's going on with you?' Beth's tone was a calm one, which wasn't in keeping with her movement, as she paced hastily around the kitchen, oscillating between the kettle and the toaster, which had seemingly completed their tasks at precisely the same time.

'A few weeks ago, you didn't turn up to Jack's, instead accompanying a client to the hospital where you spent a large part of the day. You barely spoke to me about that. Now you're telling me you need to take some time out on your own. This just isn't like you. What aren't you telling me, Toby?' Beth asked.

Whilst she appeared calm on the outside, he felt sure on the inside things were very different. At this moment he hated what he was doing. He and Beth had always enjoyed a very communicative relationship. They had no secrets, and had been open and honest with each other throughout their marriage. He had spoken to her briefly about Olivia, but of course, was limited as to what he could and could not say. He knew he wasn't able to tell her the whole truth, hell did he even know the whole truth himself? All he could do was try to reassure her and ask her to trust him.

'The nature of my work means sometimes things can just get too much.'

'You have Richard.'

'Not on speed dial I don't'.

Breaking boundaries

Whilst he had intended to highlight Richard was his supervisor, not his friend, he was conscious this may have sounded a little flippant. He looked up tentatively, as if bracing himself, and noticed Beth had now ceased what she was doing and was looking directly back at him. Her head was tilted, her eyebrows raised.

'That's not what I meant Toby.'

'I'm sorry, I didn't mean it like that.'

'How exactly did you mean it?' she snapped.

'I can't confide in Richard every time I have a bad day. It's a professional arrangement, not a personal one.'

'Isn't this a professional issue?'

He paused for a moment, unsure how to respond.

'Perhaps. I don't know.'

'What do you know Toby?'

Beth's tone was now sounding harsher and that calmness evident moments earlier had now disappeared. She was frustrated.

'I don't want to leave the house on an argument,' he said offering an olive branch.

'I'm not sure why you're leaving the house at all.'

'That's not fair.'

Now it was Toby's turn to feel the frustration. He felt attacked, interrogated, and wasn't fond of the feeling. Regardless, he remained adamant he wasn't leaving Beth for the weekend with any animosity between them. He held out his arms and gestured for Beth to embrace him for a hug. This was his way of calling a truce; it was their way. She

Breaking boundaries

took a step towards him, opened her arms and rested her head on his shoulders. The feeling of Beth close to him had always been enough to soothe Toby no matter what he was thinking or feeling. It had never failed in the past, and it didn't fail now. As he squeezed her tightly, he smelled her hair and felt the frustration dissipate. He was desperate to open up to Beth, but until he could understand his own feelings, he felt sure he would be unable to convey them to anybody else. He knew something wasn't right and hoped the weekend would give him the physical and emotional space to better understand what that was. As he exited the house, Toby felt a splash of rain fall onto his head, prompting him to look up to the sky. It was bleak and overcast. The wind was picking up, and Toby felt certain a storm was imminent.

'Please be safe,' Beth shouted, as Toby loaded the car.

'I'll call you when I get there.'

He sounded his horn and Beth's look of anguish was the last thing he saw before driving away.

The small country pub Toby had opted to stay at was around an hour's drive for him. He had carefully selected somewhere far enough away to provide a complete change of scenery, yet close enough so he could return quickly in an emergency. It was out in the country and would offer the tranquillity Toby felt he needed. There were only a handful of rooms and the geographical isolation boasted beautiful

Breaking boundaries

countryside to explore, which would allow Toby to acquaint himself with nature. He knew any phone signal would be at a premium, and this was an added benefit to him rather than a hindrance. He didn't want to be contactable. Beth had the address and number of where he was staying, and that was all he needed. As he drove, he thought about Beth, the argument still fresh in his mind. The look on her face as he had driven away, had left him feeling subdued. They rarely exchanged cross words, which meant when they did, it would usually affect them both significantly. He felt bad but wasn't sure whether this was for the argument, or for deciding to take time out on his own at short notice, and expecting Beth to be okay with it. He rarely did anything for himself, and believed this was out of necessity rather than desire. Still, he had been feeling the cramps in his stomach since he started the engine, and they were showing no signs of easing. The rain was getting heavier, visibility was getting worse and the winds were picking up. The storm had well and truly set in, and Toby found his wipers even at full speed, were no match for the torrential rain bouncing off his windscreen. He slowed down and considered pulling over to see if the weather would improve, but knew this would have been in hope rather than expectation. As he looked down at his sat-nav, he sighed at the realisation he was still over half an hour from his destination. He slowed down further. The dual carriageway was almost empty, even though it was

Breaking boundaries

only eleven in the morning. He grinned to himself as he questioned what sort of idiot would risk driving any sort of distance in this weather. The grin quickly turned to a frown as he realised his plans to go for a walk before checking in at two o'clock, were now dashed, meaning he would now likely have to sit in the bar for an extended lunch on his own, whilst he waited for his room to be prepared. His mind wandered. Suddenly he was thinking about Olivia. He hadn't seen her for an appointment since the hospital incident, and she had no further appointments scheduled at this time. He thought about her plight, about Tyler, an innocent child caught in a difficult environment through no fault of his own. He had been led to believe by Olivia that Tyler had been safe, but her confession from her hospital bed had now raised questions about this. He'd wrestled with his conscience but ultimately didn't feel there was enough to betray Olivia's confidence and disclose to the authorities. He'd had an indirect experience with social services with more than one client previously, and knew once that process began, there was no turning back, and the impact could be devastating. He'd seen it tear families apart, children ripped away from one, or even both parents. He knew the hurt this could cause and had resolved, only if he was certain a child was in continuous danger, would he ever explore this avenue. Whilst Eric had lost his temper and struck Tyler in the heat of the moment, Olivia had not stated this behaviour had ever been

Breaking boundaries

repeated. Although he didn't believe Tyler was in imminent danger, he couldn't say the same for Olivia. He had witnessed bruising and of course, the burn on her arm, but had told Richard he didn't believe there were any signs of escalation. Did he really believe this? What was his remit as a therapist? He was limited and knew his job wasn't to try and fix his clients. He wasn't supposed to become emotionally invested in their situation. He provided a service, not a friendship. Still...

Suddenly an unwanted image entered his head. He tried to shake it, but it only became more imposing, like he was being forced to watch a movie scene he was desperately trying to turn away from. He imagined Olivia being raped by her husband. He thought about the brutality involved. He'd never met Eric but could picture his face, and smell the alcohol on his breath as he took what he wanted. He saw Olivia's face, her body finally going limp as she submitted after putting up such a brave fight. He saw Eric simply walk away, grinning, pleased with himself after exerting control over her. He saw Olivia, dazed, defiled. Then he was present again. What was happening to him? Where had these images come from? He had taken time out to remove himself from anything that resembled Olivia Stanton, yet here she was, in her own way, following him, present. He was losing control. Toby Reynolds, a composed, laid-back individual was losing control. He smiled at the thought of the words

Breaking boundaries

laid-back forming part of his epitaph before being drawn back to the road. Visibility was low, and the momentary lapse in concentration by Toby had been just enough to see his car drift to the left towards the embankment. He quickly jerked the steering wheel to the right, but it was too late and as he found himself with no control over the speed or direction of his car, he thought of Beth's parents and wondered whether he would meet the same fate. As the car rolled to a stop, everything was quiet, and Toby's eyes closed. He came around to the sound of sirens which seemed to be getting closer and was able to make out the flashing blue lights approaching in the background. He tried to move.

'Stay still buddy, help is on the way.'

A strange voice attached to a strange face. Where was he? What was happening to him? It felt surreal, almost like he was watching through somebody else's eyes. Panic set in and he started to thrash around.

'Hey, hey, try and keep still, you don't want to cause any more damage,' said the voice again.

More damage? What did he mean? Why was he talking about damage? This did nothing to quell Toby's panic and he began to wonder what he had woken up to. It certainly felt like a nightmare, except now he couldn't simply wake Beth to make it better. Beth! He tried to speak, but only managed a few syllables.

'My wi....'.

Breaking boundaries

Then darkness, a silence. A tranquillity that felt soothing, and peaceful.

'Joe, we need to stabilise him, and quickly.'

Toby's eyes rolled open momentarily. The flashing blue lights were now just yards away. One of the men was leaning over him.

'Can you tell me your name?'

Toby heard the words but didn't feel capable of answering. The man spoke again.

'You've been in an accident. We're going to get you out of here as quickly as possible and get you to the hospital.'

Out of where? thought Toby. He was conscious enough to realise he was still sitting in his car, seatbelt fastened but had no concept of where he was or indeed why several people were surrounding him, seemingly working with a certain urgency.

'Joe, are the fire brigade on their way? I think we're going to need to cut him out of here.'

Who's Joe? he thought. Why is he here?

'They're on their way Rob, but in the meantime, we need to keep him conscious and try and assess what we are dealing with here.' Toby heard the words, but they made no sense to him. Everything seemed a blur. He felt tired, so very tired. All he wanted to do was to close his eyes.

'Stay with me.' A tap on the face, and a stroke on the head from this stranger. Who was he?

'Toby'. The word was slurred, but just about comprehendible.

Breaking boundaries

'Toby, is that your name? My name is Rob and this is my colleague, Joe. We're paramedics. You've been in an accident. We're waiting for the fire brigade to arrive to help us get you out of here, so I just need you to keep still. Is there anybody we can call for you?'

Toby just about understood the question but lay silent for a moment. He was still trying to piece together what had happened, when the man dressed in green, who went by Rob, spoke again.

'Toby, is there somebody we can call?'

'My wife.'

The words were uttered slowly, but enough for the paramedic to understand.

'Toby, what's the name of your wife?'

No response.

'Toby, stay with me.'

Then silence. The sirens had stopped, so peaceful. All the voices had disappeared now, it was just Toby. Serenity. His eyes closed, and that was the last time he would be conscious at the scene. When his eyes next opened, the first image he saw was the shape of a woman. He squinted to try and make out the figure and became impatient waiting for his eyes to adapt to the daylight. At first, there were no sounds, then slowly he could make out voices, but not close to him. No, they were at a distance and they moved around. He tried to move but felt a sharp pain which seemed to span from his chest to his abdomen. He looked down and noticed his right hand was heavily bandaged. He attempted

Breaking boundaries

to raise it to take a closer look, but there was little movement and he decided not to force the issue. His head was sore, but it didn't feel like it was pain from a wound, more like a severe headache. As his eyes began to accustom themselves to the light, he was able to make out the image, who he now realised was asleep in the chair at the side of his bed.

'Beth!'

He felt bad for shouting so loudly, inevitably a move which would wake her. In reality, his voice had been little more than a whisper, and Beth had not even stirred.

He stared at her for a moment. She looked so peaceful, with her natural beauty flowing. Whether she was dressed for an occasion, or simply a day in the garden, Toby felt Beth carried herself so well. It was her caring nature which he admired most, however, and whilst he hadn't told her as much recently, he felt incredibly lucky to have her as his wife. She had always created stability for Toby, her unconditional love and unwavering support, a source of strength for him. The thought of ever hurting her induced a guilt and sense of sadness he had never experienced before. Yet he knew in the last few months, he had not been as open with her as he should have been. However, there would be time to make amends, and Beth didn't hold grudges. Something else he admired about her. He tried to sit up but again was prevented from doing so by a sharp pain in his ribcage. As he turned his head to

Breaking boundaries

the side, he noticed a glass of water on the table next to his bed and reached for it to soothe his dry mouth. As he did so, he quickly realised he had no grip in his left hand, and the glass was sent tumbling to the floor. Beth awoke with a jolt and let out a brief scream before she was able to gather her thoughts and realise what was happening.

'Toby, you're awake,' she exclaimed.

'Beth.'

His voice was still a whisper, likely due to the sore throat he had from his mouth being so dry. He wondered if he was dehydrated. A nurse had heard the commotion and had entered his hospital room. She asked him how he was feeling before proceeding to clear up the smashed glass and spilt water. Toby was apologetic, but the nurse dismissed the accident. She was kind and reassuring, and he appreciated this. He wondered how many patients she would see in a day and how she was able to maintain that calm persona, in what must be an extremely difficult environment. She checked his blood pressure and told him a doctor would be along shortly to look in on him and answer any questions he may have. She asked if there was anything Toby needed before exiting the room with the same calmness with which she had entered it moments earlier. He turned to Beth.

'Hey.'

His voice was faint and raspy, and speaking seemed an effort. Beth had now moved her chair next to his bed, where moments earlier there had

Breaking boundaries

been broken glass and a pool of water. She looked at him with a sympathetic smile and took hold of his hand gently.

'How are you feeling?'

'I've been better.'

She said nothing, simply squeezing his hand and moving closer to rest her head on his shoulder. Toby could feel her warm breath on his skin, and it felt comforting. As he looked down at her, he could see her body shaking and suddenly realised his shoulder was wet. He wanted to comfort her but didn't have enough movement to raise his arm. His voice was still hoarse, and he felt helpless. He had dedicated his life so far to helping and comforting strangers, and now the person who meant the most to him was laid here, vulnerable, and he felt powerless. Beth looked up at him and wiped her eyes.

'Sorry, I know this isn't what you need.'

'It's okay,' he replied softly.

'Toby, do you remember anything about the accident?'

He shook his head slowly as if straining to remember.

'You were in a car crash. You left the road and veered down an embankment. They had to cut you out.'

Toby took a deep breath, trying to take in what Beth was saying, whilst also trying to keep in the emotion. He closed his eyes tightly.

Breaking boundaries

'I remember it was raining, conditions were bad,' he said opening them again.

'I should never have let you go.'

'This isn't your fault.'

'Toby, this brought everything back for me. I relived that night I lost my parents, and kept thinking what if I lost you too?'

'I understand.'

'No, you don't.' Beth had raised her voice, let go of his hand and had moved back, staring intently at him.

'You don't get it, Toby. Everything that happened that night, I have relived over and over. On the surface, I am this happy and carefree individual, but underneath I'm in turmoil most days. Do you know the times when I feel ok about things when I forget for a while when I am smiling Toby, and smiling genuinely rather than wearing a mask?'

Toby was looking straight into her eyes, he could see the pain behind them. He didn't speak. Beth didn't open up much, he knew this was important to her, and though he couldn't say anything right now to make things better, he could listen. She continued.

'The pain of losing my parents, the fear of losing people, of being abandoned. That all ends when I'm with you.'

'Beth...'

She raised her hand, gesturing for him to allow her to finish.

Breaking boundaries

'Toby, I love that you do what you do, your altruism and dedication to your clients are so admirable. But I know it consumes you, and as much as your clients need their therapist, I wonder if sometimes you realise that I need my husband. When I got the phone call from the police, I was taken back to the hospital room where I was told my parents had died. I thought I'd lost you. I was so afraid of what was facing me. I can't do this without you Toby.'

She paused and Toby looked up at her.

'Do what Beth?'

'This, life, everything. I need you. I need you more than your clients do, but you just don't seem to see it.'

'Beth I'm always here…'

She interrupted him, her voice getting louder, her face displaying a look of exasperation.

'Your mind has been elsewhere Toby, and that's what I need the most,' she finished.

'I'm sorry, I hadn't realised. Why didn't you say anything?'

'I would never put you in a position of potentially having to choose between your work and your wife.'

'I'd choose you in an instant.'

Beth looked at him and smiled. She moved closer to him and gently kissed his forehead.

'I know I have to take some time to figure out how I can better balance my work and home life,' Toby continued as she drew back from the kiss.

Breaking boundaries

'Well, you're going to be taking some time out now that's for sure.'

Toby looked at her puzzled.

'Three broken ribs, a broken hand and internal bleeding, which required surgery.'

'That would explain the chest pains and the reason why that poor glass met its demise.'

Beth laughed and quickly held her hand to her mouth as if feeling a sudden attack of guilt for doing so. She was only too aware Toby was lying there badly injured, having just been through an incredibly traumatic experience, and was mindful not to risk trivialising this in any way.

'In the grand scheme of things, it could have been a lot worse Toby. They had to cut you out of the car and said you were drifting in and out of consciousness. Thankfully, a driver in another car stopped and called the emergency services. He stayed with you until the ambulance and fire service arrived. He may well have saved your life.'

'I don't remember anything.'

Toby's voice began to crack as he realised the severity of what he had been through. He wasn't concerned about the physical impact on himself, his wounds would heal over time. He was more worried about the psychological effect this had had on Beth. He gestured for her to walk around to the opposite side of the bed, where he slowly moved his one good hand and held hers tightly, as she placed her head on his shoulder. They remained like this for several minutes, saying nothing, until Toby spoke.

Breaking boundaries

'I would like to find the person who was responsible for saving my life.'

'I don't know if he gave his details at the scene, but I can find out.'

'Maybe you could ask Mike?'

Mike was a mutual friend, whom they had met a few years ago when he and his wife had attended the funeral of an old school friend of Beth's. They had got talking at the wake and found they had much in common. It had been a particularly emotional funeral for various reasons, but Mike had provided much-needed laughter, later at the gathering, and they had all been friends ever since. Mike was a little older than Toby at fifty-one, but he was athletically built and incredibly intelligent. He also happened to be a Detective Inspector in the police, having been on the force for twenty years. He had knowledge, and he had contacts. If anybody could trace this individual, it would be Mike.

'I'll call him tomorrow. I would say he would want to know about your accident, but I am almost sure knowing Mike, he would already be aware.'

'He probably knew before I'd even crashed,' Toby said with a smile.

They looked at each other and giggled for a moment, before Toby grimaced with pain, holding his ribs. The laughter quickly vanished, and a more solemn look appeared on Beth's face. She composed herself and took a deep breath.

'Are you ready to tell me what's going on?'

Breaking boundaries

Toby knew he could no longer trivialise or dismiss what was happening to him.

'Something's changed in me recently, professionally, and I'm frightened.'

'Does this have anything to do with that client?'

Toby stared at her intently, paused for a moment, and then looked away without saying anything. He had answered her question without saying a word.

'Have you spoken to Richard about this?'

'Yes.'

'And?'

'And what?'

'For God's sake Toby, I'm your wife, not your parent.'

'I'm sorry.'

'For what? For being emotionally absent the last few months? For not being open with me about how you're feeling? For taking off and leaving me, nearly dying as a result? For devoting your time to a client and still not understanding the impact this is having on you, on us? What exactly are you fucking sorry about?'

Toby looked at her startled. He had never seen Beth this angry before and struggled to recall a time when she had used expletives in the aggressive manner in which she was doing now. He hadn't lied to her, but he hadn't been honest with her either. He knew he could have spoken to her without breaching client confidentiality. He had just chosen not to, and at this moment, he had no idea why, but he regretted it.

Breaking boundaries

'I've been struggling. I haven't wanted to admit it to myself, and by telling somebody else, I make it real. I don't want this to be real Beth.'

'Don't want what to be real?'

'All of it. The anxiety, the worry, the fear, everything.'

'I don't understand,'

'I've never been affected by a client, like this one. I can't explain what it is, but something doesn't sit right and I'm afraid.'

'What are you afraid of Toby?'

'That's the thing. I don't know. All I know is that there is this deep-seated fear that something is going to happen. It's not rational, but still, I can't shake it.'

Beth grabbed his hand tight and squeezed. Toby was now visibly upset, the sight of which was enough for her not to ask any further questions, regardless of the fact she perhaps had more now than when they had begun the conversation. After a while, once the sobbing had subsided, Toby pulled Beth to him and whispered in her ear.

'I think I know what I need to do.'

Beth hugged him for a moment as his head relaxed back against the pillow. She didn't reply, just kept her head tucked in tight next to his. By the time she pulled away, Toby's eyes had closed and there was a faint rasping sound coming from his mouth. It had been a long day for him, and after just a few hours awake, his body needed to rest, to recuperate. Perhaps more so, his mind also needed

Breaking boundaries

to mend. He may have been broken physically, but his conversation with Beth highlighted he was also broken emotionally right now. She got up from the bed and moved back to the reclining chair in the corner of the room, taking care to first draw the curtains before she settled. The only way she would leave the hospital was with Toby. She lay there for a while deep in thought, staring at her husband, wondering how he would recover, and not just physically. This had been extremely traumatic for her, dragging up suppressed memories of the fateful night she was orphaned as a young girl. Her eyes started to close. It wasn't late, but it had been an emotionally charged twenty-four hours, and she had slept very little in that time. She stood up to grab a jumper which was folded in her bag, as the temperature had now dropped. Settling back into her chair, and adjusting her pillow, she pulled the throw over her for added warmth. As she did this, she took one last glance at Toby, now peacefully in a deep slumber, and whispered in his direction.

'I hope for your sake you do.'

Then the room fell almost silent, with only the faint sounds of sleep emanating from its two occupants.

Breaking boundaries

11

Toby sat in his practice, quietly reflecting. It had been two months since his accident, and whilst his physical scars had healed nicely, emotionally he was struggling to process what had happened. He hadn't seen a client since his release from the hospital, and had no idea when, or even if, he would be ready to do so again. The ordeal had terrified him, what he remembered of it anyway, but his state of mind which had led up to it frightened him more. Toby had always been content with his levels of self-awareness, yet recently, had begun to question just how well he knew himself. Beth had been supportive, she always was, but he knew he had hurt her, and he owed it to them both to figure out what was happening to him. He had spoken with Richard, who of course had been concerned about *him*, but who had also expressed concern for Olivia, questioning the therapeutic relationship. After a long conversation, they had both agreed that the best course of action would be for Toby to try and draw Olivia's therapy to a conclusion. As his absence from Psychotherapy was currently indefinite, he saw this as the ideal opportunity to propose that Olivia consider continuing her work with somebody else. When Toby made this decision, the relief he felt was something he had never experienced before. It was only then that he realised just how emotionally draining working with Olivia had been. He smiled to himself as he took another sip of his coffee.

Breaking boundaries

Although he wasn't practising, he had been driving out to the practice occasionally to see if he could find the passion he had had only months before. So far, this had been in vain, and though he felt quiet reflection in his chair was cathartic, any thought of having somebody sat opposite him filled him with dread. It was this that he was struggling to understand. Even ahead of his very first client session, he hadn't experienced this level of anxiety. Toby was never one for taking time off, but this had been welcome, and Beth had recognised the notable uplift in his mood since he took that decision. In those moments of complete honesty, he was able to admit to himself that he was unsure if he would ever take to the therapist's chair again. He stared at the empty chair opposite and thought about all the clients he had worked with over the years, but still, could only see an empty chair. By now he wasn't sure what to feel. He felt nothing being here, but there was a trace of sadness that a career he had once loved so much, he felt nothing but ambivalence towards in this moment. His concentration was broken by his phone vibrating vigorously. It would no doubt be Beth checking in on him. As he went to pick up the phone, he noticed the number was withheld. Pausing for a moment, he wondered whether or not to answer it. Realising it may be important and could be something pertaining to the accident, he pulled the phone to his ear as he pressed to answer.

'Toby Reynolds.'

Breaking boundaries

At first nothing, but a faint breathing down the line. Toby spoke again.

'Hello, can you hear me?'

No response, but the breathing was getting heavier, more frantic. He pulled the phone away from his ear and went to hang up.

'Toby, it's Olivia,' came the whisper from the other end. He froze. He had known he would need to have a conversation with her at some point but hadn't felt ready to do it just yet. As with all of his clients, he had told her he was taking some time out after the accident. She had wished him a speedy recovery and respected his privacy, which he had appreciated, but still, this had come too soon for him. Some of his other clients had moved on to other therapists to continue their work, and others had opted to wait for Toby to recover, but Olivia was the one client he had yet to have that detailed conversation with.

'Toby, are you there?'

'Yes.'

'I need to see you.'

'Olivia, I'm not seeing clients right now.'

'I know that, but this is urgent, you're the only one I can trust.'

'I'm sorry, I have no idea when I am going to be back, if at all....'

She interrupted him.

'What do you mean if at all?'

She said this sharply but sounded panicked.

Breaking boundaries

'I mean right now I don't know what my future is going to look like.'

'You can't leave me.'

Toby looked up, startled. Olivia's words reverberated through his mind. This was everything he had feared. She had become attached, reliant on him. He was in trouble.

'The steps you have taken, the things you have achieved, that's been about you, not me. I'm just like any other therapist.'

'You're not like any other therapist, Toby,' she snapped.

'I have a friend whom I can recommend....'

A knock at the door broke Toby's concentration. It was getting dark out, and the rain had now set in. He rose out of his chair and walked towards the door hesitantly. As he opened it, he saw a bedraggled figure, shivering, in a thin raincoat, hood pulled up to hide the face. As the hood was slowly pulled down, Toby noticed it was a short-haired woman whom he didn't recognise. Then as she slowly turned around to face him, she became instantly recognisable. For a moment they simply stood and stared at each other, and it was difficult to understand which of them looked most uncomfortable.

'I didn't know who else to turn to, I'm sorry.'

'How did you know I would be here?'

'I took a chance, I guess.'

'Olivia, I'm not seeing clients right now, and this isn't a scheduled appointment. I'm sorry.'

Breaking boundaries

'Please can I come in, just for a moment?'

Toby desperately wanted to say no, to exercise some assertion, something which Beth always felt he lacked. He wanted to close the door, not just on Olivia, but on therapy in general. He'd always worked with passion and endeavour, but right now, both of these eluded him. Things had changed since the accident. He had changed. He was, however, still somebody who genuinely cared, a people person, and the weather outside was dreadful. He couldn't without conscience turn somebody away in such appalling conditions. He moved to the side and gestured for Olivia to come in. Handing her a towel to dry herself, Toby turned up the fire before taking a seat. For a moment no words were exchanged, but Toby was mindful he didn't want to make this more awkward than it already was. He smiled.

'You cut your hair.'

'Do you like it?'

'It's more important that you like it,' he replied.

'Always the therapist.'

Toby wasn't sure how to take this. He didn't feel like a therapist and hadn't done for a few weeks now, and this made him nervous, because this, whatever this was, then became personal rather than professional. He sat silently, contemplating the situation.

'I have always felt so comfortable speaking to you. You've helped me so much. You've shown me it's ok to feel vulnerable. I no longer blame myself for what has happened to me.'

Breaking boundaries

'I'm pleased you have found therapy so useful, but you didn't come to tell me this.'

Olivia regarded him with a look which he thought imitated a child being caught out lying. He was aware he may have sounded harsh, but whilst he was uncomfortable simply turning her away into the stormy night, he was more uncomfortable engaging with her over any prolonged period. The gym, a coincidence; the supermarket, unfortunate. But this, this was planned. Toby pondered.

'You're right, I didn't come here to tell you that.'

'Why did you come here?'

'I was afraid... am afraid,' she replied correcting herself.

'What are you afraid of?'

'I'm not ready to let therapy go just yet. I'm feeling stronger, finding myself, but this has been my crutch whilst I'm learning to walk again if you know what I mean?'

'Olivia...'

She interrupted him.

'Toby I can't do this without you.'

Those words. He had heard those same words from Beth in his hospital bed. Olivia was now visibly emotional. Toby handed her the tissue box and she thanked him before dabbing her eyes. Her mascara was now smudged across her face. It seemed what the weather had started, her tears had finished. The fire was crackling, and the flickering of the flames was hypnotic. Toby thought about how therapeutic it

Breaking boundaries

felt. He wondered whether it was as comforting for his clients as it was for him.

'I'm sorry.'

'You don't have to apologise for getting upset,' Toby said as he turned to reach for his drink.

'I'm not.'

Toby wore a perplexed look as he turned his head back to face Olivia.

'You've taught me this is a safe place and it's ok to get upset. I'm apologising for everything. For coming here, and for putting you in this position, but I wasn't sure what else to do. I've held things in for years, never spoken to anybody about how I've been feeling. It has left me drained. Since I started to come to therapy though, it has felt like a weight has been lifted off my shoulders. Slowly, I have been releasing everything that has amassed inside of me for all these years, and it feels good.'

She stopped for a moment and Toby wondered whether to interject, but ultimately decided not to.

'Therapy is helping me to build the strength to do what I need to do. You are helping me to build that strength, Toby.'

'It is you who is building that strength, Olivia. I just provide the setting to facilitate that.'

'You're too modest. You're an amazing therapist, and I'm sure all of your clients would agree.'

'Not all perhaps.'

Toby was reminded of Amanda Benson, a woman whose son Dean, he had worked with a couple of years ago. It had been a difficult case and Toby had

Breaking boundaries

found himself on several occasions having to reaffirm the boundaries with Amanda around confidentiality. Dean was eighteen, not particularly engaging, and it had been evident from the first session that he had only been there because his mother had effectively given him an ultimatum. He wasn't rude, but he was very clear about not seeing the point of therapy, and didn't feel it was going to do anything for him. Toby had seen him for four sessions, and after each one, he would receive a call or text message from Amanda to see what progress her son had been making. She had probed around what he had been disclosing, but Toby had been very clear that he couldn't discuss the case at all with her, and if she wanted to know how her son's therapy was progressing, she should perhaps ask him. Naturally, Toby knew Dean would not disclose anything to his mum, because she would then be aware he wasn't engaging particularly. Alternatively, he could have lied to her, and told her what he believed she wanted to hear, but had he done this, she wouldn't be contacting Toby for information. Ultimately, the case ended awkwardly with Amanda Benson accusing Toby of taking her money, and not helping her son. In what little bits he had been able to obtain from Dean, Toby believed his mother was more than likely a contributing factor in the way her son was feeling and behaving, but of course, he kept this theory to himself. She had given him a negative review, something he was unable to fully defend himself against without

Breaking boundaries

breaching confidentiality. He had discussed the case with Richard, and as he had anticipated, Richard had said whilst the outcome was unfortunate, it was more of a reflection on Amanda and Dean Benson than it was on him. He had asked Amanda Benson if she would like to make an official complaint to his accrediting body, but she had declined, and he had felt comfortable enough to move on past the unpleasant experience.

Olivia stared at him for a moment, appearing to hang on to his last comment.

'Oh?'

'If a client has unreasonable expectations of therapy, they can seek to apportion blame when those expectations are inevitably not met.'

'And that's usually the therapist?'

Toby smiled without replying.

'Is your job not to make people better?'

'Is that what you think therapy is?'

'You've made me better.'

'Have I?'

'You don't think I'm better?' she asked crestfallen.

'I don't think I have made you better. There's a difference,' Toby clarified.

'I don't follow.'

'I'm not debating whether or not you are better. The only person who truly knows that is you.'

'Then what are you saying?'

'That it's the client who is ultimately responsible for any improvement in their situation, not the therapist.'

Breaking boundaries

'But you ask the right questions, you make observations, make me realise things.'

'I do only two of those.'

Olivia said nothing, waiting in anticipation for Toby to elaborate. Toby sensed her curiosity but remained silent.

'I'm confused,' she said.

'I do ask questions and I do make observations. These are things I have control over. What I don't have any control over is how my clients respond. That's on them.'

'What does that even mean?'

'It means I cannot make you or any other client *realise* anything. You choose to be receptive to what you are exploring or discovering in a session. I simply plant the seeds. Any growth is beyond my control, and that's how it should be in therapy.'

'I think you're understating what you do,' she said with a smile.

'That's kind of you to say, but I assure you, it's not the case.'

'So ultimately, the client does all the work right?'

Whilst she said this with a grin and a hint of a sarcastic tone like she didn't believe it, Toby was very calm and forthright in his response.

'That's right. All I do is provide a safe space for you to explore, to be vulnerable. I merely facilitate the process. The hard work isn't undertaken in the therapy room Olivia, well not the real hard work anyway. Remember, your therapist can never really influence how you react, how you interact, or how

Breaking boundaries

you compartmentalise or prioritise. That's all on you. So, when I say I haven't fixed you, it's not about downplaying my role, it's about ensuring you don't downplay yours.'

Olivia looked down at her feet. Toby sensed there was more to her visit than simply asking him to remain as her therapist. She had never struck him as being desperate, and he had often thought she had more strength than she perhaps gave herself credit for. He picked up his mug and went to take another sip of his coffee. Realising it was cold as it touched his lips, he grimaced, but in a diplomatic way. Had he been on his own, the coffee would have exited through his mouth back into the cup, rather than down his throat, but as he had company, he resisted this urge, uncomfortably swallowing instead. He wasn't sure whether Olivia had noticed, but when he turned his head, after placing his cup back down on his coffee table, he saw she was still looking down at the floor.

'If this is the last time I see you, I need to tell you something, something I can't speak about, with anybody else. If I cannot convince you to be my therapist any longer, and I respect your decision, I just need to have a few more minutes with you, because I'm worried, really worried.'

Toby's face changed. His body stiffened and he was swiftly aware of his heart beating rapidly in his chest. He was anxious, he was wary, and he felt out of his depth. He questioned what he was doing here, how a relaxing evening, taking some time out

Breaking boundaries

to reflect, had ended up in a therapy session. Except this wasn't a therapy session, and this made things worse. This now became something which was off the record, and if he wasn't her therapist right now, what was he?

'May I use your bathroom?'

'I'm sorry?'

'Your bathroom Toby, would it be ok if I used it?'

'Oh, yes, of course,' he said snapping out of his daydream.

Olivia had almost certainly been aware of him being deep in thought for what had felt to Toby like several minutes but had realistically been around thirty seconds. She rose out of her seat and walked past him into the back room where the toilet was situated, brushing his legs with hers on the way through. Toby sat there in silence for a few moments, wondering what she was about to disclose, and whether or not he had the emotional capacity to hear it right now. She had been very open and graphic in her description of some of the abuse she had been subjected to. He deliberated how it could get much worse than that, but didn't dare allow his mind to wander for long enough to propose an answer. As he saw it, he was faced with three choices here. He could listen to what Olivia had to say and then reach an amicable ending with her; alternatively, he could tell her he didn't feel like he was the right person to be speaking with her right now, and recommend she go and speak to somebody else; or finally, he could avoid any

Breaking boundaries

potential conflict or awkwardness by telling her she could make an appointment to see him professionally. He sighed and felt exasperated knowing these were the only three options available to him, and none of them was without their problems. He didn't feel he could simply ask her to leave now. As a person, he wouldn't turn away somebody who had built up the courage to confide in him. However, he was wary about the alternative and firmly believed if he engaged her, he would likely hear something which would be serious enough to take up headspace he simply didn't have right now. His reasoning had left him with no other choice than to offer Olivia a formal session, in the process continuing as her therapist. This was against his better judgement and Richard's advice. More importantly for him, he had promised Beth from his hospital bed that he knew what needed to be done. He hadn't lied to her, he did know what had to be done, carrying that out was proving problematic though. He felt angry, powerless and dejected. The accident had presented him with a way out, but Olivia's presence suddenly drew him back in. He knew he needed to take control of the situation, and redefine professional boundaries. He had allowed this client to consume him, in a manner that no other client had done so previously. He needed to change this; it was the only way he could justify still seeing her. Toby didn't fear Olivia, he feared how he felt when he was around her. He didn't believe she was manipulative, simply

Breaking boundaries

desperate, and from that desperation arose her issues with boundaries. He would be clear with expectations from the offset. The trepidation he had experienced previously with Olivia had its roots firmly planted in that feeling of not being in control. He heard the toilet flush, followed by the sound of the tap. You always knew when the taps had been turned on by the loud groan from the pipes, largely in part due to the age of the building. It was rare clients utilised the facilities, and Toby had grown accustomed to the sound, so it didn't bother him so much these days. She reappeared and walked past Toby to take her seat, thanking him in the process.

'Olivia…'

'Toby it's ok, I know what you are going to say.'

'You do?'

'That you can't see me anymore, and I understand. I just need five minutes of your time, and then I promise I'll leave. You've helped me in ways that you couldn't imagine.'

He sat focused on Olivia, wondering what was coming next. He didn't feel equipped. He had been caught off guard and felt ill-prepared for having any sort of in-depth conversation with another person. She opened her mouth to speak, but it was Toby who spoke first.

'When did you cut your hair?'

Now it was Olivia's turn to be caught off guard. She clearly hadn't anticipated that question as she stuttered through her answer.

'Erm, about two weeks ago, I think.'

Breaking boundaries

'It's quite a change.'

'That was the point.'

Then it hit him, the reason why she was here, the reason she had cut her hair. He looked up at her, his face twisting at the sudden realisation. Olivia knew. No words needed to be exchanged, he could see that she now realised he'd figured it out. He couldn't say anything, and knew that that one question he had felt was a harmless deflection, an attempt to keep things light, a distraction perhaps, had done him more harm than he could imagine. He felt angry but hid it. At least he got that right he thought to himself. The situation had begun as uncomfortable but had now descended into something where Toby yearned for uncomfortable again. It had now gone way beyond this, and there was no option to ask Olivia to hold onto this until he could make an appointment to see her. He had initiated this, and he now had to deal with the consequences. He was now fairly certain he knew what was coming. Baggy clothes, a dishevelled look and cropped hair. This was a concerted effort to make herself look less appealing, not uncommon in somebody who had been subjected to a traumatic or brutal event. He felt a shiver as he began to piece things together, hoping desperately he was wrong, but knowing this was simply hope and not expectation.

'That's what I wanted to tell you, Toby. This time I couldn't keep it in. It happened again; he raped me.'

Breaking boundaries

Toby felt the colour drain out of his face. Even though he had heard this many times before, and had anticipated hearing it again here, it still impacted him. He felt relieved a little upon realising he still had empathy, and he still had compassion. He had said that when things stopped impacting him, he should walk away from therapy. He wondered whether this was a good indication that he wasn't ready to move away from the profession just yet.

'I'm so sorry, I can't imagine how you must be feeling right now.'

'Pretty shit to be honest. I feel weak and not in control.'

'Why do you feel weak?'

'Because I just let him do it…again.'

'Did you say no?'

'Yes, but it made no difference.'

'Saying no takes strength, it's not a sign of weakness.'

Olivia just sighed and bowed her head. She had struggled to look Toby in the eye whilst she had been speaking to him.

'Did you call the police?'

'They wouldn't believe me,' she replied with a resignation in her voice.

'Why do you feel they wouldn't believe you?'

'Toby, have you seen the percentage of rape cases that end up in a prosecution? How can you prove it wasn't consensual when you are married? It would simply be my word against his.'

Breaking boundaries

'I have a friend in the force. I could give you his card if you would like an informal chat with him. He's really good.'

'I can't risk making things worse.'

She had been raped twice now by her husband, one of those resulting in pregnancy. He had been physically abusive towards her and there was evidence of control. Toby wondered how much worse things could get for her. Whilst he could disclose to the authorities what Olivia had told him, the truth was he wasn't legally obligated to do so. As sad as her situation was, he wasn't there to fix it. He wasn't her saviour and as her therapist, couldn't be persuasive in any way. It was about her, and regardless of his personal feelings, he needed to be without agenda. It was a moral and ethical dilemma, because whilst he felt like he had a duty of care to his clients if they didn't feel they were in imminent danger, breaching their trust could have far worse consequences on more than one level. He couldn't put her in danger. He sat there quietly, waiting for Olivia to continue.

'We hadn't slept together in months. I guess it pissed him off. I mean he would occasionally try, but I would always have an excuse.'

'How would he react on such occasions?'

'I could tell he was annoyed, and sometimes we would argue about it, but…'

'But what?'

'But he never turned violent. He was frustrated, but he accepted it, but this time it was different.'

Breaking boundaries

'Different how?'

'He had this rage. I could see it in his eyes. It was that same look I saw all those years ago when he first did it to me. I knew what was going to happen. I was powerless, and all I could do was just brace myself.'

'That must have been terrifying for you,' Toby said softly.

'You know what the worst thing was? I spent the next few days questioning what I must have done wrong for that to happen. I looked at ways to blame myself. Hell, even now I'm justifying his behaviour.'

'Perhaps you're looking for explanations.'

'What do you mean?'

'There is a difference between seeking an explanation and seeking justification. Trying to find answers doesn't mean you are excusing what he did.'

'I think I get what you mean,' she said in a way that made Toby question whether she actually did.

He looked at her sympathetically. Whatever anxiety he had felt had disappeared now. When he looked at Olivia, he saw a vulnerable and damaged individual, for whom he couldn't help but feel sorry. He knew discharging her could be detrimental to her health, and his personal and professional oath was to keep clients safe. He could work through his own stuff, with the help of Richard, and Beth. She had built up a therapeutic relationship, and had found her safe place, a place where she could feel vulnerable without judgment or consequence. This

Breaking boundaries

was something which could take a lot of time for clients, with some never reaching that point. Ending therapy with Olivia now could damage her ability to trust others and have a profound impact on any future relationships. He simply couldn't risk this and knew what he had to do.

'It's getting late, and I should be heading home. Perhaps we should make an appointment for you, to give you the time to work through this?'

'Toby, that would be so helpful. You're the only one I feel comfortable talking to. Thank you.'

'How about next Thursday at five?

'I'll be here. I can't thank you enough.'

Toby got up out of his seat and walked to the door. The rain had abated; the wind had died down, and he noticed his fire had gone out. Oliva took her coat, which had dried nicely by now and pulled it on, carefully fastening it up. She walked past Toby, who was now holding the door open for her, and stepped out into the night. She turned to him.

'Thank you, Toby, for everything.'

'Goodnight Olivia.'

At that Toby closed the door and sank back into his seat. He paused for a moment, wondering whether he had made the right decision. He thought about Olivia's situation and felt a sense of sorrow. More than this, he felt helpless. He knew in his job he had no control over his client's situation, but he cared, too damn much sometimes. He closed his eyes but knew with the warmth of the room if he allowed himself just a few moments, there was a

Breaking boundaries

danger he would fall asleep. He pulled himself up out of his chair, and took his cup into the kitchen, taking care to remove the bits of coffee which had not successfully dissolved. As he turned off the light and locked the door, he thought about Tyler, and wondered how much he would ever know about his father. He thought about Olivia, her ordeal, her resignation and despair. Then he thought about Eric. He thought about the type of person he was, and whether he would be charming on the surface. He thought about his motives, and wondered if there was an end game with him. He considered some of the abusers he had worked with, the similarities to Eric. As he made his journey home, he continued to think about the evening. He thought of Olivia, Tyler and Eric. But mostly, he thought about Eric.

Breaking boundaries

12

They didn't often go out, but tonight was a special occasion. Beth looked radiant, as she always did, and with little effort. Toby stood admiring her beauty.

'Close your mouth, Mr Reynolds, a drool patch on your shirt would not be a good look,' she teased catching him staring.

'You're as beautiful now as when we first met.'

He pulled Beth close and wrapped his arms around her, giving her a firm and exaggerated kiss. Of course, this wasn't just about their anniversary, and it wasn't simply about how she looked now. The kiss had more meaning behind it than most others. It was a thank you for how she had supported him; it was sorry for what he had put her through; it was a promise to get their lives back to how they used to be.

'Happy anniversary beautiful.'

'Your lipstick now matches mine, Toby.'

'Ah shit,' he laughed as he darted for the bathroom to clean his face.

Beth giggled, shaking her head as he frantically scrubbed at his lips. He reappeared seconds later and sat on the bed, waiting for her to finish getting ready. He knew how lucky he was, but still worried sometimes he took her for granted. The last twelve months had thrown them some challenges, and Toby felt he was to blame. It was *he* who had become distant, due to his work. *He* who had

Breaking boundaries

decided to take time out as a result, and *he* had lost concentration on the road when conditions had been treacherous. Beth's role had been simple. She had supported him through it all, unconditionally and without judgment. Only once had she really expressed how she had been feeling. Toby, however, knew this had not been in the moment, and had instead built over time, something else he was responsible for. He watched her as she straightened her hair. She turned to him.

'What do you think?'

'Are you trying to catch me out?' he said shaking his head slowly.

'Whatever do you mean?'

'Did you think I wouldn't remember?' Toby teased.

Beth looked at him with a grin, put down her straighteners and walked towards him.

'It's exactly how you wore it on our wedding day. You looked beautiful then, and you look beautiful now,' he continued.

'Uggghhh. Too much romance,' she replied as she ran away from him laughing. Toby, feeling romantic, chased her for another embrace. His love for her grew by the day, though he didn't tell her nearly enough.

The evening felt quiet as they made their way to the restaurant. This was perhaps a reflection on the wintery conditions Toby thought. The weather wasn't freezing, but it wasn't far off, and as Beth

Breaking boundaries

waited for the heaters in the car to work their magic, she joked that a meal at home in front of the warm fire seemed more favourable at this moment in time. Toby turned up the heating as they made their way onto the main road, battling for warmth in the biting conditions. The restaurant was about twenty miles away. Toby had been a nervous driver since the accident, but he ensured, as soon as he was physically able to do so, he returned to driving. He had worried that the longer he left it, the harder it would be to get back behind the wheel. Not only did he need his own transport, but he had always enjoyed driving, and wasn't ashamed to admit he was a bit of a petrolhead. Toby's car had been damaged beyond repair, which Beth had teased had hurt him more than his injuries. Against her wishes, Toby had used the insurance money to buy an even sportier car, and whilst he enthused over it, she had been much more muted on its arrival, ambivalent almost. The route was pleasant, and after a short while on the main road, they would enter the countryside for a stretch, which in the daytime presented picturesque views, but at night, felt a little more isolating. Although a little anxious, Toby felt relieved he was doing the journey in the dark. His focus had to be solely on the conditions of the road, and the last thing he needed right now was any sort of distraction. They turned onto the dual carriageway and Toby squeezed the accelerator producing a sudden grunt from the engine. A large

Breaking boundaries

grin spread across his face as he did so. Beth looked at him mockingly and sighed.

'It's just a phase Beth, just a phase. He'll grow out of it.' She said out loud.

Toby let out a hearty laugh, Beth giggling with him shaking her head.

'You're not jealous, are you?'

'That you love your car more than me? Of course not.'

'That's not true...I love you both the same, Toby said, trying to maintain a straight face, but bursting into laughter. Beth looked at him smiling, open-mouthed.

'It won't be long until this car replaces me.'

'Don't be silly.'

He paused and glanced at Beth for a moment.

'It can't cook like you do!'

They again broke into laughter, but Toby reached for Beth's hand.

'You know how much I love you, don't you?'

'I do, now how do I change the radio station on this thing?'

Just as Toby was about to answer, they were startled by the sound of a horn. They had only been on the dual carriageway for one junction, and were now making their way along the more scenic route. The roads were narrow, and the overgrown trees meant careful navigation was required in places. The car behind seemed impatient, flashing its lights incessantly at Toby. He had slowed down significantly, partly due to nervousness, and partly

Breaking boundaries

due to the conditions outside. Whilst it was cosy inside the car, the display was showing the outside temperature to be just two degrees. Toby looked in his central mirror and noticed the car was incredibly close to him. He could just about make out the driver was male, heavyset with a beard.

'What the hell is this guy's problem?'

Beth looked over her shoulder out of the back window.

'Toby, just pull to the side and let him pass.'

'There isn't any space. Remember what happened last time I got too close to an embankment?'

The stretch they were on contained continuous blind bends, which made overtaking incredibly difficult unless you were prepared to take the risk nothing was approaching on the other side of the carriageway. Toby felt uneasy, for himself, but more so for Beth. She had been involved in the accident that had seen both of her parents perish. She also had to take that phone call from the police informing her that her husband had been rushed to hospital after being involved in a serious road accident. She had experienced that fear of losing somebody else she loved in the same circumstances she had lost her parents. It had been a lot for her to handle, and he wondered just how much it must have affected her. The lights again flashed. Toby looked in his mirror and saw the individual was now gesticulating.

'Clearly, he's in a rush Toby, just pull over and let him past.'

Breaking boundaries

'You mean just stop?'

'Yes.'

'What if he stops as well?'

'Why would he?'

'I don't know Beth, I have no idea what this guy's motives are, but for some reason, he seems agitated, and I'm not keen on finding out why.'

Ironically Toby himself was becoming agitated.

'Then accelerate.'

Toby glanced at her tentatively, looked down at his speedometer, and pushed his foot down on the accelerator. The car grunted, the gear shifted down and Toby began to move away from the car behind. He felt relief knowing that a patch of straight road was coming up where he would feel more comfortable opening up the car. Suddenly out of nowhere, the vehicle which moments ago had been behind him drew up next to him. The driver stared at Toby for a moment before speeding off into the distance. Toby felt himself shaking, his heart beating quickly. Beth reached for his hand and squeezed it.

'It's ok Toby, he was probably just in a rush. This wasn't about you.'

He took a deep breath and eased up on the accelerator.

'Why is my body in shock Beth? What's going on? What's happening to me?' Beth now noticed him shaking and realised he was having flashbacks.

'Toby, pull over for me darling,' she said reassuringly.

Breaking boundaries

He slowed the car down to a stop, finding a small verge to move partially onto to avoid blocking the road. Now just the low humming of the engine. Beth undid her seatbelt and wrapped her arms around him. She was mindful not to do this too tight as he was having a panic attack, and the last thing she wanted him to feel was constricted. They remained like that for a couple of minutes, with no words spoken, and then just sat holding hands. After a short while Beth turned to him and asked if he wanted them to turn back. Toby had reasoned they were over half-way there and he didn't want an impatient stranger and his own anxiety to ruin their evening. Beth held out her hand. Toby switched off the engine and placed the key in her hand. They exited the car and exchanged places. Beth adjusted her seat and her mirror before starting the engine and turning to Toby.

'Ready?' she asked squeezing his hand.

'Ready.'

The rest of the journey had been uneventful, but the delay had caused them to lose their table at the restaurant, which had been very specific in explaining to Toby and Beth their twenty-minute policy. Toby had tried to call from the car to explain, however, whilst one of the perks of the countryside was the ability to cut yourself off from the outside world, the downside of this was the lack of masts to allow any sort of phone signal. Though they had been rigid in their policy, the restaurant had been understanding and had juggled some things around

Breaking boundaries

to accommodate them at a later time. Unfortunately, however, this came with a seventy-minute wait, which left them with the choice of either being seated in the bar area or returning later. They had passed a country pub less than a mile back and decided to drive back there for a drink before returning to the restaurant for their table.

The pub was quiet, warm, and had a traditional look. Toby much preferred pubs with an old-fashioned feel to them. He felt they were more inviting and attracted a type of drinker there to savour the selection of drinks on offer, and enjoy the surroundings, rather than simply getting inebriated watching some sporting event. On the occasions he and Jack would catch up, they would head to a pub close to Jack's in the countryside. It felt to Toby like the world had moved on and left it behind, and that was just fine by him. They had no interest in pub crawling, preferring instead to remain in the one place for the evening. Good company, good surroundings and good beer, Toby couldn't ask for any more. They chose a seat next to the open fire which roared ferociously, whilst mesmerising its audience with its bright, flickering flames. Beth rubbed her hands together as they raised their glasses and toasted their anniversary. The years had not been without challenges, but Toby had never felt their relationship was anything other than strong. In Beth, he had found his soul mate, his best friend, and there had never been a doubt in his mind

Breaking boundaries

that they would grow old together. He raised his glass and smiled at her, taking a moment to admire her beauty. Beth was one of these people who could throw on a baggy jumper and a pair of jeans, and still glow. He was reminded of her natural beauty as he reached out for her hand across the table.

'Happy anniversary beautiful.'

'Where are you looking?' she replied squeezing his hand as she smiled back at him. This was one of the things Toby enjoyed the most. They could have fun, not take each other or life too seriously, enjoy the moment. His smile suddenly disappeared as he thought about the last few months, and how he had missed this, lost sight of what was important. He had fallen victim to becoming too immersed in his work, something he had vowed never to do. The nature of his work meant the ability to be able to separate his personal and professional self was absolutely vital. He felt he had always managed this in the past, and though things would affect him, he left them in his practice, or talked it through with Richard. But something had changed, and no amount of reflection had provided him with a definitive answer as to what had brought about this change. He was wary, but the overriding feelings he was currently experiencing were sadness and guilt. He felt sad because he knew whilst he had been physically present, emotionally he had been elsewhere at times. The guilt he felt was purely about the impact this had had on Beth. He had been

Breaking boundaries

challenging to live with and he knew it. He had been coy with Beth and though he had tried to convince himself this was to protect her; he had realised it was more to protect himself. Ethically, so far, he had not contravened any boundaries, and done his utmost to remain professional. This had of course conflicted with his own morals, but he felt all choices he had made, he had made so with professional integrity. What didn't sit comfortable with him, however, was why he felt like he couldn't be more open with his wife. Was there a part of him that somehow felt the relationship with Olivia Stanton was inappropriate? Was he worried that Beth would be suspicious? How could she though? He didn't even know what was happening, what he was feeling, why he had reacted in this way to his client.

'Toby you're distracted.'

'No, right now, I'm thinking clearly.'

He had lied. Why?

'This is a beautiful place, feels cosy,' Beth said with a content smile.

'When you look outside, and see the trees covered in frost, it makes you grateful you have the fire as company,' Toby replied.

'We should do this more often.'

'What, have anniversaries? Sorry darling, they're an annual thing, nothing I can do about that.'

Beth playfully slapped his hand.

'You know what I mean. Have more time together out of the house,' she said.

'It's nice.'

227

Breaking boundaries

'It's nice that you are working less.'

'Beth…'

She waved her hand at him.

'I'm sorry, it's just I am really happy to have my husband around a little more. You seem happier.'

Toby looked at her. He knew it was never about the number of hours he had been working, but hadn't told Beth that. Something else he had kept from her, he thought.

'Fancy another one before we head off?'

Beth stared at her empty glass.

'Better make this one a lemonade if I'm driving.'

Toby leant over the table and gave her a kiss.

'Thank you,' he said tenderly.

'For what?'

'Just for being you, and always knowing the right thing to say.'

At this, Toby got out of his seat and made his way past the fire to the bar. The bar was quiet. In one corner there were a couple who looked deep in conversation. There looked to be quite an age difference, and Toby wondered whether it was a mother and son. As he observed for a moment, he saw the way they looked at each other, and realised his initial assessment had been incorrect. He smiled and turned to his right. A man, perhaps in his forties, was sat there with a newspaper in one hand, and what looked like a soft drink in the other. He was dressed casually, but still looked smart. He was well built, Toby estimated around six feet tall. He seemed completely immersed in the article he was

Breaking boundaries

reading, oblivious to the surroundings. Toby admired this, and often wondered how some people could feel so comfortable being solitary in a social setting. There was a strange paradox, he thought, to somebody heading to a place full of people to seek solitude. As Toby stood contemplating, the man caught Toby's gaze, and aimed a pleasant smile and nod in his direction. Toby felt a little awkward, like he had just been caught looking into the girls changing room at school, but returned the courtesy. He ordered two lemonades and headed back to the table where Beth was sat waiting patiently.

'You're not drinking?' she asked?

'It wouldn't feel right.'

'Ever the gentleman,' she quipped.

Toby blushed a little. She was having fun, but still there were certain things that elicited an involuntary reaction from him, and compliments of any sort, were right at the top of that list.

'Who's the guy at the bar?'

'What makes you ask that?'

'You were staring at him for long enough. I thought with that much effort, you may have at least got his number,' Beth teased.

Toby laughed loudly, and quickly placed his hand over his mouth to muffle the sounds. He glanced around to ensure he hadn't drawn attention to himself. Beth sat opposite, head on the table, with her arms wrapped around it, shaking with fits of uncontrollable laughter. She had been a lot more clandestine in her amusement than Toby. He loved

Breaking boundaries

this aspect of their relationship, and realised just how much he had missed this, as it hadn't been there since some time before the accident. His job was serious, it was emotional, which was why he had always tried to maintain a homelife which wasn't. He felt like he had been heading the wrong way down a one-way street, and wondered how long he had been doing this. More importantly he wondered how he had allowed it to happen. He was very self-aware, and had Richard for the moments when introspection failed him. How had it got to this? Beth looked down at her watch.

'We should be leaving. We don't want to lose our table for a second time in one night.'

'We still have plenty of time, don't panic,' Toby reasoned.

'It's not panic dear, it's hunger.'

Toby chuckled.

'Not wishing to get between you and your food, I will make a hasty retreat to the toilet and then we can head off.'

'Don't be long,' she shouted after him.

'Wouldn't dare,' came the reply, Toby's voice fading as he disappeared into the background.

He was stood washing his hands when a man exited the cubicle, and came and stood at the sink beside him. An awkward, yet courteous smile was exchanged, before a moment of silence, broken only by the sound of the tap. Toby looked over at

Breaking boundaries

the man and noticed a tattoo on the man's forearm, a date in Roman numerals.

'The day my sister died.'

'I'm sorry?'

'The tattoo, it's the date of my sister's death.'

'I'm sorry, I didn't mean to stare,' Toby said apologetically,

'It's ok, I'm not offended.'

Another moment of awkward silence followed, and Toby was reminded again how uncomfortable he was conversing with people outside of his professional setting.

'Anything interesting in the news today?'

It was the man's turn to look puzzled.

'You were reading a newspaper at the bar, when I was ordering my drinks.'

'Ah yes, so I was. Not much going on, but I think maybe that's a good thing. There always seems to be so much negativity in the news, I rarely read an uplifting story these days. To be honest, I don't know why I still buy the bloody thing.'

'Why do you buy it?'

The man smiled at Toby.

'I'm an optimist. I guess I live in hope. I haven't seen you in here before. New to the area?'

'We don't live locally... my wife and I that is,' Toby clarified.

'To be honest neither do we.' the man replied.

'I came across this place whilst out for a drive last year. I was thirsty and it was incredibly cold, but something looked so warm and inviting. Now I drive

Breaking boundaries

out here every so often, and just take some time out for myself.'

'Sounds like escapism,' Toby grinned.

'It does, doesn't it?'

'There are much worse places to escape to I can imagine.'

'There are just a handful of regulars here, because of its positioning. It's a short taxi ride for the few houses within the vicinity, but it's not really walkable. It's tranquil, and about as far removed from city life as you could get. That's why I like it.'

'How often do you escape here?' Toby asked inquisitively.

'I try to drive out here once every couple of weeks if I can.'

'Ah, that would explain the soft drink in your hand.'

'You are perceptive good sir,' the man said with a broad smile, before continuing.

'I'm not really a drinker anyway. I wouldn't say I am tee-total, but I am not that far away. Alcohol and I have never really been friends. When I was a lot younger, I had a skirmish with the law, my fault entirely, and I accepted that, but alcohol played a big part, and it was most unpleasant. That was the first and last time I have ever had a brush with the law, and I aim to keep it that way. On special occasions I will have a drink, but I moderate it.'

'I admire that.'

The man smiled at Toby and having both finished washing their hands, they now stood facing each

Breaking boundaries

other conversing in the most peculiar of settings, Toby thought.

'I was never reliant on it, but I guess I felt I was. I thought I needed alcohol to become a more likeable person. Turns out it made me into a less likeable person. I went through a little therapy, and it made me realise that I was fine just the way I was. I learned to accept myself.'

'Therapy can do that.'

'Are you talking from experience?' the man asked.

'Perhaps not experience in the same way you're thinking.'

The man looked at Toby, curiously.

'I'm a Psychotherapist,' Toby clarified.

'Ah, I see. Well, I have nothing but admiration for you guys. My therapist was great, she really helped me.'

'I'm glad to hear that.'

'To be honest, I probably should contact her. A while back, I had a traumatic experience. Since then, I haven't been sleeping properly, and still can't get rid of these unwanted images.'

'Perhaps talking to somebody would help?'

'I guess.'

'Addressing trauma in therapy inevitably means re-living it. That's never an easy thing to conceptualise. Many people simply wish to forget and move on. Of course, that's not always so easy.'

'You're very wise.'

Breaking boundaries

'Not really, just experienced in my field, as I'm sure you are in yours. What is it you do?' Toby asked politely.

'I guess you could say I am a kind of engineer.'

'Sounds interesting.'

'It's really not!'

They both laughed for a moment, but Toby noticed the man's smile begin to fade, replaced instead with a more troubled look.

'Can I ask you a question?'

'Of course.'

'Do people ever forget something that's traumatic? I mean can you really ever get over something like that?'

'It's not an easy question to answer, but I wonder whether it is about getting over it, or simply learning to accept it. One of the key things when it comes to trauma is processing it, being able to make sense of your experience. When I say make sense, I mean have a logical understanding of what has happened. Sometimes we spend a lot of time trying to look for reason or justification, and it's not always there.'

'I don't even know why it has affected me, I mean nobody died,' the man said almost dismissively.

'Perhaps it resonated with you in some way?'

'Maybe.'

Toby glanced down at his watch. He had been in here longer than Beth would have expected, and they had reservations.

'I should be going,' he said with a warm smile, before extending his hand.

Breaking boundaries

'Toby.'

'Rick.'

They shared a joke about the merits of shaking hands after each had used the sink, and Toby headed swiftly out of the door to Beth. She was waiting for him, coat on, keys in hand, head tilted with a look that let Toby know she was a little frustrated.

'Sorry, sorry,' Toby said now picking up pace as he realised they were again running late.

'I got talking to somebody in there, lost track of time.'

Beth rolled her eyes. Toby had a tendency to do this, usually at the most inopportune moments. He was reminded of her telling him that his passion for people was a blessing and a curse at the same time, and wondered whether this was an example of what she meant. As they exited the pub, the cold breeze was biting, neither of them being overly enamoured with swapping a cosy open fire for sub-zero temperatures. They quickly headed for the car, not wishing to be exposed to the winter elements any longer than they had to. Beth entered at the driver's side and swiftly switched on the engine to allow the heaters to activate. Waiting a few moments to allow the ice on the windows to clear, they huddled for warmth. After a couple of minutes, she clicked the paddle located on the steering wheel to reverse, carefully navigating her way out of the tight space. She stopped for a moment, shifted the gear to drive and placed her hand on Toby's knee.

Breaking boundaries

They exchanged a smile as he placed his hand on hers and squeezed. Then Beth pulled out of the warmly lit car park and into the frosty night for the short journey to the restaurant.

Breaking boundaries

13

Rosie Johnson looked down at her feet. She cut a hesitant figure. Toby had worked hard to build a rapport with his client, but it was taking time, and he needed to be patient. He looked up at the clock and felt relieved there were only ten minutes left. His relief came solely from the fact she had said little in the session, and Toby struggled with sessions that contained so many silences. She had been subdued today, explaining to him she had been involved in an unpleasant exchange with her husband, just the previous evening. They had been married for five years, but she had disclosed that she had felt pressured into the wedding by her family, and wasn't sure whether she had actually wanted to go through with it. Rosie was a young woman, twenty-six years of age, with long blond hair and an athletic figure. She had felt sure her husband had been having an affair, and admitted she herself had been tempted by somebody else last year.

'I'm sorry, I haven't said much today, have I?'

'That's okay,' Toby said not wishing to add to her troubles.

'I know, I just feel overwhelmed at the moment. I think the argument last night drained me. We've argued before, but this felt different.'

'Different how?'

'It felt personal, nasty.'

'What did you argue about?'

Breaking boundaries

'I accused him of having an affair, again,' Rosie said despondently.

'This isn't the first time?'

'No, I've had my suspicions for a while now. I confronted him a couple of months ago, but he convinced me I had it wrong.'

Toby studied Rosie for a moment. He was interested to know if she was questioning her husband or herself. He drew breath and responded.

'And do you?'

'Do I what?'

'Have it wrong?'

'This time, when I asked him, I saw it on his face, in his eyes. He denied it of course, but his face didn't lie.'

'I'm sorry.'

She looked up and stared at Toby. Then a tiny smile appeared, but he knew it camouflaged a deeper sadness. Even if she wasn't happy in her marriage, the prospect of a relationship ending was never easy, particularly not in these circumstances. Rosie looked down at her feet again, like a naughty child waiting outside the office of the headteacher. She looked beaten, and he felt sorry for her. For a couple of minutes there was a quietness in the practice, with just the faint humming of the fridge in the distance, breaking the silence. Toby glanced at the clock again and reminded Rosie that the session was drawing to a close. She looked relieved, Toby thought. Though she hadn't been her usual engaging self, it had been an emotional session for

Breaking boundaries

her, and she now had a lot to process. She thanked Toby and made her way out of the practice and onto the street, blending in with the masses, before fading into the background. Toby poured himself a drink and looked at his diary. He had reduced his client hours since the accident, limiting himself to no more than twelve in a week, spread over three days. Beth had been supportive, relieved by all accounts. She had seen first-hand the emotional turmoil he had been experiencing as a result of his job but was also pleased to have him around the house a little more. He had been concerned with the potential financial implications, but they had sat together and thrashed out the finer details, ultimately deciding they could take the hit. Beth had reasoned, the gain for Toby's emotional wellbeing, would significantly outweigh the loss of income. Deep in thought, he jumped at the sound of a knock at the door. He rose up out of his seat to answer it, in the process noticing the sky was looking overcast. It was only the middle of the afternoon, but you could have been forgiven for thinking it was early evening. The winter had well and truly arrived, and Toby felt grateful for the open fire providing a glowing warmth, in stark contrast to the conditions outside. Olivia greeted Toby and walked into the practice. She removed her coat and scarf and took the seat nearest the fire. She looked subdued and whilst Toby couldn't be sure, he thought he had noted a bruise peering out from under her bra strap, which had been partially on display when she had bent

Breaking boundaries

down to put her phone in her bag. Toby gave her a moment before speaking.

'How have you been?'

'Last week has been difficult. I've been really looking forward to seeing you.'

'I'm sorry to hear things have been difficult for you.'

'I'm guessing you need to know why it has been difficult right?'

'There is nothing I *need* to know. It's simply a case of what you *want* me to know.'

'I think I want and need to talk about this. Eric and I had a fight, well he had a fight with me anyway.'

'Are you okay?' Toby asked with concern.

'A little bruising, but mainly just shook up.'

Toby noticed her body language change. She suddenly dropped eye contact with him, instead looking down at her feet which were now swinging back and forth. For a moment he thought she had regressed back to a time when she felt safe, childhood quite possibly. She began massaging her right shoulder, slowly moving it in small circles as if it had stiffened. Noticing this Toby questioned her about it.

'Is that painful?'

'It's the one I dislocated.' She paused for a moment and then continued.

'It's the one he dislocated when he threw me down the stairs.'

Toby looked at her with what he feared was pity. He knew all he could provide was a safe

Breaking boundaries

environment for her. There was nothing he could say right now that would change Olivia's situation.

'I'm frightened,' she sobbed.

'Did you call the police?'

'No, and you can't either. Please Toby, I know you said if you fear your client or anybody else is in danger you may disclose that information to somebody else, but you can't.'

Olivia sounded panicked, desperate almost as she pleaded with him. The very mention of the police had clearly startled her, but this wasn't uncommon among abuse victims. One of the main reasons they tended not to come forward was through fear. Toby had seen this time and time again with clients who had been victims of prolonged domestic abuse. He thought for a moment. Legally, he wasn't obligated to intervene. Disclosing if he felt a client or somebody else may be in danger was a personal caveat, he added to breaching confidentiality. There was no legal dilemma here, that was very clear. What he was facing was a moral one. He wanted to help all his clients, but it was not his job to fix them or their situation. His choice here was quite simple. He either, disclosed his fears to the authorities, potentially putting his client at more risk as well as potentially irreversibly damaging their therapeutic relationship. Or, he respected her wishes and maintained confidentiality, knowing this may keep her and her son in an abusive environment. Whilst the options were obvious, the answer for Toby,

Breaking boundaries

unfortunately lacked any simplicity, and for a moment he sat silently pondering.

'Toby?'

Olivia had now leaned forward, pushing her fringe back above her eyes and staring at him intently. For a moment he couldn't figure whether she looked frightened or threatening.

'I'm going to leave him Toby. I have started to put things into place for Tyler and I. Hopefully we will soon be free of him. I'm sad for Tyler, and I honestly don't know how he will react, but what sort of mother would I be, if I knowingly placed him in danger?'

'Do you fear for his safety?'

'Eric's hit him before. It's only a matter of time before he does it again. I think Eric is starting to resent him.'

'Resent him?'

'Tyler is almost seven, and he's smart. He sees what happens, and it pushes him closer to me. The closer he gets to me, the more he removes himself from Eric. Eventually Tyler will say or do something that really antagonises him. Do you understand what I mean?'

'You believe Eric will feel Tyler has chosen you over him?'

'Yes, and he will feel isolated. I'm not concerned about his feelings, I'm concerned about how he responds to them, especially when it could endanger my son.'

Breaking boundaries

Toby noted her choice of words here, '*my son*'. Olivia was slowly removing Eric from not only her life, but that of her son's also. She didn't see him as a partner anymore, or even a co-parent. She hadn't uttered the words father or husband, and she spoke about him with contempt and disdain. Toby believed she had already begun the process of separation, with Eric oblivious. Olivia sat back in her chair, legs crossed, expressionless. Her anxiety had now seemingly disappeared, the panic subsided. Instead in front of him sat this assured and confident young woman, but he was mindful this could simply mask her vulnerability.

'I have a friend who is an estate agent. I talked to her the other day, about an hour after Eric had attacked me actually.'

'Okay.'

'She said she loved our house and asked why we were moving.'

'What did you tell her?' Toby asked.

'That we weren't moving, but I was.'

'I see.'

'Yeah, she went quiet for a while, probably didn't know what to say.'

'It's a big step, it must have taken a great deal of courage,' Toby replied.

'Isn't it about time I stood up for myself?'

Toby interpreted this as a rhetorical question, but even if this wasn't how it was meant, he had no inclination to answer it, he knew better. The look on

Breaking boundaries

her face told Toby she also knew it wasn't a question he would, or indeed could, answer.

'I need some perspective,' she said suddenly less assured.

'Are you having doubts?'

Olivia shuffled further back into her chair and put her head in her hands, letting out a sigh in the process. She rubbed her face several times before sitting forward. She gazed around the room, her breathing loud, but rhythmic, deep in thought, seemingly searching for her words. It almost looked like she was trying to find some inspiration. Finally, she answered him.

'It's not that I'm having doubts. I know what has to happen. I am just fearful of the consequences. Whether I like it or not, he's Tyler's dad. I'm never going to be rid of him, am I?' she said with a resignation.

'How would co-parenting work for you?'

'It wouldn't. How can I let Tyler be around him if I fear for his safety? How could I be sure he wasn't poisoning Tyler against me?

'It sounds like you're conflicted.'

Olivia bowed her head and looked down at the floor once again. She was agitated, yet controlled in the same manner, if that was even possible. Toby thought it was like she was trying to remove any trace of Eric but had realised the enormity of doing this.

Breaking boundaries

'There is always going to be that link through Tyler. He will always be in my life, won't he? Unless of course...'

Olivia paused for a moment.

'Unless what?'

She raised her head, slowly meeting Toby's eyes.

'Unless he's dead.'

Toby held her gaze for a moment, waiting for Olivia to elaborate. She sat silently; her face expressionless. Toby waited, uncomfortably, his heart skipping several beats. Olivia smirked at him.

'You don't think I am serious, do you?'

'Are you?'

'You don't need to worry; it wasn't a statement of intent. Besides, with his temper, I'm much more likely to end up dead than he is.'

She laughed, but it was a nervous laugh. She was all over the place tonight, Toby thought, oscillating between confidence and despair. Initially he felt she was lucid and clear in her mind, but now he wasn't so sure. *She* wasn't so sure. Still, he felt relieved.

'Olivia how are you feeling, I mean how are you really feeling?'

'I think I'm done with all of this.'

'That's what you are *thinking*. Tell me what you're *feeling*.'

'I feel trapped, lost, without any direction. I feel desperate and I feel lonely.'

She was becoming animated, her frustration tangible. Her voice was getting louder, and Toby

Breaking boundaries

knew he had tapped into something here. This was good. She was finally releasing what she was really feeling. He smiled inwardly as Olivia continued.

'I feel cheated, I feel weak, and I feel like a fucking failure. I feel like I have wasted years and given everything to some son of a bitch who in return, has given me a couple of black eyes, a dislocated shoulder, and a burn mark for good measure. Oh, and to add to that, he has raped me. Is that enough for you? Is that what you wanted to hear?'

Now she was visibly shaking. She was angry, and Toby knew this was coming from a place of intense pain and fear. He gave her a moment to catch her breath and compose herself. He knew the anger wasn't aimed at him.

'It's not about what I want to hear, it's about what you want to say,' he said calmly.

'I'm sorry, I didn't mean to get angry with you.'

'You didn't.'

'Well, I shouted.'

'I don't believe I was the one you were really shouting at.'

'What do you mean?' she asked curiously.

'I mean, I'm not the subject of your anger.'

'Oh, you mean Eric?'

'Not just him.'

She looked at him confused.

'It sounds like some of the anger is being directed internally.'

'Do you think I blame myself?'

Breaking boundaries

'Do you?'

'Maybe I do, I don't know.'

'It's common for abuse victims to question themselves and self-blame, but this is part of a careful manipulation from the abuser.'

'Oh great, so I am weak minded as well, I give up,' she laughed.

Her laugh was a nervous one and he knew she found this situation anything but funny.

'Victims aren't weak Olivia. They are often subjected to prolonged and careful manipulation. In many cases, people don't realise it's happening.'

'I think I'm conflicted,' she managed.

'Perhaps that's natural considering your situation?'

He posed this as a question, but knew it was a veiled statement. Being in an abusive relationship was difficult enough, and even without children, could throw up certain dilemmas. When children were involved however, this added complexity. Olivia had previously said she felt Eric was a good dad. It wasn't always easy to differentiate between somebody as a parent and as a partner, and Toby admired this. Whilst he had never been in this position personally, he couldn't imagine saying positive things about a person who had caused you physical and psychological pain, was an easy thing to do.

'I thought I had things figured out before I came here,' Olivia said with a frustration which was difficult to hide.

Breaking boundaries

'If you're now questioning that, perhaps you already had doubts?'

'I have more questions than answers, but it has helped to talk it through. I think I know what needs to be done, I just need to figure out the best way to do it.'

Toby a forced smile but didn't respond. This was her battle, and he didn't have the answers for her, it wasn't his job. Sometimes it could be difficult, but ultimately any change, any action, any reaction, had to come from the client.

The rest of the session had taken a different direction with Olivia focusing on Tyler and how he was doing at school. His behaviour had been declining to such an extent his teacher had called her to discuss the situation. Olivia had expressed a fear that Tyler's anger was coming from what he was seeing from his father, that he was starting to identify with him. Toby had questioned whether the anger could actually be a manifestation of the pain he is experiencing if he is witnessing distressing things in the household. She had left the practice telling Toby she was going to take a walk to clear her head, gain some perspective. As always Toby reflected for a few moments after his client had left. He valued this reflective time and would sit in silence for a while before writing up his case notes. Olivia was his last client of the day. He finished his paperwork and washed up his cup. On it a picture of he and Beth on a trip to Switzerland. No matter how difficult his day may have been, that picture never

Breaking boundaries

failed to make him smile. He placed it back on his desk and headed for the door. There was a gentle breeze and the skies looked dark and overcast. Toby thought the temperature was fresh, which in his eyes meant it was cool, but in a refreshing way. The breeze certainly added to this he thought, as he buttoned up his coat and headed for the car. He was able to park relatively close by, something he was even more grateful for when the harsh winters would present themselves. He walked briskly, taking in some of the scenery along the way. The trees were now beginning to shake rigorously as the gentle breeze transitioned into something more resembling of a storm. Toby picked up the pace, wary of having to make the journey home in adverse conditions. Whilst the crash had not impacted his ability to drive, he was certainly more cautious, and would avoid driving in challenging conditions where possible.

Seatbelt fastened and about to start the engine, Toby suddenly noticed his phone, which was on the passenger seat, was lit up, displaying an incoming call. As he picked up the phone, he stared at it for a moment, realising it was a withheld number. Marketing probably, he thought, rejecting the call. The engine started with a roar, but before he could let out the obligatory excited sound which usually accompanied this, his phone rang again. He was now curious. Marketing callers usually only tried once. Whoever this was, they were clearly needing

Breaking boundaries

to speak with him. He shifted the car back into Park and picked up the phone. Though he could speak freely whilst driving, after the crash he had made every attempt to minimise any distraction when out on the road.

'Toby Reynolds.'

Silence on the other end. He could hear somebody breathing and wondered whether it was a new client, perhaps one who was consumed with anxiety. It took a lot of courage to contact a therapist in person, and for somebody displaying high levels of anxiety, it could be an incredibly daunting experience.

'Is anybody there?'

Suddenly a voice from the other end.

'Toby, I need your help.'

The voice was instantly recognisable. The trepidation wasn't around who it was, it was around what he may be about to hear. For a moment he remained silent. In truth he had been caught cold, and had no idea how to respond.

'I'm sorry for calling you, I know I shouldn't, but I didn't know who else to turn to.'

Toby took a deep breath and closed his eyes. He needed to be sensitive, but assertive here. This...this right here is what he had been wary about since he first met Olivia Stanton. He had managed to convince himself she respected the therapeutic boundaries, and that what he saw was a strong and independent woman. Now he worried she had not only become reliant on him but had

Breaking boundaries

formed an unhealthy attachment in the process. He felt anger, not aimed towards Olivia, but inwardly. He had allowed himself to be talked into continuing to see her as a client when he had been reluctant to do so. Now he was faced with an extremely uncomfortable situation, of which he could see no positive conclusion. This wasn't the first time she had called him like this. More importantly, she had left his practice a matter of minutes ago.

'Olivia, I…'

He was cut off abruptly.

'I know what you're going to say and believe me I feel as uncomfortable about this as you do, but I had nowhere else to turn. I feel despair, and I'm worried about what I might do. Do you hear me Toby? I'm worried about my own actions.'

She stopped as if waiting for Toby to say something. He wondered what she meant by that last part.

'Olivia, there are people who can help you, professionals. I'm just a Psychotherapist, this isn't my remit.'

'You are more than a Psychotherapist Toby. You're kind, intelligent and you actually care. In fact, you care more than most of my friends or family. That's the reason why I called you. You care Toby, you fucking care.'

Her voice had elevated and had a desperate sound to it. She was pleading with him. Toby thought back to a conversation he and Beth had previously had, where she had told him he cared too

Breaking boundaries

much. Did he? Was this problematic? Had his own actions through therapy created this situation, this dependency? Everything that was happening now, in this moment, it suddenly felt like he had caused it.

'Olivia, what do you think you need from me?'

'Think? Don't fucking patronise me.'

He didn't like her tone, and he wasn't used to her throw away profanities either.

'I'm sorry Toby, I'm desperate. Ten minutes ago, when I left our session, I felt ok, good almost. I felt like I had a plan, and that Tyler and I could be safe, maybe even happy. For the first time in as long as I can remember, I had clarity'.

'Had'. This implied something had happened, but Toby was mindful not to ask Olivia what had changed, as this would undoubtedly open the conversation up, and what he was trying to do was to close it down. He wasn't successful.

'When I got to my car, he had left me a voicemail. It was nasty, threatening. Clearly, he had been drinking, but Tyler is with him. What sort of a person gets drunk whilst looking after a child?'

'Have you considered going to the police?'

'I deleted it immediately. Didn't even get to the end. What's the point anyway? He would talk his way out of it.'

'I'm not sure how I can help Olivia, I'm just your therapist.'

'I need you to come and meet me. I need you to help me get out of here.'

'I can't do that, I'm sorry.'

Breaking boundaries

'Please Toby, I'm begging you. If not for me, for Tyler.'

'If you feel either of you are in danger, I would strongly recommend calling the police,' he said firmly.

'I can't, and you can't either.'

'I'm not the person who can change your situation, Olivia. I can't take pain away from clients. That all comes from within. There are organisations who can support you, help to keep you safe, keep both of you safe. I can get you the details if you like?'

'No, it's ok, I need to figure this one out for myself.'

'Olivia...'

'I'm sorry to have bothered you, Toby. You're right, this isn't your problem.'

'It isn't that I don't care about my clients, but as a Psychotherapist, it can never be my problem. The therapy isn't about me, and I'm not in a position to provide a resolution. I simply offer an environment where you can find your own. I hope you understand.'

'Sorry to disturb you,' she replied as if she had not heard what he had just said.

The phone went dead, and just like that Toby felt he could breathe again. He sat for a few minutes, trying to gain some perspective on the conversation with Olivia. She had sounded desperate, almost broken and had come to him for help. What help she sought, however, wasn't clear. He was certain it

Breaking boundaries

would have taken a lot for her to reach out to him, in these circumstances, but he needed to maintain professional boundaries. He was her therapist; she was his client. They weren't friends or colleagues, and although Toby felt bad for the situation she was in, there was no legal obligation for him to disclose any of what she had told him. He had discussed his concerns with her, but she had been perspicuous in the fact she did not wish him to contact the police on her behalf, something she had repeated more than once. He felt uneasy. Why would she want him to go and meet her? What did she think he would, or in fact could, do? He sat with his chin resting on his hands and stared up at the sky. The wind had died down a little, and whilst the rain hadn't ceased, it had become much lighter. As Toby made his way home, he wondered whether Olivia was safe. He thought about Eric, and wondered what was pushing him to abuse. The obvious answer was control, but it didn't feel as straightforward as that. The abusive moments seemed to be sporadic, and the way Olivia conveyed them, were most often fuelled by alcohol. So, he could be a nasty drunk, but Toby knew that was very different to somebody who would carry out prolonged and calculated bouts of abuse. Something didn't feel quite right to him. Olivia was his client, but he possessed a real interest in Eric. As he pulled up outside his house, he felt relieved to see Beth through the window, standing in the dining room, setting the table. She looked up and flashed Toby the smile which always

Breaking boundaries

made him feel safe. Though he smiled back, it was forced and masked something which was now more than simply a passing concern. He had remained professional, and reiterated boundaries with Olivia, but something told him this wasn't the end of it. He was worried he was already in deeper than he should be, a feeling which made him desperately uncomfortable. He knew he should speak to Richard, but had no idea where to start, considering Richard's word of warning to him previously. He felt isolated, out of control, like he was in a car careering towards a cliff edge with somebody else behind the wheel. His heart rate began to increase, and he felt a sudden panic. He quickly adjusted his posture and began some breathing techniques to try and calm himself down. After a couple of minutes, Toby was calm again, but whilst the physical symptoms had dissipated, emotionally he was still in panic mode. He had always had a metaphorical wall between his private and personal life, but he felt this had now been breached. No client had ever before contacted him outside of therapy and requested to meet with him. He had never taken a client to the hospital or met any of their family members, and had never bumped into a client at the gym. The more he thought about this, the more he began to question whether the previous unscheduled meetings had in fact been coincidental. The more questions he asked, the less this all made sense, and the more concerned he became that he was already out of his depth and sinking.

Breaking boundaries

14

Jack greeted him with a hug, a meaningful hug which signified how long it had been since the pair had seen each other. The last time they had made plans, Toby had never arrived, and though Jack had understood the situation, there remained an element of guilt on Toby's part for letting him down. Today was different, however. Toby wasn't the hired help; this was simply respite for him. He had felt himself slipping emotionally, and Beth had suggested he take some time out with Jack. He didn't judge and was about as laid back as you could get. Toby wasn't sure what he needed right now, but he was certain of what he didn't need, and that was drama and judgment. Jack signalled for Toby to come in, and they headed through the narrow hallway towards the lounge. The farmhouse was an old building with wooden beams and stone walls. It was picturesque, and about as far removed from modernity as you could get. There was a large stove in the kitchen, which heated the house except for the lounge area. It was this room Toby loved most due to it housing a beautiful wood burner. In the winter the fire would be roaring, with the bright flames lighting up the room, creating an ambience you couldn't help but be mesmerised by. Toby took a seat next to the fire as Jack went to get them both a drink. It was only the middle of the morning, but the warmth and sound of the fire could quite easily induce drowsiness within its guests. Jack returned

Breaking boundaries

with two glasses of Pepsi, and placed one on a small table in front of Toby, before taking a seat himself. He was a simple character, and that wasn't doing him any disservice. He dedicated much of his time to the farm, but when he wasn't immersed in farm work, he didn't take life too seriously. He was light-hearted and fun to be around, and that's what Toby needed right now. He didn't often engage in deep conversation, but he was wise, and although he would sometimes come across as a little docile, the occasional judgments of him lacking intelligence were ill-placed.

'How've you been?'

Toby took a sip of his drink and then exhaled a long breath, searching for a measured response. Jack had called him out of the blue and invited him over for the weekend, an offer Beth had actively encouraged him to take up. Toby hadn't told Beth about the call with Olivia, he hadn't told anyone. The fact he had not told Richard was significant. He knew he would have a succinct response, and he knew what that response would be. What worried Toby most, is why he feared that response. It wasn't because he worried about drawing Richard's ire, it was because he knew he couldn't comply. This realisation had impacted him profoundly as it confirmed his worst fears...he was in too deep, and he didn't know how to get out. He felt trapped, and cornered, but had no idea how to convey that to Jack, or whether indeed he wanted to. Jack picked

Breaking boundaries

up on Toby's hesitance and laughed heartily in an attempt to lighten the mood and relax Toby.

'That good huh? It's been a while my friend.'

'I'm sorry about that.'

'What are you sorry about?' Jack asked, still grinning.

'I know I let you down.'

'You didn't let me down; you had an emergency. Besides, I managed, I always do.'

Toby smiled and stared into his glass.

Jack continued. 'I came to see you in hospital you know.'

'I feel bad that I have no recollection,' Toby said glumly.

'You were unconscious, I wouldn't expect you to.'

They both laughed, which seemed to release some of the tension Toby had been feeling.

'Besides I had a good catch-up with Beth, well she lectured me on my lifestyle,' Jack said smiling.

'That sounds like Beth.'

'She never left your side you know.'

'I know. I'm so lucky to have her. I don't deserve her really.'

Toby's face dropped under a sudden wave of emotion.

'Toby, we've known each other for a long time, right?'

'You're my oldest friend Jack.'

'And you know I'm not known for my deep conversation?'

Breaking boundaries

Toby smiled. He admired the fact Jack was to the point, but he knew occasionally, he had a much more sensitive side to him. He also knew Jack had something to say.

'The day you were supposed to come to see me, Beth called looking for you.'

'She never said anything.'

'She was worried about you and asked me if I knew anything.'

Toby was about to speak, but Jack waved his hands at him, before continuing.

'Don't be angry with her, you know she's your biggest fan, Toby.'

'I'm sorry you were put in that position.'

'She was really concerned, and you know Beth is quite laid back, so for her to be worried…'

'I know,' Toby interrupted.

Knowing people were worried was one thing, but hearing about the impact he was having on loved ones only added to the guilt and regret he was already feeling.

'You've never talked about your work with me Toby.'

'There's a reason for that.'

'Except that once a few months back,' Jack continued.

Toby suddenly looked up, alarmed. He hadn't realised he had ever spoken to Jack about his work, a throwaway comment perhaps?

'You don't remember?' Jack said picking up on Toby's alarm.

Breaking boundaries

Toby shook his head slowly, mouth now slightly ajar in puzzlement. His heart began to beat faster, and he felt panicked that he couldn't remember something so recent. What if the crash had caused memory loss? What had he said? Had he breached confidentiality? How else would Jack know about a client, and why were he and Beth discussing this in the first place?

'You didn't say anything other than you had a challenging case which was unique in its own right.'

Toby's relief was palpable as Jack gave him a strange look.

'Did Beth put you up to inviting me here today?' he asked.

'She adores you, Toby. You're very lucky you have somebody who looks out for you the way she does.'

'So that's a yes then,' Toby replied, shaking his head.

'She's not wrong though, is she?'

Toby sat back in his chair and turned towards the fire.

'How do you manage to get anything done in the winter?'

'What do you mean?'

'Is there not a temptation to just close the curtains, shut out the outside world and sit in the company of this thing of beauty?' he said waving an arm in the direction of the log burner, which was now in full effect.

Breaking boundaries

'I'm not sure my animals would appreciate that,' Jack said grinning.

Toby smiled, but it was a tentative smile.

'What's troubling you, Toby?'

'What makes you think something is troubling me?'

'I've known you for a long time, and when you feel uncomfortable, you drop eye contact and change the subject.'

Toby turned towards Jack and smiled.

'And here was me thinking you were just a farmhand.'

'I have my moments.'

Toby said nothing at first, and just looked down at the floor. Then he leaned forward and cupped his chin with his hands, something he did in therapy when he was about to provide an insightful response to a client.

'Jack, I think I'm in trouble.'

'What sort of trouble?'

'I know it sounds strange, but I don't know. It's just a feeling I have that something isn't right and something bad is going to happen.'

'You're not often wrong with this stuff Toby.'

'That's what worries me. This is the one time I desperately want to be wrong.'

'Is this to do with that client you mentioned to me, you know the interesting case, the one Beth also talked about?'

Toby took a slow and deep breath, frantically searching for the right words, cautiously considering

Breaking boundaries

what he could and could not say. He didn't wish to add breaching confidentiality to his list of concerns right now. He kept it succinct.

'Yes.'

He felt relief. He hadn't spoken to anybody about the phone call, and it had felt like a dead weight, not only resting on him but pushing down on his chest, making it difficult to breathe. He wondered whether this was how his clients felt, the ones who would begin talking at pace, and show no signs of relenting until the session was about to expire. He used the analogy of releasing the valve on a pressure cooker when speaking about these types of sessions. This wasn't the first time he had likened his own experience to that of his clients, and the thought of being vulnerable terrified him. Here he was, about to talk to somebody else about his trepidation and concerns in hope of finding his own answers. This felt very much like therapy, and it made him feel uncomfortable. As he looked up, he saw Jack sitting back, hands placed on his knees waiting for him to elaborate, a technique Toby used with his clients. Another similarity.

'I have been practising for nearly sixteen years, and I have never crossed a boundary. I have worked with many clients, and of course, some cases have been challenging due to their very nature, but I have always found a way through, and remained in control.'

He paused and bowed his head, searching for the right words to continue.

Breaking boundaries

Jack, noting that he was struggling interjected. 'What's going on buddy?'

'I'm worried I may have been pulled into something I really shouldn't be a part of.'

'With a client?'

'Yes.'

'Have you crossed a boundary, Toby?'

'I don't know. I don't think so, but I have found myself in positions I have not wanted to be in, and this has led me to begin to question myself, my practice, my ethics.'

Jack looked at him, confused.

'I know you, Toby, if you ever crossed a boundary, there would be a damn good reason for it. You're as sincere as they come.'

'I used to think that too Jack.'

'What are you involved in here?'

'That's the problem. I don't actually know, but there's something, and I feel like I am slipping out of my depth.'

'Toby, you're not making any sense.'

Jack was right, he wasn't making any sense, but wasn't that the problem? He was trying desperately to make sense of a situation, which made little sense at all. How could he possibly explain this to somebody else, when he didn't understand it himself?

'There are guidelines and boundaries in my profession. You don't see friends as clients, and you don't see clients as friends.'

'And you've broken this?'

Breaking boundaries

Toby ignored Jack's question.

'Client communication should be almost entirely limited to therapy. The only exceptions to this are when appointments need to be confirmed or rescheduled. You don't liaise with clients outside of therapy. Do you know why Jack?'

'Because they're not your friends?'

'Precisely, but also you don't want them to develop an unhealthy attachment to you. It can detract from the work you're doing with them. If they start to see you as a friend, they stop seeing you as a therapist. If they start to tell you about everyday things, they stop telling you about the really important things, the things which are underlying. Most importantly, the moment their time with you becomes about catching up, it ceases to be about therapy. That then provides a moral and ethical dilemma. What are they paying you for?'

'I'd never looked at it like that before,' Jack said curiously.

'So, you understand we do everything we can to maintain those boundaries. We work incredibly hard to ensure our clients don't become reliant on us. We use therapy to empower them to explore and find their own answers. But why do you think we do this?'

'So, they can become self-reliant,' Jack replied hesitantly.

'Precisely. So, they are reliant only upon themselves because that way when they encounter challenges in the future, they are more equipped to

Breaking boundaries

process and deal with them, as opposed to finding a therapist to do it for them. We don't fix people, Jack, we simply provide a setting where they either fix themselves or realise they don't actually need fixing.'

This felt good. Toby was flowing now, feeling the weight lifting as he opened up to Jack. He knew this wasn't simply about the phone call. It was about the hospital visit, it was about the conversation in the gym, it was about the call she had made to him out of the blue before stopping by his practice to plead with him not to leave her as a client. He didn't doubt her sincerity, he didn't doubt her motives, he just doubted her methods. But then he knew desperation was an extremely powerful emotion and could influence people in very different ways. Toby paused and took a deep breath, before taking a sip of his drink. He looked over at Jack, who had remained transfixed. His face looked focused which wasn't something you could say too often about somebody who simply rolled with life and didn't take himself too seriously. As Toby placed his glass back on the table next to him, he began tapping his leg with his hand, looking up into the air, considering how to proceed, and where he was going with this.

'Sometimes you meet a client who piques your interest, I mean really piques your interest. Occasionally you can reflect upon the reason behind this and find your answer, but on other occasions, you remain in the dark. It's natural to sometimes think about clients and their situation

Breaking boundaries

away from therapy, it's inevitable when you consider the nature of the work, and how things can resonate with us all. But there's a boundary Jack, a metaphorical limit as to how often this should occur.'

He paused and inhaled slowly through his nose.

'And this client is having that effect on you?'

'It's worse than that. I'm pushed to distraction in moments I shouldn't be. There have been times when I have been with Beth, but my mind has been elsewhere.'

'Do you have feelings for this person?'

'That's the thing, I don't. There's no physical attraction to her, I don't fantasise about being with her, but there is just something there, and I'm worried.'

'That it could cost you your career? Your marriage?'

Toby gave Jack a serious look. Without dropping his gaze and with some hesitation he responded.

'My life.'

'Your life? What the hell have you got yourself into Toby?'

'Jack, what I'm about to tell you, I haven't told anybody else, and never can, but I need to get this out.'

Jack held his hand up to Toby as though signalling to stop what he was saying.

'Toby, this sounds serious. If you're only going to tell one person, are you sure you want it to be me?'

Toby gave a wry smile.

Breaking boundaries

'Believe it or not Jack, you're the perfect person to tell.'

Jack looked at him and said nothing but gestured for Toby to go ahead.

'Do you remember the day of the crash?'

'I remember it well, the conditions were treacherous.'

'The conditions didn't cause the crash. Of course, they didn't help, but they weren't responsible for me ending up unconscious in a ditch.'

Jack looked at him, and whilst the confused look on his face suggested he had questions, he remained silent.

'I was distracted Jack, I lost my concentration.'

'What distracted you?'

'Not what, but who.'

Jack's face suddenly dropped as the realisation of what he was about to hear hit him. He looked like a kid who had just solved a puzzle but was underwhelmed with the prize.

'Your client?' he said tentatively.

Toby nodded his head slowly, before placing it into his hands. This was the first time he had spoken so candidly about his situation. He felt relief, but now there was no disguising the fact that saying it out loud had suddenly made it real for him. He could no longer pretend he had this under control; because he now knew he didn't. Although he believed the decrease in clients each week was just what he needed, he knew deep down, this simply papered over the cracks.

Breaking boundaries

'I'm worried I'm spiralling out of control Jack. I paint on this smile for Beth and pretend I have it together, but I don't. It feels like a relationship I'm not able to end.'

'I'm not sure what to say, Toby. Who's that guy you talk to about your cases?'

Toby laughed. He admired Jack's blunt nature, one of the reasons he enjoyed spending time with him.

'You mean Richard, my clinical supervisor?'

'Yeah him. Can you talk to him about it?'

'Not anymore. We spoke about it previously, and he told me what I already knew. The problem isn't that I don't know what to do, it's that I seem unable to actually do it.'

'Toby, I don't know what to say. It feels like you just wasted your phone a friend.'

At this, they both broke out into laughter. Toby didn't need anybody to fix this for him, he didn't need anybody to offer up opinions on the situation. He needed somebody whom he could trust, somebody who would sit there and listen without passing judgment.

'No Jack, I got it spot on. Thank you.'

'I haven't done anything.'

'More than you think buddy.'

Toby got out of his chair and finished the remainder of his drink. He had been there little over an hour but had got what he needed. He came confused and desolate but was leaving with some clarity, a plan even. He thanked Jack for his time

Breaking boundaries

and company, and they shared a hug before Toby exited. As he opened the door of his car, Jack shouted after him.

'You take care Tobes, promise me you won't do anything stupid.'

Toby looked back at Jack, with a faint, tentative smile, but didn't reply. Then in an instant, he was gone.

Though the wind was biting, the sun had peeked through the clouds, and whilst this hadn't done much for the temperature, it had certainly made driving conditions much more pleasant. Toby adjusted his sunglasses and admired the rural surroundings as he drove cautiously through the narrow, winding roads. He felt a strange calmness after his conversation with Jack. Talking it through had made it real, however, and Toby could no longer hide the fact that the situation wouldn't simply resolve itself. His attention switched now to the inevitable question he would need to find an answer to. How should he proceed? He knew his only option was to wind down his therapy with Olivia, but this presented two immediate problems in his mind. Firstly, he was unsure how quickly he could draw her therapy to a close, and how he would convey this to her. There was now little doubt in his mind that Olivia had formed an unhealthy attachment to him, but what he hadn't yet figured out was what degree of reliance there was sat underneath this. Toby believed she saw him as more of her rescuer

Breaking boundaries

than her therapist, and that in itself raised ethical concerns. Secondly, and perhaps most importantly, there is how she would react to Toby discharging her. He feared she would see this as rejection, and was worried about what this might do to her. Part of him still believed, that whilst he had always acted with the best of intention, his actions had contributed to her attachment. He had, in reality, enabled her. He felt responsible and knew there would be a fallout from whatever happened next, it simply became about minimising the impact. As he pulled up outside the house, Beth opened the door and flung out her arms.

'You weren't long at Jack's.'

'I got just what I needed.'

'And what was that?'

'Perspective.'

'Do you feel better?' she asked hopefully.

'I feel more prepared.'

'That wasn't my question.'

'I know, but it's all I have right now,' he replied.

As she closed the door, Beth's smile waned, and a worried look appeared.

'Toby...'

'Beth please, I just want to have a peaceful afternoon, just the two of us,' he interrupted. This was as close to being assertive as Toby got, and she knew he was serious whenever his usual passive nature took a back seat. Beth had selected the movie, a comedy, which Toby felt had been done deliberately to remove the slight tension there

Breaking boundaries

had been between them since he had arrived home. It had worked, and they sat throughout the early parts of the afternoon cuddled together, laughing. For Toby, however, behind the laughter sat a great deal of anxiety, and as hard as he had tried, he had found himself periodically distracted. Beth hadn't noticed, well at least he didn't think she had. As the closing credits began, she stood up, tapped Toby playfully on the knee and headed to the kitchen to pour them both a drink.

'Wine shelf, spirit cabinet or the fridge?'

'Surprise me,' Toby replied.

'Maybe I won't bring anything then,' Beth said giggling.

'Or maybe you could also cut us both a piece of that lemon cake whilst you're there,' he shouted after her as she disappeared out of view. Beth reappeared and threw a cushion at him, before dashing into the kitchen to avoid any retaliation. Toby sat smiling for a moment. With his job, he cherished the lighter side of their marriage. Without him saying a word, Beth usually always knew when he needed to laugh. His thoughts were disrupted by his phone vibrating rigorously at his side. It wasn't a number he recognised but written below the number was a message in capital letters. As he read it the colour left his face and he felt sick.

'I CAN'T LIVE LIKE THIS ANYMORE. THANK YOU FOR GIVING ME THE COURAGE TO DO

Breaking boundaries

WHAT I HAVE TO DO. I'M SORRY FOR EVERYTHING. OLIVIA.'

For a brief moment, he was paralysed, physically and emotionally. She was going to kill herself. He thought about calling the police but realised he would be wasting precious time. She lived in a quiet rural area about fifteen minutes from him, but Toby felt if he drove quickly and traffic was kind to him, he could be there in less than that, quicker than the police anyway. He could call them from the car. A human life was at stake here and nothing else mattered to him right now. At this moment he had no regard for professional ethics or boundaries. She had messaged him for a reason, and Toby wondered whether it was a plea for help out of desperation, rather than a goodbye. Surely she wouldn't leave Tyler? Then a darker thought entered his mind. What if she planned to take him with her? What if she had justified to herself that this was the only way that he wouldn't suffer at the hands of his father? It would be the one act which would be irreversible and would do the most damage to Eric. It would be her ultimate revenge. He ran into the hallway as Beth was exiting the kitchen, walking towards him with a bottle of wine in one hand and two pieces of cake on a plate in the other. He stopped and stared at her with a concerned look on his face.

'I need to go.'

Breaking boundaries

'Go where?' Beth replied with a sudden panicked look of her own.

'I'll explain later, but this is urgent.'

'Toby, what's going on?' She was now raising her voice.

'Damn it, Olivia, you just need to trust me, I don't have time for this.'

As he rushed through the door, the last thing he noticed was Beth standing in the hallway, open-mouthed with a look of both bewilderment and disappointment on her face. He would have some explaining to do, but right now she couldn't be his priority. As he sped away from the house, he didn't feel a sense of guilt. He reasoned he was doing the right thing, and Beth would understand this, eventually. Beth would be fine; his marriage would be fine. Olivia on the other hand was anything but fine and right now needed him more than Beth.

Breaking boundaries

15

Toby screeched onto the main road, his clock was showing twenty-past three. He knew he needed to call the police, and quickly, but wasn't sure what he was supposed to say. The message could have had more than one meaning behind it, perhaps he had misinterpreted it. He was being led by a feeling in the pit of his stomach. Olivia had been cryptic. What if he had misconstrued what she was saying? What if the police felt he was wasting their time, and there was nothing of substance in the report, or worse still, they arrived, and everything was normal? If this was the case, he may actually be placing her in danger. Still, the feeling remained. He reasoned with himself that he would prefer to be wrong and do something, than right and do nothing. His mind was made up. Just as he went to dial, a call came through from Beth. As the call answered, he cursed the auto-answer facility he had activated in the car the previous week. He had thought it would be a convenient addition to his driving experience, but this felt decisively inconvenient.

'You called me Olivia,' came the voice from the other end of the phone.

'Huh?'

'Before you left, you called me Olivia.'

Toby sighed. He hadn't realised he had done this but had no reason to believe she was being disingenuous.

Breaking boundaries

'Beth, I'm sorry, I really can't talk, I have an emergency.'

'What the hell is going on with you Toby? What have you got yourself into?'

'I promise I'll explain, but I really can't talk right now.'

'Toby if you value me and our marriage, you'll tell me what's going on.'

There was a brief pause as he gathered his thoughts and considered how he could possibly explain the situation.

'I have reason to believe somebody I am working with may be in imminent danger.'

'Jesus, have you called the police?'

'I was about to, but if I can get there quickly and she is still alive, I believe I can save her.'

'Still alive?'

'Beth I have to go.'

'Toby, I'm...' but Toby had already hung up and was calling the police. The roads were quiet, and he estimated he was only around five minutes away.

'Which emergency services do you require?'

'Police, please,' he said hastily, yet politely.

There was a brief pause before Toby heard another voice on the end of the phone.

'You're through to the police, what's the nature of your emergency?'

'I have a concern for somebody's welfare.'

'Are you with them now?'

'No.'

Breaking boundaries

'Okay, I'll get somebody out there straight away. Do you have an address?'

Toby paused for a moment. He had learned of her address at the hospital when needing to provide details to the receptionist. His mind was actively racing, yet he drew a blank. He knew panic could have this effect on you but knowing that didn't help him. He would be able to drive there as he knew the area, but the name of the road eluded him.

'Sir, do you have an address for us?' the voice now sounding a little impatient.

'I can't remember, I just know where it is.'

Toby panicked and hung up, not knowing why, and having no clear idea of what he was going to do next. He would now need to call the police once he arrived at the scene, with the address at hand. He approached a set of traffic lights and cursed as they turned red just as he drew near to them. He looked out of the window and noticed a bus shelter to his left. A man and a woman sat close to each other. Toby couldn't figure out whether they were displaying romance, or simply huddled for warmth in the biting winter conditions. On the side of the shelter was a movie poster advertising a new cinema release, a psychological thriller called '*Slow Burn*'. The movie told the story of a woman who had been accused of murdering her husband after being subjected to years of traumatic abuse. Toby stared at the poster for a moment, unaware that the lights had now changed. He didn't move. He was hypnotised by the plotline, emboldened just yards

276

Breaking boundaries

away from him. The cars behind had now started to sound their horns, ultimately deciding to move around him perhaps thinking he was broken down. Some of the drivers gesticulated angrily, whilst others just shook their heads. All the while Toby sat there, staring out of the window, absorbed, thinking. Then suddenly it hit him, a realisation that made him feel cold, and drained the colour from his cheeks. He could feel his heart rate increase so significantly that he thought it was going to beat right out of his chest. He had developed a feeling in the pit of his stomach. Toby was experienced working with panic in others, but as a recipient, this was unfamiliar ground. He took a deep breath and composed himself. He was right. Olivia wouldn't leave Tyler, and she wouldn't take him with her either. She wasn't planning on going anywhere. Jesus, she wasn't going to kill herself. She was going to kill her husband. This changed things. Toby was out of his depth, but only a couple of minutes away. He hit the accelerator, unaware the lights had now changed to red, which drew angry responses from the cars coming from the other direction. He was oblivious to the fact he narrowly avoided a collision with a turning car, his mind clouded by what he was going to find when he arrived at the Stantons. Toby had broken into a sweat and was now physically shaking. The dial on the speedometer moved quickly, spurred on by the roar of the engine. The caution Toby had exercised whilst driving since the crash, was a distant memory as he sped through

Breaking boundaries

the roads and into the quiet village where Olivia's house was situated. The village was quaint, charming some would say, but there was no time to admire the surroundings. As he turned up the long track which led up to the house, Toby feared what he was going to find. Would Olivia really go through with this, or was it simply a cry for help? Was she looking for Toby to come to her rescue before she acted in a way that would change her life forever? But what if he had this wrong? What if she did in fact plan to end her own life? Toby was aware it wasn't inconceivable for people who felt controlled or trapped to see this as their only way out. Maybe Olivia was taking back control, all the while punishing Eric by forcing him to live with the effects for the rest of his life.

As he reached the top of the drive, he applied his brakes gently, not wishing to draw attention to himself. The first thing he noticed was there were two cars on the drive. He knew one of these to be Olivia's and assumed by the private registration plate, that the other belonged to her husband, Eric. As he jumped out of the car he was struck by the quietness. There was no commotion, in fact, it was eerily quiet. He approached the front door and then stopped. Should he knock? What if he burst into the house, and this had all been a misunderstanding? How would he explain who he was, his presence? But even if he knocked, what was he expecting to happen? He felt conflicted. He either breached

Breaking boundaries

confidentiality or risked wasting valuable time. Toby thought for a moment. He knew as soon as he entered the house, he would be faced with one of three things. Either Olivia would be dead, Eric would be dead, or he would have got there in time. Then he was suddenly alerted to a fourth option. What if there was no intention? What if this was about her getting his attention? The last time they had spoken, he had rejected her. She had asked him to go and meet her, and Toby had refused. His mind was awash with conflicting thoughts. Whatever the eventuality, his presence here meant that Olivia was no longer his client, and that made up his mind for him. He cupped his hands together over his forehead and peered through the window. No sign of life. He then moved to the lounge window which was a little more difficult to see through due to the curtain nets. He squinted but was unable to make any figures out. He darted around the back of the house to see if there were any signs of life. Nothing. The bedroom, he thought. It's more difficult to see into an upstairs room, more privacy. Now he had no option, he needed to enter the house. Adrenalin had taken over, and Toby had given no thought to the fact he had still not called the police. He was here alone. The house was detached and sat back on its own grounds, which meant privacy was not a problem. The nearest house, Toby estimated, was probably about a hundred yards away. He moved toward the back door and slowly turned the handle. It was unlocked. He took a deep breath and

Breaking boundaries

cautiously entered. There was an unnerving silence about the house, Toby strained to see if he could hear any sounds at all. He wasn't sure what he was expecting, but in his mind, whatever was awaiting him wouldn't be good, it was simply a matter of how bad it was. He had entered through the kitchen and as he absorbed the surroundings, he noticed it was tidy, undisturbed almost. The room was relatively dark but for the clock on the oven, illuminated in the corner of the room. Another thought crossed his mind, which stopped him in his tracks. What if Olivia intended to use Toby as a means to escape? What if he was the bait? An unexplained stranger in your house responding to a message sent by your wife. This would be enough to arouse suspicion in most people. Eric, however, had more than a casual relationship with anger, and in the heat of the moment, his actions would be unpredictable. How could he possibly begin to explain who he was and why he had entered the house on his own accord? Then there was confidentiality. The only way to avoid breaking this would be to lie. The thoughts overwhelmed him and the shaking which had subsided, now returned. His heart was racing, and he was frantically trying to gather his thoughts, but something here just didn't feel right. He still had time to leave, and call the police. Hell, why hadn't he called the police? Then it struck him. He wanted to fix her, he had assumed the role of her rescuer. That daydream where he had imagined bursting through the door and saving Olivia from Eric's

Breaking boundaries

clutches. What if this was it? Never had he doubted himself so much than in this moment. He couldn't turn back now, he was in too deep. On the other hand, what was he expecting to find? Realistically, what could he do? He wasn't a fighter. He felt trapped. The indecision left him momentarily catatonic. Right here, right now, he wasn't a therapist, he was simply a concerned individual trying to prevent something awful from happening. Prevent? Could he really prevent anything, or was he too late? He looked down at his watch. Surveying the room, his eyes were drawn to the clock on the oven. It felt like he had been here for a while, but in reality, it had only been a couple of minutes. He drew in a long and deep breath and slowly moved towards the archway, which would lead out of the kitchen, but where to, he had no idea. His heart was still racing and his desperate attempts to calm himself proved fruitless. Still, he was surrounded by silence, and whilst normally this may point to calmness, a serenity, when he put that into context and considered the marital background, her message, and the fact the door was left unlocked with both cars out front, this wasn't a good sign. His chain of thought was interrupted, but not by anything in the house, by a realisation. If this was a crime scene, he was not only disturbing it but now leaving traces of himself all over it. He panicked and wanted to run; run back to the safety and comfort of his life with Beth; run as far away from this house and Olivia Stanton as he possibly could. But

Breaking boundaries

something held him back. Part of this was a feeling he was already in too deep, and leaving the house now, if it was indeed a crime scene, could make him look suspicious. On the other hand, he may be able to prevent the situation from escalating, or better still, stop it from happening in the first place. He moved through the archway, which led to a corridor all the while increasing his anxiety levels with every step. In front of him was a room, door closed. To the left, a long stretch of hallway which he assumed opened out to another area of the house, possibly the living room. He cautiously made his way to the door and gently turned the handle to enter. The room was small, and nicely decorated, but not especially tidy. On the wall hung a family portrait. Toby thought they looked so happy, not a forced happy you sometimes see in a photograph, but a natural happy. On the floor lay several large plush toys, with boxes of various action figures and board games scattered around the room. Some had been placed on the shelf, others just lay unattended on the floor, in no specific order. This was Tyler's playroom. Tyler! Where was he? He again looked down at the floor. Was this how it normally looked or did it look like it had been left in a rush? He was overthinking, and it served him no benefit. The unease he had felt walking through somebody else's house, uninvited, began to fade as a deeper concern emerged. Olivia would surely never hurt her son, but what if he had seen something? What if she had acted in the heat of the moment and hurt

Breaking boundaries

him…or worse? He stopped and began to doubt the decision he had made. He looked back at the door through which he had just entered and thought how easy it would be for him to make his way back to the kitchen and out of the house. Nobody knew he was here. He could disappear into the darkness, and nobody would be wise to his presence. He turned and walked back towards the door. Suddenly he was startled by the smashing of glass followed by a door slamming. It had come from the other end of the house but was loud enough to get his attention. There was a door to the left. This door however was solid wood, so Toby didn't have the luxury of being able to see what awaited him on the other side. Now moving quickly and without hesitation, he burst through it, bracing himself as he did so. He gasped, loudly. His mind struggled to process what his eyes were seeing. His heart appeared to skip several beats, before increasing to what surely must have been a medically dangerous rate. He stared in disbelief, unable to speak, unable to move. He had heard some disturbing accounts of personal traumas but had only ever lived these vicariously through his clients. This was *his* trauma, *his* story, and he didn't like the narrative. He felt sick, not just mild nausea, but physically sick. Probably the shock. He battled to think rationally but found himself running off emotion and adrenaline. He tried to survey the room, but no matter how hard he tried, his eyes were unable to leave the image slowly coming into focus in front of him; an image which

Breaking boundaries

would be forever etched in his memory. He closed his eyes, partly to get perspective, and partly because he hoped if he did this for long enough, he would wake up in his own bed, in Beth's arms, safe from this nightmare. When he opened his eyes, an unkempt figure with clothes stained with blood was walking towards him, knife in hand. Toby noticed the large blade and thought if it had a thirst for blood, that thirst had been well and truly quenched. A sudden fear washed over him as the figure walked closer and stopped just inches away. The knife which had been raised was now facing down as he stood paralysed with fear, face to face with its owner. There was a silence, only disturbed by the hollow breathing of the person in front of him. He wanted to run but was struck by a sudden paralysis, the type you usually experience in dreams when you are desperately trying to flee something unthinkable. There was no logical feeling, this was panic, but in a strangely subdued form. Terror maybe. He felt trapped, powerless, and in fear for his life. He felt vulnerable, like whatever was about to happen was out of his hands. He felt completely out of control. As his breathing increased, and the sweat poured down his cheeks, the figure raised the hand containing the knife and moved towards Toby. He closed his eyes, wondering if he would ever open them again.

Breaking boundaries

16

Toby instinctively clasped his hand around the handle of the knife as it was thrust into his hands. He squirmed at the feel of the blood on his skin. As he had stepped back, he realised he had also got traces of blood on his clothes, and wondered how he would explain this to Beth. Right now, though, this was the least of his worries. He looked down at the knife for a moment, in shock, in disbelief. What had he walked into? He raised his head back up slowly and was finally able to find his voice to break the silence.

'What have you done?' he asked so slowly and purposefully that his bewilderment couldn't be hidden.

Ordinarily, he wouldn't have been so direct and accusatory, but with his knowledge of her situation as well as the evidence in front of him, he felt like there was little chance he had it wrong. Olivia stood, barely able to make eye contact. She looked in shock, and Toby thought he should console her, but all he could think about was whatever awaited him in the next room, did so missing a large amount of blood. There was no response.

'Olivia, what the hell has happened here?'

She was in shock, and Toby knew he would have to act fast to stand any chance of salvaging anything at all from this situation. He took both of her hands and crouched down in an attempt to appear less imposing.

Breaking boundaries

'Olivia, I need you to talk to me, who else is in the house? Are you okay?'

Olivia took several deep breaths and composed herself. She squeezed Toby's hands, finally, he had reached her, he thought.

'I don't know where to start,' she replied.

'Why don't you start by telling me whose blood that is on the knife.'

It was more of a directive than a question, but Toby felt there were more important things to worry about than whether or not he was being overly assertive. As he took in the surroundings, his eyes settled on the door Olivia had just come through. She noticed him staring and grabbed his wrist tightly as he made a stride towards it. Toby looked down at his hand and then moved his eyes slowly to meet Olivia's. He was confused and then it dawned on him. If he was right about her; if this was pre-meditated; if she really had carried out the unspeakable act it now looked increasingly likely she had done, then he was no longer in the company of a vulnerable woman, he was in the company of a murderer. If she was capable of killing somebody who had wronged her, and Toby didn't comply, his life was also now in danger. He had to tread carefully, for his freedom, for his life. At that moment he wondered whether he really knew anything about her. She had done this in therapy, switched from a despondent and vulnerable victim to a self-assured and confident woman. He noticed it the very first time she had done it and had always

Breaking boundaries

remained troubled about how she could produce two very contrasting personas in such a short space of time. He questioned who the real Olivia was; a vulnerable woman, subjected to heinous abuse over a prolonged period, who had finally snapped and fought back. He prevented his mind from considering the alternative. He didn't want to feel vulnerable, frightened, in fear of his life, but if she was a calculated, cold-blooded killer, this was an inevitability. She had loosened her grip on his wrist and then suddenly let go as she looked down, like she had been in a daze and had just become conscious again.

'Toby I'm sorry, I didn't mean to...' She stopped suddenly and looked directly into his eyes. They seemed vacant, she looked lost, helpless.

'I didn't mean to do it. He attacked me,' she continued.

'Your message...'

'I was going to leave him. I had packed a case, just enough for a few nights, whilst I figured out a long-term plan.'

She pointed to a suitcase in the corner of the room, which Toby had not noticed previously. Why would he?

Olivia continued.

'I should have left a long time ago, but I didn't have the courage. Talking to you gave me that courage Toby.'

Breaking boundaries

'When you said you couldn't take it anymore, and that you were sorry for everything, I was worried that...'

'That I might take my own life?'

'Yes.'

'I would never leave Tyler. I was saying sorry because I know I have put you in a difficult position on more than one occasion, a position I don't believe any therapist should ever be in with their clients. That's what I am sorry for, and Toby, I truly am.'

Toby didn't reply. He was still tentatively trying to piece things together, considering what to do next.

'He came home early and saw the suitcase,'

'Huh?' Toby had been interrupted from his thoughts and hadn't fully grasped what she had said.'

'He wasn't due home until later this evening. I was just grabbing a few things when he came back unexpectedly. I had left a note on the table, not that he deserved an explanation. I did it for Tyler. I don't want him growing up without a father figure, and mostly, he is good with him. Anyway, he came home early whilst I was still in the bedroom and stumbled upon the note. He raced up the stairs and began shouting at me aggressively, screaming that I wasn't taking his son away from him. He grabbed me by the throat and pinned me to the wall. I managed to kick out hard enough to force him to release me and ran down the stairs. He caught up to me and began a volley of physical abuse. I

Breaking boundaries

managed to wrestle free and ran towards the front door in the hallway. He raced after me and grabbed me by the hair pulling me back into the middle of the lounge. As I struggled to break free, that's when it happened.'

'What happened?'

'I stabbed him, well not intentionally I don't think.'

'You don't think?'

Toby was confused. How could you not know whether you had intentionally stabbed somebody or not?

'I didn't mean to kill him.'

'Where did the knife come from?'

'I had it hidden in my bedside drawers, for protection.'

'Protection against who?' Toby asked, before realising the answer was glaringly obvious.

'Him Toby, him.'

'Olivia we need to...'

Olivia continued as though Toby hadn't spoken. It felt like she was becoming manic, her speech getting faster and more panicked.

'I heard him come in and knew what would happen when he found the note. I wasn't going to let the son of a bitch hurt me anymore.'

Toby felt cold. Her story made sense on the surface, yet it didn't make any sense at all. Was there an intent or was it a case of self-defence? Did she fear for her life or deliberately extinguish his?

'We need to call the police.'

Breaking boundaries

Olivia took hold of Toby's hand, seemingly oblivious to his suggestion. It felt like he was having a separate conversation with her from the one she was having with him. He couldn't reach her.

'Olivia, I need you to stop for a moment, take a deep breath and look at me, okay?'

She held still and looked at him. She was shaking now, visibly in shock.

'If I walk through that door now, what am I going to find?'

She screwed her face up, like Toby had just insulted her, and pulled away from him, then she smiled at him.

'Karma,' she said coldly.

He now felt worried. Was this the grief talking, the shock perhaps?

'I'm sorry Toby, I'm not sure what I'm supposed to feel right now. I am struggling to feel anything aside from relief that these shackles which have bound me for so long, have suddenly been removed. I never wanted this though. I just wanted him to let me go, to let me have a life away from him. I would never have stopped him from being a dad, I wouldn't do that to Tyler, but I don't think he would have ever just let me go. I need you to understand that Toby. I'm not a bad person.'

'There may still be time,' shouted Toby heading for the door with Olivia chasing after him. If Eric was still alive, there may be an outside chance of Tyler not having to grow up without his father.

Breaking boundaries

He barged through the door and stopped in his tracks. There in the middle of the lounge floor lay a figure, face down and in a small pool of blood, which seemed to be coming from one side. The sight of it was too much for him, and Toby felt tears begin to run down his cheeks. He made his way over to the body slowly and leaned over to try and feel a pulse. He couldn't, but he was in shock and the adrenaline was running high, so couldn't be sure. He was now knelt and realised he was covered in blood. This looked bad, but right now Eric was his main concern. He would deal with any repercussions later. Eric may be an abuser, a rapist, a vicious individual, but he was also a father, a human being, and Toby didn't believe anybody deserved to die. He had vehemently condemned the death penalty during a rather heated debate at university. It stood for everything he opposed. He now found himself in a situation where he needed to placate Olivia. He needed to convince her to call the emergency services, to give Eric a chance of survival if of course there was any. He needed to convince her that he was worth saving, but considering Olivia believed she would never be free of him unless he was dead, this may prove difficult. He rose to his feet and stood contemplating for a moment. He couldn't see Eric's face, nor did he want to. His hair was hidden by a bobble hat, his hands the only things on display and not covered. Toby was hit by a sudden fear, and he felt his heart begin to race. He was having a panic attack. Olivia must have

Breaking boundaries

seen that same vacant look in him that he had witnessed in her moments earlier. So far, he was holding everything in, but barely. He felt like he had been struck with aphasia and paralysis at the same time as he struggled to speak or move. The room felt smaller, the walls appeared to be closing in on him. As each second ticked by, the situation became graver. Time was of the essence, but the link between his mind and body appeared to have been severed. What had been a large lounge area when he had entered it, now appeared to be nothing more than a box room. There was a symbolic parallel between the room constricting him metaphorically and the panic doing so physically. The room, now no bigger than a telephone box to him, began to spin. The ticking of the large clock on the wall, became louder with each movement, to the point where it felt like it would explode at any moment. He could now just about make out that he was in the room alone. He closed his eyes, desperately hoping when he opened them again, he would be somewhere else, anywhere but here. Still, he didn't move.

Breaking boundaries

17

The flashing lights illuminated the darkening skies. A while earlier the sirens had disturbed the tranquillity in what was ordinarily a quiet neighbourhood. It was a pleasant area, with only a few houses meticulously placed to offer privacy and seclusion. Yet for one house, that privacy would never be known again, and the incident that had taken place that afternoon would ensure the lives of its occupants would be changed forever. The Stantons had not stood out for any reason, remaining a relatively private family, but happy to exchange a courteous greeting with the neighbours. One ambulance had already left hastily, Toby assumed with Eric Stanton. Another was currently parked at the bottom of the track having assessed Toby and Olivia for any injuries. Olivia was being spoken to by two police officers. Toby noticed she was in handcuffs. He was standing with Mike Thomas, who wasn't only a Detective Inspector in the police, but also a friend of his and Beth's. Toby was in shock, and though he had blood on his hands, which he had managed to smear on his shirt, none of it belonged to him. He looked up at Mike, with a distant expression on his face. He tried to speak but only managed to mutter something incoherent.

'Are you injured?' Mike asked him.

Still, in a trance-like state, Toby looked down at his hands.

Breaking boundaries

'This, this, this isn't mine,' he stuttered.

'Toby, how the hell have you ended up at a crime scene with traces of blood on you which I can now only assume, belong to the victim?'

Toby started to become more lucid but still spoke softly and slowly.

'Am I being interviewed?'

'That was rhetorical, but there will need to be a formal interview, it's a very serious incident.'

Mike looked at Toby. It was overtly clear he was struggling both physically and emotionally.

'Call your solicitor, Toby.'

'Do I need one?'

'I would recommend you have legal counsel during a formal police interview. It's for your own protection.'

'I have nothing to hide.'

'Ultimately that's your decision, I can only advise. I would think very carefully about it if I were you.'

'Can I call Beth?'

Mike looked at Toby with a degree of sympathy but shook his head.

'You're facing a charge of attempted murder. At this moment in time, we're not able to allow you to have contact with anybody else. It's protocol, I'm sorry. You'll be able to speak to Beth after the interview.'

Toby sank to his knees, head in his hands. He felt deflated, but more so, frightened. He felt angry, not just with Olivia, but with himself for being drawn into her world. He thought about the formal interview he

Breaking boundaries

was about to endure and began to shake at the prospect of having to explain the situation. Hell, he couldn't even make sense of it, so how was he supposed to convince somebody else? He knew he'd have to explain Olivia, his relationship with her. Fuck, what was he even able to say? With everything that had happened that day, and all that had preceded it, Toby still felt the most trepidation around the prospect of explaining all of this to Beth. He had promised her several months back he knew what needed to be done. She had been at his bedside, and he had promised her. He had lied, but not intentionally. At the time he felt in control of the situation, but now, looking back, he realised he never was. Naturally, she would be angry, but that wasn't what bothered Toby. It was her inevitable disappointment in him he would struggle to handle. How would he ever be able to regain her trust after this? The last time he had spoken to her, he had cut her off sharply, moments after calling her by his client's name. He had never felt so ashamed, and the recurring thought that Beth deserved better, compounded his dejection.

'Toby I'm afraid I am going to have to place you in handcuffs.'

'What?' Toby shouted jumping back.

'It's just procedure, but a necessary one.'

Toby held out his hands, which he was unable to keep still. Mike attached the handcuffs and led him to the car. He cautioned him as they walked briskly, a young female officer accompanying them. He had

Breaking boundaries

never felt as afraid as he did right now, and whilst paramedics and police surrounded the scene, he felt alone. As the police car headed off to the station, Toby took a final glance behind him questioning every decision he had made, not just over the last twenty-four hours, but the last eight months or so. He closed his eyes in disbelief and felt a strong sense of anger, directed more towards himself than Olivia. Everything he had done had come from a good place, but this had come at a great cost to him. Even if by some miracle he was able to practice after this, his reputation would be significantly diminished, and any potential clients would likely avoid him. Who could blame them? This however wasn't his main concern. His main concern was losing his freedom, his marriage. He stood on the precipice of ruin. As the crime scene became a distant view through the rear window, he placed his head in his hands, feeling only numbness. The warm, salty tears began to trickle down his face and onto his palms. He had recovered from a car crash which had nearly cost him his life, but that physical healing seemed easy in comparison to what now lay ahead for him, psychologically.

As he entered the police station, Toby felt the muscles in his legs give way, and were it not for the fact he had Mike and another officer escorting him, he would have collapsed to the floor. He stood there in a daze as he was presented to the custody sergeant, who was having the details of the arrest

Breaking boundaries

explained to him. Toby was asked several questions, personal questions about his health, and whether he had any previous history of self-harm or suicide attempts. It all felt surreal, and humiliating, to such an extent he felt relief when he was eventually escorted to a cell. The cell was empty aside from a buzzer.

'There's no toilet.'

The only words which Toby could manage right now, spoken only faintly.

'We need to preserve forensic integrity, Toby. If you need the toilet, just press that buzzer on the wall. We cannot risk any potential evidence being contaminated. My colleague from the CSI department here is going to take your clothes and swab you.'

Toby looked at the individual, dressed in a full white body suit, which he assumed was to prevent any cross-contamination. His heart sank.

'Am I a suspect?'

'You were discovered at the scene of an attempted murder with the victim's blood on your hands and clothes. Naturally, we have some questions for you.'

Toby couldn't manage a response. Just hearing those words made the situation real. All he could now feel was panic.

'If your story checks out, the evidence will support this Toby. Are you sure you don't want a solicitor?'

'Don't they just tell you to sit there and say no comment?' Toby asked dismissively.

Breaking boundaries

'You've been watching too many police dramas.'

Mike raised a slight smile, but Toby knew the person in front of him now wasn't his friend, he was an officer of the law investigating a serious crime, in which Toby was a suspect.

'I have nothing to hide and will cooperate fully.'

'Suit yourself,' Mike replied, and Toby couldn't decide whether Mike commended him for his endeavour for honesty, or thought him a fool for declining legal representation. He sat there, unaware of time. There was nothing to do but think, and alone time with his thoughts wasn't something Toby relished right now. His clothes had been taken for evidence. Evidence? For what? His fingerprints were on the knife and the blood on his clothes was that of murder victim Eric Stanton. Then a cold and dark thought passed through his mind. What if Olivia blamed him? The evidence would support her story. What if rather than plead self-defence, she simply blamed Toby? Had this been her plan all along? Had she ever seen him as a therapist, or simply a scapegoat? He panicked and wondered whether now would be a good time to call a solicitor.

'Sir, the suspect about to be interviewed on the charge of attempted murder, he's a...' Mike stuttered, struggling to find the right words.

'He's what, Detective inspector?'

'I know him and his wife, on a personal level,' Mike Thomas disclosed.

'I'll get another officer to conduct the interview.'

Breaking boundaries

'Sir, with your permission, I'd like to be able to sit in.'

'Mike you're too close to the suspect, you need to take a step back.'

'He trusts me. I believe he'll feel more comfortable speaking freely with me present.'

The Chief Inspector was Clive Sutherland, who looked older than his fifty-five years. He had been in the force for thirty-five years, and it had taken its toll. Whilst they didn't always see eye to eye, Mike respected Clive, and always thought he was fair. He felt valued by him as an officer and as far as bosses went, believed he could have done much worse.

'You believe you can remain impartial?'

'Have I ever given you a reason to doubt my integrity before Sir?'

'You've never interviewed a friend before Mike.'

'In the interview room, he is a suspect, not a friend Sir.'

'What are your thoughts on this one?'

'You mean do I think he did it?'

'Yes.'

'Anybody is capable of committing a crime. If he did it, the evidence will lead straight to him.'

'That's not what I asked.'

Mike Thomas sighed and took a deep breath.

'It's not in his character, but I'll remain open-minded.'

'What about the other suspect, the woman?'

'She's been taken to another station, Bridgford, I believe.'

Breaking boundaries

The Chief Inspector screwed his face up and pondered for a moment, before exhaling a deep breath and turning towards the young sergeant standing next to them, who had remained an observer up until now.

'Sergeant Williams, are you happy to lead this? Detective Inspector Thomas will sit in'

'Yes sir,' she replied as she looked across at Mike with a tentative smile. A smile which said she didn't want to undermine her superior but was also mindful this was an opportunity to impress the Chief Inspector. She began to move off down the corridor towards the cell containing Toby. As Mike moved to walk with her, Clive Sutherland grabbed him gently by the arm.

'Mike, I don't need to remind you, guilty or innocent, this needs to be by the book. You got me?'

Mike nodded but didn't reply. He turned and headed down the corridor to join Nadia Williams, who was standing waiting patiently for him.

Toby was deep in thought when he was alerted to Mike and a second officer approaching his cell. The second officer, a young woman, had a friendly face, reassuring. Toby thought she had the kind of face which could catch people off guard, the kind which could convince people to confess without her opening her mouth. As he was led to the interview room, he noticed there was an eerie quietness to the station. There was a chill in the air, and he could

Breaking boundaries

feel the goose bumps on his flesh. He wondered if the station was actually cold, or whether the chill he was feeling was more of a psychological reaction to an extremely distressing situation.

The first thing Toby noticed about the room was that all the furniture seemed fixed to the floor. He assumed this was to eliminate any possibility of a prisoner using the furniture in an attack. The room seemed soulless. It was tiled from floor to ceiling, to add to the soundproofing no doubt, he thought. There was something odious in the air, which Toby couldn't place. He was afraid, very afraid. This was official, and he knew he wasn't there voluntarily, he was under arrest and a suspect in a very serious crime. He was seated at the side of the table furthest away from the door. Quick escape for the officers should things turn nasty he thought. Toby noticed in the corner there was a small black machine, which he guessed would record the interview. He felt better for having Mike there, but again reminded himself that Mike was an on-duty officer of the law, and this was a formal police interview. Mike stared down at his notes, twisting his pen through his fingers as he did so. Toby had never seen him in official capacity before; he'd never had a need to. The female officer rose to her feet and pressed the button on the black machine. The name 'Toby Reynolds' appeared. It all felt so official, and any thought of Toby being seen as somebody simply helping officers with their enquiries had disappeared. He was a suspect, there

Breaking boundaries

was no disguising this. The female officer drew breath and offered a slight smile, but Toby didn't feel its warmth.

'This interview is being conducted in an interview room at Oxton police station and is being recorded. It may be given in evidence if your case is brought to trial. At the conclusion of the interview, I will give you a notice explaining what will happen to the recording and how you can obtain a copy of it, should you wish to do so.'

Toby was now noticeably shaking. The officer paused for a moment upon realising this, perhaps fearing he was about to pass out. Toby drew a deep breath and sat up in his seat. Nadia Williams continued.

'The date is the 23rd November 2022 and the time by my watch is five fifteen in the evening. I am Sergeant 4295 Nadia Williams in the major crimes department based at Oxton police station. Also present is Detective Inspector 5408 Mike Thomas, also based at Oxton police station. Can you confirm your full name and date of birth please?'

'My name is Toby Nathan Reynolds, and I was born on the 19th January 1984.'

'And for the purpose of the recording, can you confirm there are no other persons present in this room?'

'I confirm there are no others present,' Toby said obligingly, making a concerted effort to show he was cooperating.

Breaking boundaries

'Before I begin asking questions, I must remind you that you do not have to say anything, but it may harm your defence if you do not mention, when questioned, something which you later rely on in court. Anything you do say, may be given in evidence.'

Toby looked confused, not by what Nadia Williams had said specifically, but by his very presence in this situation, in a police interview room, as a suspect.

'Let me break this down for you. You do not have to answer my questions, but if the case does go to trial, then a judge, a jury or a magistrate may draw their own inferences as to the reasoning behind your refusal to answer the questions I have asked today. As the interview is being recorded, it may be played in court for anyone present to hear. Do you understand?'

Toby could manage no words but was able to nod his head slowly. He was lost, but clinging to the vain hope that the truth wouldn't sound too insane to be believable. He wanted to believe both the evidence and the truth would exonerate him, but he couldn't help but think that he wouldn't be the first innocent person to be wrongfully convicted. He could feel the colour slowly draining out of his cheeks, and again wondered whether he had made the right decision to refuse legal counsel. He had hoped it would make them believe he had nothing to hide, but now he wasn't so sure.

Breaking boundaries

'Toby Reynolds, you have been arrested on suspicion of attempted murder. What can you tell me about the offence in question?'

'He's still alive?'

Toby was relieved but confused. The amount of blood. Surely, he couldn't have survived it, could he? Did Olivia know he had survived? Why was he still thinking of Olivia? He wanted to hate her, but knew she wasn't the reason he was here. He was the reason he was here. He had a choice, and whether that came from a desire to do the right thing or not, he had to live with the consequences. Blaming her wouldn't help him.

'He's critical, but there's a chance he could make it. You sound surprised. Why is this?'

'There seemed so much blood,' Toby stuttered.

Nadia Williams appeared to ignore Toby's answer, instead preparing her first question.

'Why don't we start from the beginning. Tell me in your words what you know about the offence in question.'

Mike was focused on Toby, his face expressionless. Toby wasn't sure whether he was being judged, or whether Mike was genuinely interested to see how somebody who he would consider a friend, had ended up a suspect in an attempted murder case.

'Earlier today I received a text message from Olivia Stanton. It was cryptic, but I thought she was in danger. I believed she was going to take her own life.'

Breaking boundaries

'For the purpose of the tape, Olivia Stanton is a co-suspect in the attempted murder of Eric Stanton,' Nadia Williams said with an officious tone.

Toby felt a shiver run down his spine, not at the mention of Olivia's name, but at the mention of his own in association with attempted murder. The reality set in again. Sergeant Williams continued.

'Did you call the police?'

'I knew she didn't live far away, so I set off with the thought I may be able to help her if I got there quick enough. I called the police from the car, but when the operative asked me for the address I just froze. I knew how to get there, but I couldn't remember the street. I panicked and just hung up.'

'What happened from there?'

'I arrived at the house and could see there were two cars in the drive. At that point I had begun to question things,' Toby answered.

'Question things?'

'Something didn't feel right. When I noticed both cars I wondered...'

He paused and looked down at his feet. His heart felt like it was about to beat right out of his chest.

'What did you wonder Toby?'

Toby slowly lifted his head and looked Nadia Williams directly in the eye.

'I wondered whether her life wasn't the one in danger,' he said slowly.

'What made you think that?' she asked with a look of genuine intrigue.

Breaking boundaries

'I saw a poster on a bus stop as I was stopped at a set of lights. Then I started to think of the circumstances, the things that had led up to this moment. I wanted to be wrong, but I think I knew deep down I wasn't.'

'When you talk about a set of circumstances, it would suggest that this wasn't something which was impulsive, rather something which had been building, yes?'

'I guess so,' Toby replied cautiously.

'You guess so?'

'I mean yes, I thought in that moment that something may have happened, and she may have snapped, fought back.'

'Fought back? Can you elaborate on that please?'

This was the moment Toby had been dreading since his arrest, the thing that had strangely dominated his thoughts whilst he was sat in the cold, empty cell awaiting the police interview. He wondered what he was able to disclose without breaching client confidentiality, and then something struck him. His career was most likely over. She was no longer a client, and he was being questioned for attempted murder. He knew he was innocent, but she could implicate him at any point. He still had a lot left to lose, and being reproached over his professional ethics was the least of his worries.

'The abuse, physical and sexual.'

Breaking boundaries

'Okay Toby, I think we need to take a step back here. How long have you known Olivia Stanton, and in what capacity?'

'She is…was, a client of mine. I have known her for around eight months.'

'May I ask the nature of your work?' 'I'm a psychotherapist,' Toby replied.

'I can appreciate this must be awkward for you, but let me remind you, you are being questioned in line with a very serious crime, attempted murder. It's in your best interest to tell us anything you know which may help us with our investigation.'

Toby swallowed hard at the very sound of those words. *Attempted murder.* He also felt increasingly anxious at the prospect of having to speak in detail about his work with a client. Aside from supervision, he had never discussed a client before. Regardless of the gravity of the situation, the prospect of doing so made him feel uncomfortable, like he was committing an act of betrayal. He wasn't though. He had tried to save Olivia from herself. He had tried to save Eric from Olivia. Now it was time for him to think about saving himself.

'Olivia came to me presenting as an abuse victim. Her marriage had contained emotional and unspeakable acts of physical and sexual abuse. She was just like any other client I had worked with, except…'

He broke off.

'Except what?' Nadia Williams probed.

Breaking boundaries

'Except she wasn't. She wasn't like any other client. On more than one occasion I thought about referring her to another therapist, but I always felt I was in control of the situation. Now looking back, I realise I never was.'

'Did you have reservations about her?'

'I was worried she may have had an issue with boundaries, but I never imagined it would end like this.'

'I'd like to get back to the afternoon in question. What happened when you arrived at the house Toby?'

'I looked for signs of life. I didn't want to just enter somebody's property. I walked around the back and found the door unlocked. I slowly made my way through a couple of rooms and found myself in the dining room. As I entered, I saw Olivia holding a knife with blood on her clothes. I will never forget that look in her eyes. She looked vacant, completely lost.'

'Then what happened?'

'She walked towards me, and I panicked. I thought she was going to stab me. I froze to the spot, but she just...'

His voice began to crack once again. Reliving events which were still so raw proved too much, and he began to sob. It was hard to understand what he was feeling, as there was so much. Anger, resentment, sadness, fear. Nadia Williams gave him a slight smile. Perhaps she didn't see him as a suspect after all he thought. Then he imagined how

Breaking boundaries

many guilty people had sat in this chair and protested their innocence.

'In your own time Toby.'

He continued.

'We walked through into the lounge area. I had to see it. I had to see what she had done. I hoped it wasn't too late, but when I looked at him, I really thought it was.'

'Did you touch Mr Stanton?'

'I don't know. Yes, I think so. I bent down to check his pulse but couldn't feel anything.'

'Why didn't you call the police at that point?'

'I guess I was afraid.'

'Of Olivia Stanton?'

'Maybe. I saw a different side to her. It was like the years of abuse had finally taken their toll.'

'Go on.'

'The whole situation petrified me. I panicked, my head was cloudy, but I knew I had to call the police, I just needed to find a way.'

'How did you manage to convince Olivia?' Nadia Williams asked probingly.

'I didn't. I made an excuse that I needed the bathroom. When I got out of earshot, that's when I made the call.'

He looked over at Mike, who was sat taking notes. His expression hadn't given anything away about what he was thinking. Toby again wondered if he believed him. He must have heard stories like this many times, people doing their utmost to convince him they are innocent. Why should he be

Breaking boundaries

any different? Mike and Nadia Williams exchanged a look, and Toby wondered what it meant. Did they think his story was a little too convincing? Did it sound contrived? She looked down at the notepad she had been scribbling on.

'Is the victim known to you?' she asked.

'Not personally. I only know what Olivia has disclosed about him. I've also seen some of his work…'

Toby stopped suddenly as Nadia Williams and Mike Thomas stared at each other in puzzlement for a moment.

'His work?'

'Burn marks and bruises.'

'She showed you these?'

'I saw the burn mark at the gym.'

'At the gym? Do you make a habit of seeing your clients outside of their sessions Toby?' Nadia Williams asked in a manner which made Toby feel like he was being judged.

He wasn't sure how to reply to this. He feared he was digging himself into a hole. This didn't reflect well on him.

'No, I bumped into her. I have a personal training session weekly. She just happened to be there one day when I was leaving.'

He realised how crazy this sounded. He was struggling to believe it himself, so what chance did he have of convincing them?

'What else did Olivia Stanton tell you about her husband?'

Breaking boundaries

'I'm not so sure how to answer this. What I mean is I don't feel comfortable answering that question,' Toby replied, feeling cornered.

'We're trying to get a picture of what happened, and the more information you are able to provide, the more chance we have of that picture being accurate,' Nadia Williams replied, somewhat frustratedly.

'I know she was worried about her son. She said she had called the police before, but they hadn't seemed interested. She presented as somebody who was genuinely living in fear.'

Mike leant over to Nadia Williams and whispered something in her ear. She looked confused but stood up from her chair and walked over to the tape recorder in the corner of the room. She pressed a button.

'Interview suspended at seventeen thirty-five.'

Toby felt consumed by a sudden dread. What had Mike whispered to her? Why was the interview suspended? Did they not believe him?

'We're just going to take a short break, Toby, we need to check a few things out,'

Mike Thomas moved towards the door and opened it, Nadia Williams followed him out. Toby sat there, staring around the room, wondering, just wondering. He thought of Beth, and what he would give to have her by his side right now. He could hear a very faint murmuring of a conversation outside, but the sound proofing was too good for him to make out any coherent sentences.

311

Breaking boundaries

Mike Thomas straightened his tie and composed himself, deep in thought.

'We need to check that original call he made to the police, make sure the timings work out. It would also be worth having another listen to the 999 call. There are several things he has said in there which we should be able to corroborate, if of course they are true.'

'What are you thinking sir?'

'Right now, I don't know, but I want to be thorough. He hasn't given much away about Olivia Stanton, I almost get the impression he's protecting her.'

'The bit about Eric Stanton's work you mean?'

Mike didn't answer Nadia Williams' question. He looked troubled.

'What do we know about Olivia Stanton? Does she have any previous?'

'I'm not sure, want me to take a look?' Nadia Williams asked.

'No, you listen to the 999 call again and let me know your thoughts. Can you also verify he is telling the truth about the original call? Can we get hold of that recording?'

'Of course, sir.'

'I'm going to go and see what we can find out about Olivia Stanton, and maybe get more of an insight into why he's protecting her.'

Nadia Williams nodded and headed off in the direction of the front desk, whilst Mike Thomas

Breaking boundaries

walked briskly towards his office. He wasn't in there long.

Breaking boundaries

18

Olivia Stanton sat opposite Sergeants Amanda Stone and Luke Meadows. They were both experienced officers with over twenty-five years of service between them. The suspect's face was expressionless, giving nothing away. This didn't seem to faze them, and their demeanour suggested they were confident they would soon discover whether this was a display of shock by an innocent person, or a quiet confidence of a guilty one. At this moment, she didn't know whether her husband would live or die, they didn't know whether this had been self-defence through provocation, or a premeditated attack. Olivia slowly lifted her head, her appearance understandably dishevelled, her manner subdued. Her clothes had been taken for processing; all other possessions had been bagged for evidence. The interview had been suspended after only a few minutes, when Olivia had reported feeling unwell, which had coincided with Sergeant Stone detailing the charge she was facing. Sergeant Meadows leaned over to resume the recording of the interview.

'The time is seventeen thirty and the interview with Olivia Stanton is now resuming after a short break. Presents are Sergeant Amanda Stone, Sergeant Luke Meadows, and suspect Olivia Stanton. Olivia, for the purpose of the recording, can you please confirm no other persons are present?'

Breaking boundaries

'No other persons are present,' she replied without even looking up.

'Also, for the purpose of the recording, can you please confirm you have been offered legal representation, but have declined it under your own free will?'

'I associate solicitors with people who are guilty or devious, of which I am neither,' Olivia Stanton replied confidently.

Amanda Stone looked down at her notes, exchanged a look with Luke Meadows, and began.

'Olivia, can you tell us what you know about the incident on the afternoon of the 23rd November at your residence, involving the stabbing of your husband, Eric Stanton?'

'I was at home packing when Eric returned early, unexpectedly. He had been away for a couple of days and wasn't due back until the following afternoon. I had the locks changed when he left, as originally, I was going to stay in the house and pack his things, you know leave them on the driveway.'

'What changed your mind?' asked Amanda Stone

'I realised as long as he knew where we were, he would never leave us alone. We would always be living in fear, and I couldn't have that life for my son. After years of abuse, I had finally built up the courage to leave him, to free us both from the emotional and physical abuse he would inflict upon us. I had packed one case which I had left in the dining room. The plan was to go and collect Tyler,

Breaking boundaries

that's our son, and get as far away from Eric as possible.'

'You said you had the locks changed. How did Eric enter the premises?'

'He threw a brick through the window and unlocked the door from the inside. It was the smashing of the glass that startled me. I guess he then saw the case in the dining room, because the next thing I knew he was charging up the stairs swearing at the top of his voice.'

'That must have been terribly frightening for you. What happened next?' Amanda Stone continued.

'He grabbed me and threw me to the floor, punching me in the face. I tried to run past him down the staircase, but he caught up to me and grabbed me by the hair. We wrestled, and I managed to kick out and run past him, but I couldn't get to the front door in time. He grabbed me again and threw me to the floor before jumping on top of me. We struggled and then...' She broke off as her head dropped and she began to cry. Amanda Stone gave her a sympathetic smile.

'In your own time Olivia,' she said

'I didn't mean to kill him. I just wanted to leave. If he'd just let me go....' She paused, and looked down into her lap, forlorn.

'Olivia, can you tell us how the knife came to be in your possession?'

'It was under the bed. After he had raped me for the second time, I made a decision it would never happen again. When I heard the window smash

Breaking boundaries

then the sound of him running up the stairs screaming at me, I quickly grabbed the knife and placed it in my pocket. I feared what he was about to do. You have to understand I couldn't go through that again, I just couldn't.'

'Can you tell us what happened next?'

'I don't remember much in the immediate aftermath. The next time I was lucid, I had wandered into the dining room after hearing a noise. That's when I saw Toby…Toby Reynolds.'

'The man at the scene with you?' Amanda Stone asked.

'Yes.'

'And how do you know Toby Reynolds?'

'He's my therapist.'

The two officers looked at each other perplexed. Olivia Stanton recognised this and quickly elaborated.

'He has helped me a lot in the last few months. I sent him a message to thank him, and I think he panicked.'

'What did that message say Olivia?' Amanda Stone asked, intrigued.

'That I couldn't continue the way I was, that I was sorry.'

'What did you mean by that, why were you apologising to your therapist?'

Amanda Stone's voice was becoming more inquisitive, and with every answer, Olivia was providing, the look of confusion on her face grew.

Breaking boundaries

'The intention was to finally leave, to run away. I was sorry because I haven't been the best client.'

'In what way?'

'Toby ended up in hospital with me after I collapsed in a supermarket. We weren't there together, it was just coincidence, but I felt bad he got pulled into that. He's the only one I have been able to trust, and he is the only one who has never judged me, apart from Tyler of course, but he's too young to be anything other than innocent.'

'Why would he drive to your property?'

'What do you mean?' Olivia replied a little defensively.

'You're telling us you intended to leave your husband and move away. You then sent a message to your therapist to let him know of your plans. Why would he then drive to your house? Either there's more to this relationship than you're telling us, or he thought the message meant something else. Which one is it?'

Olivia looked surprised and was unsure how to answer the question. She tried to speak, but nothing intelligible surfaced. Luke Meadows leant forward, cleared his throat and spoke for the first time in the interview.

'Olivia, we need to have a clear picture of what happened, and what we know is there was a third person at the crime scene. What we don't know is what they were doing there. So, again, why would a therapist rush to the house of one their clients?'

Breaking boundaries

'I don't know, perhaps you should ask him that,' Olivia said flippantly.

She was becoming agitated and looked pale. The officers could see this was taking its toll on her, but the questions were vital in allowing them to piece together the events leading up to the incident. They needed her to be physically and emotionally capable to endure the interview. At this moment in time, she was neither.

'I think we need to take another break Olivia, give you some time to try and clear your head a little. This must be difficult for you.'

Luke Meadows rose to his feet and pressed the button on the digital recorder. The dynamics in the room were fluctuating with the officers caught between seeing her as a victim and seeing her as a suspect. She wasn't easy to read.

'Interview suspended at seventeen fifty.'

The two officers exited the room leaving Olivia Stanton alone. Her face was ashen as they closed the door. This was the second time they had needed to suspend the interview since they had begun, and they were only really beginning to scratch the surface. They had only walked a few yards when Amanda Stone stopped and grabbed the arm of Luke Meadows.

'What's your feeling on this one?'

'I'm not sure. As she tells it, she is a victim of domestic abuse who has fought back.'

'You think there's more to it?'

Breaking boundaries

Luke Meadows paused for a moment and formed an expression which suggested he was unsure, unconvinced.

'The therapist. Something just doesn't fit there,' he replied.

'It's a strange one. As soon as we questioned her about it, she became defensive, her whole demeanour changed.'

'What are your thoughts, Amanda?'

'I think Toby Reynolds could hold the key to this investigation.'

'He's currently being questioned over at Oxton. We need to see what we can find out about him. Do we have anything from forensics yet?'

'I'll go check.'

'Thank you,' Luke Meadows replied as they headed off to her office. Meanwhile, Olivia Stanton sat in the interview room, staring vacantly at the wall. She hadn't moved since the officers had left, her face still giving no indication of whether she was an innocent victim or a cold-blooded killer.

Breaking boundaries

19

The door opened, startling Toby, and in walked Mike Thomas. Toby glanced behind him, but Mike was alone. He closed the door and took a seat in the chair opposite, but not before walking over to the machine to check it wasn't recording. Toby sensed a conversation off the record was about to take place yet felt more curious than anxious.

'Toby, you need to be honest with us.'

'I am, Mike...Detective Inspector Thomas,' he quickly corrected himself.

'Why are you protecting her?'

'What makes you think I'm protecting her?'

'Some of your answers have been bordering on justification. You have to understand that doesn't look good.'

'I'm trying to explain, not justify,' Toby replied hastily.

'It's our job to find the explanation Toby; it's yours to provide us with answers to our questions. If we want your opinion, we will be very clear in asking for it. You got me?'

Toby looked at Mike like a child who had just been told off. Had he really been trying to justify Olivia's actions? Was he protecting her? Then something else struck him. Mike's language, his tone. Did he have suspicions of Olivia. What did he know that Toby didn't?

'Toby, I'm not sure Olivia Stanton is who you think she is.'

Breaking boundaries

'I don't understand.'

Toby felt cold, he didn't like where this was heading.

'We deal in facts Toby, cold hard facts. We don't speculate in what we don't know, we create a narrative using what we do know. Does that make sense?'

Toby nodded, but it didn't make sense to him. None of this did. Olivia had been subjected to prolonged abuse and had defended herself. She was as much a victim as Eric Stanton, wasn't she? What was he missing here?

'Earlier, you stated Olivia Stanton had reported a case of domestic abuse to the police, is that correct?'

'Yes, that's what she told me, that she had feared for her son,' Toby replied.

'Did she tell you what the outcome of that report was?'

'No, I don't recall her going into detail.'

'The reason for that Toby is that report was never made, well perhaps not in the way you might think it was anyway.'

'I'm not sure I understand what you're saying.'

'I pulled up her file Toby. There is a record of a call for a domestic disturbance from that address, but she didn't make the call…Eric Stanton did.'

Toby stared in disbelief at Mike. Everything he had been made to believe in the last eight months was now unravelling before him. Her past, her present, had this all been lies? No, it couldn't have

Breaking boundaries

been, there would have been inconsistencies in her story, he would have undoubtedly noticed these over the months. She had been consistent; she had been convincing. Maybe Eric had called the police to cover up his own abusive behaviour. It wasn't unheard of, an abuser going to great lengths to convince others they were in fact a victim.

'He called the police?' Toby asked surprised.

'He called the police, but there's perhaps something else you should be aware of.'

'What's that?'

'The son wasn't at the property at the time.'

Toby bowed his head. He wasn't sure what to think. It felt like Mike believed his version of events, which should have caused him to feel relief, but he couldn't, not right now. He felt disconsolate around the legitimacy of what he was hearing. If Mike was right, it would likely mean Toby was exonerated, but it would also mean he had been deceived by a client, and had failed to recognise any warning signs, which would have likely occurred. On the other hand, if Mike was wrong, Toby wouldn't question his professional ability, however he risked losing his freedom. It wasn't that he was torn between the outcome, of course he wanted to walk out of here a free man. It was more when he suddenly realised that whatever the outcome, there were consequences.

'*Therapy is helping me to build the strength to do what I need to do,*' Toby muttered quietly as he

Breaking boundaries

slowly looked up at Mike, with a dazed look on his face.

'Toby?'

'What if that wasn't about leaving him? What if it was about killing him?'

Mike looked confused; Toby wasn't making any sense.

'She said therapy had given her the strength to do what she needed to do. Those were her words, I remember them distinctly. I thought she meant she was building her self-confidence to leave him, to live independently. What if that wasn't her intention? What if it was never about leaving him, but killing him? What if it wasn't impulsive self-defence, but pre-meditated?'

'Leave us to ask the questions Toby, your job is simply to tell us what you know. You have to be honest; we're not looking for your opinion. If you withhold any information, which we later discover, you're going to arouse suspicion, and you don't want that.'

'Why are you telling me this?' Toby asked him with a hint of suspicion.

Mike Thomas drew a deep breath, and looked Toby in the eye.

'Do you know how many police interviews I've been involved in?'

Toby shook his head slowly.

'More than I can remember. I've worked hundreds of cases from disturbing the peace to murder, from indecent exposure to rape. I know when somebody

Breaking boundaries

is bullshitting me. I have a good feel for what a criminal looks and sounds like, and you don't match that profile.'

'You believe I'm telling the truth?'

'I don't believe what you've told us has been disingenuous, but I do believe there are things you're holding back. I'm advising you now off the record, whatever loyalty you have to this woman, I'm almost certain it is not reciprocated.'

'What do you mean?'

'Let's just say Olivia Stanton may not be the person you believe her to be. She has a form for losing her temper.'

'Eric Stanton was the real victim of domestic abuse?'

'I've already told you more than I should, you need to think about yourself here, and not worry about her, because I'm pretty sure in her interview right now, she's not thinking of you.'

Toby closed his eyes, his head slumped. There was silence for a few moments, which was ultimately interrupted by the reappearance of Sergeant Nadia Williams. As she walked in, she looked surprised to see Mike Thomas alone with Toby, her suspicion not helped no doubt, by the palpable atmosphere in the room. As she walked back to her chair her eyes were moving slowly between her superior and the suspect. She placed her notepad meticulously on the desk in front of her and cleared her throat. She paused for a moment, but said nothing, before rising out of her seat and

Breaking boundaries

making a movement towards the digital recorder. As she pressed the button, she did so without taking her eyes off Toby or Mike.

'Interview resumed at eighteen forty-five. Presents are Detective inspector Mike Thomas, Sergeant Nadia Williams, and suspect Toby Reynolds. Toby can you please confirm no other persons are present in the interview room.'

Toby shook his head.

'Toby, we need verbal confirmation please,' she followed up with.

'Sorry, yes, I mean no, there are no other persons present in the room,' he stuttered. He was nervous and rattled by what Mike had just told him. He began to replay some of the sessions in his head, desperately trying to ascertain whether there had been anything he had missed, that could have given any indication Olivia Stanton was disingenuous at best, manipulative at worst. There was something he kept coming back to however. What did she have to gain by all of this? What was her end game? He didn't get the opportunity to think about these questions in any depth, swiftly brought back into the moment by Nadia Williams.

'We've listened to the original 999 call, and it does appear to corroborate your story. We've also listened to the call when you reported the stabbing of Mr Stanton. Toby, we need to revisit a few things please, just so we can get a clearer understanding of what happened.'

Breaking boundaries

Toby was looking down at the floor, emptily. The reality of the situation was now beginning to set in, not what he thought the reality was, but what it actually was. He wondered how many times he would need to relive the event before they believed his innocence. He again thought about Olivia, but quickly brought his mind back to this own situation. Mike's message had been clear, Toby couldn't risk jeopardising his own freedom, or even obstructing a criminal investigation due to misplaced loyalty. He had always lived by the professional mantra of believing your clients, but this didn't extend to criminal investigations. He wasn't the police, it wasn't his job to find the answers, speculation had no place here. His case notes were factual, not conjecture, he knew he needed to adopt that same stance now. He sat up, straightened his shoulders and took a deep breath.

'I'm ready.'

'Can you begin by telling us your movements on November 23rd 2022?'

'I had been with a friend in the morning, until just after lunch. I got home to Beth, that's my wife, in the early afternoon. Then I received the text message from Olivia, and the rest you know.'

'We're going to need the name of that friend please.'

'Sure, his name is Jack Newby.'

Nadia Williams pushed a piece of blank paper along with a pen across the desk to Toby.

Breaking boundaries

'Can you write down the contact details for Mr Newby please?' she asked.

Toby took the pen and paper and wrote down Jack's details before sliding them back across the desk.

'What time did you receive the message from Olivia Stanton? Please keep in mind before you answer, we have your phone in our possession and it will be very easy to check the validity of your answer.'

Her voice had sounded stern, and Toby worried about the sudden change. It wasn't only him who picked up on this, as Mike Thomas glanced across at her, with a less than warm look on his face. Toby had cooperated; he hadn't tried to hide anything. Was she angry at finding him and Mike speaking alone, without her present? Did she feel excluded? Had she felt undermined, and was now trying to prove a point by displaying a level of authority? Whatever the reasoning, her reassuring tone had now disappeared. Toby began to bite his fingernails, something he hadn't done in a long time. This was his go to in times of extreme anxiety and discomfort.

'It was around three fifteen in the afternoon, I think. I know I was on the road a few minutes later.'

'What happened then,' came the next question, curt and abrupt. For a moment he felt angry, confused as to why he was being asked the same questions again, when he had already been over this. Inside he was screaming… '*I already fucking told you this, why are you not listening to me? You*

Breaking boundaries

have a notepad right there in front of you and it's been there the whole time. Have you not written anything down? Why are you making me relive this?' In reality, his response was much less inflammatory.

'I thought I could help her...'

'I'm not asking for your thoughts Toby, just the facts.'

Toby looked surprised. Had she reeled him in by presenting as approachable, to now hit him with something much harsher? His moment of optimism after speaking with Mike alone had all but dissipated, replaced with a genuine fear, a resignation that Nadia Williams believed him to be guilty and was going to go all out to prove it.

'I'm sorry. I got into my car and drove to her house,' he qualified.

'Tell us again what you found when you arrived there.'

'I looked through the front window and couldn't see anything.'

'You didn't think of knocking?'

'I didn't know what to do, I was in a panic. If I had it wrong, if I knocked and Eric answered, how would I explain who I was, or what I was doing there?'

'What happened then?'

'I moved around the back to see if I could see anything and noticed the door was unlocked. I couldn't hear anything, so I crept in slowly through the kitchen, through what looked like a child's

Breaking boundaries

playroom, and then into the dining room. That's where I saw Olivia.'

'Was she already in the room?'

'No, I was looking around and she startled me. I guess she must have heard me.'

'You told us earlier you noticed her as soon as you entered the dining room. Now you're saying, she entered the room after you. Which one is it?'

Toby looked shocked. He hadn't intentionally lied and knew recollection could be affected in traumatic circumstances. He stuttered, but Nadia Williams didn't give him the opportunity to answer.

'What did she say when she saw you?'

He composed himself, still wondering why his own story had been inconsistent.

'She didn't say anything, well not at first. It was like she hadn't even noticed I was there. She just walked towards me with a blank look. I could see she was holding a knife and that it had blood on it, her top was also stained. She was in shock. Even after she placed the knife in my hands, she still remained silent.'

'When did you first see Eric Stanton?'

'I asked her what had happened, if there was anybody else in the house. That's when she finally spoke. All she said was that she hadn't meant to do it, that he'd attacked her.'

Nadia Williams took a sip of water and looked down at her notes. Toby realised he hadn't answered her question at all. He was rambling now,

Breaking boundaries

and he was sure both the officers sat opposite had recognised this. He quickly continued.

'I'm sorry, I, I…' he stuttered, before again looking down into his lap and pausing for a moment. He knew he would have to answer the question but needed to calm himself first. He took several deep breaths and then steadied himself before continuing.

'I peered over her shoulder at the door she had entered the room through. I knew something terrible lay behind it and started to move in its direction, but she grabbed my wrist. Eventually she let go and I walked through the door. The image I was met with will stay with me for the rest of my life.'

Toby lowered his head into his hands, tears began to flow down his face, not for the first time since his arrest. He felt defeated and knew even if he walked out of here a free man, he would be a prisoner to the trauma for many years to come.

'In your own time Toby. What did you see?'

Toby looked up and wiped his eyes with his hand.

'There was a body in the middle of the room, face down, motionless on the floor. His face was covered, and though I had never seen Eric Stanton before, I presumed it to be him.'

Nadia Williams sat upright and buttoned up her blazer. She stared intently at Toby, which did nothing to shake the intense bout of anxiety he was feeling.

'Here's where I'm having trouble Toby. Perhaps you can help me out. You receive a text message

Breaking boundaries

from a person whose life you believe to be in danger. You call the police but are not entirely sure where you are going so you hang up. You arrive at the address and clearly have concerns, yet you don't call the police. You then entered the house and were faced with somebody wielding a knife, covered in blood, yet you don't call the police. She then relinquished the knife, unarming herself and you both stood over the stab victim. Still, you remained in the house, still you decided against calling the police. Why is it Toby, given the opportunities you had to flee the scene and call us, you chose not to do so? Why did you delay making that call, therefore wasting valuable time for Eric Stanton who lay there critically injured? What am I not understanding here?'

Nadia Williams had become increasingly more animated, which culminated in her banging the desk. Toby flinched in surprise and recoiled at her sudden movement. He looked to Mike, but realised there was no ally in that direction. He was on his own and suddenly regretted not having a solicitor, somebody on his side. He'd been naïve, but with the best of intentions. He had thought it would be a simple matter of explaining the situation and being released. Before he had left the house, he had thought this was self-defence, thought Eric Stanton had been a perpetrator, an abuser. Mike's disclosure had now caused him to question everything he thought he knew about Olivia Stanton. Toby knew Olivia had lied to him, but right now, he

Breaking boundaries

wasn't sure just how deep those lies ran. Had she omitted certain things in therapy, embellished others? Or had her whole persona been an act? He was on his own in here and found himself wondering what Olivia's interview looked like. Mike had been right. His only loyalty should be to himself, to Beth and his family. Nadia Williams was now staring at him expectantly. Toby closed his eyes for a moment to try and find some composure. He felt angry that his integrity was being questioned; angry that he had acted with good intentions and it had blown up in his face; angry that at every point he had tried to make a measured decision as to what the right and safe thing to do was; angry again at himself for getting involved in this and not seeing it coming, or seeing it coming and not being able to do anything about it. He wasn't sure which one. He opened his eyes and glanced between Mike Thomas and Nadia Williams. It was time to lay everything bare.

'As a person, I've always distinguished between doing things right and doing the right thing, in my mind of course,' he began.

Nadia Williams and Mike Thomas exchanged a look which was one of intrigue. Toby thought they were perhaps both wondering where he was going with this, but he knew, and soon enough, they would too.

'I don't always get things right. What I mean by that is sometimes I make bad decisions, but never

Breaking boundaries

deliberately so. I always want to do the right thing, it's who I am as a person.'

'What are you telling us Toby?' Mike Thomas asked.

'I think I made some bad decisions today, but every decision I made was done so trying to do the right thing. I know how this looks, but you have to believe I went to the house to try and save a life, not take one.'

'Toby when we arrived and you exited the house, Olivia Stanton looked angry and surprised. Why was this?' Mike Thomas asked him.

'She hadn't wanted me to call the police. She was worried the police wouldn't believe her. She said she needed time to process things, to get her story straight.'

'So, she didn't want you to call the police after she had stabbed somebody in self-defence. Did this not arouse suspicion in your mind?'

'I thought she was desperate, but I had no intention of covering anything up. I just had to figure out a way to get on my own and then try to distract her for long enough for the police to arrive.'

'Because you thought there was more to this than she was telling you?'

'Perhaps. Like I say, she wasn't thinking straight.'

'Toby, right now you could be charged as a co-conspirator. I'd think very carefully about where your loyalties lie here,' Nadia Williams interjected, now with a more relaxed tone.

Breaking boundaries

'There isn't anything more I can tell you, I'm sorry. I didn't see the incident, I only arrived on the scene in the aftermath. I'm not an eyewitness, and you must believe, neither am I a co-conspirator.'

There was a knock at the door. Sergeant Nadia Williams rose out of her seat and moved towards the digital recorder.

'Interview suspended at twenty twenty-eight. She walked toward the door and opened it. Toby could hear the voice of a man, but it was only a whisper. She closed the door and the conversation continued. After a few seconds, the door opened slightly and she gestured for Mike Thomas to join her outside. Toby grew increasingly more concerned about the situation he found himself in, wondering what was happening out of earshot. Had some evidence been found, somehow linking him to the crime? His stomach was consumed with so much tension, no position provided any relief. Now all he could hear was the ticking of the clock. It felt late, like he had been there all day, but in reality, it was only eight thirty and he had been here no more than a few hours. He desperately wanted this to be over. He wanted Beth, he needed Beth. The door swung open, and Mike Thomas and Nadia Williams stood staring at Toby from the doorway. For a moment, all that could be heard was the faint sound of a telephone ringing in the distance.

Breaking boundaries

20

The time was now just after seven in the evening and Sergeants Amanda Stone and Luke Meadows were seated, with Olivia Stanton sat opposite. Formalities completed, Amanda Stone spoke first.

'Olivia, can you tell us what happened once you realised Toby Reynolds was in your house?' Amanda Stone began.

'It's all a bit of a haze, but I remember just giving him the knife. I didn't want it in my hands, I didn't want it anywhere near me. I was in shock, I couldn't believe what had happened.'

'What did Toby Reynolds say when you handed him the knife?'

'He asked me what had happened. I feel really sorry for him, walking into a crime scene like that. He didn't deserve to see it.'

'And what did he see Olivia?'

'We walked into the lounge area, where Eric was on the floor. At this point his face was covered. I was glad really,' Olivia replied.

'Did either of you attempt to move him, or make any contact with him at all?'

'I think Toby grabbed his hand to feel for a pulse, but that was it.'

'Then what happened?'

'We called the police and left the house.'

Luke Meadows had been busy writing notes during the questioning. He flipped the page back,

Breaking boundaries

appearing to circle something and looked Olivia directly in the eyes.

'There are a few things we just need some clarity on Olivia if that's ok?' he said.

'I'm happy to answer any questions, but I don't see what else I could add. I've told you every detail about the attack.'

'There's quite a gap between when you said the attack took place, and when you called the police. Why is this?'

'As I said, I was in a state of shock, Toby was comforting me. I thought it was too late, I thought Eric was already gone. When I managed to gain some perspective, I called.'

'But you didn't, did you Olivia? We have a recording of the call. Toby Reynolds made it, not you. What's really interesting about that call is how quiet his voice was, barely more than a whisper. It was almost like he was making a concerted effort not to be overheard. Why do you think that was?' Luke Meadows asked suspiciously.

Olivia looked startled, inconsistencies in her story were starting to appear, and it hadn't gone unnoticed by the two officers.

'I didn't mean I literally made the call. I asked Toby to do it, as I was too shaken and incoherent to speak to anybody.'

Amanda Stone wrote something down on a piece of paper and slid it across the table in the direction of her colleague. He looked down, then across at her, before continuing.

Breaking boundaries

'Olivia, when you exited the house and realised the police were in attendance, it was reported that you looked startled, then began shouting at Toby Reynolds. Why was that?'

'It wasn't the fact the police were there, it was the number of flashing lights and officers which shocked me. It made it real.'

'Why were you shouting at Toby Reynolds?'

'As we were leaving the house, Toby had made a comment about Eric. I took exception to it and that's what the officer observed.'

'Would you care to tell us what he said?' Amanda Stone asked inquisitively.

'I'm not sure if I should say this, as I don't want him to get into trouble.'

'Why would you get him into trouble?'

'I don't know. I don't want you to think badly of him. It felt out of character and not what I would expect from somebody in his position.'

'Olivia, what did Toby Reynolds say to you as you exited the house?' Amanda Stone repeated.

'He said Eric had the face of an abuser, that he got what he deserved and Tyler would be better off without him. He said the guilt would be outweighed by the relief. Eric was still the father of my son, and whilst I wanted him away from us, I didn't want him dead. Do you understand what I mean?'

Neither officer answered her question. Their questioning was going somewhere, and they weren't about to be knocked off stride.

Breaking boundaries

'Olivia, did Toby Reynolds ever meet your husband?'

'Not to my knowledge.'

'And when he arrived on the scene you said Eric was positioned on his front with his face covered. Is that correct?'

'Yes, I believe so.'

'You also said neither of you moved Eric, the only contact being Toby grabbing his wrist to feel for a pulse, is that right?'

'Yes. Why are you asking me this again?'

'If Toby Reynolds had never met your husband, and when he arrived on the scene your husband was positioned in a manner which concealed his face, how would Toby know what he looked like to make such a comment?'

'Perhaps he saw a photograph on his way through my house. There are plenty on the walls,' Olivia replied calmly.

'Or perhaps you weren't angry at something he said, but something he did,' Amanda Stone interjected forcefully.

'Like what?' Olivia asked in an innocent manner.

'Like calling the police perhaps.'

Olivia sat there stunned. The brief moment of arrogance had been displaced by disbelief. Luke Meadows straightened the notes in front of him and addressed Olivia.

'We've had the chance to speak with the team at the scene, as well as the medical professionals treating your husband. Yes, he is still alive by the

Breaking boundaries

way, and whilst he is not out of danger just yet, we have reason to be optimistic that he will make a full recovery. We will be very interested to hear his version of events. You see a testimony is always accompanied by evidence. If a suspect is telling the truth, the evidence will tell us; if a suspect is lying, the evidence will tell us. Allow me to explain to you what the evidence has told us so far.'

Olivia shuffled in her chair. One look at her eyes and her body language told you she was fearful of what she was about to hear. Luke Meadows took a sip of his coffee and sat back in his chair. Amanda Stone rose to her feet, leaning forward with her hands placed on the table, looking Olivia Stanton directly in the eyes.

'You described being subjected to a brutal attack which involved being hit, jumped on, and thrown to the floor, yet you have no marks on you. No defensive wounds at all. You told us you wrestled near the front door, an area which was covered in broken glass, yet neither of you have any injuries consistent with this. This would suggest the window was either broken after your husband lay unconscious on the floor, or that struggle didn't happen the way you are telling us. Either way, your claim is not supported by the evidence. You stated you had been living in fear, and kept a knife close by for protection, yet you were careless enough to leave your back door unlocked allowing an individual to walk right into your house undetected. It's almost like you were expecting somebody.'

Breaking boundaries

Olivia held her head in her hands, visibly distressed at what was unfolding before her. They didn't believe her, the evidence didn't support her story, but Amanda Stone wasn't finished there.

'Olivia, you told us you've had the locks changed recently, with the sole purpose of preventing your husband from re-entering the house. We now know this to be untrue. In addition to this, the medical team found lacerations on your husband's hands. What do you think that tells us?'

Olivia just shrugged her shoulders slowly without speaking.

'It tells us he was defending himself from an attack. Your husband had five stab wounds. That's not self-defence, it's a pre-meditated attack, fuelled by anger. The evidence doesn't lie Olivia, and it's piling up against you. Nothing you have told us has been substantiated. You may have hoped murdering your husband would release the shackles, but in actuality your lies have tightened them.'

She couldn't speak, her defence unravelling before her very eyes. There was no escape now, and Amanda Stone still wasn't finished.

'When somebody attempts to cover up a crime, you always find it's the small details which give them away, things you wouldn't even think to consider, like CCTV footage for example.'

'We don't have CCTV.'

Breaking boundaries

'No, but the house that faces the bottom of your drive does, and we managed to pull the footage from it. What do you think it showed?'

Olivia again shrugged her shoulders.

'It showed your husband's car turning onto your drive yesterday lunchtime, where it has remained since. We know he didn't return unexpectedly this afternoon as you described. He was already in the house. What we would like to know is why you lied to us?'

She said nothing, she wasn't going to give them the satisfaction, not right now. The inconsistencies in her story had been exposed. Amanda Stone looked at her, a slight sympathetic smile on her face.

'We are piecing together the what, we already know the how, but what we're struggling with is the why. What was your motive for trying to murder your husband? We know this wasn't self-defence.'

Still Olivia Stanton sat silently. Now sloped in her chair, arms folded, she looked a shadow of the confident figure she portrayed only hours ago. She had only recently celebrated her thirty-fourth birthday, but on the wrong side of a formal interview, she suddenly looked much older.

'Olivia, don't you have anything you'd like to say?' asked Luke Meadows. Olivia Stanton sat up straight in her chair. A grin slowly spread across her face. She leaned forward glancing firstly at Luke Meadows, then Amanda Stone, before sitting back

Breaking boundaries

on her seat and crossing her legs. She briefly looked up at the clock on the wall.

'I think I'll have that solicitor now.'

Breaking boundaries

21

Nadia Williams was the first to take her seat, followed by Mike Thomas, who seemed to linger in the doorway for a while. He looked preoccupied and his expression gave nothing away about his mood or his thinking. As he finally took his seat he looked over at Nadia Williams, before focusing on Toby.

'Olivia Stanton has confessed Toby. There is nothing that implicates you. Your story checked out, you're a free man.'

'I don't understand. You say she confessed? Confessed to what?'

'Attempted murder.'

Toby started to sway, but Mike Thomas' quick thinking meant he caught him before he fell to the floor.

'Get me a glass of water,' he bellowed at Nadia Williams, before lying Toby down carefully on his side. He was conscious and hadn't passed out, but he was in shock and needed a moment to compose himself. Toby felt weak, physically and emotionally. He felt like he should have been elated that he had been exonerated, but he knew his ordeal was far from over. There were so many questions, but he had no idea where to begin. He gestured to sit up, speaking no words at first. With the assistance of the two officers, he positioned himself back on his chair.

'Are you ok?' Nadia Williams asked him with an aura of concern. Her demeanour had changed in an

Breaking boundaries

instant. Now he was no longer a suspect, the edge in her voice had disappeared and she seemed much more sympathetic.

'I'm just struggling to understand all this I guess.'

'I'm not going to ask the nature of your sessions with her, I don't need to. The shock on your face tells me everything I need to know,' she said calmly.

'I'm not sure what you mean.'

'I mean, it's now clear to us you didn't see this coming.'

'If I'd have had any inclination somebody was at risk, my personal and professional ethics would have seen me report it immediately.'

Mike Thomas straightened his jacket and clasped his hands together, resting his chin on them in the process.

'But you did Toby, and you foolishly decided to try and play the hero. Had she not confessed, that decision could have led to an outcome so much worse for you. In future, I would think very carefully about your role with your clients,' he warned.

'My career as a Psychotherapist was over the moment I got into my car this afternoon. I just didn't realise it at the time.'

'I'm sorry to hear that Toby. You clearly care about your clients, perhaps a little too much,' Nadia Williams responded.

'Toby, is there anybody you would like to call?'

'Why did she do it?' Toby asked seemingly oblivious to the question.

'Toby, did you hear what I said?'

Breaking boundaries

'Yes, but I need to know why she did it?'

'That's not something we are at liberty to share with you Toby. It's also not something we have a clear answer to right now. Why is it important to you anyway?'

'What if I've been manipulated?'

'In what way?' Mike Thomas asked with genuine curiosity.

There was no cohesion, Toby was simply verbalising whatever entered his head. He himself had no idea where this was leading, so what chance did they have?

'What I'm trying to understand is, was it down to chance that I ended up at a crime scene today, or was that her intention all along? Was I ever her therapist, or simply her alibi?'

'Toby, we don't have the details right now, we have just been advised by the investigating officer at the station where Olivia is being questioned, that she has confessed, and hasn't implicated you or anybody else. We will get to know the details in time, but the important thing right now is that you're no longer a suspect.'

'She was so convincing.'

He was talking out loud, not specifically to them, but still their interest was piqued.

'I'm sorry?' Nadia Williams asked.

'At the crime scene, she was so convincing, but looking back there were signs I should have recognised.'

Breaking boundaries

'These things are often obvious with hindsight Toby. Try not to give yourself a hard time over this.'

Mike Thomas sounded genuine, and for the first time, Toby caught a glimpse of the man whom he considered a friend.

'She asked me to cover up a crime. I tried to reason with her, but she was adamant. Now I know why. Then outside, when the police arrived, she flew into a rage accusing me of betraying her.'

'You threw her into a panic because everything she had planned out was now having to change, due to the unexpected police presence. She knew at that moment she was in trouble. She didn't have the time to create a whole new story, and ultimately that would have been her downfall. You're the psychotherapist Toby, you know why she was angry.'

'What about the abuse she suffered?'

Mike Thomas made a movement to answer, but Nadia Williams reached over and tapped his arm before leaning forward and addressing Toby.

'Toby there are still a few things we're piecing together. We have several narratives at the moment, but one of those is that Olivia Stanton has never been the victim of domestic abuse.'

'Not all victims report it,' Toby said defensively, as though offended.

'We're well aware of that, and haven't discarded anything so far, but right now there is no evidence that links her to being an abuse victim, however…'

'However what?' Toby interrupted.

Breaking boundaries

She stopped for a moment and looked over at Mike Thomas, perhaps seeking approval to proceed down this line. He nodded and she continued.

'We have reason to believe she may have been a perpetrator.'

Toby had heard this previously from Mike but had convinced himself it was an isolated incident where she had merely defended herself. He hadn't wished to consider the alternative, as it would not only bring into question his work with Olivia, but also his ability as a therapist to identify a client's deceit. He paused for a moment, deceit was a strong word, but if what he was hearing was true, and he had no reason to believe it wasn't, then deceit was an accurate description. She had created a false narrative, spun a web of lies, projected effectively. If she was the abuser and had presented as a victim, she had cleverly manipulated Toby into looking in the wrong direction. Of course, his focus would be on her as a victim, why wouldn't it be? What reason did he have at the time to doubt her sincerity? The more he thought about it, the more confused he became. He kept returning to the question of why?

'This has been quite an ordeal for you. I'd suggest you call your wife and head on home, try to get a good night's sleep. We know where you are if we need anything further,' Mike Thomas said in a soft, sympathetic voice. He had seen a different side to Mike today and wondered whether their friendship would ever be the same again. Then a thought struck him. Mike was more senior than Nadia

Breaking boundaries

Williams, but it had been her who had led the interview. Mike had said very little, so what had his role been? Why was he there?

Toby looked up at the ceiling and closed his eyes for a brief moment, wondering whether Mike Thomas had been there to try and coax a confession out of him. He didn't allow his mind to wander any further with this. Right now, he didn't care whether Mike had been friend or foe. He just wanted to get out of this place and begin his long journey to getting his life back on track, whatever that looked like. In a quiet town where very little happens, this would be all over the national papers. He knew there would be a chance somehow his name would crop up and he would have to deal with that in due course, but right now all he wanted was the safe and loving arms of Beth. But how could he even begin to explain all of this to her? He had been naïve but had no idea to what depths this naivety had run. He had trusted his client and his judgment; both had let him down. Whilst his freedom may still be intact, his career was in tatters. Even if his reputation withstood this, the inevitable internal persecution which would follow, would cast continuous judgment on his work, making his position as a therapist untenable. He opened his eyes and looked at the two officers sat opposite him.

'I think I'd like to go home now please,' he said in little more than a whisper.

Breaking boundaries

'I'll walk you down to the cell area where your property will be returned to you. We also have a few questions we need to ask,' Amanda Thomas said.

'Thank you.'

The custody sergeant wasn't far behind them. He sat with Toby for a few moments and asked him questions about his wellbeing. The irony wasn't lost on Toby. He was asked whether he was leaving with any injuries and whether he had any suicidal tendencies. He wasn't sure whether this was a genuine concern about his health, or a mere exercise to cover the backs of the police. Either way it didn't last long, and he didn't give it a second thought as he was escorted towards the main doors.

As Toby exited the police station, he switched on his phone. There were several missed calls from Beth with three voicemails, each one sounding more frantic. He had questions, he needed answers, and in due time he would get them, but for now he wanted to erase anything which held any link to Olivia Stanton. He dialled Beth and waited for her to answer, which she did after the first ring.

'Toby, where the hell are you? Are you okay?'

He took a deep breath and for a moment couldn't find the right words.

'Toby are you there, where are you? What's happened?'

Finally, he found the words to speak, but it was muffled due to the outpouring of emotion. In between the sobbing Beth was able to understand that he was at the police station. She arrived shortly

Breaking boundaries

afterwards, rushing to embrace him. That's how they remained for a few minutes, until they got into the warm car and headed home. No words were exchanged during the drive, Beth focusing as much on Toby as the road, squeezing his hand periodically to make sure he was okay. Toby sat staring ahead of him, out of the window, the symbolism of the long dark road in front of them not lost on him.

Breaking boundaries

22

Toby stood at the entrance of the hospital. A week had passed since he had been arrested on suspicion of attempted murder, and he had slept very little in that time. To Beth he had spoken only briefly about the ordeal. To others, not at all. The media had picked up the story as he knew it would, and he had been identified as the third person at the scene. The focus of course wasn't on him, but the mere association meant almost all of his clients had contacted him to end their therapy during the subsequent week. Toby understood the reasoning, though nobody directly mentioned or even alluded to the incident. He knew his career was over, and now had to live with the choices he had made. He wasn't angry or upset. He wasn't anything really, and that was the problem. He had avoided Richard, not because there was no longer the need for their professional relationship, but because Richard had tried to warn him, and Toby hadn't heeded this. He knew Richard wouldn't judge him; he wouldn't be angry. He would be disappointed, and that was what Toby couldn't face, not right now. He'd spent much of his time replaying things in his mind, not simply the incident, but the whole situation with Olivia. He had revisited her case notes and analysed every session, every communication, every meeting, chance or scheduled, but still he didn't have the answers. He had to know the truth though. He had been torn with his feelings and was still struggling to

Breaking boundaries

believe she wasn't a victim, in some way. If he could find something, anything, which would suggest she had simply snapped after years of abuse, then maybe, just maybe, her therapy with him hadn't been a lie. At this thought, Toby suddenly realised something, something which had not dawned on him before. He wasn't just the third person at the scene, he was the third victim. He didn't like to think of himself as a victim, but he'd suffered at the hands of Olivia Stanton. What he needed to do now was find out just how much. He was hoping to find some of those answers at the Royal City hospital, where Eric Stanton was now recovering, having been moments from death just one week earlier. Toby hadn't requested to see him and was taking a chance that Eric would be receptive to his visit. All of his thoughts over the past week had led him here. Beth had been patient, but it had been hard on her. Toby was happier in his own company right now, and when he and Beth were together, few words were exchanged. They had spent the odd evening cuddled on the sofa with a movie, but Toby's mind had been elsewhere. He didn't worry about his marriage, but he worried about the impact this had had on Beth, and wondered how long she could withstand his withdrawal. He walked over to the reception desk. A middle-aged woman greeted him with a reassuring smile, asking him how she could assist.

'I'm here to visit Eric Stanton.'

'Are you a family member or friend?'

Breaking boundaries

'Neither. I'm just a well-wisher,' Toby said half raising a smile.

The woman looked confused, and for a moment there was a silence between them, before she asked for Toby's name.

'My name is Toby Reynolds. He's not expecting me.'

The smile on the woman's face disappeared, and Toby knew she'd made the link. He sighed, shook his head and looked away, recognising this was his life now. Whenever people realised who he was, the silent judgment would begin. He hadn't done anything wrong; he had been cleared, but that wouldn't matter. It was guilt by association. Another consequence of his choices, he thought.

'Let me give the ward a call. If you just take a seat, I'll be with you shortly.'

Toby watched as the woman picked up the phone. She seemed to be deep in conversation, much more than simply asking whether Eric Stanton was well enough to have visitors. Finally, she hung up the phone, got up from behind her desk, and walked towards him.

'Mr Stanton is on the fourth floor. You can either take the lifts just behind you or if you prefer, the staircase is just over there to your right. If you head to the reception desk on the ward, one of the nurses will show you to his room.'

'Thank you,' Toby said contemplating whether the stairs would be a better option as it would give him some thinking time. The woman didn't reply, instead

Breaking boundaries

nodding her head in acknowledgment before turning and walking back to her desk. Toby was feeling tired with the lack of sleep starting to catch up on him, so he opted for the lift. As the lift doors opened on the fourth floor, he realised he had no idea how to start the conversation. What if Eric Stanton didn't want to see him? What if he had questions for Toby which he couldn't answer? What if he blamed him or thought Toby was somehow involved after all? He turned back towards the lift, and considered whether or not to get back in it. Perhaps it would be much easier to find his own answers, draw his own conclusions rather than risk hearing things which may make him feel uncomfortable. No, he had to do this. He reasoned there was more to gain than to lose and set off towards the main desk. The nurse had been pleasant and if she had known who he was, she hadn't shown it. They walked down the corridor, neither of them speaking until they reached room two which was the last room on the right hand-side. The nurse knocked at the door and paused for a moment before opening it slightly and peering in.

'We have a visitor for you Eric.'

And just like that Toby was face to face with the man, who only a week ago he had been accused of trying to murder. He took a step forward into the room, and the nurse closed the door. Eric Stanton was sat up in bed and for the first time Toby could see his face. There was a silence, not an awkward silence, more a moment of contemplation as both men stared at each other. The face looked familiar

Breaking boundaries

to Toby, but he was having difficulty placing it. He knew he had seen this man before, but he couldn't remember where. Then his eyes were drawn to a tattoo on the man's arm, Roman numerals depicting a date. In an instant he was able to piece it together. He had met Eric Stanton before, spent time talking with him, without ever realising who he was.

'The man in the bar right? Rick?' Toby said tentatively.

Eric Stanton, smiled.

'I thought I recognised you, It's Tony isn't it?'

'Toby actually,' he corrected.

'Sorry. Yes, Toby of course. Now I remember. The therapist, right?'

'You're Eric Stanton?'

'Not many people call me that, I go by Rick.' His face suddenly stiffened, and Toby noticed his lips start to quiver.

'I'm sorry, I don't know where this has come from.'

'No need to apologise,' Toby responded waving away Eric's apology.

Eric dabbed his eyes and sat up in an attempt to stave off the emotion he had suddenly been overcome by.

'Please take a seat,' he said gesturing towards the chair placed at the bottom corner of his bed.

'Thank you.'

'I am led to believe it's because of you, I'm still here. Who would have thought a stranger I randomly struck up a conversation with, in a pub

Breaking boundaries

toilet of all places, would be responsible for saving my life just weeks later.'

Toby felt embarrassed that somebody whom he had had such a low opinion of, someone whom he had judged without meeting, someone whom he had fantasised about hurting, was thanking him.

'They told me you were the one who called for help.'

'They?'

'The police.'

Toby realised that sitting in front of Eric now, he had no idea what he wanted from him. Leading up to this moment he had been so sure of the questions he needed answering, but suddenly things felt different. The picture Toby had built up of Eric Stanton was of an abusive husband, a rapist, a bully who craved control. This however, had all come from Olivia Stanton, the woman currently incarcerated for attempted murder. It was her who had created the narrative, and Toby knew at least some of the things she had told him had been untrue. Maybe that was why he was here...to see whether any of what she had told him had been genuine, or whether her whole persona had been false. What did he expect though? Was Eric Stanton likely to admit he was a rapist, an abuser, a violent drunk? Then he knew what it was he needed to know. He needed to know if Olivia had been damaged to such an extent, that it had transformed her into a vengeful, emotionless killer, or whether she had carefully selected her victim. He needed

Breaking boundaries

some kind of closure, and the more he could piece together, and the more he was able to understand, the better chance he would have of obtaining this.

'I know you were seeing my wife as a client.'

'I'm not sure how to respond to that,' Toby replied cautiously.

'I knew she was attending therapy, and she had mentioned your name. Strangely, she had also described your wife to me, so after we had met in the pub, and I saw you leaving with your wife, I pieced it together.'

Toby looked stunned. This was unfamiliar ground for him, and he was out of his comfort zone. Several things went through his mind, the first being he had just uncovered another lie from Olivia. She had maintained her husband knew nothing of her therapy. Eric's face began to change. He didn't look angry, more puzzled, like somebody deep in thought frantically searching for some understanding. Toby's heart began to race, and he felt a resignation about what would inevitably follow. He knew Eric would likely have as many questions for him as he had for Eric. He should have anticipated this, yet he felt unprepared.

'Toby I hope you don't mind my asking, but how the hell did you end up at my house in the first place?'

There it was. The one question he hadn't wanted to be asked. This exposed him on so many levels. He hadn't prepared for this, though he thought it was perhaps the most obvious place for Eric to

Breaking boundaries

start. He would have asked that same question in Eric's position, so why had he not anticipated this? Toby closed his eyes for a moment and considered lying. He thought about being economical with the truth, giving Eric enough to satisfy his curiosity, but not enough to risk getting drawn into a conversation he was desperately trying to avoid. He knew he couldn't lie though. Not only was he sure he would be caught out; he felt he owed it to Eric to be honest with him. The man had nearly died at the hands of his wife. He had a child, and it wasn't clear whether he had been guilty of domestic abuse or not. Toby owed him the opportunity to at least provide his side of the story. He inhaled slowly, placed both hands on his knees and steadied himself.

'Olivia had sent me a message. I thought she was going to take her own life.'

'She knew you'd come.'

Toby looked confused.

'She must have made quite an impression on you,' Eric continued with a slight grin.

'Why do you say that?'

'She knew you'd come Toby, Olivia doesn't leave anything to chance. I've seen her manipulate her way through many situations throughout the years. You're not the first person to fall victim to her.'

'What makes you think I'm a victim?' Toby asked.

'How many other clients have you rushed to see in their own home? How many other clients have you wound up at a crime scene with? How many

Breaking boundaries

other clients have you ended up being arrested for?' Eric said calmly.

Toby fell silent. He had no comeback. As difficult as it was to acknowledge, Eric Stanton was right. Toby was a victim here, but if Eric saw him as a victim, it meant he didn't blame him, and that was something at least.

'I don't blame you Toby, how can I? Like I said, you saved my life.'

'I thought you were gone. I checked for your pulse but couldn't find one.'

'Whilst I knew Olivia was seeing a therapist, I never knew why.'

'It's not uncommon for people to keep therapy private,' Toby replied a little coyly.

'I considered it myself you know. After we'd spoken, I thought about contacting somebody, but I wouldn't know what to say.'

'Many people feel that way.'

For a brief moment, the room descended into a quietness, only disturbed by the occasional noise of a nurse rushing down the corridor to the rooms opposite. Toby looked at Eric and began to speak, but only murmured. Eric smiled at him.

'You want to know why she did it, don't you?'

'What makes you say that?'

'It's the question you've been dying to ask since you got in here.'

'How do you know?'

'Why else would you be here?'

'Do you know why she did it?' Toby asked him.

Breaking boundaries

'I have my theories, but only Olivia would be able to tell you why she wanted me dead.'

'I see,' Toby replied curiously.

'I had threatened to leave her, take Tyler with me.'

'You were going to leave her?' Toby asked, now feeling confused.

'There's only so much one man can take Toby. The last three years have been hell. She was controlling, and had a temper on her, which surfaced mostly when she didn't get her own way. I probably should have left long before now, but it was complicated.'

'Complicated how?'

Eric Stanton sighed carefully considering how to proceed.

'Olivia is a complex person. She brought a lot of emotional baggage into the relationship, but I thought I could help her, show her there was a different side to life other than what she had experienced.'

Toby's eyes were firmly fixed on Eric. He was captivated by him.

Eric speaking so openly without prompts, made it easier for Toby. The less he was required to speak, the better. Eric continued.

'Her upbringing was rough, but it was her ex-partner who really damaged her. He had beaten her repeatedly and even...' His voice cracked and he swallowed hard, almost like he was reliving a personal trauma. Toby didn't drop eye contact but

361

Breaking boundaries

sat quietly contemplating. Eric would open up in his own time and in his role, moments of silence were commonplace.

'He even raped her,' Eric finally managed.

'I'm sorry.'

'It was the alcohol with him, she said. So, when she found out I abstained from drinking, I think she felt reassured. He was convicted of the rape ultimately, but I suppose that's scant consolation for her. She never got over it, hell would anybody? It left her angry and suspicious.'

Toby coiled back in his chair for a moment and thought about what he was hearing. Physical violence, rape, both alcohol fuelled, this sounded familiar. Suddenly he realised why Olivia had sounded so convincing, why she had been overcome with emotion when talking about her ordeal. It was real. She was re-living actual events, only changing one detail, the perpetrator. Toby felt a moment of relief. He hadn't missed any warning signs, because there weren't any. The relief was short-lived, replaced by a swift realisation that it wasn't entirely inconceivable that Eric was lying. The part Toby was struggling with was what he would have to gain by doing so. He wasn't under any police investigation as far as he knew; he hadn't been under any obligation to see Toby today. He found himself reflecting back to the comment by Mike about the domestic disturbance which had been reported at the house, reported by Eric, not Olivia as she had claimed.

Breaking boundaries

'You say she had a temper. Did you ever fear for your safety?' Toby asked.

'Not at first, but there was one particular occasion where I ended up locking myself in the bathroom. She was hammering on the door making threats. Thankfully Tyler wasn't there, but she was relentless. Eventually, I called the police. It felt like the only way I could get her to calm down.'

'What made her so angry?'

'She thought I was seeing somebody else, picked up my work phone and saw a message from one of the receptionists. It was just a bit of banter, but there was no reasoning with her.'

'Had this happened before?' Toby asked, now realising he was probing.

'You mean the angry outburst or the suspicion?'

'Both I guess.'

'She had been suspicious of me since we first met, but I'd always hoped I would be able to talk her round, gain her trust, and show her I wasn't like Carl. That was the name of her ex-partner. The angry outbursts became more frequent after Tyler hit three. I think he had always been a distraction for her, pacified her to an extent. The irony huh? When he went to school that distraction was gone, she had more time in her own head, and for Olivia that wasn't a good place to be.'

Toby shuffled in his chair to get comfortable. The Olivia that Eric Stanton was presenting to him was very different to the person he had seen as a client. This both confused and saddened him. He was still

Breaking boundaries

unsure what to believe, but the more he listened to Eric, the more things started to fall into place, and the less chance there was of him being wrong.

'Can I ask you something, Toby?'

'Of course,' Toby said wondering what was coming next.

'In your line of work, how do you know if somebody is lying to you?'

The question took Toby by surprise, and he wasn't sure how to answer. What he was less sure of however, was why Eric Stanton had asked it in the first place. Was this about him or Olivia? Toby reached for his jacket removed a bottle of water from the pocket and took a sip. He screwed the top back on and placed the bottle back before adjusting his trousers which had rode up over his ankles during the process.

'It's not always easy, sometimes there are tell tail signs, like details may change, but ultimately, it's not my role to detect whether somebody is genuine or not. If somebody wishes to use therapy to create a false story, that's their thing, not mine.'

Eric was smiling, almost grinning Toby thought.

'Why do you ask?' Toby said with genuine intrigue.

'I was wondering how convincing my wife was.'

Toby looked perplexed. What would prompt Eric Stanton to make such a comment? He had spent the last few minutes trying to explain her actions, almost to the point of defending her, yet now it felt like he was changing direction. Toby couldn't read him.

'I'm assuming she didn't tell you she threw herself down the stairs dislocating her left shoulder in the process? It's why she struggles to raise her arm. She did some serious damage.'

'Why would she throw herself down the stairs?'

Eric began to answer, but Toby was oblivious, distracted by a realisation. Her story *had* changed. How had he not recognised this at the time? When she had first described the incident, it had been her left shoulder, but in a later session she had been massaging her right shoulder, stating this was the one Eric had been responsible for dislocating. There *were* inconsistencies in her story, he just hadn't realised it at the time. What else had she lied about? Had any of it been true? He felt cold, angry that he could have been deceived. He had dedicated his life to investing everything he had emotionally into his clients, never feeling that he needed anything in return from them. He had moments ago told Eric that if clients lied it was their thing and not his, but he now knew her lies had impacted him, and that was his thing. Eric, noticing Toby's vacant look, had stopped talking. Toby, having been staring out of the window, turned back to face Eric.

'Were there other occasions when she self-harmed?' Toby asked.

'I wouldn't call it self-harm Toby. She did it with a very clear intention, to get at me. I once watched

Breaking boundaries

her put her arm on the stove during an argument, gloating she would tell people I was responsible. I tried to reason with her, but when she got that crazed look in her eye, she was beyond listening to reason. That's why I stayed. I was terrified of what she might say about me. She can be very convincing, and plays the victim incredibly well.'

The burn, Toby thought. The burn he had seen on her arm at the gym. It hadn't been by coincidence. She had wanted him to see it. This was all starting to make sense now.

'What happened when you called the police?' Toby asked changing the direction of the conversation.

'What do you think happened? They were sceptical. She turned on the tears; she could be very convincing. They took statements from us both separately, recorded it as a domestic dispute, and were on their way. Could you imagine if she had called them? I'd have been tossed in a cell for the night with no questions asked.'

'It must have been very traumatic for you,' Toby replied noting Eric was getting slightly animated.

'One of only two occasions when I have been genuinely fearful of her.'

'When was the other?'

'Last week when she plunged a knife into my back.'

He said this with humour, and Toby wondered how he could be so nonchalant about a brutal attack that almost cost him his life. He seemed very laid

Breaking boundaries

back, not at all like Olivia had described him. Toby couldn't imagine him losing his temper, but as he knew, appearances could be deceptive, people could put on a show. Toby just nodded his head slowly; no words would have sounded appropriate in this situation.

'The first one hurt, the next one I didn't even feel, the rest must have occurred after I had already passed out. I'm told she stabbed me five times in total.'

Toby swallowed hard. He wanted to ask if anything had provoked it but knew a question of this nature risked Eric believing he was trying to justify it, which he wasn't. He wondered if he was still searching for something to explain why she had done this. He was struggling to believe this was premeditated and without provocation, but so far Eric Stanton hadn't given him anything to suggest otherwise.

'You know what the most painful part was?'

Toby shook his head, not taking his eyes off Eric.

'The fact that my wife hates me so much, she wanted to kill me. The physical pain will ease, but psychologically, that thought will forever haunt me. Sure we argued, and I'm not perfect, but for my own wife to want me dead, I don't know.'

His voice lowered to a whisper as he tried to compose himself. Toby had come here for answers, but he wasn't sure he was looking in the right place. He knew there was only one person who could give him what he was looking for, but the very thought of

Breaking boundaries

seeing her was enough to set his heart racing. He got up from his chair and walked over to Eric, who had now laid down.

'Thank you for seeing me today, I know this can't have been easy for you, any of it. I wish you all the best in your recovery.'

He turned to walk away, but Eric grabbed his hand, startling Toby. He looked him straight in the eye, with a pained look on his face. As Toby looked him in the eye, he realised Eric looked troubled, and wondered how much trauma sat behind those eyes.

'I have to know Toby, did you have any idea she was capable of this?'

Toby froze. How could he answer that question? What was Eric looking for here? Somebody, to blame perhaps? Toby bowed his head for a moment before responding.

'If I had any inclination that any of my clients posed an immediate threat to themselves or others, I would report it.'

'I didn't ask if you were concerned about her carrying out an attack like this, I asked if you thought she was capable of it.'

Toby needed to tread carefully. He risked being drawn into something, and whilst he wasn't entirely sure what that something was, he had a feeling it wouldn't be pleasant. He was cautious, and suddenly felt very uncomfortable in Eric Stanton's presence. Eric's demeanour had changed. He no longer seemed that approachable and talkative man Toby had met in the pub. As he looked into his

Breaking boundaries

eyes, he now saw something very different, something which frightened him. The eyes didn't reflect kindness or affability, instead, they seemed angry and vengeful. Toby had often spoken about there being a victim of some sort buried deep within every perpetrator, but now he wondered whether it was possible he was staring at a perpetrator surfacing from within a victim. He composed himself, preparing for what was now inevitably going to be an extremely uncomfortable end to their conversation. He was fairly certain he now knew what this was about. It wasn't about Eric believing him to be complicit, it was a rage rising out of the pain that he had tried for years to reach Olivia, but it had not been enough. She had sought her answers elsewhere. She didn't turn to her husband for comfort; she didn't turn to her husband for support; she didn't turn to her husband to help her find her own answers…she turned instead to her therapist, another man, and that was where the pain had come from. He hadn't been enough, he had failed. What Eric didn't realise is that Toby too had failed. She had alluded to finding the strength through therapy to make the changes she felt she needed to make, and Toby hadn't picked up on her desperation. He hadn't realised just how damaged by her trauma Olivia Stanton had been. Without realising it, he was answering Eric's question in his own mind. He couldn't possibly have known she was capable of this because only now was he beginning to realise that the Olivia Stanton he saw

Breaking boundaries

as a client, and this Olivia Stanton were two very different people. At this, he jerked his hand away from the grasp of Eric's and provided him with a detailed answer to his question. Whether Eric believed it or not didn't matter to him. He now had more of a picture of Olivia's background, but his answers didn't lie here, not with Eric Stanton.

'Eric, sometimes when we work with clients, we may get a feeling they are withholding information or avoiding answering certain questions. In most cases, this is because talking about those things can be incredibly painful, so we naturally protect ourselves by avoiding them. Sometimes we deliberately suppress memories, and they are buried so deep, they can be difficult to access. Sometimes, and it's a rare occurrence, but sometimes, clients will have an agenda and will deliberately mislead a therapist. There can be many reasons behind this, but not all have a sinister origin. In those situations, unless it is patently obvious, we as therapists, are none the wiser. You find most knowledge in hindsight, not foresight. So, when you ask me if I thought Olivia was capable of what she did, during my time with her, absolutely not. If I were to look back now, could I identify any discrepancies or inconsistencies? Quite possibly, but this is only made possible with the knowledge I now have of the situation. Do you understand what I'm saying?'

Eric lay there silently, not taking his eyes off Toby. He had hung on to his every word and was

Breaking boundaries

processing Toby's response. Toby didn't wait around for any acknowledgement. He gave Eric a tentative smile as he turned to exit.

'I wish you a speedy recovery and thank you for your time.'

At that, he was out of the door and walking briskly down the staircase. He was shaking a little, it had felt quite intense in there. As he made his way out of the main hospital doors, he stopped to take several deep breaths in an attempt to steady himself before he got back into the car. He looked up at the window of Eric Stanton's hospital room, half expecting him to be watching, but he wasn't. As he walked to his car Toby knew he had one more place to visit, one more person to see before he could start to find some closure. The thought of this sent him into a panic, but he knew what needed to be done. He wondered if she would see him, and part of him hoped she wouldn't, but this was the final part of the jigsaw, and if he wanted to sleep again, and return his life to anything resembling normality, he would need to sit opposite Olivia Stanton one more time.

Breaking boundaries

23

Toby sat patiently awaiting the appearance of Olivia. As he did so he studied his surroundings and felt grateful he was only there as a visitor. Two months ago, that very thought would have been absurd, but two weeks ago, on that fateful afternoon, it had felt a distinct possibility. Olivia had been on remand since her arrest, currently awaiting a trial date. There had been a strange contrast in his emotions, an oscillation between hyper anxious and serenity. He wasn't here through want, he was here through need, a necessity almost. He hadn't had the intention of seeing Olivia, but the visit to the hospital had left him with doubts, and he felt Olivia Stanton was the only person who could settle those doubts, one way or another. The question was, would she? What would be in it for her? Part of Toby wondered whether she would enjoy being in control, seeing him desperately searching for answers only she had; seeing his emotional anguish, knowing she had the power to end or prolong it. Was she sadistic enough to get off on that? Toby thought of all he had done for her, both in and out of practice, but was drawn back to the moment he had called the police. This had taken the situation out of her control and, thrown her plans into disarray. Olivia had set the scene and created the back story, but Toby's call to the police had changed all of that. Suddenly, her story of self-defence didn't match the evidence at the crime scene. This would ultimately, be her

Breaking boundaries

undoing. She may hold him responsible for her incarceration, for not being able to watch her son grow up, not being able to take a walk or a drive at her leisure. If he was right, and it was about control, he wondered just how bitter she would be now having the most basic of things ordinarily taken for granted, regimented, or restricted. One word kept leaping to the forefront of his mind… betrayal. Is this how she saw it? Could it be possible she felt he had betrayed her at the time she needed his loyalty most?

A door swung open, and in walked Olivia, accompanied by a stern-looking officer. The first thing that struck Toby was her appearance. Her shoulders were slumped, and she looked dishevelled like she had slept in her clothes. He felt sympathy for her and couldn't help thinking about the stark contrast between the Olivia he had worked with as a client, and the one approaching him now. There was a look of resignation about her, like the reality of her situation had finally set in. She took a seat and aimed a slight smile in his direction. Toby couldn't determine whether this was done out of politeness or anxiety, but he didn't respond. For a moment they sat there in awkward silence, almost like they were two people on their first date, neither wanting to begin the conversation. He felt an uncertainty, and like when he had visited Eric Stanton, now he was here sitting in front of Olivia, he was unsure where to begin.

Breaking boundaries

It was Olivia who spoke first.

'How have you been?'

Toby felt like he should be angry with her. She had lied to him, the depths of which he was not yet aware. She had taken advantage of him both as a therapist and as a person, his good nature. Yet still, looking at her dejected figure across the table, he felt a tinge of sadness. He didn't like to see anybody suffer, and Olivia looked like a pale shadow of the woman he had met, physically that is. He remembered his belief that behind all perpetrators there was somewhere a victim and clung to the hope that she had been misunderstood in some way, that she wasn't a scorned woman obsessed with revenge. He wasn't sure why he felt like this. Perhaps it was because he had built up a relationship with her for close to a year, and it was difficult to see her in this position, or perhaps he didn't want to believe she had drawn him into her narrative and he had been fooled by it, manipulated no less. He smiled to himself thinking about the irony that the same thing which had been responsible for him getting into therapy in the first place was now responsible for ending his career. Regardless of the inner conflict, he didn't want to add to her situation and knew his responses would need to be measured.

'I've been okay. How are you?' he managed.

'Well it's not the Hilton, but I guess I'll have to get used to it.'

Breaking boundaries

Toby laughed but knew her humour was masking a deep sadness, a fear. This would likely be her home for some time depending on how the courts saw it.

'My solicitor says I could get anything from a few years to life imprisonment. I've cooperated with the investigation and confessed, which will be taken into consideration, but you know...'

'I'm sorry.'

'For what? You didn't do this Toby. I have to take responsibility for what happened.'

'Do you regret it?'

The words just slipped out, and Toby felt regret at asking such a question, but perhaps this was what he was looking for. Maybe seeing her show some remorse at what she did to her husband, to the father of her son, would help him to find some closure, to see there was a humane side to her.

'If I'm going to be in here for life, I regret that I didn't kill that son of a bitch,' she laughed. The laugh seemed somehow disingenuous, and Toby saw something in her eyes, something he didn't like. Strangely, it was that same look he had seen in the eyes of Eric Stanton the previous week. He had his answer there but couldn't figure out why there was so much hatred. She had lied about the attack, lied about previously calling the police and lied about her physical injuries. Something didn't seem right though. Something was missing. If her entire story was a lie, why would she still want her husband dead? Then he thought back to that moment with

Breaking boundaries

Eric when he began to feel uneasy. At the time it was only a passing feeling, but now it was growing into real doubt. What secret was Eric Stanton hiding, and why did Olivia want him dead so badly?

'Can I ask you a question?'

'Sure,' Toby replied with a tentative tone which suggested he was worried about what that question might be.

'Why did you come here today? Since I was told you had requested to visit, I've been wondering why you would want to see me.'

Toby shuffled in his chair, gazing around the room before settling back on Olivia. There was a smell about the place which wasn't pleasant, but he couldn't place it. There was a faint murmur coming from people desperately trying to have private conversations in surroundings which were anything other than private. Finally, he composed himself, resting his arms on the table.

'My career is over, my marriage on the rocks, and emotionally I'm in a place I have never wished, nor did I ever expect, to be in. I guess I want to know why.'

Olivia sat back in her chair and stared at Toby for a moment. Her face gave nothing away about how she was feeling or what she was thinking. 'What makes you think I can provide you with those answers?' she asked.

'I believe you're the only one who can. I thought Eric may be able to provide some answers, but...'

Breaking boundaries

He stopped as though he had spoken out of turn. Olivia now wore a look that was very easy to identify. She was angry. The very mention of his name had incensed her as she banged her hand on the table. Toby jumped back in surprise as an officer walked over to see what the commotion was. She then took a deep breath, placed the palms of her hands on the table and smiled at Toby.

'You've been to see him?'

'Yes, is that a problem?'.

He wondered why this was important to him. He didn't need her permission or her validation, but there was something, something about her which still bugged him. Whatever that something was, it had kept him talking to her at the gym for longer than he should have, it had kept him at the hospital, it had prevented him from referring her to another therapist, and ultimately it had led to him racing to a crime scene for her.

'What did he tell you?' she asked abruptly, seemingly ignoring his question.

'That he had been the real victim of abuse, that you had a temper, that he was planning to leave, and that's why you stabbed him.'

'He's lying', she quickly interrupted.

Toby sat there for a moment contemplating. Suddenly it occurred to him that he didn't trust either of them, and it was entirely plausible that both were lying. Was he wasting his time here, chasing his tail? Would he really find the answers he had been

Breaking boundaries

seeking, the answers he needed to allow himself to move forward with his life?

'You don't believe me, do you?'

'It's difficult to know what or whom to believe. I know it was him who called the police for the domestic disturbance, not you.'

'How do you know that?' she asked aggressively.

'That doesn't matter.'

Toby sat up straight and removed his jacket.

'Can you tell me again which shoulder you dislocated?'

'Excuse me?'

Olivia appeared agitated, offended.

'You told me on two occasions about your shoulder being dislocated by Eric. I'm just wondering which shoulder it was?'

'Why does that matter?'

'Because it changed Olivia, and that's not a detail you just forget.'

'I don't follow.'

'When you first told me about the injury, you told me it was your left shoulder. In a later session you were massaging your right shoulder, and said it was the one that he had injured when he had thrown you down the stairs. I didn't realise at the time, but....'

'You're mistaken,' she interrupted.

'I thought I was, hoped I was. But when I checked your case notes, I realised I wasn't.'

'Look, Toby, I wasn't entirely honest with you, and I may have exaggerated certain things, but you have to believe he isn't a good man.'

Breaking boundaries

'This isn't about whether he is a good person or not.'

'Then what is it about?'

Toby swallowed hard.

'Why me?' he finally asked.

'You think you're that fucking special, that I would pick you out?'

'Did you?'

'You're half right, I did pick you out, but you're not anything special. I knew you'd be easy to manipulate.'

Olivia sat back, a smirk had spread across her face like she was suddenly enjoying this. *Like a switch being flicked*, he thought, before remembering this wasn't the first time had had thought this.

'Why?' he asked, not sure he really wanted to know.

'Oh Toby, for somebody so well qualified, you're incredibly naïve.'

Toby had never seen this side to her, even when seeds of doubt had been planted, he never envisaged this. He had little doubt now that the person sat in front of him was the real Olivia Stanton. These weren't the words of somebody living in fear, they weren't the incoherent ramblings of somebody who had lost touch with reality. This was somebody who had complete control.

'If you had only listened to me, and not called the police when you did, you wouldn't be sat here now looking so uneasy.'

Breaking boundaries

'Calling the police when I did, reduced your charge to attempted murder,' he snapped back.

'I'd rather spend more time in here knowing the bastard was dead.'

'What about Tyler?' Toby asked lowering his voice.

'I did this for him.'

'How did you do this for him?'

'Toby, you don't know Eric, you don't know his past or what he is capable of. Tyler would be better off without having a father like him.'

'Do you think he'd see it like that?'

'Because of you he is now stuck with his father and will grow up without his mother. Why did you have to get involved, I only needed you as an alibi?'

'An alibi? That's what this was?'

'You don't think I actually needed therapy, do you?'

Toby thought about the irony, that somebody in her position who would say such a thing, would almost certainly benefit from therapy. He felt dejected, used somewhat, and wondered how he could have been drawn into her world, her game, her revenge. He thought about Richard and his word of caution, that he ignored; he thought about Beth and her word of caution, that he ignored; he thought about his promise to Beth, which he broke. He thought about the last fifteen years and all the clients he had worked with. He thought about the countless thank you cards he received as well as the occasional tipple as a Christmas present.

380

Breaking boundaries

Suddenly, none of this mattered. All the things he had proudly achieved as a therapist over the years, none of it mattered. All he could think about was the one client who had taken everything from him. She had lied and manipulated her way through therapy, and now he was left with nothing. Olivia continued.

'Your mistake was coming to the house. You had no right to be there,' she said angrily.

'I thought you were going to kill yourself.'

'You were supposed to think that.'

'It added to your narrative of the abuse victim didn't it? It was to make your story more believable. You were planning to have me as a witness all along, weren't you?'

'Give the man a prize,' she tormented in a sadistic tone she made no attempt to hide.

'You knew I'd never disclose to the police. You were very careful not to give me too much that I believed you or anybody else were in danger. Back then I saw it as desperation, but now I recognise it for what it actually was.'

'And what's that Toby?'

'A carefully calculated act. You were playing a role the entire time, yet I...'

'Never realised what was going on? Never realised that you were playing a lead role in the act?' she interrupted now seemingly enjoying herself.

Toby fell silent, mouth open in disbelief. He had come here with the hope that Olivia would provide the missing pieces of the jigsaw, perhaps giving him

Breaking boundaries

some respite from the emotional torture he had been inflicting on himself trying to find answers he simply didn't have. He was supposed to leave here feeling lighter, but instead felt his psychological wellbeing decline with every sentence she spoke. She was hostile, yet obliging in the same manner, and he realised that after knowing her for nearly a year, it was entirely possible that this was the first time she was being honest with him. Yet her honesty was being delivered in a tactless way, and she showed no concern about its impact. He had served his purpose, become a major thorn in her side, and she had no hesitation in letting him know how she felt. He felt bruised, she likely recognised this, but her brutal onslaught wasn't finished, not by a long way. She leaned closer to him and smiled, but this wasn't a smile which emitted warmth, it was cold and punishing.

'I spent weeks studying your every movement. I knew about your marriage, your past time, your friend Jack, everything. The one thing I wrestled with at the time was the fact you had no children. Ideally, I needed somebody who could empathise with a mother, fearing for the safety of her child, but everything else about you was perfect. You were far enough away that we wouldn't operate in the same circles, but close enough geographically for me not to arouse suspicion. I read your website several times, oh that website Toby. Bravo by the way for the award. You seemed so dedicated to your clients, and I knew you specialised in abuse, which made you the perfect candidate.'

'You tracked me?'

'Don't look so surprised Toby, you're facing a killer, remember?'

'Is that how you see yourself?'

'It's how others see me, isn't it?' she replied angrily.

'Was anything you told me real?'

'Does it matter?'

Toby shrugged his shoulders and wondered whether she was getting more out of this than him. Was that the reason she had agreed to see him, to chip away at his self-confidence, his self-worth, to make him question himself as not only a therapist, but a person? Was this her revenge for him effectively ruining her otherwise perfectly executed plan? She had been methodical, planned every last detail, but she had made one very distinctive mistake. She had never believed that Toby would blur the lines, step over the boundaries, when she had sent that message. He now realised his presence at the Stanton household was beyond justification on a professional level. He had spent countless hours reasoning he did the right thing, but he wasn't beyond reproach for his actions. Even if the proceeding events had never occurred, that decision he made to get into his car and drive to her house would bring serious questions around his professional integrity and ability to maintain boundaries. There was an irony there, that he had

Breaking boundaries

been concerned about Olivia's ability to maintain boundaries, yet ultimately it had been his downfall. He looked at her, now feeling a little more settled.

'The physical injuries. Did you do them to yourself?'

'The scar on my ankle was a childhood accident, and I am sure Eric told you about the burns. I've never dislocated my shoulder, but I had to work hard to make you believe I had. What is it they say, if you're going to be a good liar you have to have a good memory? Well clearly that was one minor detail I tripped up on.' Toby thought for a moment, confused at what he was hearing. Eric Stanton had said Olivia had thrown herself down the stairs and dislocated her shoulder, but here she was denying she had ever sustained such an injury. Which one of them was lying? Then it struck him. Eric's version would further validate the belief he was the victim, and she was the perpetrator. She had nothing to lose by lying, but he had much to gain.

Toby addressed her.

'In one of your sessions, you told me that therapy was helping you to build the strength to do what you needed to do. It stuck with me at the time, but the words only became relevant with hindsight. It was cryptic, almost like you were enjoying confessing to something without anybody else realising what you were doing?'

'It was rather fun watching you empathise, oblivious to who and what you were empathising

Breaking boundaries

with. I put on quite an act, didn't I?' she replied revelling in the moment.

She was playing to her audience, getting off on the fact she was in control, and had been right from the first time they had met, he just hadn't realised it. She was in full flow now, and Toby had no desire to spend any more time in her company than was absolutely necessary.

'Was cutting your hair and changing your appearance also part of your story?'

'I knew you'd notice. Regardless of everything, you had a very good reputation as a therapist. I researched the behaviour of abuse victims, emotional, physical and sexual; their demeanour, how they dress, common reactions. I knew female rape victims would sometimes cut their hair, stop wearing makeup, wear baggy clothes to make themselves less attractive.'

Toby was stopped in his tracks, that last part. Why would Olivia need to research the reactions of rape victims when she herself was one? He thought back to his visit with Eric. He had told Toby that Olivia's ex-partner had been imprisoned for her rape. Surely, he wouldn't lie about something which could be verified or disproved so easily? Then he realised why Olivia had said this. This was just part of her game, her act. She was letting him know she wasn't a victim, and she wasn't weak. Toby considered for a moment whether or not to challenge her, but decided there was little to gain in antagonising her further.

Breaking boundaries

'In most cases, rape isn't about physical attraction or even sexual gratification. It's about power and control, sometimes even revenge.'

The whole time she had been looking directly at him, but now her gaze dropped to her hands which she had clasped together and rested on the table. Toby looked at the clock, positioned at the top of the wall facing him. He didn't have much time left and knew this was his final chance, because when he walked out of those prison gates, he wouldn't be returning. He continued.

'That night when you called me and said you had to see me one more time...'

He didn't have to finish; she knew exactly where this was going.

'After your crash, you told me you were taking some time out,' she interrupted.

'That must have thrown your plans into disarray,' he said in an accusatory tone.

Where had that come from? He was unexpectedly overcome with an anger he'd not experienced in a very long time. He'd felt like the wounded victim throughout this conversation, but suddenly he was displaying a confidence and aggression which took him by surprise. She recognised this, but rather than bite back, she simply smiled at him as if to let him know his efforts hadn't gone unnoticed but weren't enough to rattle her. She was letting him know she was still in control here.

Breaking boundaries

'I knew the longer you stayed away, the more likely it was that you wouldn't return. I couldn't have that; I hadn't finished with you.'

'Finished with me?' Toby said with surprise.

'You still don't get it, do you?'

'Why don't you enlighten me.'

He was goading her. She was getting a perverse pleasure from explaining to him blow by blow how she had used and manipulated him. She had no intention of leaving anything out, he just needed to ask the right questions.

'It was never about therapy Toby. It wasn't about building trust or any sort of therapeutic relationship. It was a theatrical performance, and you played a starring role.'

She suddenly broke into a fit of uncontrollable laughter, which drew attention from others intrigued by the commotion. Toby wasn't sure where to look. He felt more embarrassed than uncomfortable.

'You know what?' she finally managed. 'All that time you thought you were working on me, but in reality, it was you who was being worked on.'

'That night, you weren't just in the area, were you?' he asked now piecing things together.

'I was going to leave you a note, but when I drove by the practice and the lights were on, I saw my opportunity. The weather was treacherous. A soaking-wet female fresh from a brutal rape was perfect for drawing sympathy. I drove to the supermarket, bought a pair of scissors, and hacked

Breaking boundaries

at my hair. It wasn't the cleanest of cuts, but it did the job.'

Toby sat in disbelief at what he was hearing. Strangely it wasn't his presence at a crime scene, nor his arrest, which had effectively ended his career. It was Olivia Stanton. He would never be able to sit with a client again without suspicion; in fact, his trust in people had now disappeared. This had clearly impacted his marriage as his suspicion had spared nobody, not even Beth. He wanted to ask, why him? What had he done to deserve any of this? He already knew the answer though. It all came down to the choice he made that day to go to her house. Up to the point where she realised, he had called the police, this had likely not been personal. It hadn't been about him, but now it was. Because of him, Eric was still alive, and Olivia was in prison, most likely for a long time. This was now about her exacting some kind of revenge on him. She was twisting the knife, and on this occasion, she would be sure to see it through.

He'd got what he came for. He took slight comfort in knowing that the reservations he had about her were justified, but still felt angry that he had allowed himself to be manipulated. She had played the role very well, but she had underestimated Toby's commitment to helping people. He had come to realise when it came down to a choice, this came above everything else, including maintaining boundaries. He had perfectly captured it when he told the police that whilst he didn't always do things

Breaking boundaries

in the right way, he always endeavoured to do what he thought was the right thing. He knew now this had never been about him, he was a mere pawn in a very sinister game being played by a very conniving and vengeful woman. Still, there was one more thing which piqued his curiosity. Olivia had admitted that she had lied and fabricated physical evidence. So, if Eric Stanton hadn't raped her, hadn't been responsible for dislocating her shoulder or burning her arm, hadn't subjected her to a volley of psychological abuse...He broke off his thought and stared at Olivia intently for a moment.

'Why?'

'Why what?' she replied curiously.

'You went to extreme lengths to convince me that Eric was an abusive husband. If it was all a lie, why did you want him dead?'

'When you visited him at the hospital, what were your thoughts on him?' she asked calmly.

Toby wasn't sure what Olivia was driving at but was intrigued enough to play along.

'He seemed fragile,' Toby said in a guarded manner.

'No, what did you *really* think of him, Toby? What did you *see*?'

'There was a moment when I wondered...'

'Wondered what?' she interrupted, as though trying to guide him down a specific path.

'I saw something in his eyes that made me feel uncomfortable. I can't describe what it was, I spent

Breaking boundaries

a lot of time trying to figure it out afterwards, but there was just something there.'

'About eighteen months ago my car was in the garage, so I took Eric's into town to run some errands. As I was driving down a country lane, I hit a pothole and blew a tyre. I know my way around a car, so headed to the boot to locate the spare. Do you want to know what was tucked away underneath it?'

Toby, moved back in his chair, hypnotised. Morbid curiosity was telling him he needed to find out more, but part of him questioned whether he could physically absorb any more shock, and he knew this wasn't heading towards a happy ending. He couldn't manage a response, which gave Olivia the impetus she needed to continue.

'A pair of underwear, a pair of women's underwear. They were worn, soaked in what I assumed was semen, but you know what else?'

Toby shook his head, engrossed.

'There were traces of blood. Blood! What does that tell you?'

'I don't know,' Toby mustered.

'It likely wasn't consensual, it certainly wasn't romantic.'

'Could she not have been, you know...'

Olivia picking up on Toby's awkwardness took pity on him and finished his question for him.

'Menstruating? It's possible, and at the time that's what I tried to convince myself had happened. Then a few months later I received a private message on

Breaking boundaries

social media from a woman from his office accusing Eric of being a vile and evil man, a rapist no less.'

'Did you confront him?'

'He denied it of course, said the underwear must have been left in there by a previous owner, which I might just have believed, had it been an isolated incident. But when his colleague contacted me...' She broke off.

'How did he explain the message?'

'He told me she had been making a play for him for quite a while, and he had spurned her advances. He said at an office party she had been very suggestive, and he had rejected her in front of others. He tried to convince me she had felt humiliated, and this was her way of exacting revenge.'

'Did you believe him?'

'I wanted to, but something didn't feel right. When I thought about the timeline, I recognised that our sex life had declined around that period. He didn't seem as interested in me. Now I know why.'

'You wanted to kill him because you believed him to be a rapist?'

'Not just a rapist Toby, a serial rapist. Women would never be safe, and I couldn't risk even the remotest chance of Tyler growing up to be like his father.'

Toby looked perplexed and suddenly felt a shiver run down his spine. He had known there was something more to Eric under the surface, but he

Breaking boundaries

could never have imagined the secret he was hiding.

'He'd done this before? How do you know?' Toby asked.

'I dug into his past and followed the paper trail. His ex-girlfriend was the first person I spoke to, but then there was somebody at his high school. Fucking high school Toby, a kid.'

'Was any of this reported?'

'The school investigated, but the girl wouldn't go to the police, so it was her word against his. He said it had been consensual, and she had panicked when her father had found out. The ex-girlfriend was afraid of him. He can come across as charming, but if he's crossed, he's like a caged animal. Eventually, she packed her things whilst he was at work and simply disappeared. She was difficult to locate and a little reluctant to speak to me at first.'

Toby put his head in his hands and rubbed them up and down his face slowly. He hadn't expected this and wasn't sure what to make of it. Olivia had lied to him consistently throughout her time as his client, but something told him she wasn't lying now. She didn't really have anything to gain by doing so, he thought. It would do nothing to her sentence.

'Toby when I told you he raped me that was a lie, but what isn't a lie is the fact that he tried. I managed to fight him off and he swore to me it was a drunken misunderstanding, but I knew at that point the only way he would ever stop, was if he was dead.'

Breaking boundaries

'Surely if all of you had gone to the police they would have listened?'

'Nobody else would report it, and that son of a bitch has avoided detection for this long. I didn't have the evidence, and he had the perfect excuse because I once flew into a rage and attacked him, something which is on record. I'm tainted, and he's clean so to speak.'

She took a mouthful of water and coughed as it tickled her throat on the way down.

The ones I have mentioned are the ones I know about.'

'You think there are more?' Toby asked, afraid of her answer.

'I can't be sure, but it wouldn't surprise me.'

'I don't know what to say,' Toby said having no understanding of why he was hearing this, or more importantly, what he was supposed to do with this information. He'd come here to close the door on Olivia but felt like he was instead opening the door on Eric. He now faced a dilemma, because if Olivia was telling the truth, there was a rapist on the street known to him, but not to the authorities. On the other hand, there was the possibility this was part of her game, her parting shot, her final act of revenge to plant a seed of doubt, and watch Toby agonise. He was snapped back into the moment by the sudden increase in noise, mainly chair legs being scraped along the floor as the hall began to empty. His time with Olivia was up, not just for now he thought, but forever. This chapter of his life was

Breaking boundaries

over, though he felt sure he would be dealing with the aftermath for quite some time. As he rose out of his seat, he wished Olivia the best of luck and turned to walk away.

'Toby,' she shouted after him.

He stopped and turned back around to face her as she was being carefully escorted out of the room.

'If he thinks you're suspicious of him, you're not safe. Don't be fooled by him, Toby.'

And like that Olivia Stanton was gone, not just from the room, but from his life. If this was as she had described, a theatrical performance, they had taken a bow, and the final curtain had descended.

As Toby exited the prison, he paused for a moment to reflect. He had hoped he would feel a sense of relief when he left, and even though Olivia had been brutal in her confession, he felt like he had handled this. He hadn't expected her to be warm towards him but had also not anticipated the extent of her vitriol. He was experienced enough though to be able to acknowledge that this was a reflection on her and not on him. This was the first time his trust had been so drastically misplaced, but he knew that whilst it would take time, it wouldn't change him. He would again offer his trust to people automatically without them first having to earn it. His default would change from suspicious to open-minded over time, and he would begin to allow people to get close to him once again, but right now this wasn't his concern, Eric Stanton was. He couldn't switch off

Breaking boundaries

from what Olivia had just told him, and though every fibre in his body was screaming at him to be cautious, he believed her. He couldn't explain why, and perhaps had he not met Eric himself, he would have thought differently, but he believed, even amongst all the lies she had told him, she was telling the truth where Eric was concerned. The question now was what he would do next. He couldn't think of this right now though, the emotion of the day getting the better of him. He sat on the curb next to his car, head in his hands with the tears flowing down his face. The skies were clear, though his head was anything but. He remained in that position for a few minutes until he heard footsteps approaching. He looked up and dried his eyes as the figure moved closer. It was a tall woman dressed in jeans and a baggy jumper, though she pulled the causal look off very well Toby thought. As she got within a few feet of him, Toby's heart skipped a beat, his eyes bulged and his mouth fell open. As she stopped in front of him, Toby stared into her eyes, mesmerised. He was looking right into the past, around twenty years. She didn't appear to have aged, and that natural beauty he had fallen in love with all those years back had never left her.

'George?'

For a moment they simply stood and looked at one another, before they tentatively embraced. As she pulled away, the smile she had worn disappeared, an anguished look having now replaced it.

Breaking boundaries

'I need your help, Toby,'

He took a step back, and for a moment they just stared into each other's eyes without speaking. His day had begun with Olivia Stanton and was ending with Georgina Sampson. He had no idea what trouble she was in, nor if he would be able to help, but the flame he had carried for her as a teenager had never been fully extinguished, and he knew at that moment he would give what little he had left, to her. The sun was now setting, and the wind dying down.

'Where are you heading?' he asked.

'Just drive and we can figure that out along the way.'

She placed her bag on the back seat, then opened the front door and climbed in. Toby pulled slowly out of the car park and turned onto the main road. As the prison faded into the background, they were passed by flashing lights and sirens on the opposite carriageway. For a moment he wondered, but he didn't look back.

Breaking boundaries

Breaking boundaries

About the author

Jason is a senior accredited psychotherapist and writer, based in the East Midlands, where he lives with his wife and four-year-old daughter. Originally from Yorkshire, he graduated from Leeds Metropolitan University with a Master's degree in Psychoanalytic Studies. He subsequently went on to qualify as a psychotherapist and has been running his own practice for the last ten years.

In 2021, Jason published his first solo book, **Domestic Abuse: Men Suffer Too,** however, **Breaking Boundaries** is his debut fictional novel. Jason previously spent over two years writing as a guest columnist for the local paper, and has also co-authored two CBT books, with a third in the works. In 2018, he was featured in a national magazine that had picked up one of his articles. In his spare time, he enjoys rugby, walking and reading.

Contact details:

E-mail: therapy@jasonhansoncounselling.co.uk

Facebook: Jason M Hanson - Author

Twitter: @Jason_H_author

TikTok: @jasonmhanson_author

Printed in Great Britain
by Amazon